Lazarre

Mary Hartwell Catherwood

Alpha Editions

This edition published in 2022

ISBN : 9789356717442

Design and Setting By
Alpha Editions
www.alphaedis.com
Email - info@alphaedis.com

As per information held with us this book is in Public Domain.
This book is a reproduction of an important historical work. Alpha Editions uses the best technology to reproduce historical work in the same manner it was first published to preserve its original nature. Any marks or number seen are left intentionally to preserve its true form.

PRELUDE

ST. BAT'S

"My name is Eagle," said the little girl.

The boy said nothing.

"My name is Eagle," she repeated. "Eagle de Ferrier. What is your name?"

Still the boy said nothing.

She looked at him surprised, but checked her displeasure. He was about nine years old, while she was less than seven. By the dim light which sifted through the top of St. Bat's church he did not appear sullen. He sat on the flagstones as if dazed and stupefied, facing a blacksmith's forge, which for many generations had occupied the north transept. A smith and some apprentices hammered measures that echoed with multiplied volume from the Norman roof; and the crimson fire made a spot vivid as blood. A low stone arch, half walled up, and blackened by smoke, framed the top of the smithy, and through this frame could be seen a bit of St. Bat's close outside, upon which the doors stood open. Now an apprentice would seize the bellows-handle and blow up flame which briefly sprang and disappeared. The aproned figures, Saxon and brawny, made a fascinating show in the dark shop.

Though the boy was dressed like a plain French citizen of that year, 1795, and his knee breeches betrayed shrunken calves, and his sleeves, wrists that were swollen as with tumors, Eagle accepted him as her equal. His fine wavy hair was of a chestnut color, and his hands and feet were small. His features were perfect as her own. But while life played unceasingly in vivid expression across her face, his muscles never moved. The hazel eyes, bluish around their iris rims, took cognizance of nothing. His left eyebrow had been parted by a cut now healed and forming its permanent scar.

"You understand me, don't you?" Eagle talked to him. "But you could not understand Sally Blake. She is an English girl. We live at her house until our ship sails, and I hope it will sail soon. Poor boy! Did the wicked mob in Paris hurt your arms?"

She soothed and patted his wrists, and he neither shrank in pain nor resented the endearment with male shyness.

Eagle edged closer to him on the stone pavement. She was amused by the blacksmith's arch, and interested in all the unusual life around her, and she leaned forward to find some response in his eyes. He was unconscious of his strange environment. The ancient church of St. Bartholomew the Great, or St. Bat's as it was called, in the heart of London, had long been a hived village. Not only were houses clustered thickly around its outside walls and the space of ground named its close; but the inside, degraded from its first use, was parceled out to owners and householders. The nave only had been retained as a church bounded by massive pillars, which did not prevent Londoners from using it as a thoroughfare. Children of resident dissenters could and did hoot when it pleased them, during service, from an overhanging window in the choir. The Lady Chapel was a fringe-maker's shop. The smithy in the north transept had descended from father to son. The south transept, walled up to make a respectable dwelling, showed through its open door the ghastly marble tomb of a crusader which the thrifty London housewife had turned into a parlor table. His crossed feet and hands and upward staring countenance protruded from the midst of knick-knacks.

Light fell through the venerable clerestory on upper arcades. Some of these were walled shut, but others retained their arched openings into the church, and formed balconies from which upstairs dwellers could look down at what was passing below.

Two women leaned out of the Norman arcades, separated only by a pillar, watching across the nave those little figures seated in front of the blacksmith's window. An atmosphere of comfort and thrift filled St. Bat's. It was the abode of labor and humble prosperity, not an asylum of poverty. Great worthies, indeed, such as John Milton, and nearer our own day, Washington Irving, did not disdain to live in St. Bartholomew's close. The two British matrons, therefore, spoke the prejudice of the better rather than the baser class.

"The little devils!" said one woman.

"They look innocent," remarked the other. "But these French do make my back crawl!"

"How long are they going to stay in St. Bat's?"

"The two men with the little girl and the servant intend to sail for America next week. The lad, and the man that brought him in—as dangerous looking a foreigner as ever I saw!—are like to prowl out any time. I saw them go into the smithy, and I went over to ask the smith's wife about them. She let two upper chambers to the creatures this morning."

"What ails the lad? He has the look of an idiot."

"Well, then, God knows what ails any of the crazy French! If they all broke out with boils like the heathen of scripture, it would not surprise a Christian. As it is, they keep on beheading one another, day after day and month after month; and the time must come when none of them will be left—and a satisfaction that will be to respectable folks!"

"First the king, and then the queen," mused one speaker. "And now news comes that the little prince has died of bad treatment in his prison. England will not go into mourning for him as it did for his father, King Louis. What a pretty sight it was, to see every decent body in a bit of black, and the houses draped, they say, in every town! A comfort it must have been to the queen of France when she heard of such Christian respect!"

The women's faces, hard in texture and rubicund as beef and good ale could make them, leaned silent a moment high above the dim pavement. St. Bat's little bell struck the three quarters before ten; lightly, delicately, with always a promise of the great booming which should follow on the stroke of the hour. Its perfection of sound contrasted with the smithy clangor of metal in process of welding. A butcher's boy made his way through the front entrance toward a staircase, his feet echoing on the flags, carrying exposed a joint of beef on the board upon his head.

"And how do your foreigners behave themselves, Mrs. Blake?" inquired the neighbor.

"Like French emmy-grays, to be sure. I told Blake when he would have them to lodge in the house, that we are a respectable family. But he is master, and their lordships has money in their purses."

"French lordships!" exclaimed the neighbor. "Whether they calls themselves counts or markises, what's their nobility worth? Nothing!"

"The Markis de Ferrier," retorted Mrs. Blake, nettled by a liberty taken with her lodgers which she reserved for herself, "is a gentleman if he is an emmy-gray, and French. Blake may be master in his own house, but he knows landed gentry from tinkers—whether they ever comes to their land again or not."

"Well, then," soothed her gossip, "I was only thinking of them French that comes over, glad to teach their betters, or even to work with their hands for a crust."

"Still," said Mrs. Blake, again giving rein to her prejudices, "I shall be glad to see all French papists out of St. Bat's. For what does scripture say?—'Touch not the unclean thing!' And that servant-body, instead of looking after her little missus, galloping out of the close on some bloody errand!"

"You ought to be thankful, Mrs. Blake, to have her out of the way, instead of around our children, poisoning their hinfant minds! Thank God they are playing in the church lane like little Christians, safe from even that lad and lass yonder!"

A yell of fighting from the little Christians mingled with their hoots at choir boys gathering for the ten o'clock service in St. Bat's. When Mrs. Blake and her friend saw this preparation, they withdrew their dissenting heads from the arcades in order not to countenance what might go on below.

Minute followed minute, and the little bell struck the four quarters. Then the great bell boomed out ten;—the bell which had given signal for lighting the funeral piles of many a martyr, on Smithfield, directly opposite the church. Organ music pealed; choir boys appeared from their robing-room beside the entrance, pacing two and two as they chanted. The celebrant stood in his place at the altar, and antiphonal music rolled among the arches; pierced by the dagger voice of a woman in the arcades, who called after the retreating butcher's boy to look sharp, and bring her the joint she ordered.

Eagle sprang up and dragged the arm of the unmoving boy in the north transept. There was a weeping tomb in the chancel which she wished to show him,—lettered with a threat to shed tears for a beautiful memory if passers-by did not contribute their share; a threat the marble duly executed on account of the dampness of the church and the hardness of men's hearts. But it was impossible to disturb a religious service. So she coaxed the boy, dragging behind her, down the ambulatory beside the oasis of chapel, where the singers, sitting side-wise, in rows facing each other, chanted the Venite. A few worshipers from the close, all of them women, pattered in to take part in this daily office. The smithy hammers rang under organ measures, and an odor of cooking sifted down from the arcades.

Outside the church big fat-bellied pigeons were cooing about the tower or strutting and pecking on the ground. To kill one was a grave offense. The worst boy playing in the lane durst not lift a hand against them.

Very different game were Eagle and the other alien whom she led past the red faced English children.

"Good day," she spoke pleasantly, feeling their antagonism. They answered her with a titter.

"Sally Blake is the only one I know," she explained in French, to her companion who moved feebly and stiffly behind her dancing step. "I cannot talk English to them, and besides, their manners are not good, for they are not like our peasants."

Sally Blake and a bare kneed lad began to amble behind the foreigners, he taking his cue smartly and lolling out his tongue. The whole crowd set up a shout, and Eagle looked back. She wheeled and slapped the St. Bat's girl in the face.

That silent being whom she had taken under her care recoiled from the blow which the bare kneed boy instantly gave him, and without defending himself or her, shrank down in an attitude of entreaty. She screamed with pain at this sight, which hurt worse than the hair-pulling of the mob around her. She fought like a panther in front of him.

Two men in the long narrow lane leading from Smithfield, interfered, and scattered her assailants.

You may pass up a step into the graveyard, which is separated by a wall from the lane. And though nobody followed, the two men hurried Eagle and the boy into the graveyard and closed the gate.

It was not a large enclosure, and thread-like paths, grassy and ungraveled, wound among crowded graves. There was a very high outside wall: and the place insured such privacy as could not be had in St. Bat's church. Some crusted stones lay broad as gray doors on ancient graves; but the most stood up in irregular oblongs, white and lichened.

A cat call from the lane was the last shot of the battle. Eagle valiantly sleeked her disarrayed hair, the breast under her bodice still heaving and sobbing. The June sun illuminated a determined child of the gray eyed type between white and brown, flushed with fullness of blood, quivering with her intensity of feeling.

"Who would say this was Mademoiselle de Ferrier!" observed the younger of the two men. Both were past middle age. The one whose queue showed the most gray took Eagle reproachfully by her hands; but the other stood laughing.

"My little daughter!"

"I did strike the English girl—and I would do it again, father!"

"She would do it again, monsieur the marquis," repeated the laugher.

"Were the children rude to you?"

"They mocked him, father." She pulled the boy from behind a grave-stone where he crouched unmoving as a rabbit, and showed him to her guardians. "See how weak he is! Regard him—how he walks in a dream! Look at his swollen wrists—he cannot fight. And if you wish to make these English respect you you have got to fight them!"

"Where is Ernestine? She should not have left you alone."

"Ernestine went to the shops to obey your orders, father."

The boy's dense inertia was undisturbed by what had so agonized the girl. He stood in the English sunshine gazing stupidly at her guardians.

"Who is this boy, Eagle?" exclaimed the younger man.

"He does not talk. He does not tell his name."

The younger man seized the elder's arm and whispered to him.

"No, Philippe, no!" the elder man answered. But they both approached the boy with a deference which surprised Eagle, and examined his scarred eyebrow and his wrists. Suddenly the marquis dropped upon his knees and stripped the stockings down those meager legs. He kissed them, and the swollen ankles, sobbing like a woman. The boy seemed unconscious of this homage. Such exaggeration of her own tenderness made her ask,

"What ails my father, Cousin Philippe?"

Her Cousin Philippe glanced around the high walls and spoke cautiously.

"Who was the English girl at the head of your mob, Eagle?"

"Sally Blake."

"What would Sally Blake do if she saw the little king of France and Navarre ride into the church lane, filling it with his retinue, and heard the royal salute of twenty-one guns fired for him?"

"She would be afraid of him."

"But when he comes afoot, with that idiotic face, giving her such a good chance to bait him—how can she resist baiting him? Sally Blake is human."

"Cousin Philippe, this is not our dauphin? Our dauphin is dead! Both my father and you told me he died in the Temple prison nearly two weeks ago!"

The Marquis de Ferrier replaced the boy's stockings reverently, and rose, backing away from him.

"There is your king, Eagle," the old courtier announced to his child. "Louis XVII, the son of Louis XVI and Marie Antoinette, survives in this wreck. How he escaped from prison we do not know. Why he is here unrecognized in England, where his claim to the throne was duly acknowledged on the death of his father, we do not know. But we who have often seen the royal child cannot fail to identify him; brutalized as he is by the past horrible year of his life."

The boy stood unwinking before his three expatriated subjects. Two of them noted the traits of his house, even to his ears, which were full at top, and without any indentation at the bottom where they met the sweep of the jaw.

The dauphin of France had been the most tortured victim of his country's Revolution. By a jailer who cut his eyebrow open with a blow, and knocked him down on the slightest pretext, the child had been forced to drown memory in fiery liquor, month after month. During six worse months, which might have been bettered by even such a jailer, hid from the light in an airless dungeon, covered with rags which were never changed, and with filth and vermin which daily accumulated, having his food passed to him through a slit in the door, hearing no human voice, seeing no human face, his joints swelling with poisoned blood, he had died in everything except physical vitality, and was taken out at last merely a breathing corpse. Then it was proclaimed that this corpse had ceased to breathe. The heir of a long line of kings was coffined and buried.

While the elder De Ferrier shed nervous tears, the younger looked on with eyes which had seen the drollery of the French Revolution.

"I wish I knew the man who has played this clever trick, and whether honest men or the rabble are behind it."

"Let us find him and embrace him!"

"*I* would rather embrace his prospects when the house of Bourbon comes again to the throne of France. Who is that fellow at the gate? He looks as if he had some business here."

The man came on among the tombstones, showing a full presence and prosperous air, suggesting good vintages, such as were never set out in the Smithfield alehouse. Instead of being smooth shaven, he wore a very long mustache which dropped its ends below his chin.

A court painter, attached to his patrons, ought to have fallen into straits during the Revolution. Philippe exclaimed with astonishment—

"Why, it's Bellenger! Look at him!"

Bellenger took off his cap and made a deep reverence.

"My uncle is weeping over the dead English, Bellenger," said Philippe. "It always moves him to tears to see how few of them die."

"We can make no such complaint against Frenchmen in these days, monsieur," the court painter answered. "I see you have my young charge here, enjoying the gravestones with you;—a pleasing change after the unmarked trenches of France. With your permission I will take him away."

"Have I the honor, Monsieur Bellenger, of saluting the man who brought the king out of prison?" the old man inquired.

Again Bellenger made the marquis a deep reverence, which modestly disclaimed any exploit.

"When was this done?—Who were your helpers? Where are you taking him?"

Bellenger lifted his eyebrows at the fanatical royalist.

"I wish I had had a hand in it!" spoke Philippe de Ferrier.

"I am taking this boy to America, monsieur the marquis," the painter quietly answered.

"But why not to one of his royal uncles?"

"His royal uncles," repeated Bellenger. "Pardon, monsieur the marquis, but did I say he had any royal uncles?"

"Come!" spoke Philippe de Ferrier. "No jokes with us, Bellenger. Honest men of every degree should stand together in these times."

Eagle sat down on a flat gravestone, and looked at the boy who seemed to be an object of dispute between the men of her family and the other man. He neither saw nor heard what passed. She said to herself—

"It would make no difference to me! It is the same, whether he is the king or not."

Bellenger's eyes half closed their lids as if for protection from the sun.

"Monsieur de Ferrier may rest assured that I am not at present occupied with jokes. I will again ask permission to take my charge away."

"You may not go until you have answered some questions."

"That I will do as far as I am permitted."

"Do Monsieur and his brother know that the king is here?" inquired the elder De Ferrier, taking the lead.

"What reason have you to believe," responded Bellenger, "that the Count de Provence and the Count d'Artois have any interest in this boy?"

Philippe laughed, and kicked the turf.

"We have seen him many a time at Versailles, my friend. You are very mysterious."

"Have his enemies, or his friends set him free?" demanded the old Frenchman.

"That," said Bellenger, "I may not tell."

"Does Monsieur know that you are going to take him to America?"

"That I may not tell."

"When do you sail, and in what vessel?"

"These matters, also, I may not tell."

"This man is a kidnapper!" the old noble cried, bringing out his sword with a hiss. But Philippe held his arm.

"Among things permitted to you," said Philippe, "perhaps you will take oath the boy is not a Bourbon?"

Bellenger shrugged, and waved his hands.

"You admit that he is?"

"I will again ask permission to take my charge away"

"I admit nothing, monsieur. These are days in which we save our heads as well as we can, and admit nothing."

"If we had never seen the dauphin we should infer that this is no common child you are carrying away so secretly, bound by so many pledges. A man like you, trusted with an important mission, naturally magnifies it. You refuse to let us know anything about this affair?"

"I am simply obeying orders, monsieur," said Bellenger humbly. "It is not my affair."

"You are better dressed, more at ease with the world than any other refugee I have seen since we came out of France. Somebody who has money is paying to have the child placed in safety. Very well. Any country but his own is a good country for him now. My uncle and I will not interfere. We do not understand. But liberty of any kind is better than imprisonment and death. You can of course evade us, but I give you notice I shall look for this boy in America, and if you take him elsewhere I shall probably find it out."

"America is a large country," said Bellenger, smiling.

He took the boy by the hand, and made his adieus. The old De Ferrier deeply saluted the boy and slightly saluted his guardian. The other De Ferrier nodded.

"We are making a mistake, Philippe!" said the uncle.

"Let him go," said the nephew. "He will probably slip away at once out of St. Bartholomew's. We can do nothing until we are certain of the powers behind him. Endless disaster to the child himself might result from our interference. If France were ready now to take back her king, would she accept an imbecile?"

The old De Ferrier groaned aloud.

"Bellenger is not a bad man," added Philippe.

Eagle watched her playmate until the closing gate hid him from sight. She remembered having once implored her nurse for a small plaster image displayed in a shop. It could not speak, nor move, nor love her in return. But she cried secretly all night to have it in her arms, ashamed of the unreasonable desire, but conscious that she could not be appeased by anything else. That plaster image denied to her symbolized the strongest passion of her life.

The pigeons wheeled around St. Bat's tower, or strutted burnished on the wall. The bell, which she had forgotten since sitting with the boy in front of the blacksmith shop, again boomed out its record of time; though it seemed to Eagle that a long, lonesome period like eternity had begun.

BOOK I

AWAKING

I

I remember poising naked upon a rock, ready to dive into Lake George. This memory stands at the end of a diminishing vista; the extreme point of coherent recollection. My body and muscular limbs reflected in the water filled me with savage pride.

I knew, as the beast knows its herd, that my mother Marianne was hanging the pot over the fire pit in the center of our lodge; the children were playing with other papooses; and my father was hunting down the lake. The hunting and fishing were good, and we had plenty of meat. Skenedonk, whom I considered a person belonging to myself, was stripping more slowly on the rock behind me. We were heated with wood ranging. Aboriginal life, primeval and vigor-giving, lay behind me when I plunged expecting to strike out under the delicious forest shadow.

When I came up the sun had vanished, the woods and their shadow were gone. So were the Indian children playing on the shore, and the shore with them. My mother Marianne might still be hanging her pot in the lodge. But all the hunting lodges of our people were as completely lost as if I had entered another world.

My head was bandaged, as I discovered when I turned it to look around. The walls were not the log walls of our lodge, chinked with moss and topped by a bark roof. On the contrary they were grander than the inside of St. Regis church where I took my first communion, though that was built of stone. These walls were paneled, as I learned afterward to call that noble finishing, and ornamented with pictures, and crystal sockets for candles. The use of the crystal sockets was evident, for one shaded wax light burned near me. The ceiling was not composed of wooden beams like some Canadian houses, but divided itself into panels also, reflecting the light with a dark rosy shining. Lace work finer than a priest's white garments fluttered at the windows.

I had dived early in the afternoon, and it was night. Instead of finding myself still stripped for swimming, I had a loose robe around me, and a coverlet drawn up to my armpits. The couch under me was by no means of hemlock twigs and skins, like our bunks at home: but soft and rich. I wondered if I had died and gone to heaven; and just then the Virgin moved past my head and stood looking down at me. I started to jump out of a window, but felt so little power to move that I only twitched, and pretended to be asleep, and watched her as we sighted game, with eyes nearly shut. She had a poppet of a child on one arm that sat up instead of leaning against her shoulder, and looked at me, too. The poppet had a cap on its head, and was dressed in lace, and she wore a white dress that let her neck and arms out, but covered her to the ground. This was remarkable, as the Indian women covered their necks and arms, and wore their petticoats short. I could see this image breathe, which was a marvel, and the color moving under her white skin. Her eyes seemed to go through you and search all the veins, sending a shiver of pleasure down your back.

Now I knew after the first start that she was a living girl holding a living baby, and when my father, Thomas Williams, appeared at the door of the room, it was certain I could not be in heaven. It came over me in a flash that I myself was changed. In spite of the bandages my head was as clear as if all its faculties were washed and newly arranged. I could look back into my life and perceive things that I had only sensed as a dumb brute. A fish thawed out after being frozen, and reanimated through every sparkling scale and tremulous fin, could not have felt its resurrection more keenly. My broken head gave me no trouble at all.

The girl and baby disappeared as soon as I saw my father; which was not surprising, for he could not be called a prepossessing half-breed. His lower lip protruded and hung sullenly. He had heavy brows and a shaggy thatch of hair. Our St. Regis Iroquois kept to the buckskins, though they often had hunting shirts of fulled flannel; and my father's buckskins were very dirty.

A little man, that I did not know was in the room, shuffled across the floor to keep my father from entering. Around the base of his head he had a thin curtain of hair scarcely reaching his shoulders. His nose pointed upward. Its tip was the shape of a candle extinguisher. He wore horn spectacles; and knee breeches, waistcoat and coat of black like the ink which fades to brown in a drying ink-horn. He put his hands together and took them apart uncertainly, and shot out his lip and frowned, as if he had an universal grudge and dared not vent it.

He said something in a language I did not understand, and my father made no answer. Then he began a kind of Anglo-French, worse than the patois we used at St. Regis when we did not speak Iroquois. I made out the talk between the two, understanding each without hesitation.

"Sir, who are you?"

"The chief, Thomas Williams," answered my father.

"Pardon me, sir; but you are unmistakably an Indian."

"Iroquois chief," said my father. "Mohawk."

"That being the case, what authority have you for calling yourself Thomas Williams?" challenged the little man.

"Thomas Williams is my name."

"Impossible, sir! Skenedonk, the Oneida, does not assume so much. He lays no claim to William Jones or John Smith, or some other honest British name."

The chief maintained silent dignity.

"Come, sir, let me have your Indian name! I can hear it if I cannot repeat it."

Silently contemptuous, my father turned toward me.

"Stop, sir!" the man in the horn spectacles cried. "What do you want?"

"I want my boy."

"Your boy? This lad is white."

"My grandmother was white," condescended the chief. "A white prisoner from Deerfield. Eunice Williams."

"I see, sir. You get your Williams from the Yankees. And is this lad's mother white, too?"

"No. Mohawk."

"Why, man, his body is like milk! He is no son of yours."

The chief marched toward me.

"Let him alone! If you try to drag him out of the manor I will appeal to the authority of Le Ray de Chaumont."

My father spoke to me with sharp authority—

"Lazarre!"

"What do you call him?" the little man inquired, ambling beside the chief.

"Eleazer Williams is his name. But in the lodges, at St. Regis, everywhere, it is Lazarre."

"How old is he?"

"About eighteen years."

"Well, Thomas Williams," said my fretful guardian, his antagonism melting to patronage, "I will tell you who I am, and then you can feel no anxiety. I am Doctor Chantry, physician to the Count de Chaumont. The lad cut his head open on a rock, diving in the lake, and has remained unconscious ever since. This is partly due to an opiate I have administered to insure complete quiet; and he will not awake for several hours yet. He received the best surgery as soon as he was brought here and placed in my hands by the educated Oneida, Skenedonk."

"I was not near the lodge," said my father. "I was down the lake, fishing."

"I have bled him once, and shall bleed him again; though the rock did that pretty effectually. But these strapping young creatures need frequent bloodletting."

The chief gave him no thanks, and I myself resolved to knock the little doctor down, if he came near me with a knife.

"In the absence of Count de Chaumont, Thomas," he proceeded, "I may direct you to go and knock on the cook's door, and ask for something to eat before you go home."

"I stay here," responded my father.

"There is not the slightest need of anybody's watching beside the lad tonight. I was about to retire when you were permitted to enter. He is sleeping like an infant."

"He belongs to me," the chief said.

Doctor Chantry jumped at the chief in rage.

"For God's sake, shut up and go about your business!"

It was like one of the little dogs in our camp snapping at the patriarch of them all, and recoiling from a growl. My father's hand was on his hunting knife; but he grunted and said nothing. Doctor Chantry himself withdrew from the room and left the Indian in possession. Weak as I was I felt my insides quake with laughter. My very first observation of the whimsical being tickled me with a kind of foreknowledge of all his weak fretfulness.

My father sat down on the floor at the foot of my couch, where the wax light threw his shadow, exaggerating its unmoving profile. I noticed one of the chairs he disdained as useless; though when eating or drinking with white men he sat at table with them. The chair I saw was one that I faintly recognized, as furniture of some previous experience, slim legged, gracefully curved, and brocaded. Brocaded was the word. I studied it until I fell asleep.

The sun, shining through the protected windows, instead of glaring into our lodge door, showed my father sitting in the same position when I woke, and Skenedonk at my side. I liked the educated Iroquois. He was about ten years my senior. He had been taken to France when a stripling, and was much bound to the whites, though living with his own tribe. Skenedonk had the mildest brown eyes I ever saw outside a deer's head. He was a bald Indian with one small scalp lock. But the just and perfect dome to which his close lying ears were attached needed no hair to adorn it. You felt glad that nothing shaded the benevolence of his all-over forehead. By contrast he emphasized the sullenness of my father; yet when occasion had pressed there never was a readier hand than Skenedonk's to kill.

I tossed the cover back to spring out of bed with a whoop. But a woman in a high cap with ribbons hanging down to her heels, and a dress short enough to show her shoes, stepped into the room and made a courtesy. Her face fell easily into creases when she talked, and gave you the feeling that it was too soft of flesh. Indeed, her eyes were cushioned all around. She spoke and Skenedonk answered her in French. The meaning of every word broke through my mind as fire breaks through paper.

"Madame de Ferrier sent me to inquire how the young gentleman is."

Skenedonk lessened the rims around his eyes. My father grunted.

"Did Madame de Ferrier say 'the young gentleman?'" Skenedonk inquired.

"I was told to inquire. I am her servant Ernestine," said the woman, her face creased with the anxiety of responding to questions.

"Tell Madame de Ferrier that the young gentleman is much better, and will go home to the lodges to-day."

"She said I was to wait upon him, and give him his breakfast under the doctor's direction."

"Say with thanks to Madame de Ferrier that I wait upon him."

Ernestine again courtesied, and made way for Doctor Chantry. He came in quite good natured, and greeted all of us, his inferiors, with a humility I then thought touching, but learned afterwards to distrust. My head already felt the healing blood, and I was ravenous for food. He bound it with fresh bandages, and opened a box full of glittering knives, taking out a small sheath. From this he made a point of steel spring like lightning.

"We will bring the wholesome lancet again into play, my lad," said Doctor Chantry. I waited in uncertainty with my feet on the floor and my hands on the side of the couch, while he carefully removed coat and waistcoat and turned up his sleeves.

"Ernestine, bring the basin," he commanded.

My father may have thought the doctor was about to inflict a vicarious puncture on himself. Skenedonk, with respect for civilized surgery, waited. I did not wait. The operator bared me to the elbow and showed a piece of plaster already sticking on my arm. The conviction of being outraged in my person came upon me mightily, and snatching the wholesome lancet I turned its spring upon the doctor. He yelled. I leaped through the door like a deer, and ran barefooted, the loose robe curdling above my knees. I had the fleetest foot among the Indian racers, and was going to throw the garment away for the pure joy of feeling the air slide past my naked body, when I saw the girl and poppet baby who had looked at me during my first consciousness. They were sitting on a blanket under the trees of De Chaumont's park, which deepened into wilderness.

The baby put up a lip, and the girl surrounded it with her arm, dividing her sympathy with me. I must have been a charming object. Though ravenous for food and broken-headed, I forgot my state, and turned off the road of escape to stare at her like a tame deer.

She lowered her eyes wisely, and I got near enough without taking fright to see a book spread open on the blanket, showing two illuminated pages. Something parted in me. I saw my mother, as I had seen her in some past life:—not Marianne the Mohawk, wife of Thomas Williams, but a fair oval-faced mother with arched brows. I saw even her pointed waist and puffed skirts, and the lace around her open neck. She held the book in her hands and read to me from it.

I dropped on my knees and stretched my arms above my head, crying aloud as women cry with gasps and chokings in sudden bereavement. Nebulous memories twisted all around me and I could grasp nothing. I raged for what had been mine—for some high estate out of which I had fallen into degradation. I clawed the ground in what must have seemed convulsions to the girl. Her poppet cried and she hushed it.

"Give me my mother's book!" I strangled out of the depths of my throat; and repeated, as if torn by a devil—"Give me my mother's book!"

She blanched so white that her lips looked seared, and instead of disputing my claim, or inquiring about my mother, or telling me to begone, she was up on her feet. Taking her dress in her finger tips and settling back almost to the ground in the most beautiful obeisance I ever saw, she said—

"Sire!"

Neither in Iroquois nor in Iroquois-French had such a name been given to me before. I had a long title signifying Tree-Cutter, which belonged to every chief of our family. But that word—"Sire!"—and her deep reverence seemed to atone in some way for what I had lost. I sat up, quieting myself, still moved as water heaves. She put the missal on the lap of my single garment, and drew back a step, formally standing. My scarred ankles, at which the Indian children used to point, were exposed to her gaze, for I never would sit on them after the manner of the tribe. There was no restraining the tears that ran down my face. She might have mocked me, but she remained white and quiet; while I sat as dumb as a dog, and as full of unuttered speech. Looking back now I can see what passionate necessity shook me with throbs to be the equal of her who had received me as a superior.

De Chaumont's manor house, facing a winding avenue, could be seen from where we were. It was of stone, built to enclose a court on three sides, in the form that I afterwards recognized as that of French palaces. There were a great many flowers in the court, and vines covered the ends of the wings. All those misty half remembered hunting seasons that I had spent on Lake George were not without some knowledge. The chimneys and roofs of Le Ray de Chaumont's manor often looked at me through trees as I steered my boat among the islands. He was a great land owner, having more than three hundred thousand acres of wilderness. And he was friendly with both Indians and Americans. His figure did not mean much to me when I saw it, being merely a type of wealth, and wealth extends little power into the wilderness.

The poppet of a child climbed up and held to the girl's dress. She stooped over and kissed it, saying, "Sit down, Paul." The toy human being seemed full of intelligence, and after the first protest examined me fearlessly, with enchanting smiles about the mouth and eyes. I noticed even then an upward curling of the mouth corners and a kind of magic in the liquid blue gaze, of which Paul might never be conscious, but which would work on every beholder.

That a child should be the appendage of such a very young creature as the girl, surprised me no more than if it had been a fawn or a dog. In the vivid moments of my first rousing to life I had seen her with Paul in her arms; and he remained part of her.

We heard a rush of horses up the avenue, and out of the woods came Le Ray de Chaumont and his groom, the wealthy land owner equipped in gentleman's riding dress from his spurs to his hat. He made a fine show, whip hand on his hip and back erect as a pine tree. He was a man in middle life, but he reined up and dismounted with the swift agility of a youth, and sent his horse away with the groom, as soon as he saw the girl run across the grass to meet him. Taking her hand he bowed over it and kissed it with pleasing ceremony, of which I approved. An Iroquois chief in full council had not better manners than Le Ray de Chaumont.

Paul and I waited to see what was going to happen, for the two came toward us, the girl talking rapidly to the man. I saw my father and Skenedonk and the doctor also coming from the house, and they readily spied me sitting tame as a rabbit near the baby.

You never can perceive yourself what figure you are making in the world: for when you think you are the admired of all eyes you may be displaying a fool; and when life seems prostrated in you it may be that you show as a monument on the heights. But I could not be mistaken in De Chaumont's opinion of me. He pointed his whip handle at me, exclaiming—

"What!—that scarecrow, madame?"

II

"But look at him," she urged.

"I recognize first," said De Chaumont as he sauntered, "an old robe of my own."

"His mother was reduced to coarse serge, I have been told."

"You speak of an august lady, my dear Eagle. But this is Chief Williams' boy. He has been at the hunting lodges every summer since I came into the wilderness. There you see his father, the half-breed Mohawk."

"I saw the dauphin in London, count. I was a little child, but his scarred ankles and wrists and forehead are not easily forgotten."

"The dauphin died in the Temple, Eagle."

"My father and Philippe never believed that."

"Your father and Philippe were very mad royalists."

"And you have gone over to Bonaparte. They said that boy had all the traits of the Bourbons, even to the shaping of his ear."

"A Bourbon ear hears nothing but Bonaparte in these days," said De Chaumont. "How do you know this is the same boy you saw in London?"

"Last night while he was lying unconscious, after Doctor Chantry had bandaged his head and bled him, I went in to see if I might be of use. He was like some one I had seen. But I did not know him until a moment ago. He ran out of the house like a wild Indian. Then he saw us sitting here, and came and fell down on his knees at sight of that missal. I saw his scars. He claimed the book as his mother's—and you know, count, it was his mother's!"

"My dear child, whenever an Indian wants a present he dreams that you give it to him, or he claims it. Chief Williams' boy wanted your valuable illuminated book. I only wonder he had the taste. The rings on your hands are more to an Indian's liking."

"But he is not an Indian, count. He is as white as we are."

"That signifies nothing. Plenty of white children have been brought up among the tribes. Chief Williams' grandmother, I have heard, was a Yankee woman."

Not one word of their rapid talk escaped an ear trained to faintest noises in the woods. I felt like a tree, well set up and sound, but rooted and voiceless in my ignorant helplessness before the two so frankly considering me.

My father stopped when he saw Madame de Ferrier, and called to me in Iroquois. It was plain that he and Doctor Chantry disagreed. Skenedonk, put out of countenance by my behavior, and the stubbornness of the chief, looked ready to lay his hand upon his mouth in sign of being confounded before white men; for his learning had altered none of his inherited instincts.

But as for me, I was as De Chaumont had said, Chief Williams' boy, faint from blood letting and twenty-four hours' fasting; and the father's command reminded me of the mother's dinner pot. I stood up erect and drew the flowered silk robe around me. It would have been easier to walk on burning coals, but I felt obliged to return the book to Madame de Ferrier. She would not take it. I closed her grasp upon it, and stooping, saluted her hand with courtesy as De Chaumont had done. If he had roared I must have done this devoir. But all he did was to widen his eyes and strike his leg with his riding whip.

My father and I seldom talked. An Indian boy who lives in water and forest all summer and on snowshoes all winter, finds talk enough in the natural world without falling back upon his family. Dignified manners were not lacking among my elders, but speech had seemed of little account to me before this day.

The chief paddled and I sat naked in our canoe;—for we left the flowered robe with a horse-boy at the stables;—the sun warm upon my skin, the lake's blue glamour affecting me like enchantment.

Neither love nor aversion was associated with my father. I took my head between my hands and tried to remember a face that was associated with aversion.

"Father," I inquired, "was anybody ever very cruel to me?"

He looked startled, but spoke harshly.

"What have you got in your head? These white people have been making a fool of you."

"I remember better to-day than I ever remembered before. I am different. I was a child: but to-day manhood has come. Father, what is a dauphin?"

The chief made no answer.

"What is a temple? Is it a church, like ours at St. Regis?"

"Ask the priest."

"Do you know what Bourbon is, father,—particularly a Bourbon ear?"

"Nothing that concerns you."

"But how could I have a Bourbon ear if it didn't concern me?"

"Who said you had such an ear?"

"Madame de Ferrier."

The chief grunted.

"At least she told De Chaumont," I repeated exactly, "I was the boy she saw in London, that her father said had all the traits of the Bourbons. Where is London?"

The chief paddled without replying. Finding him so ignorant on all points of the conversation, or so determined to put me down, I gazed awhile at our shadow gliding in the water, and then began again.

"Father, do you happen to know who Bonaparte is?"

This time he answered.

"Bonaparte is a great soldier."

"Is he a white man or an Indian?"

"He is a Frenchman."

I meditated on the Frenchmen I dimly remembered about St. Regis. They were undersized fellows, very apt to weep when their emotions were stirred. I could whip them all.

"Did he ever come to St. Regis?"

The chief again grunted.

"Does France come to St. Regis?" he retorted with an impatient question.

"What is France, father?"

"A country."

"Shall we ever go there to hunt?"

"Shall we ever go the other side of the sunrise to hunt? France is the other side of the sunrise. Talk to the squaws."

Though rebuked, I determined to do it if any information could be got out of them. The desire to know things was consuming. I had the belated feeling of one who waked to consciousness late in life and found the world had run away from him. The camp seemed strange, as if I had been gone many years, but every object was so wonderfully distinct.

My mother Marianne fed me, and when I lay down dizzy in the bunk, covered me. The family must have thought it was natural sleep. But it was a fainting collapse, which took me more than once afterwards as suddenly as a blow on the head, when my faculties were most needed. Whether this was caused by the plunge upon the rock or the dim life from which I had emerged, I do not know. One moment I saw the children, and mothers from the neighboring lodges, more interested than my own mother: our smoky rafters, and the fire pit in the center of unfloored ground: my clothes hanging over the bunk, and even a dog with his nose in the kettle. And then, as it had been the night before, I waked after many hours.

By that time the family breathing sawed the air within the walls, and a fine starlight showed through the open door, for we had no window. Outside the oak trees were pattering their leaves like rain, reminding me of our cool spring in the woods. My bandaged head was very hot, in that dark lair of animals where the log bunks stretched and deepened shadow.

If Skenedonk had been there I would have asked him to bring me water, with confidence in his natural service. The chief's family was a large one, but not one of my brothers and sisters seemed as near to me as Skenedonk. The apathy of fraternal attachment never caused me any pain. The whole tribe was held dear.

I stripped off Doctor Chantry's unendurable bandages, and put on my clothes, for there were brambles along the path. The lodges and the dogs were still, and I crept like a hunter after game, to avoid waking them. Our village was an irregular camp, each house standing where its owner had pleased to build it on the lake shore. Behind it the blackness of wooded wilderness seemed to stretch to the end of the world.

The spring made a distinct tinkle in the rush of low sound through the forest. A rank night sweetness of mints and other lush plants mixed its spirit with the body of leaf earth. I felt happy in being a part of all this, and the woods were to me as safe as the bed-chamber of a mother. It was fine to wallow, damming the span of escaping water with my fevered head. Physical relief and delicious shuddering coolness ran through me.

From that wet pillow I looked up and thought again of what had happened that day, and particularly of the girl whom De Chaumont had called Madame de Ferrier and Eagle. Every word that she had spoken passed again before my mind. Possibilities that I had never imagined rayed out from my recumbent body as from the hub of a vast wheel. I was white. I was not an Indian. I had a Bourbon ear. She believed I was a dauphin.

What was a dauphin, that she should make such a deep obeisance to it? My father the chief, recommending me to the squaws, had appeared to know nothing about it.

All that she believed De Chaumont denied. The rich book which stirred such torment in me—"you know it was his mother's!" she said—De Chaumont thought I merely coveted. I can see now that the crude half-savage boy wallowing in the spring stream, set that woman as high as the highest star above his head, and made her the hope and symbol of his possible best.

A woman's long cry, like the appeal of that one on whom he meditated, echoed through the woods and startled him out of his wallow.

III

I sat up with the water trickling down my back. The cry was repeated, out of the west.

I knew the woods, but night alters the most familiar places. It was so dark in vaults and tunnels of trees and thickets that I might have burrowed through the ground almost as easily as thresh a path. The million scarcely audible noises that fill a forest surrounded me, and twigs not broken by me cracked or shook. Still I made directly toward the woman's voice which guided me more plainly; but left off running as my ear detected that she was only in perplexity. She called at intervals, imperatively but not in continuous screams. She was a white woman; for no squaw would publish her discomfort. A squaw if lost would camp sensibly on a bed of leaves, and find her way back to the village in the morning. The wilderness was full of dangers, but when you are elder brother to the bear and the wildcat you learn their habits, and avoid or outwit them.

Climbing over rocks and windfalls I came against a solid log wall and heard the woman talking in a very pretty chatter the other side of it. She only left off talking to call for help, and left off calling for help to scold and laugh again. There was a man imprisoned with her, and they were speaking English, a language I did not then understand. But what had happened to them was very plain. They had wandered into a pen built by hunters to trap bears, and could not find the bush-masked and winding opening, but were traveling around the walls. It was lucky for them that a bear had not arrived first, though in that case their horses must have smelled him. I heard the beasts shaking their bridles.

I found my way to the opening, and whistled. At once the woman ceased her chatter and drew in her breath, and they both asked me a question that needed no interpretation. I told them where they were, and the woman began talking at once in my own tongue and spoke it as well as I could myself.

"In a bear pen? George, he says we are in a bear pen! Take us out, dear chief, before the bear family arrive home from their ball. I don't know whether you are a chief or not, but most Indians are. My nurse was a chief's daughter. Where are you? I can't see anything but chunks of blackness."

I took her horse by the bridle and led him, and so got both the riders outside. They had no tinder, and neither had I; and all of us groped for the way by which they had come to the bear pen. The young man spurred his horse in every direction, and turned back unable to get through.

Though we could not see one another I knew that both the adventurers were young, and that they expected to be called to severe account for the lawless act they were committing. The girl, talking English, or French, or Mohawk almost in one breath, took the blame upon herself and made light of the boy's self-reproaches.

She laughed and said—"My father thinks I am with Miss Chantry, and Miss Chantry thinks I am with my father. He will blame her for letting me ride with George Croghan to meet him, and lose the way and so get into the bear pen. And she will blame my father, and your dearest Annabel will let the Count de Chaumont and Miss Chantry fight it out. It is not an affair for youth to meddle with, George."

Having her for interpreter the boy and I consulted. I might have led him back to our hunting camp, but it was a hard road for a woman and an impossible one for horses. There was no inhabited house nearer than De Chaumont's own. He decided they must return to the road by which they had come into the bear pen, and gladly accepted my offer to go with him; dismounting and leading Annabel de Chaumont's horse while I led his. We passed over rotten logs and through black tangles, the girl bending to her saddle bow, unwearied and full of laughter. It was plain that he could not find any outlet, and falling behind with the cumbered horse he let me guide the party.

I do not know by what instinct I felt my way, conscious of slipping between the wild citizens of that vast town of trees; but we finally reached a clearing and saw across the open space a lighted cabin. Its sashless windows and defective chinks were gilded with the yellow light that comes from a glowing hearth.

"I know this place!" exclaimed Annabel. "It is where the Saint-Michels used to live before they went to my father's settlement at Le Rayville. Look at the house! Nobody lives there. It must be full of witches."

Violin music testified that the witches were merry. We halted, and the horses neighed and were answered by others of their kind.

"George Croghan's grandmother was struck by a witch ball. And here her grandson stands, too tired to run. But perhaps there aren't any witches in the house. I don't believe wicked things would be allowed to enter it. The Saint-Michels were so pious, and ugly, and resigned to the poverty of refugees. Their society was so good for me, my mother, when she was alive, made me venerate them until I hated them. Holy Sophie died and went to heaven. I shall never see her again. She was, indeed, excellent. This can't be a nest of witches. George, why don't you go and knock on the door?"

It was not necessary, for the door opened and a man appeared, holding his violin by the neck. He stepped out to look around the cabin at some horses fastened there, and saw and hailed us.

I was not sorry to be allowed to enter, for I was tired to exhaustion, and sat down on the floor away from the fire. The man looked at me suspiciously, though he was ruddy and good natured. But he bent quite over before De Chaumont's daughter, and made a flourish with his hand in receiving young Croghan. There were in the cabin with him two women and two little girls; and a Canadian servant like a fat brown bear came from the rear of the house to look at us and then went back to the horses.

All the women began to speak, but Annabel de Chaumont could talk faster than the four others combined, so they knew our plight before we learned that they were the Grignon and Tank families, who were going into the west to find settlement and had made the house their camp for one night. The Dutch maid, dark and round-eyed, and the flaxen little Grignon, had respect for their elders and held their tongues while Madame Tank and Madame Grignon spoke, but Annabel de Chaumont was like a grove of sparrows. The world seemed swarming with young maids. The travelers were mere children, while the count's daughter was startling as an angel. Her clothing fitted her body like an exquisite sheath. I do not know what it was, but it made her look as slim as a dragon fly. Her white and rose pink face had a high arched nose, and was proud and saucy. She wore her hair beaten out like mist, with rich curly shreds hanging in front of her ears to her shoulders. She shook her head to set her hat straight, and turned her eyes in rapid smiling sweeps. I knew as well then as I ever did afterwards that she was bound to befool every man that came near her.

There were only two benches in the cabin, but it was floored and better made than our hunting lodges. The temporary inmates and their guests sat down in a long row before the fire. I was glad to make a pillow of a saddle near the wall, and watch their backs, as an outsider. Mademoiselle de Chaumont absorbed all eyes and all attention. She told about a ball, to which she had ridden with her governess and servants a three days' journey, and from which all the dancers were riding back a three days' journey to join in another ball at her father's house. With the hospitality which made Le Ray de Chaumont's manor the palace of the wilderness as it existed then, she invited the hosts who sheltered her for the night, to come to the ball and stay all summer. And they lamented that they could not accept the invitation, being obliged to hurry on to Albany, where a larger party would give them escort on a long westward journey.

The head of the house took up his bow, as if musing on the ball, and Annabel de Chaumont wriggled her feet faster and faster. Tireless as thistledown that rolls here and there at the will of the wind, up she sprang and began to dance. The children watched her spellbound. None of us had ever seen the many figures through which she passed, or such wonderful dancing. The chimney was built of logs and clay, forming terraces. As if it was no longer possible for her to stay on the ground she darted from the bench-end to the lowest log, and stepped on up as fearlessly as a thing of air, until her head touched the roof. Monsieur Grignon played like mad, and the others clapped their hands. While she poised so I sat up to watch her, and she noticed me for the first time by firelight.

"Look at that boy—he has been hurt—the blood is running down his cheek!" she cried. "I thought he was an Indian—and he is white!"

She came down as lightly as she had gone up, and caused me to be haled against my will to the middle of a bench. I wanted the women to leave me alone, and told them my head had been broken two days before, and was nearly well. The mothers, too keen to wash and bandage to let me escape, opened a saddle pack and tore good linen.

George Croghan stood by the chimney, slim and tall and handsome. His head and face were long, his hair was of a sunny color, and his mouth corners were shrewd and good natured. I liked him the moment I saw him. Younger in years than I, he was older in wit and manly carriage. While he looked on it was hard to have Madame Tank seize my head in her hands and examine my eyebrow. She next took my wrists, and not satisfied, stripped up the right sleeve and exposed a crescent-shaped scar, one of the rare vaccination marks of those days. I did not know what it was. Her animated dark eyes drew the brows together so that a pucker came between them. I looked at Croghan, and wanted to exclaim—"Help yourself! Anybody may handle me!"

"Ursule Grignon!" she said sharply, and Madame Grignon answered,

"Eh, what, Katarina?"

"This is the boy."

"But what boy?"

"The boy I saw on the ship."

"The one who was sent to America—"

Madame Tank put up her hand, and the other stopped.

"But that was a child," Madame Grignon then objected.

"Nine years ago. He would be about eighteen now."

"How old are you?" they both put to me.

Remembering what my father had told Doctor Chantry, I was obliged to own that I was about eighteen. Annabel de Chaumont sat on the lowest log of the chimney with her feet on a bench, and her chin in her hand, interested to the point of silence. Something in her eyes made it very galling to be overhauled and have my blemishes enumerated before her and Croghan. What had uplifted me to Madame de Ferrier's recognition now mocked, and I found it hard to submit. It would not go well with the next stranger who declared he knew me by my scars.

"What do they call you in this country?" inquired Madame Tank.

I said my name was Lazarre Williams.

"It is not!" she said in an undertone, shaking her head.

I made bold to ask with some warmth what my name was then, and she whispered—"Poor child!"

It seemed that I was to be pitied in any case. In dim self-knowledge I saw that the core of my resentment was her treating me with commiseration. Madame de Ferrier had not treated me so.

"You live among the Indians?" Madame Tank resumed.

The fact was evident.

"Have they been kind to you?"

I said they had.

Madame Tank's young daughter edged near her and inquired in a whisper,

"Who is he, mother?"

"Hush!" answered Madame Tank.

The head of the party laid down his violin and bow, and explained to us:

"Madame Tank was maid of honor to the queen of Holland, before reverses overtook her. She knows court secrets."

"But she might at least tell us," coaxed Annabel, "if this Mohawk is a Dutchman."

Madame Tank said nothing.

"What could happen in the court of Holland? The Dutch are slow coaches. I saw the Van Rensselaers once, near Albany, riding in a wagon with straw under their feet, on common chairs, the old Patroon himself driving. This boy is some off-scouring."

"He outranks you, mademoiselle," retorted Madame Tank.

"That's what I wanted to find out," said Annabel.

I kept half an eye on Croghan to see what he thought of all this woman talk. For you cannot help being more dominated by the opinion of your contemporaries than by that of the fore-running or following generation. He held his countenance in excellent command, and did not meddle even by a word. You could be sure, however, that he was no credulous person who accepted everything that was said to him.

Madame Tank looked into the reddened fireplace, and began to speak, but hesitated. The whole thing was weird, like a dream resulting from the cut on my head: the strange white faces; the camp stuff and saddlebags unpacked from horses; the light on the coarse floor; the children listening as to a ghost story; Mademoiselle de Chaumont presiding over it all. The cabin had an arched roof and no loft. The top was full of shadows.

"If you are the boy I take you to be," Madame Tank finally said, sinking her voice, "you may find you have enemies."

"If I am the boy you take me to be, madame, who am I?"

She shook her head.

"I wish I had not spoken at all. To tell you anything more would only plunge you into trouble. You are better off to be as you are, than to know the truth and suffer from it. Besides, I may be mistaken. And I am certainly too helpless myself to be of any use to you. This much I will say: when you are older, if things occur that make it necessary for you to know what I know, send a letter to me, and I will write it down."

With delicacy Monsieur Grignon began to play a whisper of a tune on his violin. I did not know what she meant by a letter, though I understood her. Madame Tank spoke the language as well as anybody. I thought then, as idiom after idiom rushed back on my memory, that it was an universal language, with the exception of Iroquois and English.

"We are going to a place called Green Bay, in the Northwest Territory. Remember the name: Green Bay. It is in the Wisconsin country."

IV

Dawn found me lying wide awake with my head on a saddle. I slipped out into the dewy half light.

That was the first time I ever thought about the mountains. They seemed to be newly created, standing up with streamers of mist torn and floating across their breasts. The winding cliff-bound lake was like a gorge of smoke. I felt as if I had reared upon my hind feet, lifting my face from the ground to discover there was a God. Some of the prayers our priest had industriously beaten into my head, began to repeat themselves. In a twinkling I was a child, lonely in the universe, separated from my dim old life, instinct with growth, yet ignorant of my own needs.

What Madame de Ferrier and Madame Tank had said influenced me less than the intense life of my roused activities.

It was mid forenoon by the sun when I reached our lodges, and sat down fagged outside my father's door, to think longer before I entered. Hunger was the principal sensation, though we had eaten in the cabin the night before, and the Indian life inures a man to fasting when he cannot come by food. I heard Skenedonk talking to my father and mother in our cabin. The village was empty; children and women, hunters and fishermen having scattered to woods and waters.

"He ought to learn books," said Skenedonk. "Money is sent you every year to be spent upon him: yet you spend nothing upon him."

"What has he needed?" said my father.

"He needs much now. He needs American clothes. He wept at the sight of a book. God has removed the touch since he plunged in the water."

"You would make a fool of him," said my father. "He was gone from the lodge this morning. You taught him an evil path when you carried him off."

"It is a natural path for him: he will go to his own. I stayed and talked with De Chaumont, and I bring you an offer. De Chaumont will take Lazarre into his house, and have him taught all that a white boy should know. You will pay the cost. If you don't, De Chaumont will look into this annuity of which you give no account."

"I have never been asked to give account. Could Lazarre learn anything? The priest has sat over him. He had food and clothing like my own."

"That is true. But he is changed. Marianne will let him go."

"The strange boy may go," said my mother. "But none of my own children shall leave us to be educated."

I got up and went into the cabin. All three knew I had heard, and they waited in silence while I approached my mother and put my hands on her shoulders. There was no tenderness between us, but she had fostered me. The small dark eyes in her copper face, and her shapeless body, were associated with winters and summers stretching to a vanishing point.

"Mother," I said, "is it true that I am not your son?"

She made no answer.

"Is it true that the chief is not my father?"

She made no answer.

"Who sends money to be spent on me every year?"

Still she made no answer.

"If I am not your son, whose son am I?"

In the silence I turned to Skenedonk.

"Isn't my name Lazarre Williams, Skenedonk?"

"You are called Lazarre Williams."

"A woman told me last night that it was not my name. Everyone denies me. No one owns me and tells whose child I am. Wasn't I born at St. Regis?"

"If you were, there is no record of your birth on the register. The chief's other children have their births recorded."

I turned to my father. The desolation of being cut off and left with nothing but the guesses of strangers overcame me. I sobbed so the hoarse choke echoed in the cabin. Skenedonk opened his arms, and my father and mother let me lean on the Oneida's shoulder.

I have thought since that they resented with stoical pain his taking their white son from them. They both stood severely reserved, passively loosening the filial bond.

All the business of life was suspended, as when there is death in the lodge. Skenedonk and I sat down together on a bunk.

"Lazarre," my father spoke, "do you want to be educated?"

The things we pine for in this world are often thrust upon us in a way to choke us. I had tramped miles, storming for the privileges that had made George Croghan what he was. Fate instantly picked me up from unendurable conditions to set me down where I could grow, and I squirmed with recoil from the shock.

I felt crowded over the edge of a cliff and about to drop into a valley of rainbows.

"Do you want to live in De Chaumont's house and learn his ways?"

My father and mother had been silent when I questioned them. It was my turn to be silent.

"Or would you rather stay as you are?"

"No, father," I answered, "I want to go."

The camp had never been dearer. I walked among the Indian children when the evening fires were lighted, and the children looked at me curiously as at an alien. Already my people had cut me off from them.

"What I learn I will come back and teach you," I told the young men and women of my own age. They laughed.

"You are a fool, Lazarre. There is a good home for you at St. Regis. If you fall sick in De Chaumont's house who will care?"

"Skenedonk is my friend," I answered.

"Skenedonk would not stay where he is tying you. When the lake freezes you will be mad for snowshoes and a sight of the St. Lawrence."

"Perhaps so. But we are not made alike. Do not forget me."

They gave me belts and garters, and I distributed among them all my Indian property. Then, as if to work a charm which should keep me from breaking through the circle, they joined hands and danced around me. I went to every cabin, half ashamed of my desertion, yet unspeakably craving a blessing. The old people variously commented on the measure, their wise eyes seeing the change in one who had been a child rather than a young man among them.

If the wrench from the village was hard, the induction into the manor was harder. Skenedonk took me in his boat, skirting the long strip of mountainous shore which separated us from De Chaumont.

He told me De Chaumont would permit my father to pay no more than my exact reckoning.

"Do you know who sends the money?" I inquired.

The Oneida did not know. It came through an agent in New York.

"You are ten years older than I am. You must remember very well when I was born."

"How can that be?" answered Skenedonk. "Nobody in the tribe knows when you were born."

"Are children not like the young of other creatures? Where did I come from?"

"You came to the tribe with a man, and Chief Williams adopted you."

"Did you see the man?"

"No. I was on the other side of the ocean, in France."

"Who saw him?"

"None of our people. But it is very well known. If you had noticed anything you would have heard the story long ago."

What Skenedonk said was true. I asked him, bewildered—"Why did I never notice anything?"

The Oneida tapped his bald head.

"When I saw you first you were not the big fellow with speaking eyes that you are to-day. You would sit from sunrise to sunset, looking straight ahead of you and never moving except when food was put in your hand. As you grew older the children dragged you among them to play. You learned to fish, and hunt, and swim; and knew us, and began to talk our language. Now at last you are fully roused, and are going to learn the knowledge there is in books."

I asked Skenedonk how he himself had liked books, and he shook his head, smiling. They were good for white men, very good. An Indian had little use for them. He could read and write and cast accounts. When he made his great journey to the far country, what interested him most was the behavior of the people.

We did not go into the subject of his travels at that time, for I began to wonder who was going to teach me books, and heard with surprise that it was Doctor Chantry.

"But I struck him with the little knife that springs out of a box."

Skenedonk assured me that Doctor Chantry thought nothing of it, and there was no wound but a scratch. He looked on me as his pupil. He knew all kinds of books.

Evidently Doctor Chantry liked me from the moment I showed fight. His Anglo-Saxon blood was stirred. He received me from Skenedonk, who shook my hand and wished me well, before paddling away.

De Chaumont's house was full as a hive around the three sides of its flowered court. A ball was in preparation, and all the guests had arrived. Avoiding these gentry we mounted stairs toward the roof, and came into a burst of splendor. As far as the eye could see through square east and west windows, unbroken forests stretched to the end of the world, or Lake George wound, sown thick with islands, ranging in size from mere rocks supporting a tree, to wooded acres.

The room which weaned me from aboriginal life was at the top of the central building. Doctor Chantry shuffled over the clean oak floor and introduced me to my appointments. There were curtains like frost work, which could be pushed back from the square panes. At one end of the huge apartment was my huge bed, formidable with hangings. Near it stood a table for the toilet. He opened a closet door in the wall and showed a spiral staircase going down to a tunnel which led to the lake. For when De Chaumont first came into the wilderness and built the central house without its wings, he thought it well to have a secret way out, as his chateau in the old country had.

"The tunnel is damp," said Doctor Chantry. "I never venture into it, though all the corner rooms below give upon this stairway, and mine is just under yours."

It was like returning me the lake to use in my own accustomed way. For the remainder of my furniture I had a study table, a cupboard for clothes, some arm-chairs, a case of books, and a massive fireplace with chimney seats at the end of the room opposite the bed.

I asked Doctor Chantry, "Was all this made ready for me before I was sure of coming here?"

"When the count decides that a thing will be done it is usually done," said my schoolmaster. "And Madame de Ferrier was very active in forwarding the preparations."

The joy of youth in the unknown was before me. My old camp life receded behind me.

Madame de Ferrier's missal-book lay on the table, and when I stopped before it tongue-tied, Doctor Chantry said I was to keep it.

"She gives it to you. It was treasured in her family on account of personal attachment to the giver. She is not a Catholic. She was brought up as good a Protestant as any English gentlewoman."

"I told her it was my mother's. It seemed to be my mother's. But I don't know—I can't remember."

My master looked at the missal, and said it was a fine specimen of illumination. His manner toward me was so changed that I found it hard to refer to the lancet. This, however, very naturally followed his examination of my head. He said I had healthy blood, and the wound was closing by the first intention. The pink cone at the tip of his nose worked in a whimsical grin as he heard my apology.

"It is not often you will make the medicine man take his own remedy, my lad."

We thus began our relation with the best feeling. It has since appeared that I was a blessing to Doctor Chantry. My education gave him something to do. For although he called himself physician to Count de Chaumont, he had no real occupation in the house, and dabbled with poetry, dozing among books. De Chaumont was one of those large men who gather in the weak. His older servants had come to America with his father, and were as attached as kindred. A natural parasite like Doctor Chantry took to De Chaumont as means of support; and it was pleasing to both of them.

My master asked me when I wanted to begin my studies, and I said, "Now." We sat down at the table, and I learned the English alphabet, some phrases of English talk, some spelling, and traced my first characters in a copy-book. With consuming desire to know, I did not want to leave off at dusk. In that high room day lingered. The doctor was fretful for his supper before we rose from our task.

Servants were hurrying up and down stairs. The whole house had an air of festivity. Doctor Chantry asked me to wait in a lower corridor while he made some change in his dress.

I sat down on a broad window sill, and when I had waited a few minutes, Mademoiselle de Chaumont darted around a corner, bare armed and bare necked. She collapsed to the floor at sight of me, and then began to dance away in the opposite direction with stiff leaps, as a lamb does in springtime.

I saw she was in pain or trouble, needing a servant, and made haste to reach her; when she hid her face on both arms against the wall.

"Go off!" she hissed. "—S-s-s! Go off! I haven't anything on!—Don't go off! Open my door for me quick!—before anybody else comes into the hall!"

"Which door is it?" I asked. She showed me. It had a spring catch, and she had stepped into the hall to see if the catch was set.

"The catch was set!" gasped Mademoiselle de Chaumont. "Break the door—get it open—anyway—Quick!"

By good fortune I had strength enough in my shoulder to set the door wide off its spring, and she flew to the middle of the room slamming it in my face.

Fitness and unfitness required nicer discrimination than the crude boy from the woods possessed. When I saw her in the ball-room she had very little more on than when I saw her in the hall, and that little clung tight around her figure. Yet she looked quite unconcerned.

After we had eaten supper Doctor Chantry and I sat with his sister where we could see the dancing, on a landing of the stairway. De Chaumont's generous house was divided across the middle by a wide hall that made an excellent ball-room. The sides were paneled, like the walls of the room in which I first came to my senses. Candles in sconces were reflected by the polished, dark floor. A platform for his fiddlers had been built at one end. Festoons of green were carried from a cluster of lights in the center of the ceiling, to the corners, making a bower or canopy under which the dancers moved.

It is strange to think that not one stone remains upon another and scarcely a trace is left of this manor. When De Chaumont determined to remove to his seat at Le Rayville, in what was then called Castorland, he had his first hold pulled down.

Miss Chantry was a blunt woman. Her consideration for me rested on my being her brother's pupil. She spoke more readily than he did. From our cove we looked over the railing at an active world.

"Madame Eagle is a picture," remarked Miss Chantry. "—— Eagle! What a name for civilized people to give a christened child! But these French are as likely as not to call their boys Anne or Marie, and it wouldn't surprise me if they called their girls Cat or Dog. Eagle or Crow, she is the handsomest woman on the floor."

"Except Mademoiselle Annabel," the doctor ventured to amend.

"That Annabel de Chaumont," his sister vigorously declared, "has neither conscience nor gratitude. But none of the French have. They will take your best and throw you away with a laugh."

My master and I watched the brilliant figures swimming in the glow of wax candles. Face after face could be singled out as beautiful, and the scant dresses revealed taper forms. Madame de Ferrier's garments may have been white or blue or yellow; I remember only her satin arms and neck, the rosy color of her face, and the powder on her hair making it white as down.

Where this assembly was collected from I did not know, but it acted on the spirits and went like volatile essence to the brain.

"Pheugh!" exclaimed Miss Chantry, "how the French smell!"

I asked her why, if she detested them so, she lived in a French family, and she replied that Count de Chaumont was an exception, being almost English in his tastes. He had lived out of France since his father came over with La Fayette to help the rebellious Americans.

I did not know who the rebellious Americans were, but inferred that they were people of whom Miss Chantry thought almost as little as she did of the French.

Croghan looked quite a boy among so many experienced gallants, but well appointed in his dress and stepping through the figures featly. He was, Miss Chantry said, a student of William and Mary College.

"This company of gentry will be widely scattered when it disperses home," she told us. "There is at least one man from over-seas."

I thought of the Grignon and Tank families, who were probably on the road to Albany. Miss Chantry bespoke her brother's attention.

"There he is."

"Who?" the doctor inquired.

"His highness," she incisively responded, "Prince Jerome Bonaparte."

I remembered my father had said that Bonaparte was a great soldier in a far off country, and directly asked Miss Chantry if the great soldier was in the ball-room.

She breathed a snort and turned upon my master. "Pray, are you teaching this lad to call that impostor the great soldier?"

Doctor Chantry denied the charge and cast a weak-eyed look of surprise at me.

I said my father told me Bonaparte was a great soldier, and begged to know if he had been deceived.

"Oh!" Miss Chantry responded in a tone which slighted Thomas Williams. "Well! I will tell you facts. Napoleon Bonaparte is one of the worst and most dangerous men that ever lived. He sets the world by the ears, and carries war into every country of Europe. That is his youngest brother yonder—that superfine gallant, in the long-tailed white silk coat down to his heels, and white small-clothes, with diamond buckles in his shoes, and grand lace stock and ruffles. Jerome Bonaparte spent last winter in

Baltimore; and they say he is traveling in the north now to forget a charming American that Napoleon will not let him marry. He has got his name in the newspapers of the day, and so has the young lady. The French consul warned her officially. For Jerome Bonaparte may be made a little king, with other relations of your great soldier."

The young man who might be made a little king was not as large as I was myself, and had a delicate and womanish cut of countenance. I said he was not fit for a king, and Miss Chantry retorted that neither was Napoleon Bonaparte fit for an emperor.

"What is an emperor?" I inquired.

"A chief over kings," Doctor Chantry put in. "Bonaparte is a conqueror and can set kings over the countries he has conquered."

I said that was the proper thing to do. Miss Chantry glared at me. She had weak hair like her brother, but her eyes were a piercing blue, and the angles of her jaws were sharply marked.

Meditating on things outside of my experience I desired to know what the white silk man had done.

"Nothing."

"Then why should the emperor give him a kingdom?"

"Because he is the emperor's brother."

"But he ought to do something himself," I insisted. "It is not enough to accept a chief's place. He cannot hold it if he is not fit."

"So the poor Bourbons found. But they were not upstarts at any rate. I hope I shall live to see them restored."

Here was another opportunity to inform myself. I asked Miss Chantry who the Bourbons were.

"They are the rightful kings of France."

"Why do they let Bonaparte and his brothers take their place?"

Doctor Chantry turned from the promenaders below and, with slow and careful speech, gave me my first lesson in history.

"There was a great civil war in France called the Revolution, when part of the people ran mad to kill the other part. They cut off the heads of the king and queen, and shut up the two royal children in prison. The dauphin died."

"What is a dauphin?"

"The heir to the throne of France was called the dauphin."

"Was he the king's son?"

"The king's eldest son."

"If he had brothers were they dauphins too?"

"No. He alone was the dauphin. The last dauphin of France had no living brothers. He had only a sister."

"You said the dauphin died."

"In a prison called the Temple, in Paris."

"Was the Temple a prison?"

"Yes."

Madame de Ferrier had said her father and some other person did not believe the dauphin died in the Temple.

"Suppose he was alive?" I hazarded.

"Suppose who was alive?" said Miss Chantry.

"The dauphin."

"He isn't."

"Did all the people believe he was dead?"

"They didn't care whether he was dead or not. They went on killing one another until this man Bonaparte put himself at the head of the army and got the upper hand of them. The French are all fire and tow, and the man who can stamp on them is their idol."

"You said you hoped you would live to see the Bourbons restored. Dead people cannot be restored."

"Oh, the Bourbons are not all dead. The king of France had brothers. The elder one of these would be king now if the Bourbons came back to the throne."

"But he would not be king if the dauphin lived?"

"No," said Miss Chantry, leaning back indifferently.

My head felt confused, throbbing with the dull ache of healing. I supported it, resting my elbow on the railing.

The music, under cover of which we had talked, made one of its pauses. Annabel de Chaumont looked up at us, allowing the gentleman in the long-tailed silk coat to lead her toward the stairs.

V

Miss Chantry exclaimed, and her face stiffened with an expression which I have since learned to know as the fear of dignitaries; experienced even by people who profess to despise the dignitaries. Mademoiselle de Chaumont shook frizzes around her face, and lifted the scant dress from her satin shod feet as she mounted the stairs. Without approaching us she sat down on the top step of the landing with young Bonaparte, and beckoned to me.

I went at her bidding and stood by the rail.

"Prince Jerome Bonaparte wants to see you. I have told him about the bear pen, and Madame Tank, and the mysterious marks on you, and what she said about your rank."

I must have frowned, for the young gentleman made a laughing sign to me that he did not take Annabel seriously. He had an amiable face, and accepted me as one of the oddities of the country.

"What fun," said Annabel, "to introduce a prince of the empire to a prince of the woods!"

"What do you think of your brother?" I inquired.

He looked astonished and raised his eyebrows.

"I suppose you mean the emperor?"

I told him I did.

"If you want my candid opinion," his eyes twinkled, and he linked his hands around his white satin knees, "I think my brother rules his family with a rod of iron."

"What will you do," I continued, "when your family are turned out?"

"My faith!" said Annabel, "this in a house favorable to the Empire!"

"A very natural question," said Jerome. "I have often asked myself the same thing."

"The king of France," I argued, "and all the Bourbons were turned out. Why shouldn't the Bonapartes be?"

"Why shouldn't they, indeed!" responded Jerome. "My mother insists they will be. But I wouldn't be the man who undertakes to turn out the emperor."

"What is he like?"

"Impossible to describe him."

"Is he no larger than you?"

Annabel gurgled aloud.

"He is not as large."

"Yet he is a great soldier?"

"A great soldier. And he is adored by the French."

"The French," I quoted, "are all fire and tow."

"Thank you!" said Annabel, pulling out her light frizzes.

"You seem interested in the political situation," remarked Prince Jerome.

I did not know what he meant by the political situation, but told him I had just heard about the Bonapartes.

"Where have you lived?" he laughed.

I told him it didn't matter where people lived; it all depended on whether they understood or not.

"What a sage!—I think I'm one of the people who will never be able to understand," said Jerome.

I said he did not look as if he had been idiotic, and both he and Mademoiselle de Chaumont laughed.

"Monsieur"—

"Lazarre Williams," supplemented Annabel.

"Monsieur Lazarre Williams, whatever your lot in life, you will have one advantage over me; you will be an American citizen."

"Haven't I that doleful advantage myself?" mourned Annabel. "A Baltimore convent, an English governess—a father that may never go back to France!"

"Mademoiselle, all advantages of nationality, of person, of mind, of heart, are yours!"

So tipping the interview with a compliment he rose up, and Annabel rose also, making him a deep courtesy, and giving him her hand to be led back to the floor. He kissed her white forefinger, and bowed to me.

"You have suggested some interesting thoughts, monsieur prince of the woods. Perhaps you may yet take your turn on the throne of France. What would you do in that case?"

"I would make the people behave themselves if I had to grind them to powder."

"Now there spoke old Louis XIV!" laughed young Jerome Bonaparte. We both bowed, and he passed down with Annabel into the hall.

I did not know what made Madame de Ferrier watch me from her distant place with widened eyes.

Miss Chantry spoke shrilly to her brother behind me.

"You will never be able to do anything with a lad who thrusts himself forward like that! He has no sense of fitness!—standing there and facing down the brother of a crowned head!—bad as the head is. Of course Mademoiselle Annabel set him on; she loves to make people ridiculous!"

I walked downstairs after Prince Jerome, threaded a way among gazing dancers, and left the hall, stung in my pride.

We do strangely expand and contract in vital force and reach of vision. I wanted to put the lake—the world itself—between me and that glittering company. The edge of a ball-room and the society of men in silks and satins, and of bewitching women, were not intended for me.

Homesickness like physical pain came over me for my old haunts. They were newly recognized as beloved. I had raged against them when comparing myself to Croghan. But now I thought of the evening camp fire, and hunting-stories, of the very dogs that licked my hand; of St. Regis, and my loft bed, of snowshoes, and the blue northern river, longing for them as the young Mohawks said I should long. Tom betwixt two natures, the white man's and the Indian's, I flung a boat out into the water and started to go home faster than I had come away. The slowness of a boat's progress, pushed by the silly motion of oars, which have not the nice discrimination of a paddle, impressed me as I put the miles behind.

When the camp light shone through trees it must have been close to midnight, and my people had finished their celebration of the corn dance. An odor of sweet roasted ears dragged out of hot ashes reached the poor outsider. Even the dogs were too busy to nose me out. I slunk as close as I dared and drew myself up a tree, lying stretched with arms and legs around a limb.

They would have admitted me to the feast, but as a guest. I had no longer a place of my own, either here or there. It was like coming back after death, to realize that you were unmissed. The camp was full of happiness and laughter. Young men chased the young maids, who ran squealing with merriment. My father, Thomas Williams, and my mother, Marianne, sat among the elders tranquil and satisfied. They were ignorant Indians; but I had no other parents. Skenedonk could be seen, laughing at the young Mohawks.

If there was an oval faced mother in my past, who had read to me from the missal, I wanted her. If, as Madame Tank said, I outranked De Chaumont's daughter, I wanted my rank. It was necessary for me to have something of my own: to have love from somebody!

Collapsed and dejected, I crept down the tree and back to the life that was now forced upon me whether I wished to continue it or not. Belonging nowhere, I remembered my refuge in the new world of books.

Lying stretched in the boat with oars shipped, drifting and turning on the crooked lake, I took exact stock of my position in the world, and marked out my future.

These things were known:

I was not an Indian.

I had been adopted into the family of Chief Williams.

Money was sent through an agent in New York for my support and education.

There were scars on my wrists, ankles, arm and eyebrow.

These scars identified me in Madame de Ferrier's mind and Madame Tank's mind as a person from the other side of the world.

I had formerly been deadened in mind.

I was now keenly alive.

These things were not known:

Who I was.

Who sent money for my support and education.

How I became scarred.

What man had placed me among the Indians.

For the future I bound myself with three laws:

To leave alone the puzzle of my past.

To study with all my might and strength.

When I was grown and educated, to come back to my adopted people, the Iroquois, draw them to some place where they could thrive, and by training and education make them an empire, and myself their leader.

The pale-skin's loathing of the red race had not then entered my imagination. I said in conclusion:

"Indians have taken care of me; they shall be my brothers."

VI

The zigzag track of the boat represented a rift widening between me and my past. I sat up and took the oars, feeling older and stronger.

It was primitive man, riding between the highlands, uncumbered, free to grasp what was before him.

De Chaumont did not believe in and was indifferent to the waif whom his position of great seigneur obliged him to protect. What did I care? I had been hidden among the Indians by kindred or guardians humane enough not to leave me destitute. They should not trouble my thoughts, and neither—I told myself like an Indian—should the imaginings of women.

A boy minds no labor in following his caprices. The long starlit pull I reckoned as nothing; and slipped to my room when daylight was beginning to surprise the dancers.

It was so easy to avoid people in the spaciousness of De Chaumont's manor that I did not again see the young Bonaparte nor any of the guests except Croghan. They slept all the following day, and the third day separated. Croghan found my room before leaving with his party, and we talked as well as we could, and shook hands at parting.

The impressions of that first year stay in my mind as I have heard the impressions of childhood remain. It was perhaps a kind of brief childhood, swift in its changes, and running parallel with the development of youth.

My measure being sent to New York by De Chaumont, I had a complete new outfit in clothes; coat, waistcoat, and small-clothes, neckwear, ruffles, and shirts, buckle shoes, stockings of mild yarn for cold weather, and thread stockings. Like most of the things for which we yearn, when I got them I did not like them as well as the Indian garments they obliged me to shed.

Skenedonk came to see me nearly every day, and sat still as long as he could while I toiled at books. I did not tell him how nearly I had disgraced us both by running secretly away to camp. So I was able to go back and pay visits with dignity and be taken seriously, instead of encountering the ridicule that falls upon retreat.

My father was neither pleased nor displeased. He paid my accounts exactly, before the camp broke up for the winter, making Skenedonk his agent. My mother Marianne offered me food as she would have offered it to Count de Chaumont; and I ate it, sitting on a mat as a guest. Our children, particularly the elder ones, looked me over with gravity, and refrained from saying anything about my clothes.

Our Iroquois went north before snow flew, and the cabins stood empty, leaves drifting through fire-holes in the bark thatch.

There have been students greedy of knowledge. I seemed hollow with the fasting of a lifetime. My master at first tried to bind me to times; he had never encountered so boundless an appetite. As soon as I woke in the morning I reached for a book, and as days became darker, for tinder to light a candle. I studied incessantly, dashing out at intervals to lake or woods, and returning after wild activity, with increased zest to the printed world. My mind appeared to resume a faculty it had suspended, and to resume with incredible power. Magnetized by books, I cared for nothing else. That first winter I gained hold on English and Latin, on French reading, mathematics, geography, and history. My master was an Oxford man, and when roused from dawdling, a scholar. He grew foolishly proud and fond of what he called my prodigious advance.

De Chaumont's library was a luscious field, and Doctor Chantry was permitted to turn me loose in it, so that the books were almost like my own. I carried them around hid in my breast; my coat-skirts were weighted with books. There were Plutarch's Lives in the old French of Amyot, over which I labored; a French translation of Homer; Corneille's tragedies; Rochefoucauld; Montaigne's essays, in ten volumes; Thomson's poems, and Chesterfield's letters, in English; the life of Petrarch; three volumes of Montesquieu's works; and a Bible; which I found greatly to my taste. It was a wide and catholic taste.

De Chaumont spent nearly all that autumn and winter in Castorland, where he was building his new manor and founding his settlement called Le Rayville. As soon as I became a member of his household his patriarchal kindness was extended to me, though he regarded me simply as an ambitious half-breed.

The strong place which he had built for his first holding in the wilderness thus grew into a cloistered school for me. It has vanished from the spot where it stood, but I shall forever see it between lake and forest.

Annabel de Chaumont openly hated the isolation of the place, and was happy only when she could fill it with guests. But Madame de Ferrier evidently loved it, remaining there with Paul and Ernestine. Sometimes I did not see her for days together. But Mademoiselle de Chaumont, before her departure to her Baltimore convent for the winter, amused herself with my education. She brought me an old book of etiquette in which young gentlemen were admonished not to lick their fingers or crack bones with their teeth at table. Nobody else being at hand she befooled with Doctor Chantry and me, and I saw for the first time, with surprise, an old man's infatuation with a poppet.

It was this foolishness of her brother's which Miss Chantry could not forgive De Chaumont's daughter. She was incessant in her condemnation, yet unmistakably fond in her English way of the creature she condemned. Annabel loved to drag my poor master in flowery chains before his relative. She would make wreaths of crimson leaves for his bald head, and exhibit him grinning like a weak-eyed Bacchus. Once he sat doting beside her at twilight on a bench of the wide gallery while his sister, near by, kept guard over their talk. I passed them, coming back from my tramp, with a glowing branch in my hand. For having set my teeth in the scarlet tart udder of a sumach, all frosted with delicate fretwork, I could not resist bringing away some of its color.

"Did you get that for me?" called Annabel. I mounted the steps to give it to her, and she said, "Thank you, Lazarre Williams. Every day you learn some pretty new trick. Doctor Chantry has not brought me anything from the woods in a long while."

Doctor Chantry stirred his gouty feet and looked hopelessly out at the landscape.

"Sit here by your dearest Annabel," said Mademoiselle de Chaumont.

Her governess breathed the usual sigh of disgust.

I sat by my dearest Annabel, anxious to light my candle and open my books. She shook the frizzes around her cheeks and buried her hands under the scarlet branch in her lap.

"Do you know, Lazarre Williams, I have to leave you?"

I said I was sorry to hear it.

"Yes, I have to go back to my convent, and drag poor Miss Chantry with me, though she is a heretic and bates the forms of our religion. But she has to submit, and so do I, because my father will have nobody but an English governess."

"Mademoiselle," spoke Miss Chantry, "I would suggest that you sit on a chair by yourself."

"What, on one of those little crowded chairs?" said Annabel.

She reached out her sly hand for mine and drew it under cover of the sumach branch.

"I have been thinking about your rank a great deal, Lazarre Williams, and wondering what it is."

"If you thought more about your own it would be better," said Miss Chantry.

"We are Americans here," said Annabel. "All are equal, and some are free. I am only equal. Must your dearest Annabel obey you about the chair, Miss Chantry?"

"I said I would suggest that you sit on a chair by yourself."

"I will, dear. You know I always follow your suggestions."

I felt the hand that held mine tighten its grip in a despairing squeeze. Annabel suddenly raised the branch high above her head with both arms, and displayed Doctor Chantry's hand and mine clasped tenderly in her lap. She laughed until even Miss Chantry was infected, and the doctor tittered and wiped his eyes.

"Watch your brother, Miss Chantry—don't watch me! You thought he was squeezing my hand—and he thought so too! Lazarre Williams is just out of the woods and doesn't know any better. But Doctor Chantry—he is older than my father!"

"We wished to oblige you, mademoiselle," I said. But the poor English gentleman tittered on in helpless admiration. He told me privately—"I never saw another girl like her. So full of spirits, and so frank!"

Doctor Chantry did not wear his disfiguring horn spectacles when Annabel was near. He wrote a great deal of poetry while the blow of parting from her was hanging over him, and read it to me of mornings, deprecating my voiceless contempt. I would hear him quarreling with a servant in the hall; for the slightest variation in his comfort engendered rages in him that were laughable. Then he entered, red-nosed, red-eyed, and bloodlessly shivering, with a piece of paper covered by innumerable small characters.

"Good morning, my lad," he would say.

"Good morning, Doctor Chantry," I answered.

"Here are a few little stanzas which I have just set down. If you have no objection I will read them."

I must have listened like a trapped bear, sitting up and longing to get at him, for he usually finished humbly, folding his paper and putting it away in his breast. There was reason to believe that he spent valuable hours copying all these verses for Annabel de Chaumont. But there is no evidence that she carried them with her when she and her governess departed in a great coach all gilt and padding. Servants and a wagon load of baggage and supplies accompanied De Chaumont's daughter on the long journey to her Baltimore convent.

Shaking in every nerve and pale as a sheet, my poor master watched her out of sight. He said he should not see his sister again until spring; and added that he was a fool, but when a creature of light came across his path he could not choose but worship. His affections had been blighted by a disappointment in youth, but he had thought he might at least bask in passing sunshine, though fated to unhappiness. I was ashamed to look at him, or to give any sign of overhearing his weakness, and exulted mightily in my youth, despising the enchantments of a woman. Madame de Ferrier watched the departure from another side of the gallery, and did not witness my poor master's breakdown. She came and talked to him, and took more notice of him than I had ever seen her take before.

In a day or two he was quite himself, plodding at the lessons, suddenly furious at the servants, and giving me fretful histories of his wrongs when brandy and water were not put by his bedside at night, or a warming-pan was not passed between his sheets.

About this time I began to know without being taught and without expressing it in words, that there is a natural law of environment which makes us grow like the company we keep. During the first six months of my stay in De Chaumont's house Doctor Chantry was my sole companion. I looked anxiously into the glass on my dressing-table, dreading to see a reflection of his pettiness. I saw a face with large features, eager in expression. The eyes were hazel, and bluish around the iris rims, the nose aquiline, the chin full, the head high, and round templed. The hair was sunny and wavy, not dark and tight fitting like that of my Indian father and mother. There would be always a scar across my eyebrow. I noticed that the lobe of my ear was not deeply divided from my head, but fashioned close to it in triangular snugness, though I could not have said so. Regular life and abundant food, and the drive of purpose, were developing all my parts. I took childish pleasure in watching my Indian boyhood go, and vital force mounting every hour.

Time passed without marking until January. The New England Thanksgiving we had not then heard of; and Christmas was a holy day of the church. On a January afternoon Madame de Ferrier sent Ernestine to say that she wished to see Doctor Chantry and me.

My master was asleep by the fire in an armchair. I looked at his disabled feet, and told Ernestine I would go with her alone. She led me to a wing of the house.

Even an Indian boy could see through Annabel de Chaumont. But who might fathom Madame de Ferrier? Every time I saw her, and that was seldom, some change made her another Madame de Ferrier, as if she were a thousand women in one. I saw her first a white clad spirit, who stood by my head when I awoke; next, a lady who rose up and bowed to me; then a beauty among dancers; afterwards, a little girl running across the turf, or a kind woman speaking to my master. Often she was a distant figure, coming and going with Paul and Ernestine in De Chaumont's woods. If we encountered, she always said, "Good day, monsieur," and I answered "Good day, madame."

I had my meals alone with Doctor Chantry, and never questioned this custom, from the day I entered the house. De Chaumont's chief, who was over the other servants, and had come with him from his chateau near Blois, waited upon me, while Doctor Chantry was served by another man named Jean. My master fretted at Jean. The older servant paid no attention to that.

Madame de Ferrier and I had lived six months under the same roof as strangers. Consciousness plowed such a direct furrow in front of me that I saw little on either side of it. She was a name, that I found written in the front of the missal, and copied over and over down foolscap paper in my practice of script:

"Eagle Madeleine Marie de Ferrier."
"Eagle Madeleine Marie de Ferrier."

She stood in her sitting room, which looked upon the lake, and before a word passed between us I saw she was unlike any of her former selves. Her features were sharpened and whitened. She looked beyond me with gray colored eyes, and held her lips apart.

"I have news. The Indian brought me this letter from Albany."

I could not help glancing curiously at the sheet in her hand, spotted on the back with broken red wafers. It was the first letter I had ever seen. Doctor Chantry told me he received but one during the winter from his sister, and paid two Spanish reals in postage for it, besides a fee and some food and whisky to the Indian who made the journey to deliver such parcels. It was a trying and an important experience to receive a letter. I was surprised that Madame Tank had recommended my sending one into the Wisconsin country.

"Count de Chaumont is gone; and I must have advice."

"Madame," I said, "Doctor Chantry was asleep, but I will wake him and bring him here."

"No. I will tell you. Monsieur, my Cousin Philippe is dead."

It might have shocked me more if I had known she had a Cousin Philippe. I said stupidly:

"Is he?"

"Cousin Philippe was my husband, you understand."

"Madame, are you married?"

"Of course!" she exclaimed. And I confessed to myself that in no other way could Paul be accounted for.

"But you are here alone?"

Two large tears ran down her face.

"You should understand the De Ferriers are poor, monsieur, unless something can be saved from our estates that the Bonapartes have given away. Cousin Philippe went to see if we could recover any part of them. Count de Chaumont thought it a favorable time. But he was too old for such a journey; and the disappointments at the end of it."

"Old! Was he old, madame?"

"Almost as old as my father."

"But you are very young."

"I was only thirteen when my father on his deathbed married me to Cousin Philippe. We were the last of our family. Now Cousin Philippe is dead and Paul and I are orphans!"

She felt her loss as Paul might have felt his. He was gurgling at Ernestine's knee in the next room.

"I want advice," she said; and I stood ready to give it, as a man always is; the more positively because I knew nothing of the world.

"Cousin Philippe said I must go to France, for Paul's sake, and appeal myself to the empress, who has great influence over the emperor. His command was to go at once."

"Madame, you cannot go in midwinter."

"Must I go at all?" she cried out passionately. "Why don't you tell me a De Ferrier shall not crawl the earth before a Bonaparte! You—of all men! We are poor and exiles because we were royalists—are royalists—we always shall be royalists! I would rather make a wood-chopper of Paul than a serf to this Napoleon!"

She checked herself, and motioned to a chair.

"Sit down, monsieur. Pardon me that I have kept you standing."

I placed the chair for her, but she declined it, and we continued to face each other.

"Madame," I said, "you seem to blame me for something. What have I done?"

"Nothing, monsieur."

"I will now ask your advice. What do you want me to do that I have not done?"

"Monsieur, you are doing exactly what I want you to do."

"Then you are not displeased with me?"

"I am more pleased with you every time I see you. Your advice is good. I cannot go in midwinter."

"Are you sure your cousin wanted you to make this journey?"

"The notary says so in this letter. Philippe died in the farm-house of one of our peasants, and the new masters could not refuse him burial in the church where De Ferriers have lain for hundreds of years. He was more fortunate than my father."

This interview with Madame de Ferrier in which I cut so poor a figure, singularly influenced me. It made me restless, as if something had entered my blood. In January the real spring begins, for then sap starts, and the lichens seem to quicken. I felt I was young, and rose up against lessons all day long and part of the night. I rushed in haste to the woods or the frozen lake, and wanted to do mighty deeds without knowing what to undertake. More than anything else I wanted friends of my own age. To see Doctor Chantry dozing and hear him grumbling, no longer remained endurable; for he reminded me that my glad days were due and I was not receiving them. Worse than that, instead of proving grateful for all his services, I became intolerant of his opinion.

"De Chaumont will marry her," he said when he heard of Madame de Ferrier's widowhood. "She will never be obliged to sue to the Bonapartes. The count is as fond of her as he is of his daughter."

"Must a woman marry a succession of fathers?"—I wanted to know.

My master pointed out that the count was a very well favored and youthful looking man. His marriage to Madame de Ferrier became even more distasteful. She and her poppet were complete by themselves. Wedding her to any one was casting indignity upon her.

Annabel de Chaumont was a countess and Madame de Ferrier was a marquise. These names, I understood, meant that they were ladies to be served and protected. De Chaumont's daughter was served and protected, and as far as he was allowed to do so, he served and protected the daughter of his fellow countryman.

"But the pride of emigrés," Doctor Chantry said, "was an old story in the De Chaumont household. There were some Saint-Michels who lived in a cabin, strictly on their own means, refusing the count's help, yet they had followed him to Le Rayville in Castorland. Madame de Ferrier lived where her husband had placed her, in a wing of De Chaumont's house, refusing to be waited on by anybody but Ernestine, paying what her keeping cost; when she was a welcome guest."

My master hobbled to see her. And I began to think about her day and night, as I had thought about my books; an isolated little girl in her early teens, mother and widow, facing a future like a dead wall, with daily narrowing fortunes. The seclusion in which she lived made her sacred like a religious person. I did not know what love was, and I never intended to dote, like my poor master. Before the end of January, however, such a change worked in me that I was as fierce for the vital world as I had been for the world of books.

VII

A trick of the eyes, a sweet turning of the mouth corners, the very color of the hair—some irresistible physical trait, may compel a preference in us that we cannot control; especially when we first notice these traits in a woman. My crying need grew to be the presence of Madame de Ferrier. It was youth calling to youth in that gorgeous winter desert.

Her windows were hoar-frost furred without and curtained within. Though I knew where they were I got nothing by tramping past and glancing up. I used to saunter through the corridor that led to her rooms, startled yet pleased if Ernestine came out on an errand. Then I would close my book and nod, and she would courtesy.

"Oh, by the way," I would turn to remark, "I was passing, and thought I would knock and ask how Madame de Ferrier is to-day. But you can tell me."

When assured of Madame de Ferrier's health I would continue:

"And Paul—how is Paul?"

Paul carried himself marvelously. He was learning to walk. Ernestine believed the lie about knocking, and I felt bolder every time I told it.

The Indian part of me thought of going hunting and laying slaughtered game at their door. But it was a doubtful way of pleasing, and the bears hibernated, and the deer were perhaps a day's journey in the white wastes.

I used to sing in the clear sharp air when I took to the frozen lake and saw those heights around me. I look back upon that winter, across what befell me afterwards, as a time of perfect peace; before virgin snows melted, when the world was a white expanse of innocence.

Our weather-besieged manor was the center of it. Vaguely I knew there was life on the other side of great seas, and that New York, Boston, Philadelphia, Baltimore and New Orleans were cities in which men moved and had their being. My country, the United States, had bought from Napoleon Bonaparte a large western tract called Louisiana, which belonged to France. A new state named Ohio was the last added to the roll of commonwealths. Newspapers, which the Indian runner once or twice brought us from Albany, chronicled the doings of Aaron Burr, Vice-President of the United States, who had recently drawn much condemnation on himself by a brutal duel.

"Aaron Burr was here once," said my master.

"What is he like?" I inquired.

"A lady-killer."

"But he is next in dignity to the President."

Doctor Chantry sniffed.

"What is even the President of a federation like this, certain to fall to pieces some fine day!"

I felt offended; for my instinct was to weld people together and hold them so welded.

"If I were a president or a king," I told him, "and men conspired to break the state, instead of parleying I would hang them up like dogs."

"Would you?"

Despising the country in which he found himself, my master took no trouble to learn its politics. But since history had rubbed against us in the person of Jerome Bonaparte, I wanted to know what the world was doing.

"Colonel Burr had a pleasant gentleman with him at the manor," Doctor Chantry added. "His name was Harmon Blennerhassett; a man of good English stock, though having a wild Irish strain, which is deplorable."

The best days of that swift winter were Sundays, when my master left off snapping, and stood up reverently in our dining-room to read his church service. Madame de Ferrier and Paul and Ernestine came from their apartment to join in the Protestant ritual; and I sat beside them so constantly that the Catholic priest who arrived at Easter to dress up the souls of the household, found me in a state of heresy.

I have always thought a woman needs a dark capping of hair, whatever her complexion, to emphasize her beauty. For light locks seem to fray out to nothing, and waste to air instead of fitly binding a lovely countenance. Madame de Ferrier's hair was of exactly the right color. Her eyebrows were distinct dark lines, and the lashes were so dense that you noticed the curling rim they made around her gray eyes. Whether the gift of looking to your core is beauty or not, I can only say she had it. And I could not be sworn what her features were; such life and expression played over and changed them every moment.

As to her figure, it was just in its roundness and suppleness, and had a lightness of carriage that I have never seen equaled. There was charm in looking at without approaching her that might have satisfied me indefinitely, if De Chaumont had not come home.

Ernestine herself made the first breach in that sacred reserve. The old woman met me in the hall, courtesied, and passed as usual. I turned behind the broad ribbons which hung down her back from cap to heels, and said:

"Oh, by the way, Ernestine, how is Madame de Ferrier? I was going to knock—"

And Ernestine courtesied again, and opened the door, standing aside for me to enter.

Madame de Ferrier sat on a bearskin before the hearth with Paul, who climbed over her and gave her juicy kisses. There was a deep wood fire, upheld by very tall andirons having cups in their tops, which afterwards I learned were called posset cups. She was laughing so that her white teeth showed, and she made me welcome like a playmate; remaining on the rug, and bidding Ernestine set a chair for me near the fire.

"It is very kind of you to spare me some time, monsieur," said Madame de Ferrier. She admonished Paul—"Don't choke your little mother."

I told her boldly that nothing but the dread of disturbing her kept me from knocking every day. We had always walked into the lodges without knocking, and I dwelt on this as one of my new accomplishments.

"I am not studying night and day," she answered. "Sophie Saint-Michel and her mother were my teachers, and they are gone now, one to heaven and the other to Castorland."

Remembering what Annabel de Chaumont said about holy Sophie I inquired if she had been religious.

"The Saint-Michels were better than religious; both mother and daughter were eternally patient with the poor count, whose troubles unsettled his reason. They had no dear old Ernestine, and were reduced to the hardest labor. I was a little child when we came to America, yet even then the spirit of the Saint-Michels seemed to me divine."

"I wish I could remember when I was a little child."

"Can you not recall anything?"

"I have a dim knowledge of objects."

"What objects?"

"St. Regis church, and my taking first communion; and the hunting, the woods and water, boats, snowshoes, the kind of food I liked; Skenedonk and all my friends—but I scarcely knew them as persons until I awoke."

"What is your first distinct recollection?"

"Your face."

"Mine?"

"Yes, yours, madame. I saw it above me when you came into the room at night."

She looked past me and said:

"You have fortunately missed some of the most terrible events that ever happened in the world, monsieur. My mother and father, my two brothers, Cousin Philippe and I, were in prison together. My mother and brothers were taken, and we were left."

I understood that she spoke of the Terror, about which I was eager to know every then unwritten detail. Doctor Chantry had told me many things. It fascinated me far more than ancient history, which my master was inclined to press upon me.

"How can you go back to France, madame?"

"That's what I ask myself every day. That life was like a strange nightmare. Yet there was our chateau, Mont-Louis, two or three days' journey east from Paris. The park was so beautiful. I think of it, and of Paul."

"And what about this country, madame? Is there nothing beautiful here?"

"The fact has been impressed on me, monsieur, that it does not belong to me. I am an emigré. In city or country my father and Cousin Philippe kept me with them. I have seen nothing of young people, except at balls. We had no intimate friends. We were always going back. I am still waiting to go back, monsieur—and refusing to go if I must."

It was plain that her life had been as restricted as mine, though the bonds were different. She was herded with old people, made a wife and mother while yet a child, nursed in shadow instead of in the hot sunshine which produced Annabel de Chaumont.

After that we met each other as comrades meet, and both of us changed like the face of nature, when the snow went and warm winds came.

This looking at her without really approaching was going on innocently when one day Count de Chaumont rode up to the manor, his horse and his attendant servants and horses covered with mud, filling the place with a rush of life.

He always carried himself as if he felt extremely welcome in this world. And though a man ought to be welcome in his own house, especially when he has made it a comfortable refuge for outsiders, I met him with the secret resentment we bear an interloper.

He looked me over from head to foot with more interest than he had ever before shown.

"We are getting on, we are getting on! Is it Doctor Chantry, or the little madame, or the winter housing? Our white blood is very much in evidence. When Chief Williams comes back to the summer hunting he will not know his boy."

"The savage is inside yet, monsieur," I told him. "Scratch me and see."

"Not I," he laughed.

"It is late for thanks, but I will now thank you for taking me into your house."

"He has learned gratitude for little favors! That is Madame de Ferrier's work."

"I hope I may be able to do something that will square our accounts."

"That's Doctor Chantry's work. He is full of benevolent intentions—and never empties himself. When you have learned all your master knows, what are you going to do with it?"

"I am going to teach our Indians."

"Good. You have a full day's work before you. Founding an estate in the wilderness is nothing compared to that. You have more courage than De Chaumont."

Whether the spring or the return of De Chaumont drove me out, I could no longer stay indoors, but rowed all day long on the lake or trod the quickening woods. Before old Pierre could get audience with his house accounts, De Chaumont was in Madame de Ferrier's rooms, inspecting the wafer blotched letter. He did not appear as depressed as he should have been by the death of his old friend.

"These French have no hearts," I told Doctor Chantry.

He took off his horn spectacles and wiped his eyes, responding:

"But they find the way to ours!"

Slipping between islands in water paths that wound as a meadow stream winds through land, I tried to lose myself from the uneasy pain which followed me everywhere.

There may be people who look over the scheme of their lives with entire complacence. Mine has been the outcome of such strange misfortunes as to furnish evidence that there is another fate than the fate we make ourselves. In that early day I felt the unseen lines tighten around me. I was nothing but a young student of unknown family, able to read and write, to talk a little English, with some knowledge of history, geography, mathematics, and Latin. Strength and scope came by atoms. I did not know then as I know now that I am a slow grower, even when making gigantic effort. An oak does not accumulate rings with more deliberation than I change and build myself.

My master told me a few days later that the count decreed Madame de Ferrier must go back to France. He intended to go with her and push her claim; and his daughter and his daughter's governess would bear them company. Doctor Chantry and I contemplated each other, glaring in mutual solemnity. His eyes were red and watery, and the nose sharpened its cone.

"When are they going?" I inquired.

"As soon as arrangements for comfortable sailing can be made. I wish I were going back to England. I shall have to save twenty-five years before I can go, but the fund is started."

If I saved a hundred and twenty-five years I could not go anywhere; for I had nothing to save. The worthlessness of civilization rushed over me. When I was an Indian the boundless world was mine. I could build a shelter, and take food and clothes by my strength and skill. My boat or my strong legs carried me to all boundaries.

I did not know what ailed me, but chased by these thoughts to the lake, I determined not to go back again to De Chaumont's house. I was sick, and my mother woods opened her arms. As if to show me what I had thrown away to haunt the cages of men, one of those strange sights which is sometimes seen in that region appeared upon the mountain. No one can tell who lights the torch. A thread of fire ran up like an opening seam, broadened, and threw out pink ravelings. The flame wavered, paled by daylight, but shielding itself with strong smoke, and leaped from ledge to ledge. I saw mighty pines, standing one moment green, and the next, columns of fire. So the mass diverged, or ran together until a mountain of fire stood against the sky, and stretched its reflection, a glowing furnace, across the water.

Flecks of ash sifted on me in the boat. I felt myself a part of it, as I felt myself a part of the many sunsets which had burned out on that lake. Before night I penetrated to the heart of an island so densely overgrown, even in spring when trees had no curtains, that you were lost as in a thousand mile forest. I camped there in a dry ravine, with hemlock boughs under and over me, and next day rolled broken logs, and cut poles and evergreens with my knife, to make a lodge.

It was boyish, unmannerly conduct; but the world had broken, to chaos around me; and I set up the rough refuge with skill. Some books, my fish line and knife, were always in the boat with me, as well as a box of tinder. I could go to the shore, get a breakfast out of the water, and cook it myself. Yet all that day I kept my fast, having no appetite.

Perhaps in the bottom of my heart I expected somebody to be sent after me, bearing large inducements to return. We never can believe we are not valuable to our fellows. Pierre or Jean, or some other servants in the house, might perforce nose me out. I resolved to hide if such an envoy approached and to have speech with nobody. We are more or less ashamed of our secret wounds, and I was not going to have Pierre or Jean report that I sat sulking in the woods on an island.

It was very probable that De Chaumont's household gave itself no trouble about my disappearance. I sat on my hemlock floor until the gray of twilight and studied Latin, keeping my mind on the text; save when a squirrel ventured out and glided bushy trained and sinuous before me, or the marble birches with ebony limbs, drew me to gloat on them. The white birch is a woman and a goddess. I have associated her forever with that afternoon. Her poor cousin the poplar, often so like her as to deceive you until ashen bough and rounded leaf instruct the eye, always grows near her like a protecting servant. The poor cousin rustles and fusses. But my calm lady stands in perfect beauty, among pines straight as candles, never tremulous, never trivial. All alabaster and ebony, she glows from a distance; as, thinking of her, I saw another figure glow through the loop-holes of the woods.

It was Madame de Ferrier.

VIII

A leap of the heart and dizziness shot through me and blurred my sight. The reality of Madame de Ferrier's coming to seek me surpassed all imaginings.

She walked with quick accustomed step, parting the second growth in her way, having tracked me from the boat. Seeing my lodge in the ravine she paused, her face changing as the lake changes; and caught her breath. I stood exultant and ashamed down to the ground.

"Monsieur, what are you doing here?" Madame de Ferrier cried out.

"Living, madame," I responded.

"Living? Do you mean you have returned to your old habits?"

"I have returned to the woods, madame."

"You do not intend to stay here?"

"Perhaps."

"You must not do it!"

"What must I do?"

"Come back to the house. You have given us much anxiety."

I liked the word "us" until I remembered it included Count de Chaumont.

"Why did you come out here and hide yourself?"

My conduct appeared contemptible. I looked mutely at her.

"What offended you?"

"Nothing, madame."

"Did you want Doctor Chantry to lame himself hobbling around in search of you, and the count to send people out in every direction?"

"No, madame."

"What explanation will you make to the count?"

"None, madame." I raised my head. "I may go out in the woods without asking leave of Count de Chaumont."

"He says you have forsaken your books and gone back to be an Indian."

I showed her the Latin book in my hand. She glanced slightly at it, and continued to make her gray eyes pass through my marrow.

Shifting like a culprit, I inquired:

"How did you know I was here?"

"Oh, it was not hard to find you after I saw the boat. This island is not large."

"But who rowed you across the lake, madame?"

"I came by myself, and nobody except Ernestine knows it. I can row a boat. I slipped through the tunnel, and ventured."

"Madame, I am a great fool. I am not worth your venturing."

"You are worth any danger I might encounter. But you should at least go back for me."

"I will do anything for you, madame. But why should I go back?—you will not long be there."

"What does that matter? The important thing is that you should not lapse again into the Indian."

"Is any life but the life of an Indian open to me, madame?"

She struck her hands together with a scream.

"Louis! Sire!"

Startled, I dropped the book and it sprawled at her feet like the open missal. She had returned so unexpectedly to the spirit of our first meeting.

"O, if you knew what you are! During my whole life your name has been cherished by my family. We believed you would sometime come to your own. Believe in yourself!"

I seemed almost to remember and perceive what I was—as you see in mirage one inverted boat poised on another, and are not quite sure, and the strange thing is gone.

Perhaps I was less sure of the past because I was so sure of the present. A wisp of brown mist settling among the trees spread cloud behind her. What I wanted was this woman, to hide in the woods for my own. I could feed and clothe her, deck her with necklaces of garnets from the rocks, and wreaths of the delicate sand-wort flower. She said she would rather make Paul a woodchopper than a suppliant, taking the constitutional oath. I could make him a hunter and a fisherman. Game, bass, trout, pickerel, grew for us in abundance. I saw this vision with a single eye; it looked so possible! All the crude imaginings of youth colored the spring woods with vivid beauty. My face betrayed me, and she spoke to me coldly.

"Is that your house, monsieur?"

I said it was.

"And you slept there last night?"

"I can build a much better one."

"What did you have for dinner?"

"Nothing."

"What did you have for breakfast?"

"Nothing."

Evidently the life I proposed to myself to offer her would not suit my lady!

She took a lacquered box from the cover of her wrappings, and moved down the slope a few steps.

"Come here to your mother and get your supper."

I felt tears rush to my eyes. She sat down, spread a square of clean fringed linen upon the ground, and laid out crusty rounds of buttered bread that were fragrant in the springing fragrance of the woods, firm slices of cold meat, and a cunning pastry which instantly maddened me. I was ashamed to be such a wolf.

We sat with our forest table between us and ate together.

"I am hungry myself," she said.

A glorified veil descended on the world. If evening had paused while that meal was in progress it would not have surprised me. There are half hours that dilate to the importance of centuries. But when she had encouraged me to eat everything to the last crumb, she shook the fringed napkin, gathered up the lacquered box, and said she must be gone.

"Monsieur, I have overstepped the bounds of behavior in coming after you. The case was too urgent for consideration of myself. I must hurry back, for the count's people would not understand my secret errand through the tunnel. Will you show yourself at the house as soon as possible?"

I told her humbly that I would.

"But let me put you in the boat, madame."

She shook her head. "You may follow, after I am out of sight. If you fail to follow"—she turned in the act of departing and looked me through.

I told her I would not fail.

When Madame de Ferrier disappeared beyond the bushes I sat down and waited with my head between my hands, still seeing upon closed eyelids her figure, the scant frock drawn around it, her cap of dark hair under a hood, her face moving from change to change. And whether I sat a year or a minute, clouds had descended when I looked, as they often did in that lake gorge. So I waited no longer, but followed her.

The fog was brown, and capped the evening like a solid dome, pressing down to the earth, and twisting smoke fashion around my feet. It threw sinuous arms in front of me as a thing endowed with life and capable of molding itself; and when I reached my boat and pushed off on the water, a vast mass received and enveloped me.

More penetrating than its clamminess was the thought that Madame de Ferrier was out in it alone.

I tried one of the long calls we sometimes used in hunting. She might hear, and understand that I was near to help her. But it was shouting against many walls. No effort pierced the muffling substance which rolled thickly against the lungs. Remembering it was possible to override smaller craft, I pulled with caution, and so bumped lightly against the boat that by lucky chance hovered in my track.

"Is it you, madame?" I asked.

She hesitated.

"Is it you, monsieur?"

"Yes."

"I think I am lost. There is no shore. The fog closed around me so soon. I was waiting for it to lift a little."

"It may not lift until morning, madame. Let me tie your boat to mine."

"Do you know the way?"

"There is no way. We shall have to feel for the shore. But Lake George is narrow, and I know it well."

"I want to keep near you."

"Come into my boat, and let me tie the other one astern."

She hesitated again, but decided, "That would be best."

I drew the frail shells together—they seemed very frail above such depths—and helped her cross the edges. We were probably the only people on Lake George. Tinder lighted in one boat would scarcely have shown us the other, though in the sky an oval moon began to make itself seen amidst rags of fog. The dense eclipse around us and the changing light overhead were very weird.

Madame de Ferrier's hands chilled mine, and she shook in her thin cape and hood. Our garments were saturated. I felt moisture trickling down my hair and dropping on my shoulders.

She was full of vital courage, resisting the deadly chill. This was not a summer fog, lightly to be traversed. It went dank through the bones. When I had helped her to a bench, remembering there was nothing dry to wrap around her, I slipped off my coat and forcibly added its thickness to her shoulders.

"Do you think I will let you do that, monsieur?"

My teeth chattered and shocked together so it was impossible to keep from laughing, as I told her I always preferred to be coatless when I rowed a boat.

We could see each other by the high light that sometimes gilded the face, and sometimes was tarnished almost to eclipse. Madame de Ferrier crept forward, and before I knew her intention, cast my garment again around me. I helped the boat shift its balance so she would have to grasp at me for support; the chilled round shape of her arm in my hand sent waves of fire through me. With brazen cunning, moreover, that surprised myself, instead of pleading, I dictated.

"Sit beside me on the rower's bench, madame, and the coat will stretch around both of us."

Like a child she obeyed. We were indeed reduced to saving the warmth of our bodies. I shipped my oars and took one for a paddle, bidding Madame de Ferrier to hold the covering in place while I felt for the shore. She did so, her arm crossing my breast, her soft body touching mine. She was cold and still as the cloud in which we moved; but I was a god, riding triumphantly high above the world, satisfied to float through celestial regions forever, bearing in my breast an unquenchable coal of fire.

The moon played tricks, for now she was astern, and now straight ahead, in that confusing wilderness of vapor.

"Madame," I said to my companion, "why have you been persuaded to go back to France?"

She drew a deep breath.

"I have not been persuaded. I have been forced by circumstances. Paul's future is everything."

"You said you would rather make him a woodchopper than a suppliant to the Bonapartes."

"I would. But his rights are to be considered first. He has some small chance of regaining his inheritance through the influence of Count de Chaumont now. Hereafter there may be no chance. You know the fortunes and lands of all emigrés were forfeited to the state. Ours have finally reached the hands of one of Napoleon's officers. I do not know what will be done. I only know that Paul must never have cause to reproach me."

I was obliged to do my duty in my place as she was doing her duty in hers; but I wished the boat would sink, and so end all journeys to France. It touched shore, on the contrary, and I grasped a rock which jutted toward us. It might be the point of an island, it might be the eastern land, as I was inclined to believe, for the moon was over our right shoulders.

Probing along with the oar I found a cove and a shallow bottom, and there I beached our craft with a great shove.

"How good the earth feels underfoot!" said Madame de Ferrier. We were both stiff. I drew the boats where they could not be floated away, and we turned our faces to the unknown. I took her unresisting arm to guide her, and she depended upon me.

This day I look back at those young figures groping through cloud as at disembodied and blessed spirits. The man's intensest tenderness, restrained by his virginhood and his awe of the supple delicate shape at his side, was put forth only in her service. They walked against bushes. He broke a stick, and with it probed every yard of the ascent which they were obliged to make. Helping his companion from bush to log, from seam to seam of the riven slope, from ledge to ledge, he brought her to a level of high forest where the fog was thinner, and branches interlaced across their faces.

The climb made Madame de Ferrier draw her breath quickly. She laughed when we ended it. Though I knew the shores as well as a hunter, it was impossible to recognize any landmark. The trees, the moss, and forest sponge under our feet, the very rocks, were changed by that weird medium. And when the fog opened and we walked as through an endless tunnel of gray revolving stone, it was into a world that never existed before and would never exist again.

There was no path. Creeping under and climbing over obstacles, sometimes enclosed by the whiteness of steam, sometimes walking briskly across lighted spaces, we reached a gorge smoking as the lake smoked in the chill of early mornings. Vapor played all its freaks on that brink. The edge had been sharply defined. But the fog shut around us like a curtain, and we dared not stir.

Below, a medallion shaped rift widened out, and showed us a scene as I have since beheld such things appear upon the stage. Within the round changing frame of wispy vapor two men sat by a fire of logs and branches. We could smell wood smoke, and hear the branches crackle, convincing us the vision was real. Behind them stood a cabin almost as rude as my shelter on the island.

One man was a grand fellow, not at all of the common order, though he was more plainly clothed than De Chaumont. His face was so familiar that I almost grasped recognition—but missed it. The whole cast was full and aquiline, and the lobe of his ear, as I noticed when light fell on his profile, sat close to his head like mine.

The other man worked his feet upon the treadle of a small wheel, which revolved like a circular table in front of him, and on this he deftly touched something which appeared to be an earthenware vessel. His thin fingers moved with spider swiftness, and shaped it with a kind of magic. He was a mad looking person, with an air of being tremendously driven by inner force. He wore mustaches the like of which I had never seen, carried back over his ears; and these hairy devices seemed to split his countenance in two crosswise.

Some broken pottery lay on the ground, and a few vessels, colored and lustrous so they shone in the firelight, stood on a stump near him.

The hollow was not a deep one, but if the men had been talking, their voices did not reach us until the curtain parted.

"You are a great fool or a great rascal, or both, Bellenger," the superior man said.

"Most people are, your highness," responded the one at the wheel. He kept it going, as if his earthenware was of more importance than the talk.

"You are living a miserable life, roving about."

"Many other Frenchmen are no better off than I am, my prince."

"True enough. I've roved about myself."

"Did you turn schoolmaster in Switzerland, prince?"

"I did. My family are in Switzerland now."

"Some of the nobles were pillaged by their peasants as well as by the government. But your house should not have lost everything."

"You are mistaken about our losses. The Orleans Bourbons have little or no revenue left. Monsieur and Artois were the Bourbons able to maintain a court about them in exile. So you have to turn potter, to help support the idiot and yourself?"

"Is your highness interested in art?"

"What have I to do with art?"

"But your highness can understand how an idea will haunt a man. It is true I live a wretched life, but I amuse myself trying to produce a perfect vase. I have broken thousands. If a shape answers my expectations, that very shape is certain to crack in the burning or run in the glaze."

"Then you don't make things to sell?"

"Oh, yes. I make noggins and crockery to sell in the towns. There is a kind of clay in these hills that suits me."

"The wonderful vase," said the other yawning, "might perhaps interest me more if some facts were not pressing for discussion. I am a man of benevolent disposition, Bellenger."

"Your royal highness—"

"Stop! I have been a revolutionist, like my poor father, whose memory you were about to touch—and I forbid it. But I am a man whose will it is to do good. It is impossible I should search you out in America to harm my royal cousin. Now I want to know the truth about him."

Madame de Ferrier had forgotten her breath. We both stood fastened on that scene in another world, guiltless of eavesdropping.

The potter shifted his eyes from side to side, seeming to follow the burr of his vessel upon the wheel.

"I find you with a creature I cannot recognize as my royal cousin. If this is he, sunk far lower than when he left France in your charge, why are two-thirds of his pension sent out from New York to another person, while you receive for his maintenance only one-third?"

The potter bounded from his wheel, letting the vessel spin off to destruction, and danced, stretching his long mustaches abroad in both hands as the ancients must have rent their clothes. He cried that he had been cheated, stripped, starved.

"I thought they were straitened in Monsieur's court," he raged, "and they have been maintaining a false dauphin!"

"As I said, Bellenger," remarked his superior, "you are either a fool or the greatest rascal I ever saw."

He looked at Bellenger attentively.

"Yet why should you want to mix clues—and be rewarded with evident misery? And how could you lose him out of your hand and remain unconscious of it? He was sent to the ends of the earth for safety—poor shattered child!—and if he is safe elsewhere, why should you be pensioned to maintain another child? They say that a Bourbon never learns anything; but I protest that a Bourbon knows well what he does know. I feel sure my uncle intends no harm to the disabled heir. Who is guilty of this double dealing? I confess I don't understand it."

Now whether by our long and silent stare we drew his regard, or chance cast his eye upward, the potter that instant saw us standing in the cloud above him. He dropped by his motionless wheel, all turned to clay himself. The eyeballs stuck from his face. He opened his mouth and screeched as if he had been started and could not leave off—

"The king!—the king!—the king!—the king!"

IX

The fool's outcry startled me less than Madame de Ferrier. She fell against me and sank downward, so that I was obliged to hold her up in my arms. I had never seen a woman swoon. I thought she was dying, and shouted to them below to come and help me.

The potter sat sprawling on the ground, and did not bestir himself to do anything. As soon as my hands and mind were free I took him by the scruff of the neck and kicked him behind with a good will. My rage at him for disregarding her state was the savage rage of an Iroquois. The other man laughed until the woods rang. Madame de Ferrier sat up in what seemed to me a miraculous manner. We bathed her temples with brandy, and put her on a cushion of leaves raked up and dried to make a seat by the fire. The other man, who helped me carry her into the ravine, stood with his hat off, as was her due. She thanked him and thanked me, half shrouding her face with her hood, abashed at finding herself lost among strangers in the night; which was my fault. I told him I had been a bad guide for a lady who had missed her way; and he said we were fortunate to reach a camp instead of stumbling into some danger.

He was much older than I, at least fourteen years, I learned afterwards, but it was like meeting Skenedonk again, or some friend from whom I had only been parted.

The heartening warmth of the fire made steam go up from our clothes; and seeing Madame de Ferrier alive once more, and the potter the other side of his wheel taking stock of his hurt, I felt happy.

We could hear in the cabin behind us a whining like that uttered by a fretful babe.

My rage at the potter ending in good nature, I moved to make some amends for my haste; but he backed off.

"You startled us," said the other man, "standing up in the clouds like ghosts. And your resemblance to one who has been dead many years is very striking, monsieur."

I said I was sorry if I had kicked the potter without warrant, but it seemed to me a base act to hesitate when help was asked for a woman.

"Yet I know little of what is right among men, monsieur," I owned. "I have been learning with a master in Count de Chaumont's manor house less than a year. Before that my life was spent in the woods with the Indians, and they found me so dull that I was considered witless until my mind awoke."

"You are a fine fellow," the man said, laying his hands on my shoulders. "My heart goes out to you. You may call me Louis Philippe. And what may I call you?"

"Lazarre."

He had a smiling good face, square, but well curved and firm. Now that I saw him fronting me I could trace his clear eyebrows, high forehead, and the laughter lines down his cheeks. He was long between the eyes and mouth, and he had a full and resolute chin.

"You are not fat, Lazarre," said Philippe, "your forehead is wide rather than receding, and you have not a double chin. Otherwise you are the image of one—Who are you?"

"I don't know."

"Don't know who you are?"

"No. We heard all that you and the potter were saying down here, and I wondered how many boys there are in America that are provided for through an agent in New York, without knowing their parents. Now that is my case."

"Do you say you have lived among the Indians?"

"Yes: among the Iroquois."

"Who placed you there?"

"No one could tell me except my Indian father; and he would not tell."

"Do you remember nothing of your childhood?"

"Nothing."

"Did you ever see Bellenger before?"

"I never saw him before to-night."

"But I saw him," said Madame de Ferrier, "in London, when I was about seven years old. It made a stronger impression on me than anything else that ever happened in my life, except"—she stopped.

"Except the taking off of my mother and brothers to the guillotine."

The man who told me to call him Louis Philippe turned toward her, with attention as careful as his avoidance when she wished to be unobserved. She rose, and came around the fire, making a deep courtesy.

"My family may not be unknown to his royal highness the Duke of Orleans. We are De Ferriers of Mont-Louis; emigrés now, like many others."

"Madame, I knew your family well. They were loyal to their king."

"My father died here in America. Before we sailed we saw this man in London."

"And with him—"

"A boy."

"Do you remember the boy well?"

"I remember him perfectly."

The wailing in the cabin became louder and turned to insistent animal howls. Instead of a babe the imprisoned creature was evidently a dog. I wondered that the potter did not let him out to warm his hide at the fire.

"Did you ever see the boy again?"

"I did not see him again until he was brought to Count de Chaumont's house last summer."

"Why to De Chaumont? Le Ray de Chaumont is not one of us. He is of the new nobility. His chateau near Blois was bought by his grandfather, and he takes his name from the estate. I have heard he is in favor with Bonaparte."

"Even we of the old nobility, prince, may be reduced to seek favor of Bonaparte."

"Heaven forbid, madame. I say nothing against him; though I could say much."

"Say nothing against Count de Chaumont. Count de Chaumont befriends all emigrés."

"I have nothing to say against Count de Chaumont. He is not of our party; he is of the new. Fools! If we princes had stood by each other as the friends of the Empire stand by their emperor, we could have killed the Terror."

The animal in the cabin by this time was making such doleful cries I said to the potter.

"Let him out. It is dreadful to be shut in by walls."

The potter, stooping half over and rolling stiffly from foot to foot in his walk, filled me with compunction at having been brutal to so pitiful a creature, and I hurried to open the door for him. The animal clawed vigorously inside, and the instant I pushed back the ill-fitted slabs, it strained through and rushed on all fours to the fire. Madame de Ferrier fled backward, for what I liberated could hardly be seen without dread.

It was a human being. Its features were a boy's, and the tousled hair had a natural wave. While it crouched for warmth I felt the shock of seeing a creature about my own age grinning back at me, fishy eyed and black mouthed.

"There!" Bellenger said, straightening up in his place like a bear rising from all fours. "That is the boy your De Ferriers saw in London."

I remembered the boy Madame Tank had told about. Whether myself or this less fortunate creature was the boy, my heart went very pitiful toward him. Madame de Ferrier stooped and examined, him; he made a juicy noise of delight with his mouth.

"This is not the boy you had in London, monsieur," she said to Bellenger.

The potter waved his hands and shrugged.

"You believe, madame, that Lazarre is the boy you saw in London?" said Louis Philippe.

"I am certain of it."

"What proofs have you?"

"The evidence of my eyes."

"Tell that to Monsieur!" exclaimed the potter.

"Who is Monsieur?" I asked.

"The eldest brother of the king of France is called Monsieur. The Count de Provence will be called Monsieur until he succeeds Louis XVII and is crowned Louis XVIII—if that time ever comes. He cannot be called Louis XVII"—the man who told me to call him Louis Philippe took my arm, and I found myself walking back and forth with him as in a dream while he carefully formed sentence after sentence. "Because the dauphin who died in the Temple prison was Louis XVII. But there are a few who say he did not die: that a dying child was substituted for him: that he was smuggled out and carried to America, Bellenger was the agent employed. The dauphin's sister is married to her cousin, the nephew of Monsieur. She herself believes these things; and it is certain a sum of money is sent out to America every year for his maintenance. He was reduced to imbecility when removed from the Temple. It is not known whether he will ever be fit to reign if the kingdom returns to him. No communication has been held with him. He was nine years old when removed from the Temple: he would now be in his nineteenth year. When I last saw him he was a smiling little prince with waving hair and hazel eyes, holding to his mother's hand"—

"Stop!"

The frenzy of half recollection came on me, and that which I had put away from my mind and sworn to let alone, seized and convulsed me. Dreams, and sensations, and instincts massed and fell upon me in an avalanche of conviction.

I was that uncrowned outcast, the king of France!

BOOK II

WANDERING

I

A primrose dawn of spring touched the mountains as Madame de Ferrier and I stepped into the tunnel's mouth. The wind that goes like a besom before sunrise, swept off the fog to corners of the sky, except a few spirals which still unwound from the lake. The underground path to De Chaumont's manor descended by terraces of steps and entered blackness.

A rank odor of earth filled it; and I never passed that way without hearkening for the insect-like song of the rattlesnake. The ground was slippery, and thick darkness seemed to press the soul out of the body. Yet I liked it; for when we reached the staircase of rock that entered the house, she would vanish.

And so it was.

She did say—"Good-night—and good-morning."

And I answered, "Good-morning and good-night."

We were both physically exhausted. My head swarmed as with sparkles, and a thousand emotions tore me, for I was at the age when we risk all on chances. I sat alone on the steps, unmindful of that penetrating chill of stone which increases rather than decreases, the longer you sit upon it, and thought of all that had been said by my new friend at the camp-fire, while the moon went lower and lower, the potter turned his wheel, and the idiot slept.

The mixed and oblique motives of human nature—the boy's will—worked like gigantic passions.

She had said very little to me in the boat, and I had said very little to her; not realizing that the camp talk, in which she took no part, separated us in a new way.

Sitting alone on the steps I held this imaginary conversation with her.

"I am going to France!"

"You, monsieur?"

"Yes, I!"

"How are you going?"

"I don't know; but I am going!"

"The Duke of Orleans did not mention such a thing."

"Bother the Duke of Orleans!"

"When are you going?"

"Now!"

"But it may not be best to go at this time."

"It is always best to go where you are!"

"Monsieur, do not throw away your future on an unconsidered move."

"Madame, I will throw away my eternity!"

Then I went back through the tunnel to the beach, stripped, and took a plunge to clear my head and warm my blood, rubbing off with my shirt.

On reaching my room the first thing I did was to make a bundle of everything I considered necessary and desirable. There was no reason for doing this before lying down; but with an easier mind I closed my eyes; and opened them to find sunset shining through the windows, and Doctor Chantry keeping guard in an arm-chair at my side.

"Nature has taken her revenge on you, my lad," said he. "And now I am going to take mine."

"I have slept all day!"

"Renegades who roam the woods all night must expect to sleep all day."

"How do you know I have been in the woods all night?"

"I heard you slipping up the tunnel stairs without any shoes on at daylight. I have not been able to sleep two nights on account of you."

"Then why don't you go to bed yourself, my dear master?"

"Because I am not going to let you give me the slip another time. I am responsible for you: and you will have me on your back when you go prowling abroad again."

"Again?" I questioned innocently.

"Yes, again, young sir! I have been through your luggage, and find that you have packed changes of clothing and things necessary and unnecessary to a journey,—even books."

"I hope you put them neatly together"—

"Nothing of the kind. I scattered them."

"Do you want me to go bare into the world?" I laughed.

"Lazarre," said my master, "you were a good lad, studious and zealous beyond anything I ever saw."

"And now I am bad and lazy."

"You have dropped your books and taken to wild ways."

"There is one thing, dear master, I haven't done: I haven't written poetry."

He blinked and smiled, and felt in his breast pocket, but thought better of it, and forebore to draw the paper out. There was no escaping his tenacious grip. He sat by and exercised me in Latin declensions while I dressed. We had our supper together. I saw no member of the household except the men, Pierre and Jean. Doctor Chantry ordered a mattress put in my room and returned there with me.

We talked long on the approaching departure of the count and Madame de Ferrier. He told me the latest details of preparation, and tremulously explained how he must feel the loss of his sister.

"I have nothing left but you, Lazarre."

"My dear master," I said, patting one of his shriveled hands between mine, "I am going to be open with you."

I sat on the side of my bed facing his arm-chair, and the dressing-glass reflected his bald head and my young head drawn near together.

"Did you ever feel as if you were a prince?"

Doctor Chantry wagged a pathetic negative.

"Haven't you ever been ready to dare anything and everything, because something in you said—I must!"

Again Doctor Chantry wagged a negative.

"Now I have to break bounds—I have to leave the manor and try my fortune! I can't wait for times and seasons—to be certain of this—to be certain of that!—I am going to leave the house to-night—and I am going to France!"

"My God!" cried Doctor Chantry, springing up. "He is going to France!—Rouse the servants!—Call De Chaumont!" He struck his gouty foot against the chair and sat down nursing it in both hands. I restrained him and added my sympathy to his groans.

"Have you as much as a Spanish real of your own, my lad?" he catechised me, when the foot was easy.

I acknowledged that I had not.

"It costs dear to travel about the world. It is not like coming down the trail from St. Regis to Lake George. How are you to travel without money?"

I laughed at the very uncertainty, and answered that money would be found.

"Found! It isn't found, I tell you! It is inherited by the idle, or gathered by the unscrupulous, or sweated and toiled for! It costs days and years, and comes in drops. You might as well expect to find a kingdom, lad!"

"Maybe I shall find a kingdom, master!"

"Oh, what a thing it is to be young!" sighed Doctor Chantry.

I felt it myself, and hugged my youth.

"Do you know how to reach the sea-port?" he continued.

I said anybody could follow the Hudson to New York.

"You're bitten, my poor lad! It's plain what ails you. You might as well try to swim the Atlantic. De Chaumont intends her for himself. And in the unjust distribution of this world, your rival has the power and you have the feelings. Stay where you are. You'll never forget it, but it will hurt less as years go by."

"Master," I said to him, "good sense is on your side. But if I knew I should perish, I would have to go!"

And I added from fullness of conviction—

"I would rather undertake to do something, and perish, than live a thousand years as I am."

Doctor Chantry struck the chair arm with his clenched fist.

"My lad, so would I—so would I!—I wish I had been dowered with your spirit!—I'm going with you!"

As soon as he had made this embarrassing resolution my master blew his nose and set his British jaws firmly together. I felt my own jaw drop.

"Have you as much as a Spanish real of your own?" I quoted.

"That I have, young sir, and some American notes, such as they are, and good English pounds, beside."

"And do you know how to reach the seaport?"

"Since I came that way I can return that way. You have youth, my lad, but I have brains and experience."

"It's plain what ails you, Doctor Chantry. And you might as well try to swim the Atlantic."

My poor master dropped his head on his breast, and I was ashamed of baiting him and began to argue tenderly. I told him he could not bear hardships; he was used to the soft life in De Chaumont's house; while my flesh had been made iron in the wilderness. I intended to take a boat from those hidden at our summer camp, to reach the head of Lake George. But from that point to the Hudson river—where the town of Luzerne now stands—it was necessary to follow a trail. I could carry the light canoe over the trail, but he could not even walk it.

The more I reasoned with him the more obstinate he became. There was a wonderful spring called Saratoga, which he had visited with De Chaumont a few years before as they came into the wilderness; he was convinced that the water would set him on foot for the rest of the journey.

"It is twenty-nine miles above Albany. We could soon reach it," he urged.

"I have heard of it," I answered. "Skenedonk has been there. But he says you leave the river and go into the woods."

"I know the way," he testily insisted. "And there used to be near the river a man who kept horses and carried visitors to the spring."

The spirit of reckless adventure, breaking through years of extreme prudence, outran youth.

"What will you do in France?" I put to him. He knew no more than I what I should do.

And there was Count de Chaumont to be considered. How would he regard such a leave-taking?

Doctor Chantry was as insensible to De Chaumont as I myself. Still he agreed to write a note to his protector while I prepared my quill to write one to Madame de Ferrier. With the spirit of the true parasite he laid all the blame on me, and said he was constrained by duty to follow and watch over me since it was impossible to curb a nature like mine. And he left a loophole open for a future return to De Chaumont's easy service, when the hardships which he willingly faced brought him his reward.

This paper he brazenly showed me while I was struggling to beg Madame de Ferrier's pardon, and to let her know that I aimed at something definite whether I ever reached port or not.

I reflected with satisfaction that he would probably turn back at Saratoga. We descended together to his room and brought away the things he needed. In bulk they were twice as large as the load I had made for myself.

He also wrote out strict orders to Pierre to seal up his room until his return. The inability of an old man to tear himself from his accustomed environment cheered my heart.

We then went back to bed, and like the two bad boys we were, slept prepared for flight.

II

"This is fine!" said Doctor Chantry, when we descended from the rough stage which had brought us across a corduroy trail, and found ourselves at the entrance of a spacious wooden tavern. "When I passed Saratoga before there were only three log houses, and the inn had two rooms below and one above. It was lighted by pine torches stuck in the chinks of the wall—and see how candles shine through these windows!"

The tavern stood in a cleared place with miles of forest around it, and a marsh stretching near by. Dusk could not prevent our seeing a few log habitations, one of them decorated with a merchant's sign. We entered among swarming crowds, a little world dropped into the backwoods. This was more surprising because we had just left behind us a sense of wild things gathering to their night haunts, and low savage cries, and visions of moose and deer through far-off arches.

A man who appeared to be the host met us, his sprightly interest in our welfare being tempered by the consciousness of having many guests; and told us the house was full, but he would do what he could for us.

"Why is the house full?" fretted Doctor Chantry. "What right have you, my dear sir, to crowd your house and so insure our discomfort?"

"None at all, sir," answered the host good naturedly. "If you think you can do better, try for lodgings at the store-keeper's."

"The store-keeper's!" Doctor Chantry's hysterical cry turned some attention to us. "I shall do nothing of the kind. I demand the best you have, sir."

"The best I can give you," amended our host. "You see we are very full of politicians from Washington. They crowd to the spring."

My master turned his nose like the inflamed horn of a unicorn against the politicians from Washington, and trotted to the fireplace where blazing knots cheered a great tap-room set with many tables and benches.

And there rested Skenedonk in silent gravity, toasting his moccasins. The Iroquois had long made Saratoga a gathering place, but I thought of this Oneida as abiding in St. Regis village; for our people did not come to the summer hunting in May.

Forgetting that I was a runaway I met him heartily, and the fawn eyes in his bald head beamed their accustomed luster upon me. I asked him where my father and mother and the rest of the tribe were, and he said they had not left St. Regis.

"And why are you so early?" I inquired.

He had been at Montreal, and had undertaken to guide a Frenchman as far as Saratoga. It is not easy to surprise an Indian. But I wondered that Skenedonk accepted my presence without a question, quite as if he had himself made the appointment.

However, the sights to be seen put him out of my head. Besides the tap-room crowded with men there was a parlor in which women of fashion walked about, contrasting with the place. They had all been to a spring to drink water; for only one spring was greatly used then; and they talked about the medicinal effects. Some men left the stronger waters, which could be had at a glittering portcullised bar opposite the fireplace in the tap-room, to chat with these short-waisted beauties. I saw one stately creature in a white silk ball costume, his stockings splashed to the knees with mud from the corduroy road.

But the person who distinguished himself from everybody else by some nameless attraction, was a man perhaps forty years old, who sat in a high-backed settle at a table near the fire. He was erect and thin as a lath, long faced, square browed and pale. His sandy hair stood up like the bristles of a brush. Carefully dressed, with a sword at his side—as many of the other men had—he filled my idea of a soldier; and I was not surprised to hear his friends sitting opposite call him General Jackson.

An inkstand, a quill and some paper were placed before him, but he pushed them aside with his glass of toddy to lift one long fore-finger and emphasize his talk. He had a resonant, impressive voice, with a manner gentle and persuasive, like a woman's: and he was speaking of Aaron Burr, the man whose duel had made such a noise in the newspapers.

He pushed them aside with his glass of toddy to lift one long forefinger and emphasize his talk.

"I disagree with you, Mr. Campbell. You are prejudiced against Mr. Burr on account of his late unfortunate affair. Even in that case I maintain every man has a right to honor and satisfaction. But he loves the Spanish on our southwestern borders no better than I do,—and you know how I love the Spanish!"

The other man laughed, lounging against the table.

"You can't believe anything ill of Aaron Burr, General."

I might have given attention to what they were saying, since here were men from Washington, the very fountain of government, if Doctor Chantry had not made me uneasy. He chose the table at which they were sitting and placed himself in the seat nearest the fire, with the utmost nicety about his own comfort. He wiped his horn spectacles, and produced his own ink and quill and memorandum from a breast pocket. I had begged the doctor to keep strict account between us, that I might pay back from my pension whatever he spent on me, and with fine spider-like characters he was proceeding to debit me with the stage fare, when another quill barred his entrance to his ink-horn.

He took off his spectacles and glared pink-eyed at the genial gentleman with sandy upright hair.

"Sir!" he cried, "that is my ink!"

General Jackson, absorbed in talk, did not notice Doctor Chantry, who half arose and shouted directly at his ear,

"Sir, that is my ink!"

He knocked the interloping quill in the direction of its owner.

The genial sandy gentleman changed countenance in a way to astonish beholders.

"Have I disputed it, sir?"

"No, sir, but you have dipped into it without asking leave."

"By God, sir, what is a fip'ny-bit's worth of ink?"

"But it's mine, sir!"

"I see, sir; you're a Yankee, sir!"

"I'm not, sir; I'm English—the finest race in the world!"

General Jackson looked him up and down as they rose fronting each other, and filled the air with dazzling words.

"I should judge so, sir, by the specimen I see before me!"

Doctor Chantry was like a fighting-cock, and it was plainly his age which kept the other from striking him. He was beginning our journey well, but I felt bound to intercept whatever fell upon him, and stood between them. The other men at the table rose with General Jackson.

"Gentlemen," I pleaded with the best words I could command in the language, "do not forget your dignity, and disturb the peace of this house for a bottle of ink!"

The quarrel was ridiculous, and the Southerners laughed. General Jackson himself again changed countenance, and gave me, I do not know why, a smile that must have been reflected from the face of a woman he adored. But my poor master showed the bull-dog; and taking him by the arm and the collar I toddled him away from that table to a dark entry, where I held him without any admonition save a sustained grip. He became like a child, weeping and trembling, and declaring that everybody was in league against him. Argument is wasted on people having such infirmity of temper. When he was well cooled I put him in an arm-chair by a fire in the ladies' parlor, and he was soon very meek and tractable, watching the creatures he so admired.

"You must go to bed as soon as you have your supper," I said to him. "The journey to Saratoga has been a hard one for you. But Skenedonk is here fortunately, and he can take you home again."

My master looked at me with the shrewishness of an elephant. I had not at that time seen an elephant. When I did see one, however, the shifting of its eyes brought back the memory of Doctor Chantry when I had him at bay by the fire.

"You are not going to get away from me," he responded. "If you are tired of it, so am I. Otherwise, we proceed."

"If you pick quarrels with soldiers and duelists at every step, what are we to do?"

"I picked no quarrel. It is my luck. Everyone is against me!" He hung his head in such a dejected manner that I felt ashamed of bringing his temperament to account: and told him I was certain no harm would come of it.

"I am not genial," Doctor Chantry owned; "I wish I were. Now you are genial, Lazarre. People take to you. You attract them. But whatever I am, you are obliged to have my company: you cannot get along without me. You have no experience, and no money. I have experience,—and a few pounds:—not enough to retire into the country upon, in England; but enough to buy a little food for the present."

I thought I could get along better without the experience and even the few pounds, than with him as an encumbrance; though I could not bring myself to the cruelty of telling him so. For there is in me a fatal softness which no man can have and overbear others in this world. It constrains me to make the other man's cause my own, though he be at war with my own interests.

Therefore I was at the mercy of Skenedonk, also. The Indian appeared in the doorway and watched me. I knew he thought there was to be trouble with the gentleman from Washington, and I went to him to ease his mind.

Skenedonk had nothing to say, however, and made me a sign to follow him. As we passed through the tap-room, General Jackson gave me another pleasant look. He had resumed his conversation and his own ink-bottle as if he had never been interrupted.

The Indian led me upstairs to one of the chambers, and opened the door.

In the room was Louis Philippe, and when we were shut alone together, he embraced me and kissed me as I did not know men embraced and kissed.

"Do you know Skenedonk?" I exclaimed.

"If you mean the Indian who brought you at my order, he was my guide from Montreal."

"But he was not with you at the potter's camp."

"Yes, he was in the hut, wrapped in his blanket, and after you drove the door in he heard all that was said. Lazarre"—Louis Philippe took my face in his hands—"make a clean breast of it."

We sat down, and I told him without being questioned what I was going to do. He gravely considered.

"I saw you enter the house, and had a suspicion of your undertaking. It is the worst venture you could possibly make at this time. We will begin with my family. Any belief in you into which I may have been betrayed is no guaranty of Monsieur's belief. You understand," said Louis Philippe, "that Monsieur stands next to the throne if there is no dauphin, or an idiot dauphin?"

I said I understood.

"Monsieur is not a bad man. But Bellenger, who took charge of the dauphin, has in some manner and for some reason, provided himself with a substitute, and he utterly denies you. Further: supposing that you are the heir of France, restored to your family and proclaimed—of what use is it to present yourself before the French people now? They are besotted with this Napoleon. The Empire seems to them a far greater thing than any legitimate monarchy. Of what use, do I say? It would be a positive danger for you to appear in France at this time! Napoleon has proscribed every Bourbon. Any prince caught alive in France will be put to death. Do you know what he did last year to the Duke d'Enghien? He sent into Germany for the duke, who had never harmed him, never conspired against him—had done nothing, in fact, except live an innocent life away from the seat of Napoleon's power. The duke was brought to Paris under guard and put in the dungeons of Vincennes. He demanded to see Bonaparte. Bonaparte would not see him. He was tried by night, his grave being already dug in the castle ditch. That lovely young fellow—he was scarcely above thirty—was taken out to the ditch and shot like a dog!"

I stood up with my hands clenched.

"Sit down," said Louis Philippe. "There is no room in the world at this time for anybody but that jealous monster."

"He shall not tie me here," I said.

"You intend to go?"

"I intend to go."

"This Bonaparte," said Louis Philippe, "has his troubles. His brother Jerome has married an American in Baltimore. A fine explosion that will make when it reaches his ears. Where are you going to land, Lazarre?"

I said that must depend on the ship I took.

"And what are you going to do when you land?"

I said I would think that out later.

Then the spirit being upon me, I burst bounds and told him impetuously that I was going to learn what the world held for me. Without means, without friends, or power or prospects, or certainty of any good results—impudent—reckless—utterly rash—"I am going," I cried, "because I must go!"

"There is something about you which inspires love, my boy," said Louis Philippe; and I heard him with astonishment. "Perhaps it comes from the mother; she was a witcher of all mankind."

"I cannot understand why any one should love so ignorant a creature, but God grant there be others that love me, too; for I have lived a life stinted of all affection. And, indeed, I did not know I wanted it until last year. When we talked late the other night, and you told me the history of all my family, the cruelest part of my lot seemed the separation from those that belonged to me. Separation from what is our own ought not to be imposed upon us even by God Himself!"

"What!" said Louis Philippe, "is he following a woman!"

My face burned, and probably went white, for I felt the blood go back on my heart. He took my hand and stroked it.

"Don't chain yourself behind that chariot. Wait a little while for your good star to rise. I wish I had money. I wish I could be of use to you in France. I wish I stood nearer to Monsieur, for your sake. Every one must love this bold pure face. It bears some resemblance to Madame Royal. The sister of the dauphin is a good girl, not many years your senior. Much dominated by her uncles, but a royal duchess. It is the fashion now to laugh at chivalry. You are the most foolish example of it I ever saw! It is like seeing a knight without horse, armor, or purse, set out to win an equipment before he pursues his quest! Yet I love you for it, my boy!"

"It would be well for me if I had more friends like you."

"Why, I can be of no use! I cannot go back to France at this time, and if I could, what is my influence there? I must wander around in foreign parts, a private gentleman eking out my living by some kind of industry. What are you going to do with the fretful old fellow you have with you?"

I groaned and laughed.

"Carry him on my back. There is no getting rid of him. He is following me to France. He is my lesson-master."

"How will you support him?"

"He is supporting me at present. But I would rather take my chances alone."

"You have another follower," said Louis Philippe. "Your Indian has been in France, and after hearing our talk at the camp, he foresaw you might be moved to this folly, and told me he intended to guide you there, or wherever you go!"

"And Skenedonk, too!"

I shook with laughter. It was so like Skenedonk to draw his conclusions and determine on the next step.

"What shall I do with them?"

"The old master can be your secretary, and as for the Indian, you can take him for your servant."

"A secretary and a servant, for an outcast without a penny to his pouch!"

"You see the powers that order us are beginning well with you. Starting with a secretary and a servant, you may end with a full household and a court! I ought to add my poor item of tribute, and this I can do. There is a ship-master taking cargo this month in New York bay, who is a devoted royalist; a Breton sailor. For a letter from me he will carry you and your suite to the other side of the world; but you will have to land in his port."

"And what will the charges be?"

"Nothing, except gratitude, if I put the case as strongly to him as I intend to do. God knows I may be casting a foul lot for you. His ship is staunch, rigged like the Italian salt ships. But it is dirty work crossing the sea; and there is always danger of falling into the hands of pirates. Are you determined?"

I looked him in the eyes, and said I was; thanking him for all his goodness to one who had so little expectation of requiting him. The sweet heartiness of an older man so far beyond myself in princely attainments and world knowledge, who could stoop to such a raw savage, took me by storm.

I asked him if he had any idea who the idiot was that we had seen in Bellenger's camp. He shook his head, replying that idiots were plentiful, and the people who had them were sometimes glad to get rid of them.

"The dauphin clue has been very cleverly managed by—Bellenger, let us say," Louis Philippe remarked. "If you had not appeared, I should not now believe there is a dauphin."

I wanted to tell him all the thoughts tossing in my mind; but silence is sometimes better than open speech. Facing adventure, I remembered that I had never known the want of food for any length of time during my conscious life. And I had a suspicion the soft life at De Chaumont's had unstrung me for what was before me. But it lasted scarce a year, and I was built for hardship.

He turned to his table to write the ship-master's letter. Behold, there lay a book I knew so well that I exclaimed——

"Where did you get my missal?"

"Your missal, Lazarre? This is mine."

I turned the leaves, and looked at the back. It was a continuation of the prayers of the church. There were blank leaves for the inscribing of prayers, and one was written out in a good bold hand.

"His Majesty Louis XVI composed and wrote that prayer himself," said Louis Philippe. "The comfort-loving priests had a fashion of dividing the missal into three or four parts, that a volume might not be so heavy to carry about in their pockets. This is the second volume. It was picked up in the Tuileries after that palace was sacked."

I told him mine must be the preceding volume, because I did not know there was any continuation. The prayers of the church had not been my study.

"Where did you get yours, Lazarre?"

"Madame de Ferrier gave it to me. When I saw it I remembered, as if my head were split open to show the picture, that my mother had read from that very book to me. I cannot explain it, but so it was."

"I am not surprised she believes, against Bellenger's evidence, that you are Louis of France."

"I will bring my book and show it to you."

We compared the volumes after supper, and one was the mate of the other.

The inn dining-room had one long table stretched down its entire length, heaped with wild meats and honey and pastries and fish in abundance. General Jackson sat at one end, and at the other sat the landlord, explaining to all his guests what each dish was, and urging good appetite. I sat by Louis Philippe, whose quality was known only to myself, with Doctor Chantry on the other side fretting for the attendance to which Jean had used him.

My master was so tired that I put him early to bed; and then sat talking nearly all night with the gracious gentleman to whom I felt bound by gratitude and by blood.

III

Dieppe, high and glaring white above the water, will always symbolize to me the gate of France. The nobility of that view remained in my thoughts when half the distance to Paris was traversed.

I could shut my eyes and see it as I lay on the straw in a post-house stable. A square hole in the front of the grenier gave upon the landscape. Even respectable houses in that part of the country were then built with few or no windows; but delicious masses of grayness they were, roofed with thick and overhanging thatch.

"The stables of France are nothing but covered dunghills," Doctor Chantry grumbled; so when I crept with the Indian to lodgings over the cattle, one of the beds in the house was hired for the gouty master. Even at inns there were two or three beds in a room where they set us to dine.

"An English inn-keeper would throw their furniture into the fire!" he cried in a language fortunately not understood.

"But we have two good rooms on the ground floor, and another for Skenedonk," I sometimes remonstrated with him, "at three shillings and sixpence a day, in your money."

"You would not see any man, let his rank be what it may," Doctor Chantry retorted, "dining in his bedroom, in England. And look at these walls!—papered with two or three kinds of paper, the bare spots hung with tapestry moth-eaten and filled with spiders! And what have we for table?—a board laid on cross-bars! And the oaken chairs are rush-bottomed, and so straight the backs are a persecution! The door hinges creak in these inns, the wind blows through—"

So his complaints went on, for there never was a man who got so much out of small miseries. Skenedonk and I must have failed to see all in our travels that he put before us. For we were full of enjoyment and wonder: at the country people, wooden shod, the women's caps and long cloaks; at the quiet fair roads which multiplied themselves until we often paused enchanted in a fairy world of sameness; at market-towns, where fountains in the squares were often older than America, the country out of which we arrived.

Skenedonk heard without shifting a muscle all Doctor Chantry's grievances; and I told him we ought to cherish them, for they were views of life we could not take ourselves. Few people are made so delicately that they lose color and rail at the sight of raw tripe brought in by a proud hostess to show her resources for dinner; or at a chicken coming upon the table with its head tucked beneath its wing.

"We are fed with poulet, poulet, nothing but poulet," said Doctor Chantry, "until the poulets themselves are ashamed to look us in the face!"

We fared well, indeed, and the wine was good, and my master said he must sustain himself on it though it proved his death. He could not march as Skenedonk and I regularly marched. We hired a cart to lift him and our knapsacks from village to village, with a driver who knew the road to Paris. When the distances were long we sometimes mounted beside him. I noticed that the soil of this country had not the chalk look of other lands which I afterwards saw to the east and north; but Napoleon was already making good the ancient thoroughfares.

When my master was on shipboard he enjoyed the sea even less than the free air of these broad stretches; for while he could cast an eye about and approve of something under the sky—perhaps a church steeple, or the color of a thatch which filled me with joy—he could not approve of anything aboard a ship. Indeed, it was pity to have no delight in cleaving the water, and in the far-off spouting of whales, to say nothing of a living world that rides in undulations. For my part, I loved even the creaking of a ship, and the uncertainty of ever coming to port, and the anxiety lest a black flag should show above every sail we passed. The slow progress of man from point to point in his experience, while it sometimes enrages, on the whole interests me; and the monotony of a voyage has a sweetness like the monotony of daily bread. I looked out of the grenier window upon the high road, and upon the June sun in the act of setting; for we had supped and gone early to rest after a hard day. Post horses were stamping underneath, all ready for some noble count who intended to make another stage of his journey before nightfall.

Small obtrusive cares, such as the desire that my shoes should last well into Paris, mingled with joy in the smell of the earth at sunset, and the looking forward to seeing Madame de Ferrier again. I wrapped myself every night in the conviction that I should see her, and more freely than I had ever seen her in America.

There was a noise of horses galloping, and the expected noble count arrived; being no other than De Chaumont with his post coaches. He stepped out of the first, and Ernestine stepped out of the second, carrying Paul. She took him to his mother. The door flew open, and the woman I adored received her child and walked back and forth with him. Annabel leaned out while the horses were changed. I saw Miss Chantry, and my heart misgave me, remembering her brother's prolonged lament at separation from her.

He was, I trusted, already shut into one of those public beds which are like cupboards; for the day had begun for us at three of the morning. But if he chose to show himself, and fall upon De Chaumont for luxurious conveyance to Paris, I was determined that Skenedonk and I should not appear. I wronged my poor master, who told me afterwards he watched through a crack of the cupboard bed with his heart in his mouth.

The pause was a very short one, for horses are soon changed. Madame de Ferrier threw a searching eye over the landscape. It was a mercy she did not see the hole in the grenier, through which I devoured her, daring for the first time to call her secretly—Eagle—the name that De Chaumont used with common freedom! Now how strange is this—that one woman should be to a man the sum of things! And what was her charm I could not tell, for I began to understand there were many beautiful women in the world, of all favors, and shapely perhaps as the one of my love. Only her I found drawing the soul out of my body; and none of the others did more than please the eye like pictures.

The carriages were gone with the sun, and it was no wonder all fell gray over the world.

De Chaumont had sailed behind us, and he would be in Paris long before us.

I had first felt some uneasiness, and dread of being arrested on our journey; though our Breton captain—who was a man of gold that I would travel far to see this day, if I could, even beneath the Atlantic, where he and his ship now float—obtained for us at Dieppe, on his own pledge, a kind of substitute for passports. We were a marked party, by reason of the doctor's lameness and Skenedonk's appearance. The Oneida, during his former sojourn in France, had been encouraged to preserve the novelty of his Indian dress. As I had nothing to give him in its place it did not become me to find fault. And he would have been more conspicuous with a cocked hat on his bare red scalp, and knee breeches instead of buckskins. Peasants ran out to look at him, and in return we looked at them with a good will.

We reached the very barriers of Paris, however, without falling into trouble. And in the streets were so many men of so many nations that Skenedonk's attire seemed no more bizarre than the turbans of the east or the white burnous of the Arab.

It was here that Skenedonk took his rôle as guide, and stalked through narrow crooked streets, which by comparison made New York, my first experience of a city, appear a plain and open village.

I do not pretend to know anything about Paris. Some spots in the mystic labyrinth stand out to memory, such as that open space where the guillotine had done its work, the site of the Bastille, and a long street leading from the place of the Bastille, parallel with the river; and this I have good reason to remember. It is called Rue St. Antoine. I learned well, also, a certain prison, and a part of the ancient city called Faubourg St. Germain. One who can strike obscure trails in the wilderness of nature, may blunt his fine instincts on the wilderness of man.

This did not befall the Indian. He took a bee line upon his old tracks, and when the place was sighted we threaded what seemed to be a rivulet between cliffs, for a moist depressed street-center kept us straddling something like a gutter, while with outstretched hands we could brace the opposite walls.

We entered a small court where a gruff man, called a concierge, having a dirty kerchief around his head, received us doubtfully. He was not the concierge of Skenedonk's day. We showed him coin; and Doctor Chantry sat down in his chair and looked at him with such contempt that his respect increased.

The house was clean, and all the stairs we climbed to the roof were well scoured. From the mansard there was a beautiful view of Paris, with forest growth drawing close to the heart of the city. For on that side of the world men dare not murder trees, but are obliged to respect and cherish them.

My poor master stretched himself on a bed by the stooping wall, and in disgust of life and great pain of feet, begged us to order a pan of charcoal and let him die the true Parisian death when that is not met on the scaffold. Skenedonk said to me in Iroquois that Doctor Chantry was a sick old woman who ought to be hidden some place to die, and it was his opinion that the blessing of the church would absolve us. We could then make use of the pouch of coin to carry on my plans.

My plans were more ridiculous than Skenedonk's. His at least took sober shape, while mine were still the wild emotions of a young man's mind. Many an hour I had spent on the ship, watching the foam speed past her side, trying to foresee my course like hers in a trackless world. But it seemed I must wait alertly for what destiny was making mine.

We paid for our lodgings, three commodious rooms, though in the mansard; my secretary dragging himself to sit erect with groans and record the increasing debt of myself and my servant.

"Come, Skenedonk," I then said. "Let us go down to the earth and buy something that Doctor Chantry can eat."

That benevolent Indian was quite as ready to go to market as to abate human nuisances. And Doctor Chantry said he could almost see English beef and ale across the channel; but translated into French they would, of course, be nothing but poulet and sour wine. I pillowed his feet with a bag of down which he had kicked off his bed, and Skenedonk and I lingered along the paving as we had many a time lingered through the woods. There were book stalls a few feet square where a man seemed smothered in his own volumes; and victual shops where you could almost feed yourself for two or three sous; and people sitting outdoors drinking wine, as if at a general festival. I thought Paris had comfort and prosperity—with hereditary kings overthrown and an upstart in their place. Yet the streets were dirty, with a smell of ancientness that sickened me.

We got a loaf of bread as long as a staff, a pat of butter in a leaf, and a bottle of wine. My servant, though unused to squaw labor, took on himself the porterage of our goods, and I pushed from street to street, keenly pleased with the novelty, which held somewhere in its volatile ether the person of Madame de Ferrier.

Skenedonk blazed our track with his observant eye, and we told ourselves we were searching for Doctor Chantry's beef. Being the unburdened hunter I undertook to scan cross places, and so came unexpectedly upon the Rue St. Antoine, as a man told me it was called, and a great hurrahing that filled the mouths of a crowd blocking the thoroughfare.

"Long live the emperor!" they shouted.

The man who told me the name of the street, a baker all in white, with his tray upon his head, objected contemptuously.

"The emperor is not in Paris: he is in Boulogne."

"You never know where he is—he is here—there—everywhere!" declared another workman, in a long dark garment like a hunting-shirt on the outside of his small clothes.

"Long live the emperor!—long live the emperor!"

I pushed forward as two or three heavy coaches checked their headlong speed, and officers parted the crowd.

"There he is!" admitted the baker behind me. Something struck me in the side, and there was Bellenger the potter, a man I thought beyond the seas in America. His head as I saw it that moment put the emperor's head out of my mind. He had a knife, and though he had used the handle, I foolishly caught it and took it from him. With all his strength he then pushed me so that I staggered against the wheel of a coach.

"Assassin!" he screamed; and then Paris fell around my ears.

If anybody had seen his act nobody refrained from joining in the cry.

"Assassin! Assassin! To the lamp post with him!"

I stood stupefied and astonished as an owl blinking in the sunshine, and two guards held my collar. The coaches lashed away, carrying the man of destiny—as I have since been told he called himself—as rapidly as possible, leaving the victim of destiny to be bayed at by that many-headed dog, the mongrel populace of Paris.

IV

The idiot boy somewhere upon the hills of Lake George, always in a world of fog which could not be discovered again, had often come to my mind during my journeys, like a self that I had shed and left behind. But Bellenger was a cipher. I forgot him even at the campfire. Now here was this poor crazy potter on my track with vindictive intelligence, the day I set foot in Paris. Time was not granted even to set the lodging in order. He must have crossed the ocean with as good speed as Doctor Chantry and Skenedonk and I. He may have spied upon us from the port, through the barriers, and even to our mansard. At any rate he had found me in a crowd, and made use of me to my downfall: and I could have knocked my stupid head on the curb as I was haled away.

One glimpse of Skenedonk I caught while we marched along Rue St. Antoine, the gendarmes protecting me from the crowd. He thought I was going to the scaffold, where many a strapping fellow had gone in the Paris of his youth, and fought to reach me, laying about him with his loaf of bread. Skenedonk would certainly trail me, and find a way to be of use, unless he broke into trouble as readily as I had done.

My guards crossed the river in the neighborhood of palaces, and came by many windings to a huge pile rearing its back near a garden place, and there I was turned over to jailers and darkness. The entrance was unwholesome. A man at a table opened a tome which might have contained all the names in Paris. He dipped his quill and wrote by candlelight.

"Political offender or common criminal?" he inquired.

"Political offender," the officer answered.

"What is he charged with?"

"Trying to assassinate the emperor in his post-chaise."

"La, la, la!" the recorder grunted. "Another attempt! And gunpowder put in the street to blow the emperor up only last week. Good luck attends him:— only a few windows broken and some common people killed. Taken in the act, was this fellow?"

"With the knife in his hand."

"What name?" the recorder inquired.

I had thought on the answer, and told him merely that my name was Williams.

"Eh, bien, Monsieur Veeleeum. Take him to the east side among the political offenders," said the master-jailer to an assistant or turnkey.

"But it's full," responded the turnkey.

"Shove him in some place."

They searched me, and the turnkey lighted another candle. The meagerness of my output was beneath remark. When he had led me up a flight of stone steps he paused and inquired,

"Have you any money?"

"No."

"So much the worse for you."

"What is the name of this prison?" I asked.

"Ste. Pélagie," he answered. "If you have no money, and expect to eat here, you better give me some trinket to sell for you."

"I have no trinkets to give you."

He laughed.

"Your shirt or breeches will do."

"Are men shut up here to starve?"

The jailer shrugged.

"The bread is very bad, and the beans too hard to eat. We do not furnish the rations; it is not our fault. The rule here is nothing buys nothing. But sleep in your breeches while you can. You will soon be ready enough to eat them."

I was ready enough to eat them then, but forbore to let him know it. The whole place was damp and foul. We passed along a corridor less than four feet wide, and he unlocked a cell from which a revolting odor came. There was no light except what strained through a loophole under the ceiling. He turned the key upon me, and I held my nose. Oh, for a deep draught of the wilderness!

There seemed to be an iron bed at one side, with a heap of rags on top. I resolved to stand up all night before trusting myself to that couch. The cell was soon explored. Two strides in each direction measured it. The stone walls were marked or cut with names I could dimly see.

I braced my back against the door and watched the loophole where a gray hint of daylight told that the sun must be still shining. This faded to a blotch in the thick stone, and became obliterated.

Tired by the day's march, and with a taste of clean outdoor air still in my lungs, I chose one of the two corners not occupied by the ill odored bed, sat down, and fell asleep, dropping my cares. A grating of the lock disturbed me. The jailer pushed a jug of water into the room, and replaced his bolts.

Afterwards I do not remember anything except that the stone was not warm, and my stomach craved, until a groan in my ear stabbed sleep. I sat up awake in every nerve. There was nobody in the cell with me. Perhaps the groan had come from a neighboring prisoner.

Then a faint stir of covering could be heard upon the bed.

I rose and pressed as far as I could into my corner. No beast of the wilderness ever had such terror for me as the unknown thing that had been my cell-mate half a night without my knowledge.

Was a vampire—a demon—a witch—a ghost locked in there with me?

It moaned again, so faintly, that compassion instantly got the better of superstition.

"Who is there?" I demanded; as if the knowledge of a name would cure terror of the suffering thing naming itself.

I got no answer, and taking my resolution in hand, moved toward the bed, determined to know what housed with me. The jug of water stood in the way, and I lifted it with instinctive answer to the groan.

The creature heard the splash, and I knew by its mutter what it wanted. Groping darkly, to poise the jug for an unseen mouth, I realized that something helpless to the verge of extinction lay on the bed, and I would have to find the mouth myself or risk drowning it. I held the water on the bed-rail with my right hand, groped with the other, and found a clammy, death-cold forehead, a nose and cavernous cheeks, an open and fever roughened mouth. I poured water on my handkerchief and bathed the face. That would have been my first desire in extreme moments. The poor wretch gave a reviving moan, so I felt emboldened to steady the jug and let drop by drop gurgle down its throat.

Forgetting the horror of the bed I sat there, repeating at intervals this poor ministration until the porthole again dawned, and blackness became the twilight of day.

My cell-mate could not see me. I doubt if he ever knew that a hand gave him water. His eyes were meaningless, and he was so gaunt that his body scarcely made a ridge on the bed.

Some beans and mouldy bread were put in for my rations. The turnkey asked me how I intended to wash myself without basin or ewer or towels, and inquired further if he could be of service in disposing of my shirt or breeches.

"What ails this man?"

He shrugged, and said the prisoner had been wasting with fever.

"You get fever in Ste. Pélagie," he added, "especially when you eat the prison food. This man ought to be sent to the infirmary, but the infirmary is overflowing now."

"Who is he?"

"A journalist, or poet, or some miserable canaille of that sort. He will soon be out of your way." Our guard craned over to look at him. "*Oui*—da! He is a dying man! A priest must be sent to him soon. I remember he demanded one several days ago."

But that day and another dragged through before the priest appeared. I sent out my waistcoat, and got a wretched meal, and a few spoonfuls of wine that I used to moisten the dying man's lips. His life may or may not have been prolonged; but out of collapse he opened his mouth repeatedly and took the drops. He was more my blessing than I was his.

For I had an experience which has ever since given me to know the souls of prisoners.

The first day, in spite of the cell's foulness, I laughed secretly at jailers and felt at peace, holding the world at bay. I did not then know that Ste. Pélagie was the tomb of the accused, where more than one prisoner dragged out years without learning why he was put there. I was not brought to any trial or examination.

But gradually an uneasiness which cannot be imagined by one who has not felt it, grew upon me. I wanted light. The absence of it was torture! Light—to vivify the stifling air, which died as this man was dying—as I should die—in blinding mirk!

Moisture broke out all over my body, and cold dew stood on my forehead. How could human lungs breathe the midnight of blackening walls? The place was hot with the hell of confinement. I said over and over—"O God, Thou art Light!—in Thee is no darkness at all!"

This anguish seemed a repetition of something I had endured once before. The body and spirit remembered, though the mind had no register. I clawed at the walls. If I slept, it was to wake gasping, fighting upward with both hands.

The most singular phase was that I reproached myself for not soaking up more sun in the past. Oh, how much light was going to waste over wide fields and sparkling seas! The green woods, the green grass—they had their fill of sun, while we two perished!

I remembered creeping out of glare under the shadow of rocks, and wondered how I could have done it! If I ever came to the sun again I would stretch myself and roll from side to side, to let it burn me well! How blessed was the tan we got in summer from steeping in light!

Looking at my cell-mate I could have rent the walls.

"We are robbed," I told his deaf ears. "The light, poured freely all over the city, the light that belongs to you and me as much as to anybody, would save you! I wish I could pick you up and carry you out where the sun would shine through your bones! But let us be glad, you and I, that there is a woman who is not buried like a whitening sprout under this weight of stone! She is free, to walk around and take the light in her gray eyes and the wind in her brown hair. I swear to God if I ever come out of this I will never pass so much as a little plant prostrate in darkness, without helping it to the light."

It was night by the loophole when our turnkey threw the door open. I heard the priest and his sacristan joking in the corridor before they entered carrying their sacred parcels. The priest was a doddering old fellow, almost deaf, for the turnkey shouted at his ear, and dim of sight, for he stooped close to look at the dying man, who was beyond confession.

"Bring us something for a temporary altar," he commanded the turnkey, who stood candle in hand.

The turnkey gave his light to the sacristan, and taking care to lock us in, hurried to obey.

I measured the lank, ill-strung assistant, more an overgrown boy than a man of brawn, but expanded around his upper part by the fullness of a short white surplice. He had a face cheerful to silliness.

The turnkey brought a board supported by crosspieces; and withdrew, taking his own candle, as soon as the church's tapers were lighted.

The sacristan placed the temporary altar beside the foot of the bed, arrayed it, and recited the Confiteor.

Then the priest mumbled the Misereatur and Indulgentiam.

I had seen extreme unction administered as I had seen many another office of the church in my dim days, with scarcely any attention. Now the words were terribly living. I knew every one before it rolled off the celebrant's lips.

Yet under that vivid surface knowledge I carried on as vivid a sequence of thought.

The priest elevated the ciborium, repeating,

"Ecce Agnus Dei."

Then three times—"Domine, non sum dignus."

I heard and saw with exquisite keenness, yet I was thinking,

"If I do not get out of here he will have to say those words over me."

He put the host in the parted mouth of the dying, and spoke—

"Corpus Domini nostri Jesu Christi custodiat animam tuam in vetam aeternam."

I thought how easy it would be to strip the loose surplice over the sacristan's head. There was a swift clip of the arm around your opponent's neck which I had learned in wrestling, that cut the breath off and dropped him as limp as a cloth. It was an Indian trick. I said to myself it would be impossible to use that trick on the sacristan if he left the cell behind the deaf old priest. I did not want to hurt him. Still, he would have a better chance to live after I had squeezed his neck, than I should have if I did not squeeze it.

The priest took out of a silver case a vessel of oil, and a branch. He sprinkled holy water with the branch, upon the bed, the walls, the sacristan and me, repeating,

"Asperges me, Domine, hyssopo, et mundabor: lavabis me, et super nivem dealbabor."

While I bent my head to the drops, I knew it was impossible to choke down the sacristan, strip off his surplice, invest myself with it and get out of the cell before priest or turnkey looked back. The sacrilege of such an attack would take all the strength out of me.

The priest said the Exaudi nos, exhorted the insensible figure, then recited the Credo and the Litany, the sacristan responding.

Silence followed.

I knew the end was approaching. My hands were as cold as the nerveless one which would soon receive the candle. I told myself I should be a fool to attempt it. There was not one chance in a hundred. I should not squeeze hard enough. The man would yell. If I were swift as lightning and silent as force, they would take me in the act. It was impossible. But people who cannot do impossible things have to perish.

The priest dipped his thumb in oil, and with it crossed the eyes, ears, nose, mouth, and hands of him who was leaving the use of these five senses and instruments of evil.

Then he placed a lighted candle in the stiffened fingers, and ended with—

"Accipe lampadem ardentem custodi unctionem tuam."

I said to myself—"I cannot do it! Nobody could! It is impossible!"

The sacristan now began to strip the altar and pack all the sacred implements into their cases: preparing his load in the center of the room.

The man was dead.

The sacristan's last office was to fix the two lighted altar candles on the head and foot railing of the bed. They showed the corpse in its appalling stillness, and stood like two angels, with the pit between them.

The sacristan rapped upon the door to let the turnkey know it was time to unlock.

I drew the thick air to my lung depths. The man who would breathe no more was not as rigid as I stood. But there was no use in attempting such a thing!

The turnkey opened a gap of doorway through which he could see the candles and the bed. He opened no wider than the breadth of the priest, who stepped out as the sacristan bent for the portables.

There was lightning in my arm as it took the sacristan around the neck and let him limp upon the stones. The tail of the priest's cassock was scarcely through the door.

"Eh bien! sacristan," called the turnkey. "Make haste with your load. I have this death to report. He is not so pretty that you must stand gazing at him all night!"

I had the surplice over the sacristan's head and over mine, and backed out with my load, facing the room.

If my jailer had thrust his candle at me, if the priest had turned to speak, if the man in the cell had got his breath before the bolt was turned, if my white surplice had not appeared the principal part of me in that black place—.

It was impossible!—but I had done it.

V

The turnkey's candle made a star-point in the corridor. He walked ahead of the priest and I walked behind. We descended to the entrance where the man with the big book sat taking stock of another wretch between officers. I saw as I shaded my face with the load, that his inattentive eye dwelt on my surplice, which would have passed me anywhere in France.

"Good-night, monsieur the curé," said the turnkey, letting us through the outer door.

"Good-night, good-night," the priest responded.

"And to you, sacristan."

"Good-night," I muttered, and he came a step after me. The candle was yet in his hand, showing him my bulk, and perhaps the small clothes he had longed to vend. I expected hue and cry, but walked on after the priest, and heard the heavy doors jar, and breathed again.

Hearkening behind and in front, on the right and the left, I followed him in the direction of what I have since learned to call the Jardin des Plantes. It is near Ste. Pélagie.

The priest, wearied by his long office, spoke only once about the darkness; for it was a cloudy night; and did not attend to my muttered response. I do not know what sympathy the excellent old man might have shown to an escaped prisoner who had choked his sacristan, and I had no mind to test it. He turned a corner, and with the wall angle between us, I eased down the sacred furniture, drew off the surplice and laid that upon it, and took to my heels up the left hand street; for the guard had brought me across the river to Ste. Pélagie.

I had no hat, and the cut of my coat showed that I had lost a waistcoat. Avoiding the little circles of yellowness made by lamp posts, I reached without mishap of falling into the hands of any patrol, a bridge crossing to an island point, and from the other side of the point to the opposite shore. At intervals along the parapet dim lights were placed.

Compared to Lake George, which wound like a river, and the mighty St. Lawrence as I remembered it, the Seine was a narrow stream. Some boats made constellations on the surface. The mass of island splitting it into two branches was almost the heart of Paris. There were other foot passengers on the bridge, and a gay carriage rolled by. I did not see any gendarmes, and only one foot passenger troubled me.

I was on the bridge above the left arm of the river when an ear trained in the woods caught his footstep, pausing as mine paused, and hurrying as mine hurried. If the sacristan had been found in Ste. Pélagie a pursuer would not track me so delicately, and neither would Skenedonk hold back on the trail. I stopped in the shade when we two were alone on the second span, and wheeled, certain of catching my man under the flare of a cresset. I caught him, and knew that it was Bellenger following me.

My mind was made up in an instant. I walked back to settle matters with him, though slaughter was far from my thoughts. I had done him no harm; but he was my enemy, and should be forced to let me alone.

The fellow who had appeared so feeble at his cabin that I opened the door for him, and so poor-spirited that his intellect claimed pity, stood up as firm as a bear at my approach, and met my eyes with perfect understanding.

Not another thing do I remember. The facts are simply these: I faced Bellenger; no blows passed; my mind flashed blank with the partial return of that old eclipse which has fallen upon me after strong excitement, in more than one critical moment. The hiatus seems brief when I awake though it may have lasted hours. I know the eclipse has been upon me, like the wing-shadow of eternity; but I have scarcely let go of time.

I could not prove that Bellenger dragged me to the parapet and threw me into the river. If I had known it I should have laughed at his doing so, for I could swim like a fish, through or under water, and sit on the lake bottom holding my breath until Skenedonk had been known to dive for me.

When next I sensed anything at all it was a feeling of cold.

I thought I was lying in one of the shallow runlets that come into Lake George, and the pebbles were an uneasy bed, chilling my shoulders. I was too stiff to move, or even turn my head to lift out of water the ear on which it rested. But I could unclose my eyelids, and this is what I saw:—a man naked to his waist, half reclining against a leaning slab of marble, down which a layer of water constantly moved. His legs were clothed, and his other garments lay across them. His face had sagged in my direction. There was a deep slash across his forehead, and he showed his teeth and his glassy eyes at the joke.

Beyond this silent figure was a woman as silent. The ridge of his body could not hide the long hair spread upon her breast. I considered the company and the moisture into which I had fallen with unspeakable amazement. We were in a low and wide stone chamber with a groined ceiling, supported by stone pillars. A row of lamps was arranged above us, so that no trait or feature might escape a beholder.

That we were put there for show entered my mind slowly and brought indignation. To be so helpless and so exposed was an outrage against which I struggled in nightmare impotence; for I was bare to my hips also, and I knew not what other marks I carried beside those which had scarred me all my conscious life.

Now in the distance, and echoing, feet descended stairs.

I knew that people were coming to look at us, and I could not move a muscle in resentment.

I heard their voices, fringed with echoes, before either speaker came within my vision.

"This is the mortuary chapel of the Hôtel Dieu?"

"Yes, monsieur the marquis, this is the mortuary chapel."

"Um! Cheerful place!"

"Much more cheerful than the bottom of the river, monsieur the marquis."

"No doubt. Never empty, eh?"

"I have been a servant of the Hôtel Dieu fourteen years, monsieur the marquis, and have not yet seen all the marble slabs vacant."

"You receive the bodies of the drowned?"

"And place them where they may be seen and claimed."

"How long do you keep them?"

"That depends. Sometimes their friends seek them at once. We have kept a body three months in the winter season, though he turned very green."

"Are all in your present collection gathering verdure?"

"No, monsieur. We have a very fresh one, just brought in; a big stalwart fellow, with the look of the country about him."

"Small clothes?"

"Yes, monsieur."

"Buckle shoes?"

"Yes, monsieur."

"Hair light and long?"

"The very man, monsieur the marquis."

"I suppose I shall have to look at him. If he had to make himself unpleasant he should have stayed at the chateau where his mother could identify him. He is one of my peasants, come to Paris to see life! I must hold my nose and do it."

"It is not necessary to hold the nose, monsieur."

"After fourteen years, perhaps not."

I heard the snap of a snuff-box lid as the marquis fortified himself.

My agony for the woman who was to be looked at turned so sharp that I uttered a click in my throat. But they passed her, and merely glanced at my next neighbor.

The old marquis encountered my fixed stare. Visibly it shocked through him. He was all gray, and curled and powdered, instead of being clipped close and smooth in the style of the Empire; an exquisite, thin-featured man, high of nose and eyebrows, not large, but completely turned out as ample man and bright spirit. The slightest fragrance of scent was in his presence, and a shade of snuff on his upper lip appeared fine supercilious hairs.

I did not look at the servant of the Hôtel Dieu. The old noble and I held each other with unflinching gaze.

"Do you recognize him, monsieur?"

"I do," the old noble deliberately answered. "I should know this face anywhere. Have him taken to my carriage directly."

"Your carriage, monsieur! He can be sent—"

"I said take him to my carriage."

"It shall be done. His eyes have opened since he came in. But they sometimes look as if they would speak! Their faces change constantly. This other man who is grinning to-night may be quite serious to-morrow."

"And by the end of the month sorry enough, eh?"

The servant of the Hôtel Dieu tittered amiably, and I knew he was going for help to lift me off the slab, when he uttered a cry of surprise. The old marquis wheeled sharply, and said:

"Eh, bien! Is this another of them, promenading himself?"

I felt the Oneida coming before his silent moccasins strode near me. He did not wait an instant, but dragged me from the wet and death cold marble to the stone floor, where he knelt upon one knee and supported me. O Skenedonk! how delicious was the warmth of your healthy body—how comforting the grip of your hunter arms! Yet there are people who say an Indian is like a snake! I could have given thanks before the altar at the side of the crypt, which my fixed eyes encountered as he held me. The marble dripped into its gutter as if complaining of my escape.

"Oh, my dear friend!" cried the servant.

Skenedonk answered nothing at all.

"Who is this gentleman," the marquis inquired, "that seems to have the skin of a red German sausage drawn tight over his head?"

"This is an American Indian, monsieur the marquis."

"An Indian?"

"Yes, monsieur; but he understands French."

"Thank you for the hint. It may save me from having a German sausage drawn tight over my head. I have heard that American Indians practice giving their friends that appearance. How do you know he understands French?"

"I think it is the man who used to come to the Hôtel Dieu years ago, when I was new in its service. He was instructed in religion by churchmen in Paris, and learned the language. Oh, my dear monsieur—I think it is Iroquois that he is called—I am aware the Americans have different manners, but here we do not go into the mortuary chapel of the Hôtel Dieu and disarrange the bodies without permission!"

Skenedonk's eyes probably had less of the fawn in them than usual. I felt the guttural sound under his breast.

"I have found him, and now I will take him."

"But that is the marquis' servant!"

"The marquis is his servant!"

"Oh, my dear monsieur the Indian! You speak of a noble of France, the Marquis du Plessy! Be satisfied," pleaded the servitor of the Hôtel Dieu, "with this other body, whom no one is likely to claim! I may be permitted to offer you that, if you are determined—though it may cost me my place!—and after fourteen years' service! It you would appease him, monsieur the marquis—though I do not know whether they ever take money."

"I will appease him," said the old noble. "Go about your errand and be quick."

The servant fled up the stairs.

"This man is not dead, my friend," said the Marquis du Plessy.

Skenedonk knew it.

"But he will not live long in this cursed crypt," the noble added. "You will get into my carriage with him, we will take him and put him in hot sheets, and see what we can do for him."

I could feel Skenedonk's antagonism giving way in the relaxing of his muscles.

But maintaining his position the Oneida asserted:

"He is not yours!"

"He belongs to France."

"France belongs to him!" the Indian reversed.

"Eh, eh! Who is this young man?"

"The king."

"We have no king now, my friend. But assuming there is a man who should be king, how do you know this is the one?"

If Skenedonk made answer in words it was lost to me. The spirit sank to submergence in the body, I remember combating motion like a drugged person.

Torpor and prostration followed the recurring eclipse as that followed excitement and shock. I was not ill; and gathered knowledge of the environment, which was different from anything I had before experienced. De Chaumont's manor was a wilderness fortress compared to this private hotel of an ancient family in the heart of Paris.

I lay in a bed curtained with damask, and looked through open glass doors at a garden. Graveled walks, bosky trees and masses of flowers, plats of grass where arbored seats were placed, stretched their vista to a wall clothed in ivy, which proved to be the end of a chapel. For high over the curtain of thick green shone a rose window. The afternoon sun laid bare its fine staining, but only in the darkness when the church was illuminated and organ music rolled from it, did the soul of that window appear struck through with light.

Strange servants and Doctor Chantry by glimpses, and the old noble and the Oneida almost constantly, were about me. Doctor Chantry looked complacently through the curtains and wished me good-morning. I smiled to see that he was lodged as he desired, and that his clothes had been renewed in fine cloth, with lawn to his neck and silk stockings for his shrunk calves. My master was an elderly beau; and I gave myself no care that he had spent his money—the money of the expedition—on foppery.

Skenedonk also had new toggery in scarfs and trinkets which I did not recognize, and his fine buckskins were cleaned. The lackeys appeared subservient to him, and his native dignity was never more impressive than in that great house. I watched my host and my servant holding interviews, which Skenedonk may have considered councils, on the benches in the garden, and from which my secretary, the sick old woman, seemed excluded. But the small interest of seeing birds arrive on branches, and depart again, sufficed me; until an hour when life rose strongly.

I sat up in bed, and finding myself alone, took advantage of an adjoining room where a marble bath was set in the floor. Returning freshened from the plunge, with my sheet drawn around me, I found one of those skilled and gentle valets who seem less men than he-maids.

"I am to dress monsieur when monsieur is ready," said this person.

"I am ready now," I answered, and he led me into a suite of rooms and showed me an array which took my breath: dove-colored satin knee breeches, and a long embroidered coat of like color, a vest sprigged with rosebuds, cravat and lace ruffles, long silk stockings and shoes to match in extravagance, a shirt of fine lawn, and a hat for a nobleman.

"Tell your master," I said to the lackey, "that he intends me great kindness, but I prefer my own clothes."

"These are monsieur's own clothes, made to his order and measure."

"But I gave no order, and I was not measured."

The man raised his shoulders and elbows with gentlest dissent.

"These are only a few articles of monsieur's outfit. Here is the key. If monsieur selects another costume he will find each one complete."

By magic as it seemed, there was a wardrobe full of fineries provided for my use. The man displayed them; in close trousers and coats with short fronts, or knee breeches and long tails; costumes, he said, for the street, for driving, riding, traveling, for evening, and for morning; and one white satin court dress. At the marquis' order he had laid out one for a ball. Of my old clothes not a piece was to be seen.

The miracle was that what he put upon me fitted me. I became transformed like my servant and my secretary, and stood astonished at the result.

VI

"Enter the prince of a fairy tale," said the Marquis du Plessy when the lackey ushered me into the garden.

It was a nest of amber at that time of sunset, and he waited for me at a table laid for supper, under a flat canopy of trees which had their tops trained and woven into a mat.

I took his hand to kiss, but he rose up and magnificently placed me in a chair opposite himself.

"Your benefits are heavy, monsieur," I said. "How shall I acknowledge them?"

"You owe me nothing at all," he answered; "as you will see when I have told you a true story. It would sound like a lie if anything were incredible in these fabulous times."

"But you do not know anything about me."

"I am well instructed in your history, by that charming attendant in fringed leather breeches, who has been acquainted with you much longer than you have been acquainted with yourself."

"Yet I am not sure of deserving the marquis' interest."

"Has the marquis admitted that he feels any interest in you? Though this I will own: few experiences have affected me like your living eyes staring out of the face of my dead king!"

We met each other again with a steady gaze like that in the mortuary chapel.

"Do you believe I am ——?"

"Do I believe you are ——? Who said there was such a person in existence?"

"Louis Philippe."

"The Duke of Orleans? Eh, bien! What does he know of the royal family? He is of the cadette branch."

"But he told me the princess, the dauphin's sister, believes that the dauphin was taken alive from the Temple and sent to America."

"My dear Lazarre, I do not say the Duke of Orleans would lie—far be it from me—though these are times in which we courageously attack our betters. But he would not object to seeing the present pretender ousted.

Why, since his father voted for the death of Louis XVI, he and his are almost outlawed by the older branch! Madame Royal, the Duchess of Angoulême, cannot endure him. I do not think she would speak to him!"

"He is my friend," I said stoutly.

"Remember you are another pretender, and he has espoused your cause. I think him decent myself—though there used to be some pretty stories told about him and the fair sentimentalist who educated him—Madame de Genlis. But I am an old man; I forget gossip."

My host gave lively and delicate attention to his food as it was brought, and permitted nothing to be overheard by his lackeys.

The evening was warm, and fresh with the breath of June; and the garden, by a contrivance of lamps around its walls, turned into a dream world after sunset faded.

It was as impossible to come to close terms with this noble of the old régime as with a butterfly. He alighted on a subject; he waved his wings, and rose. I felt a clumsy giant while he fluttered around my head, smiling, mocking, thrusting his pathos to the quick.

"My dear boy, I do not say that I believe in you; I do not observe etiquette with you. But I am going to tell you a little story about the Tuileries. You have never seen the palace of the Tuileries?"

I said I had not.

"It has been restored for the use of these Bonapartes. When I say these Bonapartes, Lazarre, I am not speaking against the Empire. The Empire gave me back my estates. I was not one of the stringent emigrés. My estates are mine, whoever rules in France. You may consider me a betwixt-and-betweener. Do so. My dear boy, I am. My heart is with my dead king. My carcass is very comfortable, both in Paris and on my ancestral lands. Napoleon likes me as an ornament to his bourgeois court. I keep my opinion of him to myself. Do you like garlic, my boy?"

I told him I was not addicted to the use of it.

"Garlic is divine. God gave it to man. A hint of it in the appropriate dish makes life endurable. I carry a piece in a gold box at the bottom of my vest pocket, that I may occasionally take it out and experience a sense of gratitude for divine benefits."

He took out his pet lump, rubbed it on the outside of his wine bottle, poured out a glassful and drank it, smiling adorably at me in ecstasy!

"We were speaking of the Tuileries. You should have seen the place when it was sacked after the flight of the royal family. No, you should not have seen it! I am glad you were gone. Mirrors were shattered, and lusters, vases, china, gold candlesticks, rolled about and were trampled on the floor. The paintings were stabbed with pikes; tables, screens, gilt stools, chairs crushed, and carpets cut to pieces; garments of all kinds strewn and torn; all that was not carried off by pillagers being thus destroyed. It was yet a horrible sight days after the mob had done their work, and slaughtered bodies of guards had been carried away, and commissioners with their clerks and assistants began to restore order."

"Did you see the Tuileries at that time, monsieur?"

"I did. I put on the clothes of one of my peasants, slumped in Jacquot's wooden shoes, and kept my mouth open as well as I could for the dust. The fantastic was yet in my blood. Exile takes that out of everybody except your royal uncle of Provence. But I knew in my heart what I would help do with that mob, if our turn ever came again!"

His dark eyes rested on the red wine as on a pool of blood.

"Sick of the ruin, I leaned out to look in the garden, from a window in the queen's own apartment. I stepped on a shelf, which appeared fixed under the window; but it moved, and I found that it could be pushed on grooves into the wall. There was a cavity made to hold it. It had concealed two armchairs placed opposite each other, so cunningly that their paneled sides yet looked a part of the thick wall. I sat down in one of them, and though the cushion was stiff, I felt something hard under it."

Monsieur du Plessy glanced around in every direction to satisfy himself that no ears lurked within hearing.

"Eh, bien! Under the cushion I found the queen's jewel-case! Diamonds—bags of gold coin—a half circlet of gems!—since the great necklace was lost such an array had not seen the light in France. The value must be far above a million francs."

The marquis fixed his eyes on me and said:

"What should I have done with it, Lazarre?"

"It belonged to the royal family," I answered.

"But everything which belonged to the royal family had been confiscated to the state. I had just seen the belongings of the royal family trampled as by cattle. First one tyrant and then another rose up to tell us what we should do, to batten himself off the wretched commonwealth, and then go to the guillotine before his successor. As a good citizen I should have turned these jewels and stones and coins over to the state. But I was acting the part of Jacquot, and as an honest peasant I whipped them under my blouse and carried them away. In my straits of exile I never decreased them. And you may take inventory of your property and claim it when we rise from the table."

My heart came up in my throat. I reached across and caught his hands.

"You believe in me—you believe in me!"

"Do I observe any etiquette with you, Lazarre? This is the second time I have brought the fact to your notice. I particularly wish you to note that I do not observe any etiquette with you."

"What does a boy who has been brought up among Indians know about etiquette! But you accept me, or you could not put the property you have loyally and at such risk saved for my family, into my hands."

"I don't accept even your uncle of Provence. The king of Spain and I prefer to call him by that modest title. Since you died or were removed from the Temple, he has taken the name of Louis XVIII, and maintained a court at the expense of the czar of Russia and the king of Spain. He is a fine Latinist; quotes Latin verse; and keeps the mass bells everlastingly ringing; the Russians laugh at his royal masses! But in my opinion the sacred gentleman is either moral slush or a very deep quicksand. It astonishes me," said the Marquis du Plessy, "to find how many people I do disapprove of! I really require very little of the people I am obliged to meet."

He smoothed my hands which were yet holding his, and exploded:

"The Count of Provence is an old turtle! Not exactly a reptile, for there is food in him. But of a devilish flat head and cruel snap of the jaws!"

"How can that be," I argued, "when his niece loves him so? And even I, in the American woods, with mind eclipsed, was not forgotten. He sent me of the money that he was obliged to receive in charity!"

"It is easy to dole out charity money; you are squeezing other people's purses, not your own. What I most object to in the Count of Provence, is that assumption of kingly airs, providing the story is true which leaked secretly among the emigrés. The story which I heard was that the dauphin had not died, but was an idiot in America. An idiot cannot reign. But the throne of France is not clamoring so loud for a Bourbon at present that the idiot's substitute must be proclaimed and hold a beggar's court. There are mad loyalists who swear by this eighteenth Louis. I am not one of them. In fact, Lazarre, I was rather out of tune with your house!"

"Not you!" I said.

"I do not fit in these times. I ought to have gone with my king and my friends under the knife. Often I am ashamed of myself for slipping away. That I should live to see disgusting fools in the streets of Paris, after the Terror was over!—young men affecting the Greek and Roman manner—greeting one another by wagging of the head! They wore gray coats with black collars, gray or green cravats, carried cudgels, and decreed that all men should have the hair plaited, powdered, and fastened up with a comb, like themselves! The wearer of a queue was likely to be knocked on the head. These creatures used to congregate at the old Feydeau theater, or meet around the entrance of the Louvre, to talk classical jargon, and wag!"

The Marquis du Plessy drew himself together with a strong shudder. I had the desire to stand between him and the shocks of an alien world. Yet there was about him a tenacious masculine strength, an adroitness of self-protection which needed no champion.

"Did the Indian tell you about a man named Bellenger?" I inquired.

"Bellenger is part of the old story about the dauphin's removal. I heard of him first at Coblenz. And I understand now that he is following you with another dauphin, and objecting to you in various delicate ways. Napoleon Bonaparte is master of France, and in the way to be master of Europe, because he has a nice sense of the values of men, and the best head for detail that was ever formed in human shape. There is something almost supernatural in his grasp of affairs. He lets nothing escape him. The only mistake he ever made was butchering the young Duke d'Enghien—the courage and clearness of the man wavered that one instant; and by the way, he borrowed my name for the duke's incognito during the journey under arrest! England, Russia, Austria and Sweden are combining against Napoleon. He will beat them. For while other men sleep, or amuse themselves, or let circumstance drive them, he is planning success and providing for all possible contingencies. Take a leaf out of the general's book, my boy. No enemy is contemptible. If you want to force the hand of fortune—scheme!—scheme!—all the time!—out-scheme the other fellow!"

The marquis rose from the table.

"I am longer winded," he said, "than a man named De Chaumont, who has been importuning Bonaparte, in season and out of season, to reinstate an American emigré, a Madame de Ferrier."

"Will Bonaparte restore her lands?" I asked, feeling my voice like a rope in my throat.

"Do you know her family?"

"I knew Madame de Ferrier in America."

"Their estate lies next to mine. And what is the little De Ferrier like since she is grown?"

"A beautiful woman."

"Ah—ah! Bonaparte's plan will then be easy of execution. You may see her this evening here in the Faubourg St. Germain. I believe she is to appear at Madame de Permon's, where Bonaparte may look in."

My host bolted the doors of his private cabinet, and took from the secret part of a wall cupboard the queen's jewel-case. We opened it between us. The first thing I noticed was a gold snuffbox, set with portraits of the king, the queen, and their two children.

How I knew them I cannot tell. Their pictured faces had never been put before my conscious eyes until that moment. Other portraits might have been there. I had no doubt, no hesitation.

I was on my knees before the face I had seen in spasms of remembrance—with oval cheeks, and fair hair rolled high—and open neck—my royal mother!

Next I looked at the king, heavier of feature, honest and straight gazing, his chin held upward; at the little sister, a smaller miniature of the queen; at the softly molded curves of the child that was myself!

The marquis turned his back.

Before I could speak I rose and put my arms around him. He wheeled, took my hand, stood at a little distance, and kissed it.

We said not one word about the portraits, but sat down with the jewel-case again between us.

"These stones and coins are also my sister's, monsieur the marquis?"

He lifted his eyebrows.

"I had ample opportunity, my dear boy, to turn them into the exchequer of the Count of Provence. Before his quarrel with the late czar of Russia he maintained a dozen gentlemen-in-waiting, and perhaps as many ladies, to say nothing of priests, servants, attendants of attendants, and guards. This treasure might last him two years. If the king of Spain and his majesty of Russia got wind of it, and shut off their pensions, it would not last so long. I am too thrifty a Frenchman to dissipate the hoards of the state in foreign parts! Yet, if you question my taste—I will not say my honesty, Lazarre—"

"I question nothing, monsieur! I ask advice."

"Eh, bien! Then do not be quite as punctilious as the gentleman who got turned out of the debtor side of Ste. Pélagie into an alley. 'This will not do,' says he. So around he posts to the entrance, and asks for admittance again!"

"Catch me knocking at Ste. Pélagie for admittance again!"

"Then my advice is to pay your tailor, if he has done his work acceptably."

"He has done it marvelously, especially in the fitting."

"A Parisian workman finds it no miracle to fit a man from his old clothes. I took the liberty of sending your orders. Having heard my little story, you understand that you owe me nothing but your society; and a careful inventory of this trust."

We were a long time examining the contents of the case. There were six bags of coin, all gold louis; many unset gems; rings for the hand; and clusters of various sorts which I knew not how to name, that blazed with a kind of white fire very dazzling. The half-way crown was crusted thick with colored stones the like of which I could not have imagined in my dreams. Their names, the marquis told me, were sapphires, emeralds, rubies; and large clear diamonds, like beads of rain. When everything was carefully returned to place, he asked:

"Shall I still act as your banker?"

I begged him to hide the jewel box again, and he concealed it in the wall.

"We go to the Rue Ste. Croix, Lazarre, which is an impossible place for your friend Bellenger at this time. Do you dance a gavotte?"

I told him I could dance the Indian corn dance, and he advised me to reserve this accomplishment.

"Bonaparte's police are keen on any scent, especially the scent of a prince. His practical mind would reject the Temple story, if he ever heard it; and there are enough live Bourbons for him to watch."

"But there is the Count de Chaumont," I suggested.

"He is not a man that would put faith in the Temple story, either, and I understand he is kindly disposed towards you."

"I lived in his house nearly a year."

"He is not a bad fellow for the new sort. I feel certain of him. He is coaxing my friendship because of ancient amity between the houses of Du Plessy and De Ferrier."

"Did you say, monsieur, that Bonaparte intends to restore Madame de Ferrier's lands?"

"They have been given to one of his rising officers."

"Then he will not restore them?"

"Oh, yes, with interest! His plan is to give her the officer for a husband."

VII

Even in those days of falling upon adventure and taking hold of life with the arrogance of young manhood, I knew the value of money, though it has always been my fault to give it little consideration. Experience taught me that poverty goes afoot and sleeps with strange bed-fellows. But I never minded going afoot or sharing the straw with cattle. However, my secretary more than once took a high hand with me because he bore the bag; and I did mind debt chasing my heels like a rising tide.

Our Iroquois had their cottages in St. Regis and their hunting cabins on Lake George. They went to church when not drunk and quarrelsome, paid the priest his dues, labored easily, and cared nothing for hoarding. But every step of my new life called for coin.

As I look back on that hour the dominating thought rises clearly.

To see men admitting that you are what you believe yourself to be, is one of the triumphs of existence. The jewel-case stamped identification upon me. I felt like one who had communicated with the past and received a benediction. There was special provision in the way it came to me; for man loves to believe that God watches over and mothers him.

Forgetting—if I had ever heard—how the ancients dreaded the powers above when they had been too fortunate, I went with the marquis in high spirits to the Rue Ste. Croix. There were pots of incense sending little wavers of smoke through the rooms, and the people might have peopled a dream. The men were indeed all smooth and trim; but the women had given rein to their fancies.

Our hostess was a fair and gracious woman, of Greek ancestry, as Bonaparte himself was, and her daughter had been married to his favorite general, the marquis told me.

I notice only the unusual in clothing; the scantiness of ladies' apparel that clung like the skin, and lay upon the oak floor in ridges, among which a man must shove his way, was unusual to me.

I saw, in space kept cleared around her chair, one beauty with nothing but sandals on her feet, though these were white as milk, silky skinned like a hand, and ringed with jewels around the toes.

Bonaparte's youngest sister stood receiving court. She was attired like a Bacchante, with bands of fur in her hair, topped by bunches of gold grapes. Her robe and tunic of muslin fine as air, woven in India, had bands of gold, clasped with cameos, under the bosom and on the arms. Each woman seemed to have planned outdoing the others in conceits which marked her own fairness.

I looked anxiously down the spacious room without seeing Madame de Ferrier. The simplicity, which made for beauty of houses in France, struck me, in the white and gold paneling, and the chimney, which lifted its mass of design to the ceiling. I must have been staring at this and thinking of Madame de Ferrier when my name was called in a lilting and excited fashion:

"Lazarre!"

There was Mademoiselle de Chaumont in the midst of gallants, and better prepared to dance a gavotte than any other charmer in the room. For her gauze dress, fastened on the shoulders so that it fell not quite off her bosom, reached only to the middle of the calf. This may have been for the protection of rosebuds with which ribbons drawn lengthwise through the skirt, were fringed; but it also showed her child-like feet and ankles, and made her appear tiptoe like a fairy, and more remarkable than any other figure except the barefooted dame. She held a crook massed with ribbons and rosebuds in her hand, rallying the men to her standard by the lively chatter which they like better than wisdom.

Mademoiselle Annabel gave me her hand to kiss, and made room for the Marquis du Plessy and me in her circle. I felt abashed by the looks these courtiers gave me, but the marquis put them readily in the background, and delighted in the poppet, taking her quite to himself.

"We hear such wonderful stories about you, Lazarre! Besides, Doctor Chantry came to see us and told us all he knew. Remember, Lazarre belonged to us before you discovered him, monsieur the Marquis du Plessy! He and I are Americans!"

Some women near us commented, as seemed to be the fashion in that society, with a frankness which Indians would have restrained.

"See that girl! The emperor may now imagine what his brother Jerome has done! Her father has brought her over from America to marry her, and it will need all his money to accomplish that!"

Annabel shook the rain of misty hair at the sides of her rose pink face, and laughed a joyful retort.

"No wonder poor Prince Jerome had to go to America for a wife! Did you ever see such hairy faced frights as these Parisians of the Empire! Lazarre fell ill looking at them. He pretends he doesn't see women, monsieur, and goes about with his coat skirts loaded with books. I used to be almost as much afraid of him as I am of you!"

"Ah, mademoiselle, I dread to enter paradise."

"Why, monsieur?"

"The angels are afraid of me!"

"Not when you smile."

"Teach me that adorable smile of yours!"

"Oh, how improving you will be to Lazarre, monsieur! He never paid me a compliment in his life. He never said anything but the truth."

"The lucky dog! What pretty things he had to say!"

Annabel laughed and shook her mist in great enjoyment. I liked to watch her, yet I wondered where Madame de Ferrier was, and could not bring myself to inquire.

"These horrible incense pots choke me," said Annabel.

"I like them," said the marquis.

"Do you? So do I," she instantly agreed with him.

"Though we get enough incense in church."

"I should think so! Do you like mass?"

"I was brought up on my knees. But I never acquired the real devotee's back."

"Sit on your heels," imparted Annabel in strict confidence. "Try it."

"I will. Ah, mademoiselle, any one who could bring such comfort into religion might make even wedlock endurable!"

Madame de Ferrier appeared between the curtains of a deep window. She was talking with Count de Chaumont and an officer in uniform. Her face pulsed a rosiness like that quiver in winter skies which we call northern lights. The clothes she wore, being always subdued by her head and shoulders, were not noticeable like other women's clothes. But I knew as soon as her eyes rested on me that she found me changed.

De Chaumont came a step to meet me, and I felt miraculously equal to him, with some power which was not in me before.

"You scoundrel, you have fallen into luck!" he said heartily.

"One of our proverbs is, 'A blind pig will find an acorn once in a while.'"

"There isn't a better acorn in the woods, or one harder to shake down. How did you do it?"

I gave him a wise smile and held my tongue; knowing well that if I had remained in Ste. Pélagie and the fact ever came to De Chaumont's ears, like other human beings he would have reprehended my plunging into the world.

"We are getting on tremendously, Lazarre! When your inheritance falls in, come back with me to Castorland. We will found a wilderness empire!"

I did not inquire what he meant by my inheritance falling in. The marquis pressed behind me, and when I had spoken to Madame de Ferrier I knew it was his right to take the hand of the woman who had been his little neighbor.

"You don't remember me, madame?"

"Oh, yes, I do, Monsieur du Plessy; and your wall fruit, too!"

"The rogue! Permit me to tell you those pears are hastening to be ready for you once more."

"And Bichette, monsieur—is dear old Bichette alive?"

"She is alive, and draws the chair as well as ever. I hear you have a little son. He may love the old pony and chair as you used to love them."

"Seeing you, monsieur, is like coming again to my home!"

"I trust you may come soon."

They spoke of fruit and cattle. Neither dared mention the name of any human companion associated with the past.

I took opportunity to ask Count de Chaumont if her lands were recovered. A baffled look troubled his face.

"The emperor will see her to-night," he answered. "It is impossible to say what can be done until the emperor sees her."

"Is there any truth in the story that he will marry her to the officer who holds her estate?"

The count frowned.

"No—no! That's impossible."

"Will the officer sell his rights if Madame de Ferrier's are not acknowledged?"

"I have thought of that. And I want to consult the marquis."

When he had a chance to draw the marquis aside, I could speak to Madame de Ferrier without being overheard; though my time might be short. She stood between the curtains, and the man in uniform had left his place to me.

"Well, I am here," I said.

"And I am glad," she answered.

"I am here because I love you."

She held a fold of the curtain in her hand and looked down at it; then up at me.

"You must not say that again."

"Why?"

"You know why."

"I do not."

"Remember who you are."

"I am your lover."

She looked quickly around the buzzing drawing-room, and leaned cautiously nearer.

"You are my sovereign."

"I believe that, Eagle. But it does not follow that I shall ever reign."

"Are you safe here? Napoleon Bonaparte has spies."

"But he has regard also for old aristocrats like the Marquis du Plessy."

"Yet remember what he did to the Duke d'Enghien. A Bourbon prince is not allowed in France."

"How many people consider me a Bourbon prince? I told you why I am here. Fortune has wonderfully helped me since I came to France. Lazarre, the dauphin from the Indian camps, brazenly asks you to marry him, Eagle!"

Her face blanched white, but she laughed.

"No De Ferrier ever took a base advantage of royal favor. Don't you think this is a strange conversation in a drawing-room of the Empire? I hated myself for being here—until you came in."

"Eagle, have you forgotten our supper on the island?"

"Yes, sire." She scarcely breathed the word.

"My unanointed title is Lazarre. And I suppose you have forgotten the fog and the mountain, too?"

"Yes."

"Lazarre!"

"Yes, Lazarre."

"You love me! You shall love me!"

"As a De Ferrier should; no farther!"

Her lifted chin expressed a strength I could not combat. The slight, dark-haired girl, younger than myself, mastered and drew me as if my spirit was a stream, and she the ocean into which it must flow. Darkness like that of Ste. Pélagie dropped over the brilliant room. I was nothing after all but a palpitating boy, venturing because he must venture. Light seemed to strike through her blood, however, endowing her with a splendid pallor.

"I am going," I determined that moment, "to Mittau."

The adorable curve of her eyelids, unlike any other eyelids I ever saw, was lost to me, for her eyes flew wide open.

"To ——"

She looked around and hesitated to pronounce the name of the Count of Provence.

"Yes. I am going to find some one who belongs to me."

"You have the marquis for a friend."

"And I have also Skenedonk, and our tribe, for my friends. But there is no one who understands that a man must have some love."

"Consult Marquis du Plessy about going to Mittau. It may not be wise. And war is threatened on the frontier."

"I will consult him, of course. But I am going."

"Lazarre, there were ladies on the ship who cursed and swore, and men who were drunk the greater part of the voyage. I was brought up in the old-fashioned way by the Saint-Michels, so I know nothing of present customs. But it seems to me our times are rude and wicked. And you, just awake to the world, have yet the innocence of that little boy who sank into the strange and long stupor. If you changed I think I could not bear it!"

"I will not change."

A stir which must have been widening through the house as a ripple widens on a lake, struck us, and turned our faces with all others to a man who stood in front of the chimney. He was not large in person, but as an individual his presence was massive—was penetrating. I could have topped him by head and shoulders; yet without mastery. He took snuff as he slightly bowed in every direction, shut the lid with a snap, and fidgeted as if impatient to be gone. He had a mouth of wonderful beauty and expression, and his eyes were more alive than the eyes of any other man in the assembly. I felt his gigantic force as his head dipped forward and he glanced about under his brows.

"There is the emperor," De Chaumont told Eagle; and I thought he made indecent haste to return and hale her away before Napoleon.

The greatest soldier in Europe passed from one person to another with the air of doing his duty and getting rid of it. Presently he raised his voice, speaking to Madame de Ferrier so that, all in the room might hear.

"Madame, I am pleased to see that you wear leno. I do not like those English muslins, sold at the price of their weight in gold, and which do not look half as well as beautiful white leno. Wear leno, cambric, or silk, ladies, and then my manufactures will flourish."

I wondered if he would remember the face of the man pushed against his wheel and called an assassin, when the Marquis du Plessy named me to him as the citizen Lazarre.

"You are a lucky man, Citizen Lazarre, to gain the marquis for your friend. I have been trying a number of years to make him mine."

"All Frenchmen are the friends of Napoleon," the marquis said to me.

I spoke directly to the sovereign, thereby violating etiquette, my friend told me afterwards, laughing; and Bonaparte was a stickler for precedent.

"But all Frenchmen," I could not help reminding the man in power, "are not faithful friends."

He gave me a sharp look as he passed on, and repeated what I afterward learned was one of his favorite maxims:

"A faithful friend is the true image."

VIII

"Must you go to Mittau?" the Marquis du Plessy said when I told him what I intended to do. "It is a long, expensive post journey; and part of the way you may not be able to post. Riga, on the gulf beyond Mittau, is a fine old town of pointed gables and high stone houses. But when I was in Mittau I found it a mere winter camp of Russian nobles. The houses are low, one-story structures. There is but one castle, and in that his Royal Highness the Count of Provence holds mimic court."

We were riding to Versailles, and our horses almost touched sides as my friend put his hand on my shoulder.

"Don't go, Lazarre. You will not be welcome there."

"I must go, whether I am welcome or not."

"But I may not last until you come back."

"You will last two months. Can't I post to Mittau and back in two months?"

"God knows."

I looked at him drooping forward in the saddle, and said:

"If you need me I will stay, and think no more about seeing those of my own blood."

"I do need you; but you shall not stay. You shall go to Mittau in my own post-carriage. It will bring you back sooner."

But his post-carriage I could not accept. The venture to Mittau, its wear and tear and waste, were my own; and I promised to return with all speed. I could have undertaken the road afoot, driven by the necessity I felt.

"The Duchess of Angoulême is a good girl," said the marquis, following the line of my thoughts. "She has devoted herself to her uncle and her husband. When the late czar withdrew his pension, and turned the whole mimic court out of Mittau, she went with her uncle, and even waded the snow with him when they fell into straits. Diamonds given to her by her grandmother, the Empress Maria Theresa, she sold for his support. But the new czar reinstated them; and though they live less pretentiously at Mittau in these days, they still have their priest and almoner, the Duke of Guiche, and other courtiers hanging upon them. My boy, can you make a court bow and walk backwards? You must practice before going into Russia."

"Wouldn't it be better," I said, "for those who know how, to practice the accomplishment before me?"

"Imagine the Count of Provence stepping down from playing royalty to do that!" my friend laughed.

"I don't know why he shouldn't, since he knows I am alive. He has sent money every year for my support."

"An established custom, Lazarre, gains strength every day it is continued. You see how hard it is to overturn an existing system, because men have to undo the work they have been doing perhaps for a thousand years. Time gives enormous stability. Monsieur the Count of Provence has been practicing royalty since word went out that his nephew had died in the Temple. It will be no easy matter to convince him you are fit to play king in his stead."

This did not disturb me, however. I thought more of my sister. And I thought of vast stretches across the center of Europe. The Indian stirred in me, as it always did stir, when the woman I wanted was withdrawn from me.

I could not tell my friend, or any man, about Madame de Ferrier. This story of my life is not to be printed until I am gone from the world. Otherwise the things set down so freely would remain buried in myself.

Some beggars started from hovels, running like dogs, holding diseased and crooked-eyed children up for alms, and pleading for God's sake that we would have pity on them. When they disappeared with their coin I asked the marquis if there had always been wretchedness in France.

"There is always wretchedness everywhere," he answered. "Napoleon can turn the world upside down, but he cannot cure the disease of hereditary poverty. I never rode to Versailles without encountering these people."

When we entered the Place d'Armes fronting the palace, desolation worse than that of the beggars faced us. That vast noble pile, untenanted and sacked, symbolized the vanished monarchy of France. Doors stood wide. The court was strewn with litter and filth; and grass started rank betwixt the stones where the proudest courtiers in the world had trod. I tried to enter the queen's rooms, but sat on the steps leading to them, holding my head in my hands. It was as impossible as it had been to enter the Temple.

The fountains which once made a concert of mist around their lake basin, satisfying like music, the marquis said, were dried, and the figures broken. Millions had been spent upon this domain of kings, and nothing but the summer's natural verdure was left to unmown stretches. The foot shrank from sending echoes through empty palace apartments, and from treading the weedy margins of canal and lake.

"I should not have brought you here, Lazarre," said my friend.

"I had to come, monsieur."

We walked through meadow and park to the little palaces called Grand and Petit Trianon, where the intimate life of the last royal family had been lived. I looked well at their outer guise, but could not explore them.

The groom held our horses in the street that leads up to the Place d'Armes, and as we sauntered back, I kicked old leaves which had fallen autumn after autumn and banked the path.

It rushed over me again!

I felt my arms go above my head as they did when I sank into the depths of recollection.

"Lazarre! Are you in a fit?" The Marquis du Plessy seized me.

"I remember! I remember! I was kicking the leaves—I was walking with my father and mother—somewhere—somewhere—and something threatened us!"

"It was in the garden of the Tuileries," said the Marquis du Plessy sternly. "The mob threatened you, and you were going before the National Assembly! I walked behind. I was there to help defend the king."

We stood still until the paroxysmal rending in my head ceased. Then I sat on the grassy roadside trying to smile at the marquis, and shrugging an apology for my weakness. The beauty of the arched trees disappeared, and when next I recognized the world we were moving slowly toward Paris in a heavy carriage, and I was smitten with the conviction that my friend had not eaten the dinner he ordered in the town of Versailles.

I felt ashamed of the weakness which came like an eclipse, and withdrew leaving me in my strength. It ceased to visit me within that year, and has never troubled me at all in later days. Yet, inconsistently, I look back as to the glamour of youth; and though it worked me hurt and shame, I half regret that it is gone.

The more I saw of the Marquis du Plessy the more my slow tenacious heart took hold on him. We went about everywhere together. I think it was his hope to wed me to his company and to Paris, and shove the Mittau venture into an indefinite future; yet he spared no pains in obtaining for me my passports to Courland.

At this time, with cautious, half reluctant hand, he raised the veil from a phase of life which astonished and revolted me. I loved a woman. The painted semblances of women who inhabited a world of sensation had no effect upon me.

"You are wonderfully fresh, Lazarre," the marquis said. "If you were not so big and male I would call you mademoiselle! Did they never sin in the American backwoods?"

Then he took me in his arms like a mother, and kissed me, saying, "Dear son and sire, I am worse than your great-grandfather!"

Yet my zest for the gaiety of the old city grew as much as he desired. The golden dome of the Invalides became my bubble of Paris, floating under a sunny sky.

Whenever I went to the hotel which De Chaumont had hired near the Tuileries, Madame de Ferrier received me kindly; having always with her Mademoiselle de Chaumont or Miss Chantry, so that we never had a word in private. I thought she might have shown a little feeling in her rebuff, and pondered on her point of view regarding my secret rank. De Chaumont, on the other hand, was beneath her in everything but wealth. How might she regard stooping to him?

Miss Chantry was divided between enforced deference and a Saxon necessity to tell me I would not last. I saw she considered me one of the upstarts of the Empire, singularly favored above her brother, but under my finery the same French savage she had known in America.

Eagle brought Paul to me, and he toddled across the floor, looked at me wisely, and then climbed my knee.

Doctor Chantry had been living in Paris a life above his dreams of luxury. When occasionally I met my secretary he was about to drive out; or he was returning from De Chaumont's hotel. And there I caught my poor master reciting poems to Annabel, who laughed and yawned, and made faces behind her fan. I am afraid he drew on the marquis' oldest wines, finding indulgence in the house; and he sent extravagant bills to me for gloves and lawn cravats. It was fortunate that De Chaumont took him during my absence. He moved his belongings with positive rapture. The marquis and I both thought it prudent not to publish my journey.

Doctor Chantry went simpering, and abasing himself before the French noble with the complete subservience of a Saxon when a Saxon does become subservient.

"The fool is laughable," said the Marquis du Plessy. "Get rid of him, Lazarre. He is fit for nothing but hanging upon some one who will feed him."

"He is my master," I answered. "I am a fool myself."

"You will come back from Mittau convinced of that, my boy. The wise course is to join yourself to events, and let them draw your chariot. My dislikers say I have temporized with fate. It is true I am not so righteous as to smell to heaven. But two or three facts have been deeply impressed on me. There is nothing more aggressive than the virtue of an ugly, untempted woman; or the determination of a young man to set every wrong thing in the world right. He cannot wait, and take mellow interest in what goes on around him, but must leap into the ring. You could live here with me indefinitely, while the nation has Bonaparte, like the measles. When the disease has run its course—we may be able to bring evidence which will make it unnecessary for the Count of Provence to hasten here that France may have a king."

"I want to see my sister, monsieur."

"And lose her and your own cause forever."

But he helped me to hire a strong traveling chaise, and stock it with such comforts as it would bear. He also turned my property over to me, recommending that I should not take it into Russia. Half the jewels, at least, I considered the property of the princess in Mittau; but his precaution influenced me to leave three bags of coin in Doctor Chantry's care; for Doctor Chantry was the soul of thrift with his own; and to send Skenedonk with the jewel-case to the marquis' bank. The cautious Oneida took counsel of himself and hid it in the chaise. He told me when we were three days out.

It is as true that you are driven to do some things as that you can never entirely free yourself from any life you have lived. That sunny existence in the Faubourg St. Germain, the morning and evening talks with a man who bound me to him as no other man has since bound me, were too dear to leave even briefly without wrenching pain. I dreamed nightly of robbers and disaster, of being ignominiously thrust out of Mittau, of seeing a woman whose face was a blur and who moved backward from me when I called her my sister; of troops marching across and trampling me into the earth as straw. I groaned in spirit. Yet to Mittau I was spurred by the kind of force that seems to press from unseen distances, and is as fatal as temperament.

When I paid my last visit at De Chaumont's hotel, and said I was going into the country, Eagle looked concerned, as a De Ferrier should; but she did not turn her head to follow my departure. The game of man and woman was in its most blindfold state between us.

There was one, however, who watched me out of sight. The marquis was more agitated than I liked to see him. He took snuff with a constant click of the lid.

The hills of Champagne, green with vines, and white as with an underlay of chalk, rose behind us. We crossed the frontier, and German hills took their places, with a castle topping each. I was at the time of life when interest stretches eagerly toward every object; and though this journey cannot be set down in a story as long as mine, the novelty—even the risks, mischances and wearinesses of continual post travel, come back like an invigorating breath of salt water.

The usual route carried us eastward to Cracow, the old capital of Poland, scattered in ruined grandeur within its brick walls. Beyond it I remember a stronghold of the Middle Ages called the fortress of Landskron.

The peasants of this country, men in shirts and drawers of coarse linen, and women with braided hair hanging down under linen veils, stopped their carts as soon as a post-carriage rushed into sight, and bent almost to the earth. At post-houses the servants abased themselves to take me by the heel. In no other country was the spirit of man so broken. Poles of high birth are called the Frenchmen of the north, and we saw fair men and women in sumptuous polonaises and long robes who appeared luxurious in their traveling carriages. But stillness and solitude brooded on the land. From Cracow to Warsaw wide reaches of forest darkened the level. Any open circle was belted around the horizon with woods, pines, firs, beech, birch, and small oaks. Few cattle fed on the pastures, and stunted crops of grain ripened in the melancholy light.

From Cracow to Warsaw is a distance of one hundred and thirty leagues, if the postilion lied not, yet on that road we met but two carriages and not more than a dozen carts. Scattering wooden villages, each a line of hovels, appeared at long intervals.

Post-houses were kept by Jews, who fed us in the rooms where their families lived. Milk and eggs they had none to offer us; and their beds were piles of straw on the ground, seldom clean, never untenanted by fleas.

Beggars ran beside us on the wretched roads as neglected as themselves. Where our horses did not labor through sand, the marshy ground was paved with sticks and boughs, or the surface was built up with trunks of trees laid crosswise.

In spacious, ill-paved Warsaw, through which the great Vistula flows, we rested two days. I knelt with confused thoughts, trying to pray in the Gothic cathedral. We walked past it into the old town, of high houses and narrow streets, like a part of Paris.

In Lithuania the roads were paths winding through forests full of stumps and roots. The carriage hardly squeezed along, and eight little horses attached to it in the Polish way had much ado to draw us. The postilions were young boys in coarse linen, hardy as cattle, who rode bare-back league upon league.

Old bridges cracked and sagged when we crossed them. And here the forests rose scorched and black in spots, because the peasants, bound to pay their lords turpentine, fired pines and caught the heated ooze.

Within the proper boundary of Russia our way was no better. There we saw queer projections of boards around trees to keep bears from climbing after the hunters.

The Lithuanian peasants had few wants. Their carts were put together without nails. Their bridles and traces were made of bark. They had no tools but hatchets. A sheepskin coat and round felt cap kept a man warm in cold weather. His shoes were made of bark, and his home of logs with penthouse roof.

In houses where travelers slept the candles were laths of deal, about five feet long, stuck into crevices of the wall or hung over tables. Our hosts carried them about, dropping unheeded sparks upon the straw beds.

In Grodno, a town of falling houses and ruined palaces, we rested again before turning directly north.

There my heart began to sink. We had spent four weeks on a comfortless road, working always toward the goal. It was nearly won. A speech of my friend the marquis struck itself out sharply in the northern light.

"You are not the only Pretender, my dear boy. Don't go to Mittau expecting to be hailed as a novelty. At least two peasants have started up claiming to be the prince who did not die in the Temple, and have been cast down again, complaining of the treatment of their dear sister! The Count d'Artois says he would rather saw wood for a living than be king after the English fashion. I would rather be the worthless old fellow I am than be king after the Mittau fashion; especially when his Majesty, Louis XVIII, sees you coming!"

IX

Purposely we entered Mittau about sunset, which was nearer ten o'clock than nine in that northern land; coming through wheat lands to where a network of streams forms the river Aa. In this broad lap of the province of Courland sat Mittau. Yelgava it was called by the people among whom we last posted, and they pronounced the word as if naming something as great as Paris.

It was already July, St. John's day being two weeks gone; yet the echoes of its markets and feastings lingered. The word "Johanni" smote even an ear deaf to the language. It was like a dissolving fair.

"You are too late for Johanni," said the German who kept the house for travelers, speaking the kind of French we heard in Poland. "Perhap it is just as well for you. This Johanni has nearly ruined me!"

Yet he showed a disposition to hire my singular servant from me at a good wage, walking around and around Skenedonk, who bore the scrutiny like a pine tree.

The Oneida enjoyed his travels. It was easy for him to conform to the thoughts and habits of Europe. We had not talked about the venture into Russia. He simply followed me where I went without asking questions, proving himself faithful friend and liberal minded gentleman.

We supped privately, and I dressed with care. Horses were put in for our last short post of a few streets. We had suffered such wretched quarters on the way that the German guest-house spread itself commodiously. Yet its walls were the flimsiest slabs. I heard some animal scratching and whining in the next chamber. On the post-road, however, we had not always a wall betwixt ourselves and the dogs.

The palace in Mittau stood conspicuous upon an island in the river. As we approached, it looked not unlike a copy of Versailles. The pile was by no means brilliant with lights, as the court of a king might glitter, finding reflection upon the stream. We drove with a clatter upon the paving, and a sentinel challenged us.

I had thought of how I should obtain access to this secluded royal family, and Skenedonk was ready with the queen's jewel-case in his hands. Not on any account was he to let it go out of them until I took it and applied the key; but gaining audience with Madame d'Angoulême, he was to tell her that the bearer of that casket had traveled far to see her, and waited outside.

Under guard the Oneida had the great doors shut behind him. The wisdom of my plan looked less conspicuous as time went by. The palace loomed silent, without any cheer of courtiers. The horses shook their straps, and the postilion hung lazily by one leg, his figure distinct against the low horizon still lighted by after-glow. Some Mittau noises came across the Aa, the rumble of wheels, and a barking of dogs.

When apprehension began to pinch my heart of losing my servant and my whole fortune in the abode of honest royal people, and I felt myself but a poor outcast come to seek a princess for my sister, a guard stood by the carriage, touching his cap, and asked me to follow him.

We ascended the broad steps. He gave the password to a sentinel there, and held wide one leaf of the door. He took a candle; and otherwise dark corridors and ante-chambers, somber with heavy Russian furnishings, rugs hung against the walls, barbaric brazen vessels and curious vases, passed like a half-seen vision.

Then the guard delivered me to a gentleman in a blue coat, with a red collar, who belonged to the period of the Marquis du Plessy without being adorned by his whiteness and lace. The gentleman staring at me, strangely polite and full of suspicion, conducted me into a well-lighted room where Skenedonk waited by the farther door, holding the jewel-case as tenaciously as he would a scalp.

I entered the farther door. It closed behind me.

A girl stood in the center of this inner room, looking at me. I remember none of its fittings, except that there was abundant light, showing her clear blue eyes and fair hair, the transparency of her skin, and her high expression. She was all in black, except a floating muslin cape or fichu, making a beholder despise the finery of the Empire.

We must have examined each other even sternly, though I felt a sudden giving way and heaving in my breast. She was so high, so sincere! If I had been unfit to meet the eyes of that princess I must have shriveled before her.

From side to side her figure swayed, and another young girl, the only attendant in the room, stretched out both arms to catch her.

We put her on a couch, and she sat gasping, supported by the lady in waiting. Then the tears ran down her face, and I kissed the transparent hands, my own flesh and blood, I believed that hour as I believe to this.

"O Louis—Louis!"

The wonder of her knowledge and acceptance of me, without a claim being put forward, was around me like a cloud.

"You were so like my father as you stood there—I could see him again as he parted from us! What miracle has restored you? How did you find your way here? You are surely Louis?"

I sat down beside her, keeping one hand between mine.

"Madame, I believe as you believe, that I am Louis Charles, the dauphin of France. And I have come to you first, as my own flesh and blood, who must have more knowledge and recollection of things past than I myself can have. I have not long been waked out of the tranced life I formerly lived."

"I have wept more tears for the little brother—broken in intellect and exiled farther than we—than for my father and mother. They were at peace. But you, poor child, what hope was there for you? Was the person who had you in his charge kind to you? He must have been. You have grown to be such a man as I would have you!"

"Everybody has been kind to me, my sister."

"Could they look in that face and be unkind? All the thousand questions I have to ask must be deferred until the king sees you. I cannot wait for him to see you! Mademoiselle de Choisy, send a message at once to the king!"

The lady in waiting withdrew to the door, and the royal duchess quivered with eager anticipation.

"We have had pretended dauphins, to add insult to exile. You may not take the king unaware as you took me! He will have proofs as plain as his Latin verse. But you will find his Majesty all that a father could be to us, Louis! I think there never was a man so unselfish!—except, indeed, my husband, whom you cannot see until he returns."

Again I kissed my sister's hand. We gazed at each other, our different breeding still making strangeness between us, across which I yearned; and she examined me.

Many a time since I have reproached myself for not improving those moments with the most candid and right-minded princess in Europe, by forestalling my enemies. I should have told her of my weakness instead of sunning my strength in the love of her. I should have made her see my actual position, and the natural antagonism of the king, who would not so readily see a strong personal resemblance when that was not emphasized by some mental stress, as she and three very different men had seen it.

Instead of making cause with her, however, I said over and over—"Marie-Therese! Marie-Therese!"—like a homesick boy come again to some familiar presence. "You are the only one of my family I have seen since waking; except Louis Philippe."

"Don't speak of that man, Louis! I detest the house of Orleans as a Christian should detest only sin! His father doomed ours to death!"

"But he is not to blame for what his father did."

"What do you mean by waking?"

"Coming to my senses."

"All that we shall hear about when the king sees you."

"I knew your picture on the snuffbox."

"What snuffbox?"

"The one in the queen's jewel-case."

"Where did you find that jewel-case?"

"Do you remember the Marquis du Plessy?"

"Yes. A lukewarm loyalist, if loyalist at all in these times."

"My best friend."

"I will say for him that he was not among the first emigrés. If the first emigrés had stayed at home and helped their king, they might have prevented the Terror."

"The Marquis du Plessy stayed after the Tuileries was sacked. He found the queen's jewel-case, and saved it from confiscation to the state."

"Where did he find it? Did you recognize the faces?"

"Oh, instantly!"

The door opened, deferring any story, for that noble usher who had brought me to the presence of Marie-Therese stood there, ready to conduct us to the king.

My sister rose and I led her by the hand, she going confidently to return the dauphin to his family, and the dauphin going like a fool. Seeing Skenedonk standing by the door, I must stop and fit the key to the lock of the queen's casket, and throw the lid back to show her proofs given me by one who believed in me in spite of himself. The snuffbox and two bags of coin were gone, I saw with consternation, but the princess recognized so many things that she missed nothing, controlling herself as her touch moved from trinket to trinket that her mother had worn.

"Bring this before the king," she said. And we took it with us, the noble in blue coat and red collar carrying it.

"His Majesty," Marie-Therese told me as we passed along a corridor, "tries to preserve the etiquette of a court in our exile. But we are paupers, Louis. And mocking our poverty, Bonaparte makes overtures to him to sell the right of the Bourbons to the throne of France!"

She had not yet adjusted her mind to the fact that Louis XVIII was no longer the one to be treated with by Bonaparte or any other potentate, and the pretender leading her smiled like the boy of twenty that he was.

"Napoleon can have no peace while a Bourbon in the line of succession lives."

"Oh, remember the Duke d'Enghien!" she whispered.

Then the door of a lofty but narrow cabinet, lighted with many candles, was opened, and I saw at the farther end a portly gentleman seated in an armchair.

A few gentlemen and two ladies in waiting, besides Mademoiselle de Choisy, attended.

Louis XVIII rose from his seat as my sister made a deep obeisance to him, and took her hand and kissed it. At once, moved by some singular maternal impulse, perhaps, for she was half a dozen years my senior, as a mother would whimsically decorate her child, Marie-Therese took the half circlet of gems from the casket, reached up, and set it on my head.

For an instant I was crowned in Mittau, with my mother's tiara.

I saw the king's features turn to granite, and a dark red stain show on his jaws like coloring on stone. The most benevolent men, and by all his traits he was one of the most benevolent, have their pitiless moments. He must have been prepared to combat a pretender before I entered the room. But outraged majesty would now take its full vengeance on me for the unconsidered act of the child he loved.

"First two peasants, Hervagault and Bruneau, neither of whom had the audacity to steal into the confidence of the tenderest princess in Europe with the tokens she must recognize, or to penetrate into the presence," spoke the king: "and now an escaped convict from Ste. Pélagie, a dandy from the Empire!"

I was only twenty, and he stung me.

"Your royal highness," I said, speaking as I believed within my rights, "my sister tries to put a good front on my intrusion into Mittau."

I took the coronet from my head and gave it again to the hand which had crowned me. Marie-Therese let it fall, and it rocked near the feet of the king.

"Your sister, monsieur! What right have you to call Madame d'Angoulême your sister!"

"The same right, monsieur, that you have to call her your niece."

The features of the princess became pinched and sharpened under the softness of her fair hair.

"Sire, if this is not my brother, who is he?"

Louis XVIII may have been tender to her every other moment of his life, but he was hard then, and looked beyond her toward the door, making a sign with his hand.

That strange sympathy which works in me for my opponent, put his outraged dignity before me rather than my own wrong. Deeper, more sickening than death, the first faintness of self-distrust came over me. What if my half-memories were unfounded hallucinations? What if my friend Louis Philippe had made a tool of me, to annoy this older Bourbon branch that detested him? What if Bellenger's recognition, and the Marquis du Plessy's, and Marie-Therese's, went for nothing? What if some other, and not this angry man, had sent the money to America—

The door opened again. We turned our heads, and I grew hot at the cruelty which put that idiot before my sister's eyes. He ran on all fours, his gaunt wrists exposed, until Bellenger, advancing behind, took him by the arm and made him stand erect. It was this poor creature I had heard scratching on the other side of the inn wall.

How long Bellenger had been beforehand with me in Mittau I could not guess. But when I saw the scoundrel who had laid me in Ste. Pélagie, and doubtless dropped me in the Seine, ready to do me more mischief, smug and smooth shaven, and fine in the red-collared blue coat which seemed to be the prescribed uniform of that court, all my confidence returned. I was Louis of France. I could laugh at anything he had to say.

Behind him entered a priest, who advanced up the room, and made obeisance to the king, as Bellenger did.

Madame d'Angoulême looked once at the idiot, and hid her eyes: the king protecting her. I said to myself,

"It will soon be against my breast, not yours, that she hides her face, my excellent uncle of Provence!"

Yet he was as sincere a man as ever said to witnesses,

"We shall now hear the truth."

The few courtiers, enduring with hardiness a sight which they perhaps had seen before though Madame d'Angoulême had not, made a rustle among themselves as if echoing,

"Yes, now we shall hear the truth!"

The king again kissed my sister's hand, and placed her in a seat beside his arm-chair, which he resumed.

"Monsieur the Abbé Edgeworth," he said, "having stood on the scaffold with our martyred sovereign, as priest and comforter, is eminently the one to conduct an examination like this, which touches matters of conscience. We leave it in his hands."

Abbé Edgeworth, fine and sweet of presence, stood by the king, facing Bellenger and the idiot. That poor creature, astonished by his environment, gazed at the high room corners, or smiled experimentally at the courtiers, stretching his cracked lips over darkened fangs.

"You are admitted here, Bellenger," said the priest, "to answer his Majesty's questions in the presence of witnesses."

"I thank his Majesty," said Bellenger.

The abbé began as if the idiot attracted his notice for the first time.

"Who is the unfortunate child you hold with your right hand?"

"The dauphin of France, monsieur the abbé," spoke out Bellenger, his left hand on his hip.

"What! Take care what you say! How do you know that the dauphin of France is yet among the living?"

Bellenger's countenance changed, and he took his hand off his hip and let it hang down.

"I received the prince, monsieur, from those who took him out of the Temple prison."

"And you never exchanged him for another person, or allowed him to be separated from you?"

Bellenger swore with ghastly lips—"Never, on my hopes of salvation, monsieur the abbé!"

"Admitting that somebody gave you this child to keep—by the way, how old is he?"

"About twenty years, monsieur."

"What right had you to assume he was the dauphin?"

"I had received a yearly pension, monsieur, from his Majesty himself, for the maintenance of the prince."

"You received the yearly pension through my hand, acting as his Majesty's almoner, His Majesty was ever too bountiful to the unfortunate. He has many dependents. Where have you lived with your charge?"

"We lived in America, sometimes in the woods; and sometimes in towns."

"Has he ever shown hopeful signs of recovering his reason?"

"Never, monsieur the abbé."

Having touched thus lightly on the case of the idiot, Abbé Edgeworth turned to me.

The king's face retained its granite hardness. But Bellenger's passed from shade to shade of baffled confidence; recovering only when the priest said,

"Now look at this young man. Have you ever seen him before?"

"Yes, monsieur, I have; both in the American woods, and in Paris."

"What was he doing in the American woods?"

"Living on the bounty of one Count de Chaumont, a friend of Bonaparte's."

"Who is he?"

"A French half-breed, brought up among the Indians."

"What name does he bear?"

"He is called Lazarre."

"But why is a French half-breed named Lazarre attempting to force himself on the exiled court here in Mittau?"

"People have told him that he resembles the Bourbons, monsieur."

"Was he encouraged in this idea by the friend of Bonaparte whom you mentioned?"

"I think not, monsieur the abbé. But I heard a Frenchman tell him he was like the martyred king, and since that hour he has presumed to consider himself the dauphin."

- 144 -

"Who was this Frenchman?"

"The Duke of Orleans, Louis Philippe de Bourbon, monsieur the abbé."

There was an expressive movement among the courtiers.

"Was Louis Philippe instrumental in sending him to France?"

"He was. He procured shipping for the pretender."

"When the pretender reached Paris, what did he do?"

"He attempted robbery, and was taken in the act and thrown into Ste. Pélagie. I saw him arrested."

"What were you doing in Paris?"

"I was following and watching this dangerous pretender, monsieur the abbé."

"Did you leave America when he did?"

"The evening before, monsieur. And we outsailed him."

"Did you leave Paris when he did?"

"Three days later, monsieur. But we passed him while he rested."

"Why do you call such an insignificant person a dangerous pretender?"

"He is not insignificant, monsieur: as you will say, when you hear what he did in Paris."

"He was thrown into the prison of Ste. Pélagie, you told me."

"But he escaped, by choking a sacristan so that the poor man will long bear the marks on his throat. And the first thing I knew he was high in favor with the Marquis du Plessy, and Bonaparte spoke to him; and the police laughed at complaints lodged against him."

"Who lodged complaints against him?"

"I did, monsieur."

"But he was too powerful for you to touch?"

"He was well protected, monsieur the abbé. He flaunted. While the poor prince and myself suffered inconvenience and fared hard—"

"The poor prince, you say?"

"We never had a fitting allowance, monsieur," Bellenger declared aggressively. "Yet with little or no means I tried to bring this pretender to justice and defend his Majesty's throne."

"Pensioners are not often so outspoken in their dissatisfaction," remarked the priest.

I laughed as I thought of the shifts to which Bellenger must have been put. Abbé Edgeworth with merciless dryness inquired,

"How were you able to post to Mittau?"

"I borrowed money of a friend in Paris, monsieur, trusting that his Majesty will requite me for my services."

"But why was it necessary for you to post to Mittau, where this pretender would certainly meet exposure?"

"Because I discovered that he carried with him a casket of the martyred queen's jewels, stolen from the Marquis du Plessy."

"How did the Marquis du Plessy obtain possession of the queen's jewels?"

"That I do not know."

"But the jewels are the lawful property of Madame d'Angoulême. He must have known they would be seized."

"I thought it necessary to bring my evidence against him, monsieur."

"There was little danger of his imposing himself upon the court. Yet you are rather to be commended than censured, Bellenger. Did this pretender know you were in Paris?"

"He saw me there."

"Many times?"

"At least twice, monsieur the abbé."

"Did he avoid you?"

"I avoided him. I took pains to keep him from knowing how I watched him."

"You say he flaunted. When he left Paris for Mittau was the fact generally reported?"

"No, monsieur."

"You learned it yourself?"

"Yes, monsieur."

"But he must have known you would pursue him."

"He left with great secrecy, monsieur the abbé." It was given out that he was merely going to the country."

"What made you suspect he was coming to Mittau?"

"He hired a strong post-chaise and made many preparations."

"But didn't his friend the Marquis du Plessy discover the robbery? Why didn't he follow and take the thief?"

"Dead men don't follow, monsieur the abbé. The Marquis du Plessy had a duel on his hands, and was killed the day after this Lazarre left Paris."

Of all Bellenger's absurd fabrications this story was the most ridiculous. I laughed again. Madame d'Angoulême took her hands from her face and our eyes met one instant, but the idiot whined like a dog. She shuddered, and covered her sight.

The priest turned from Bellenger to me with a fair-minded expression, and inquired,

"What have you to say?"

I had a great deal to say, though the only hearer I expected to convince was my sister. If she believed in me I did not care whether the others believed or not. I was going to begin with Lake George, the mountain, and the fog, and Bellenger's fear of me, and his rage when Louis Philippe told him the larger portion of the money sent from Europe was given to me.

Facing Marie-Therese, therefore, instead of the Abbé Edgeworth, I spoke her name. She looked up once more. And instead of being in Mittau, I was suddenly on a balcony at Versailles!

The night landscape, chill and dim, stretched beyond a multitude of roaring mouths, coarse lips, flaming eyes, illuminated by torches, the heads ornamented with a three-colored thing stuck into the caps. My hand stretched out for support, and met the tight clip of my mother's fingers. I knew that she was towering between Marie-Therese and me a fearless palpitating statue. The devilish roaring mob shot above itself a forced, admiring, piercing cry—"Long live the queen!" Then all became the humming of bees—the vibration of a string—nothing!

X

Blackness surrounded the post-carriage in which I woke, and it seemed to stand in a tunnel that was afire at one end. Two huge trees, branches and all, were burning on a big hearth, stones glowing under them; and figures with long beards, in black robes, passed betwixt me and the fire, stirring a cauldron. If ever witches' brewing was seen, it looked like that.

The last eclipse of mind had come upon me without any rending and tearing in the head, and facts returned clearly and directly. I saw the black robed figures were Jews cooking supper at a large fireplace, and we had driven upon the brick floor of a post-house which had a door nearly the size of a gable. At that end spread a ghostly film of open land, forest and sky. I lay stretched upon cushions as well as the vehicle would permit, and was aware by a shadow which came between me and the Jews that Skenedonk stood at the step.

"What are you about?" I spoke with a rush of chagrin, sitting up. "Are we on the road to Paris?"

"Yes," he answered.

"You have made a mistake, Skenedonk!"

"No mistake," he maintained. "Wait until I bring you some supper. After supper we can talk."

"Bring the supper at once then, for I am going to talk now."

"Are you quite awake?"

"Quite awake. How long did it last this time?"

"Two days."

"We are not two days' journey out of Mittau?"

"Yes."

"Well, when you have horses put in to-morrow morning, turn them back to Mittau."

Skenedonk went to the gigantic hearth, and one of the Jews ladled him out a bowlful of the cauldron stew, which he brought to me.

The stuff was not offensive and I was hungry. He brought another bowlful for himself, and we ate as we had often done in the woods. The fire shone on his bald pate and gave out the liquid lights of his fawn eyes.

"I have made a fool of myself in Mittau, Skenedonk."

"Why do you want to go back?"

"Because I am not going to be thrown out of the palace without a hearing."

"What is the use?" said Skenedonk. "The old fat chief will not let you stay. He doesn't want to hear you talk. He wants to be king himself."

"Did you see me sprawling on the floor like the idiot?"

"Not like the idiot. Your face was down."

"Did you see the duchess?"

"Yes."

"What did she do?"

"Nothing. She leaned on the women and they took her away."

"Tell me all you saw."

"When you went in to hold council, I watched, and saw a priest and Bellenger and the boy that God had touched, all go in after you. So I knew the council would be bad for you, Lazarre, and I stood by the door with my knife in my hand. When the talk had gone on awhile I heard something like the dropping of a buck on the ground, and sprang in, and the men drew their swords and the women screamed. The priest pointed at you and said, 'God has smitten the pretender!' Then they all went out of the room except the priest, and we opened your collar. I told him you had fallen like that before, and the stroke passed off in sleep. He said your carriage waited, and if I valued your safety I would put you in it and take you out of Russia. He called servants to help me carry you. I thought about your jewels; but some drums began to beat, and I thought about your life!"

"But, Skenedonk, didn't my sister—the lady I led by the hand, you remember—speak to me again, or look at me, or try to revive me?"

"No. She went away with the women carrying her."

"She believed in me—at first! Before I said a word she knew me! She wouldn't leave me merely because her uncle and a priest thought me an impostor! She is the tenderest creature on earth, Skenedonk—she is more like a saint than a woman!"

"Some saints on the altar are blind and deaf," observed the Oneida. "I think she was sick."

"I have nearly killed her! And I have been tumbled out of Mittau as a pretender!"

"You are here. Get some men to fight, and we will go back."

"What a stroke—to lose my senses at the moment I needed them most!"

"You kept your scalp."

"And not much else. No! If you refuse to follow me, and wait here at this post-house, I am going back to Mittau!"

"I go where you go," said Skenedonk. "But best go to sleep now."

This I was not able to do until long tossing on the thorns of chagrin wore me out. I was ashamed like a prodigal, baffled, and hurt to the bruising of my soul. A young man's chastened confidence in himself is hard to bear, but the loss of what was given as a heritage at birth is an injustice not to be endured.

The throne of France was never my goal, to be reached through blood and revolution. Perhaps the democratic notions in my father's breast have found wider scope in mine. I wanted to influence men, and felt even at that time that I could do it; but being king was less to my mind than being acknowledged dauphin, and brother, and named with my real name.

I took my fists in my hands and swore to force recognition, if I battered a lifetime on Mittau.

At daylight our post-horses were put to the chaise and I gave the postilion orders myself. The little fellow bowed himself nearly double, and said that troops were moving behind us to join the allied forces against Napoleon.

At once the prospect of being snared among armies and cut off from all return to Paris, appalled me as a greater present calamity than being cast out of Mittau. Mittau could wait for another expedition.

"Very well," I said. "Take the road to France."

We met August rains. We were bogged. A bridge broke under us. We dodged Austrian troops. It seemed even then a fated thing that a Frenchman should retreat ignominiously from Russia.

There is a devilish antagonism of inanimate and senseless things, begun by discord in ourselves, which works unreasonable torture. Our return was an abominable journal which I will not recount, and going with it was a mortifying facility for drawing opposing forces.

However, I knew my friend the marquis expected me to return defeated. He gave me my opportunity as a child is indulged with a dangerous plaything, to teach it caution.

He would be in his chateau of Plessy, cutting off two days' posting to Paris. And after the first sharp pangs of chagrin and shame at losing the fortune he had placed in my hands, I looked forward with impatience to our meeting.

"We have nothing, Skenedonk!" I exclaimed the first time there was occasion for money on the road. "How have you been able to post? The money and the jewel-case are gone."

"We have two bags of money and the snuffbox," said the Oneida. "I hid them in the post-carriage."

"But I had the key of the jewel-case."

"You are a good sleeper," responded Skenedonk.

I blessed him heartily for his forethought, and he said if he had known I was a fool he would not have told me we carried the jewel-case into Russia.

I dared not let myself think of Madame de Ferrier. The plan of buying back her estates, which I had nurtured in the bottom of my heart, was now more remote than America.

One bag of coin was spent in Paris, but three remained there with Doctor Chantry. We had money, though the more valuable treasure stayed in Mittau.

In the sloping hills and green vines of Champagne we were no longer harassed dodging troops, and slept the last night of our posting at Epernay. Taking the road early next morning, I began to watch for Plessy too soon, without forecasting that I was not to set foot within its walls.

We came within the marquis' boundaries upon a little goose girl, knitting beside her flock. Her bright hair was bound with a woolen cap. Delicious grass, and the shadow of an oak, under which she stood, were not to be resisted, so I sent the carriage on. She looked open-mouthed after Skenedonk, and bobbed her dutiful, frightened courtesy at me.

The marquis' peasants were by no means under the influence of the Empire, as I knew from observing the lad whom he had sought among the drowned in the mortuary chapel of the Hôtel Dieu, and who was afterwards found in a remote wine shop seeing sights. The goose girl dared not speak to me unless I required it of her, and the unusual notice was an honor she would have avoided.

"What do you do here?" I inquired.

Her little heart palpitated in the answer—"Oh, guard the geese."

"Do they give you trouble?"

"Not much, except that wicked gander." She pointed out with her knitting-needle a sleek white fellow, who flirted his tail and turned an eye, quavering as if he said—"La, la, la!"

"What does he do?"

"He would be at the vines and the corn, monsieur."

"Bad gander!"

"I switch him," she informed me, like a magistrate.

"But that would only make him run."

"Also I have a string in my pocket, and I tie him by the leg to a tree."

"Serves him right. Is the Marquis du Plessy at the chateau?"

Her face grew shaded, as a cloud chases sunlight before it across a meadow. "Do you mean the new marquis, the old marquis' cousin, monsieur? He went away directly after the burial."

"What burial?"

"The old marquis' burial. That was before St. John's day."

"Be careful what you say, my child!"

"Didn't you know he was dead, *monsieur?*"

"I have been on a journey. Was his death sudden?"

"He was killed in a duel in Paris."

I sat down on the grass with my head in my hands. Bellenger had told the truth.

One scant month the Marquis du Plessy fostered me like a son. To this hour my slow heart aches for the companionship of the lightest, most delicate spirit I ever encountered in man.

Once I lifted my head and insisted,

"It can't be true!"

"Monsieur," the goose girl asserted solemnly, "it is true. The blessed St. Alpin, my patron, forget me if I tell you a lie."

Around the shadowed spot where I sat I heard trees whispering on the hills, and a cart rumbling along the hardened dust of the road.

"Monsieur," spoke the goose girl out of her good heart, "if you want to go to his chapel I will show you the path."

She tied a string around the leg of the wicked gander and attached him to the tree, shaking a wand at him in warning. He nipped her sleeve, and hissed, and hopped, his wives remonstrating softly; but his guardian left him bound and carried her knitting down a valley to a stream, across the bridge, and near an opening in the bushes at the foot of a hill.

"Go all to the right, monsieur," she said, "and you will come to the chapel where the Du Plessys are buried."

I gave her the largest coin in my pocket, and she flew back as well as the spirit of childhood could fly in wooden shoes. All the geese, formed in a line, waddled to meet her, perhaps bearing a memorial of wrongs from their husband.

The climb was steep, rounding a darkened ferny shoulder of lush forest, yet promising more and more a top of sunlight. At the summit was a carriage road which ascended by some easier plane. Keeping all to the right as the goose girl directed, I found a chapel like a shrine.

It was locked. Through the latticed door I could see an altar, whereunder the last Du Plessy who had come to rest there, doubtless lay with his kin.

I sat down on one of the benches under the trees. The ache within me went deep. But all that sunny hillcrest seemed brightened by the marquis. It was cheerful as his smile. "Let us have a glass of wine and enjoy the sun," he said in the breeze flowing around his chapel. "And do you hear that little citizen of the tree trunks, Lazarre?"

The perfume of the woods rose invisibly to a cloudless sky. My last tryst with my friend was an hour in paradise's antechamber.

The light quick stepping of horses and their rattling harness brought Madame de Ferrier's carriage quickly around the curve fronting the chapel. Her presence was the one touch which the place lacked, and I forgot grief, shame, impatience at being found out in my trouble, and stood at her step with my hat in my hand.

She said—"O Lazarre!"—and Paul beat on Ernestine's knee, echoing—"O Zar!" and my comfort was absolute as release from pain, because she had come to visit her old friend the marquis.

I helped her down and stood with her at the latticed door.

"How bright it is here!" said Eagle.

"It is very bright. I came up the hill from a dark place."

"Did the news of his death meet you on the post-road?"

"It met me at the foot of this hill. The goose girl told me."

"Oh, you have been hurt!" she said, looking at me. "Your face is all seamed. Don't tell me about Mittau to-day. Paul and I are taking possession of the estates!"

"Napoleon has given them back to you!"

"Yes, he has! I begged the De Chaumonts to let me come alone! By hard posting we reached Mont-Louis last night. You are the only person in France to whom I would give that vacant seat in the carriage to-day."

I cared no longer for my own loss, as I am afraid has been too much my way all through life; or whether I was a prince or not. Like paradise after death, as so many of our best days come, this perfect day was given me by the marquis himself. Eagle's summer dress touched me. Paul and Ernestine sat facing us, and Paul ate cherries from a little basket, and had his fingers wiped, beating the cushion with his heels in excess of impatience to begin again.

We paused at a turn of the height before descending, where fields could be seen stretching to the horizon, woods fair and clean as parks, without the wildness of the American forest, and vineyards of bushy vines that bore the small black grapes. Eagle showed me the far boundaries of Paul's estates. Then we drove where holly spread its prickly foliage near the ground, where springs from cliffs trickled across delicious lanes.

Hoary stone farmhouses, built four-square like a fortress, each having a stately archway, saluted us as we passed by. The patron and his wife came out, and laborers, pulling their caps, dropped down from high-yoked horses.

But when the long single street of stone cottages which formed the village opened its arms, I could see her breast swelling and her gray eyes sweeping all with comprehensive rush.

An elderly man, shaking some salad in a wire basket, dropped it at his feet, and bowed and bowed, sweeping his cap to the ground. Some women who were washing around a roofed pool left their paddles, and ran, wiping suds from their arms; and houses discharged their inmates, babies in children's arms, wives, old men, the simplicity of their lives and the openness of their labor manifest. They surrounded the carriage. Eagle stood Paul upon his feet that they might worship him, and his mouth corners curled upward, his blue-eyed fearless look traveled from face to face, while her gloved hand was kissed, and God was praised that she had come back.

"O Jean!" she cried, "is your mother alive?" and "Marguerite! have you a son so tall?"

An old creature bent double, walked out on four feet, two of them being sticks, lifted her voice, and blessed Eagle and the child a quarter of an hour. Paul's mother listened reverently, and sent him in Ernestine's arms for the warped human being to look upon at close range with her failing sight. He stared at her unafraid, and experimentally put his finger on her knotted cheek; at which all the women broke into chorus as I have heard blackbirds rejoice.

"I have not seen them for so long!" Madame de Ferrier said, wiping her eyes. "We have all forgotten our behavior!"

An inverted pine tree hung over the inn door, and dinner was laid for us in its best room, where host and hostess served the marquise and the young marquis almost on their knees.

When we passed out at the other end of the village, Eagle showed me a square-towered church.

"The De Ferriers are buried there—excepting my father. I shall put a tablet in the wall for Cousin Philippe. Few Protestants in France had their rights and privileges protected as ours were by the throne. I mention this fact, sire, that you may lay it up in your mind! We have been good subjects, well worth our salt in time of war."

Best of all was coming to the chateau when the sun was about an hour high. The stone pillars of the gateway let us upon a terraced lawn, where a fountain played, keeping bent plumes of water in the air. The lofty chateau of white stone had a broad front, with wings. Eagle bade me note the two dove-cotes or pigeon towers, distinctly separate structures, one flanking each wing, and demonstrating the antiquity of the house. For only nobles in medieval days were accorded the privilege of keeping doves.

Should there be such another evening for me when I come to paradise, if God in His mercy brings me there, I shall be grateful, but hardly with such fresh-hearted joy. Night descends with special benediction on remote ancient homes like Mont-Louis. We walked until sunset in the park, by lake, and bridged stream, and hollied path; Ernestine carrying Paul or letting him pat behind, driving her by her long cap ribbons while he explored his mother's playground. But when the birds began to nest, and dewfall could be felt, he was taken to his supper and his bed, giving his mother a generous kiss, and me a smile of his upcurled mouth corners. His forehead was white and broad, and his blue eyes were set well apart.

We walked until sunset in the park, by lake, and bridged stream, and hollied path.

I can yet see the child looking over Ernestine's shoulder. She carried him up stairs of oak worn hollow like stone, a mighty hand-wrought balustrade rising with them from hall to roof.

We had our supper in a paneled room where the lights were reflected as on mirrors of polished oak, and the man who served us had served Madame de Ferrier's father and grandfather. The gentle old provincial went about his duty as a religious rite.

There was a pleached walk like that in the marquis' Paris garden, of branches flattened and plaited to form an arbor supported by tree columns; which led to a summer-house of stone smothered in ivy. We walked back and forth under this thick roof of verdure. Eagle's cap of brown hair was roughened over her radiant face, and the open throat of her gown showed pulses beating in her neck. Her lifted chin almost touched my arm as I told her all the Mittau story, at her request.

"Poor Madame d'Angoulême! The cautious priest and the king should not have taken you from me like that! She knew you as I knew you; and a woman's knowing is better than a man's proofs. She will have times of doubting their policy. She will remember the expression of your mouth, your shrugs, and gestures—the little traits of the child Louis, that reappear in the man."

"I wish I had never gone to Mittau to give her a moment's distress."

"Is she very beautiful?"

"She is like a lily made flesh. She has her strong dislikes, and one of them is Louis Philippe—"

"Naturally," said Eagle.

"But she seemed sacred to me. Perhaps a woman brings that hallowedness out of martyrdom."

"God be with the royal lady! And you, sire!"

"And you!—may you be always with me, Eagle!"

"This journey to Mittau changes nothing. You were wilful. You would go to the island in Lake George: you would go to Mittau."

"Both times you sent me."

"Both times I brought you home! Let us not be sorrowful to-night."

"Sorrowful! I am so happy it seems impossible that I come from Mittau, and this day the Marquis du Plessy died to me! I wish the sun had been tied to the trees, as the goose girl tied her gander."

"But I want another day," said Eagle. "I want all the days that are my due at home."

We ascended the steps of the stone pavilion, and sat down in an arch like a balcony over the sunken garden. Pears and apricots, their branches flattened against the wall, showed ruddy garnered sunlight through the dusk. The tangled enclosure sloped down to the stream, from which a fairy wisp of mist wavered over flower bed and tree. Dew and herbs and the fragrance of late roses sent up a divine breath, invisibly submerging us, like a tide rising out of the night.

Madame de Ferrier's individual traits were surprised in this nearness, as they never had been when I saw her at a distance in alien surroundings. A swift ripple, involuntary and glad, coursed down her body; she shuddered for joy half a minute or so.

Two feet away, I worshiped her smiling eyes and their curved ivory lids, her rounded head with its abundant cap of hair, her chin, her shoulders, her bust, the hands in her lap, the very sweep of her scant gown about her feet.

The flash of extreme happiness passing, she said gravely,

"But that was a strange thing—that you should fall unconscious!"

"Not so strange," I said; and told her how many times before the eclipse—under the edge of which my boyhood was passed—had completely shadowed me. At the account of Ste. Pélagie she leaned toward me, her hands clenched on her breast. When we came to the Hôtel Dieu she leaned back pallid against the stone.

"Dear Marquis du Plessy!" she whispered, as his name entered the story.

When it was ended she drew some deep breaths in the silence.

"Sire, you must be very careful. That Bellenger is an evil man."

"But a weak one."

"There may be a strength of court policy behind him."

"The policy of the court at Mittau is evidently a policy of denial."

"Your sister believed in you."

"Yes, she believed in me."

"I don't understand," said Madame de Ferrier, leaning forward on her arms, "why Bellenger had you in London, and another boy on the mountain."

"Perhaps we shall never understand it."

"I don't understand why he makes it his business to follow you."

"Let us not trouble ourselves about Bellenger."

"But are you safe in France since the Marquis du Plessy's death?"

"I am safe to-night, at least."

"Yes, far safer than you would be in Paris."

"And Skenedonk is my guard."

"I have sent a messenger to Plessy for him," Madame de Ferrier said. "He will be here in the morning."

I thanked her for remembering him in the excitement of her home coming. We heard a far sweet call through a cleft of the hills, and Eagle turned her head.

"That must be the shepherd of Les Rochers. He has missed a lamb. Les Rochers is the most distant of our farms, but its night noises can be heard through an opening in the forest. Paul will soon be listening for all these sounds! We must drive to Les Rochers to-morrow. It was there that Cousin Philippe died."

I could not say how opportunely Cousin Philippe had died. The violation of her childhood by such a marriage rose up that instant a wordless tragedy.

"Sire, we are not observing etiquette in Mont-Louis as they observe it at Mittau. I have been talking very familiarly to my king. I will keep silent. You speak."

"Madame, you have forbidden me to speak!"

She gave me a startled look, and said,

"Did you know Jerome Bonaparte has come back? He left his wife in America. She cannot be received in France, because she has committed the crime of marrying a prince. She is to be divorced for political reasons."

"Jerome Bonaparte is a hound!" I spoke hotly.

"And his wife a venturesome woman—to marry even a temporary prince."

"I like her sort, madame!"

"Do you, sire?"

"Yes, I like a woman who can love!"

"And ruin?"

"How could you ruin me?"

"The Saint-Michels brought me up," said Eagle. "They taught me what is lawful and unlawful. I will never do an unlawful thing, to the disgrace and shame of my house. A woman should build her house, not tear it down."

"What is unlawful?"

"It is unlawful for me to encourage the suit of my sovereign."

"Am I ever likely to be anything but what they call in Mittau a pretender, Eagle?"

"That we do not know. You shall keep yourself free from entanglements."

"I am free from them—God knows I am free enough!—the lonesomest, most unfriended savage that ever set out to conquer his own."

"You were born to greatness. Great things will come to you."

"If you loved me I could make them come!"

"Sire, it isn't healthy to sit in the night air. We must go out of the dew."

"Oh, who would be healthy! Come to that, who would be such a royal beggar as I am?"

"Remember," she said gravely, "that your claim was in a manner recognized by one of the most cautious, one of the least ardent royalists, in France."

The recognition she knew nothing about came to my lips, and I told her the whole story of the jewels. The snuffbox was in my pocket. Sophie Saint-Michel had often described it to her.

She sat and looked at me, contemplating the stupendous loss.

"The marquis advised me not to take them into Russia," I acknowledged.

"There is no robbery so terrible as the robbery committed by those who think they are doing right."

"I am one of the losing Bourbons."

"Can anything be hidden in that closet in the queen's dressing-room wall?" mused Eagle. "I believe I could find it in the dark, Sophie told me so often where the secret spring may be touched. When the De Chaumonts took me to the Tuileries I wanted to search for it. But all the state apartments are now on the second floor, and Madame Bonaparte has her own rooms below. Evidently she knows nothing of the secrets of the place. The queen kept her most beautiful robes in that closet. It has no visible door. The wall opens. And we have heard that a door was made through the back of it to let upon a spiral staircase of stone, and through this the royal family made their escape to Varennes, when they were arrested and brought back."

We fell into silence at mention of the unsuccessful flight which could have changed history; and she rose and said—"Good-night, sire."

Next morning there was such a delicious world to live in that breathing was a pleasure. Dew gauze spread far and wide over the radiant domain. Sounds from cattle, and stables, and the voices of servants drifted on the air. Doves wheeled around their towers, and around the chateau standing like a white cliff.

I walked under the green canopy watching the sun mount and waiting for Madame de Ferrier. When she did appear the old man who had served her father followed with a tray. I could only say—"Good-morning, madame," not daring to add—"I have scarcely slept for thinking of you."

"We will have our coffee out here," she told me.

It was placed on the broad stone seat under the arch of the pavilion where we sat the night before; bread, unsalted butter from the farms, the coffee, the cream, the loaf sugar. Madame de Ferrier herself opened a door in the end of the wall and plunged into the dew of the garden. Her old servant exclaimed. She caught her hair in briers and laughed, tucking it up from falling, and brought off two great roses, each the head and the strength of a stem, to lay beside our plates. The breath of roses to this hour sends through my veins the joy of that.

Then the old servant gathered wall fruit for us, and she sent some in his hand to Paul. Through a festooned arch of the pavilion giving upon the terraces, we saw a bird dart down to the fountain, tilt and drink, tilt and drink again, and flash away. Immediately the multitudinous rejoicing of a skylark dropped from upper air. When men would send thanks to the very gate of heaven their envoy should be a skylark.

Eagle was like a little girl as she listened.

"This is the first day of September, sire."

"Is it? I thought it was the first day of creation."

"I mention the date that you may not forget it. Because I am going to give you something to-day."

My heart leaped like a conqueror's.

Her skin was as fresh as the roses, looking marvelous to touch. The shock of imminent discovery went through me. For how can a man consider a woman forever as a picture? A picture she was, in the short-waisted gown of the Empire, of that white stuff Napoleon praised because it was manufactured in France. It showed the line of her throat, being parted half way down the bosom by a ruff which encircled her neck and stood high behind it. The transparent sleeves clung to her arms, and the slight outline of her figure looked long in its close casing.

The gown tail curled around her slippered foot damp from the plunge in the garden. She gave it a little kick, and rippled again suddenly throughout her length.

Then her face went grave, like a child's when it is surprised in wickedness.

"But our fathers and mothers would have us forget their suffering in the festival of coming home, wouldn't they, Lazarre?"

"Surely, Eagle."

"Then why are you looking at me with reproach?"

"I'm not."

"Perhaps you don't like my dress?"

I told her it was the first time I had ever noticed anything she wore, and I liked it.

"I used to wear my mother's clothes. Ernestine and I made them over. But this is new; for the new day, and the new life here."

"And the day," I reminded her, "is the first of September."

She laughed, and opened her left hand, showing me two squat keys so small that both had lain concealed under two of her finger tips.

"I am going to give you a key, sire."

"Will it unlock a woman's mind?"

"It will open a padlocked book. Last night I found a little blank-leaved book, with wooden covers. It was fastened by a padlock, and these keys were tied to it. You may have one key: I will keep the other."

"The key to a padlocked book with nothing in it."

Her eyes tantalized me.

"I am going to put something in it. Sophie Saint-Michel said I had a gift for putting down my thoughts. If the gift appeared to Sophie when I was a child, it must grow in me by use. Every day I shall put some of my life into the book. And when I die I will bequeath it to you!"

"Take back the key, madame. I have no desire to look into your coffin."

She extended her hand.

"Then our good and kind friend Count de Chaumont shall have it."

"He shall not!"

I held to her hand and kept my key.

She slipped away from me. The laughter of the child yet rose through the dignity of the woman.

"When may I read this book, Eagle?"

"Never, of my free will, sire. How could I set down all I thought about you, for instance, if the certainty was hanging over me that you would read my candid opinions and punish me for them!"

"Then of what use is the key?"

"You would rather have it than give it to another, wouldn't you?"

"Decidedly."

"Well, you will have the key to my thoughts!"

"And if the book ever falls into my hands—"

"I will see that it doesn't!"

"I will say, years from now—"

"Twenty?"

"Twenty? O Eagle!"

"Ten."

"Months? That's too long!"

"No, ten years, sire."

"Not ten years, Eagle. Say eight."

"No, nine."

"Seven. If the book falls into my hands at the end of seven years, may I open it?"

"I may safely promise you that," she laughed. "The book will never fall into your hands."

I took from my pocket the gold snuffbox with the portraits on the lid, and placed my key carefully therein. Eagle leaned forward to look at them. She took the box in her hand, and gazed with long reverence, drooping her head.

Young as I was, and unskilled in the ways of women, that key worked magic comfort. She had given me a link to hold us together. The inconsistent, contradictory being, old one instant with the wisdom of the Saint-Michels, rippling full of unrestrained life the next, denying me all hope, yet indefinitely tantalizing, was adorable beyond words. I closed my eyes: the blinding sunshine struck them through the ivied arch.

Turning my head as I opened them, I saw an old man come out on the terrace.

He tried to search in every direction, his gray head and faded eyes moving anxiously. Madame de Ferrier was still. I heard her lay the snuffbox on the stone seat. I knew, though I could not let myself watch her, that she stood up against the wall, a woman of stone, her lips chiseled apart.

"Eagle—Eagle!" the old man cried from the terrace.

She whispered—"Yes, Cousin Philippe!"

XI

Swiftly as she passed between the tree columns, more swiftly her youth and vitality died in that walk of a few yards.

We had been girl and boy together a brief half hour, heedless and gay. When she reached the arbor end, our chapter of youth was ended.

I saw her bloodless face as she stepped upon the terrace.

The man stretched his arms to her. As if the blight of her spirit fell upon him, the light died out of his face and he dropped his arms at his sides.

He was a courtly gentleman, cadaverous and shabby as he stood, all the breeding of past generations appearing in him.

"Eagle?" he said. The tone of piteous apology went through me like a sword.

She took his hands and herself drew them around her neck. He kissed her on both cheeks.

"O Cousin Philippe!"

"I have frightened you, child! I meant to send a message first—but I wanted to see you—I wanted to come home!"

"Cousin Philippe, who wrote that letter?"

"The notary, child. I made him do it."

"It was cruel!" She gave way, and brokenly sobbed, leaning helpless against him.

The old marquis smoothed her head, and puckered his forehead under the sunlight, casting his eyes around like a culprit.

"It was desperate. But I could do nothing else! You see it has succeeded. While I lay in hiding, the sight of the child, and your youth, has softened Bonaparte. That was my intention, Eagle!"

"The peasants should have told me you were living!"

"They didn't know I came back. Many of them think I died in America. The family at Les Rochers have been very faithful; and the notary has held his tongue. We must reward them, Eagle. I have been hidden very closely. I am tired of such long hiding!"

He looked toward the chateau and lifted his voice sharply—

"Where's the baby? I haven't seen the baby!"

With gracious courtesy, restraining an impulse to plunge up the steps, he gave her his arm; and she swayed against it as they entered.

When I could see them no more, I rose, and put my snuffbox in my breast. The key rattled in it.

A savage need of hiding when so wounded, worked first through the disorder that let me see none of the amenities of leave-taking, self-command, conduct.

I was beyond the gates, bare-headed, walking with long strides, when an old mill caught my eye, and I turned towards it, as we turn to trifles to relieve us from unendurable tension. The water dripped over the wheel, and long green beard trailed from its chin down the sluice. In this quieting company Skenedonk spied me as he rattled past with the post-carriage; and considering my behavior at other times, he was not enough surprised to waste any good words of Oneida.

He stopped the carriage and I got in. He pointed ahead toward a curtain of trees which screened the chateau.

"Paris," I answered.

"Paris," he repeated to the postilion, and we turned about. I looked from hill to stream, from the fruited brambles of blackberry to reaches of noble forest, realizing that I should never see those lands again, or the neighboring crest where my friend the marquis slept.

We posted the distance to Paris in two days.

What the country was like or what towns we passed I could not this hour declare with any certainty. At first making effort and groping numbly in my mind, but the second day grasping determination, I formed my plans, and talked them over with Skenedonk. We would sail for America on the first convenient ship; waiting in Paris only long enough to prepare for the post journey to a port. Charges must at once be settled with Doctor Chantry, who would willingly stay in Paris while the De Chaumonts remained there.

Beyond the voyage I did not look. The first faint tugging of my foster country began to pull me as it has pulled many a broken wretch out of the conditions of the older world.

Paris was horrible, with a lonesomeness no one could have foreseen in its crowded streets. A taste of war was in the air. Troops passed to review. Our post-carriage met the dashing coaches of gay young men I knew, who stared at me without recognition. Marquis du Plessy no longer made way for me and displayed me at his side.

I drove to his hotel in the Faubourg St. Germain for my possessions. It was closed: the distant relative who inherited after him being an heir with no Parisian tastes. The care-taker, however, that gentle old valet like a woman, who had dressed me in my first Parisian finery, let us in, and waited upon us with food I sent him out to buy. He gave me a letter from my friend, which he had held to deliver on my return, in case any accident befell the marquis. He was tremulous in his mourning, and all his ardent care of me was service rendered to the dead.

I sat in the garden, with the letter spread upon the table where we had dined. Its brevity was gay. The writer would have gone under the knife with a jest. He did not burden me with any kind of counsel. We had touched. We might touch again. It was as if a soul sailed by, waving its hat.

"My Dear Boy:—

"I wanted you, but it was best you should not stay and behold the depravity of your elders. It is about a woman.

"May you come to a better throne than the unsteady one of France.

"Your friend and servant,
Etienne du Plessy.

"Garlic is the spice of life, my boy!"

I asked no questions about the affair in which he had been engaged. If he had wanted me to know he would have told me.

The garden was more than I could endure. I lay down early and slept late, as soon as I awoke in the morning beginning preparation for leaving France. Yet two days passed, for we were obliged to exchange our worn post-carriage for another after waiting for repairs. The old valet packed my belongings; though I wondered what I was going to do with them in America. The outfit of a young man of fashion overdressed a refugee of diminished fortune.

For no sooner was I on the street than a sense of being unmistakably watched grew upon me. I scarcely caught anybody in the act. A succession of vanishing people passed me from one to another. A working man in his blouse eyed me; and disappeared. In the afternoon it was a soldier who turned up near my elbow, and in the evening he was succeeded by an equally interested old woman. I might not have remembered these people with distrust if Skenedonk had not told me he was trailed by changing figures, and he thought it was time to get behind trees.

Bellenger might have returned to Paris, and set Napoleon's spies on the least befriended Bourbon of all; or the police upon a man escaped from Ste. Pélagie after choking a sacristan.

The Indian and I were not skilled in disguises as our watchers were. Our safety lay in getting out of Paris. Skenedonk undertook to stow our belongings in the post-chaise at the last minute. I went to De Chaumont's hotel to bring the money from Doctor Chantry and to take leave without appearing to do so.

Mademoiselle de Chaumont seized me as I entered. Her carriage stood in the court. Miss Chantry was waiting in it while Annabel's maid fastened her glove.

"O Lazarre!" the poppet cried, her heartiness going through me like wine. "Are you back? And how you are changed! They must have abused you in Russia. We heard you went to Russia. But since dear Marquis du Plessy died we never hear the truth about anything."

I acknowledged that I had been to Russia.

"Why did you go there? Tell your dearest Annabel. She won't tell."

"To see a lady."

Annabel shook her fretwork of misty hair.

"That's treason to me. Is she beautiful?"

"Very."

"Kind?"

"Perfectly."

"Well, you're not. By the way, why are you looking so wan if she is beautiful and kind?"

"I didn't say she was beautiful and kind for me, did I?"

"No, of course not. She has jilted you, the wretch. Your dearest Annabel will console you, Lazarre!" She clasped my arm with both hands. "Madame de Ferrier's husband is alive!"

"What consolation is there in that?"

"A great deal for me. She has her estates back, and he was only hiding until she got them. I know the funniest thing!"

Annabel hooked her finger and led me to a small study or cabinet at the end of the drawing-room.

A profusion of the most beautiful stuffs was arranged there for display.

"Look!" the witch exclaimed, pinching my wrist in her rapture. "India muslin embroidered in silver lama, Turkish velvet, ball dresses for a bride, ribbons of all colors, white blond, Brussels point, Cashmere shawls, veils in English point, reticules, gloves, fans, essences, a bridal purse of gold links—and worse than all,—except this string of perfect pearls—his portrait on a medallion of ivory, painted by Isabey!"

"What is this collection?"

"A corbeille!"

"What's a corbeille?"

Annabel crossed her hands in desperation. "Oh, haven't you been in Paris long enough to know what a corbeille is? It's the collection of gifts a bridegroom makes for his bride. He puts his taste, his sentiment, his"—she waved her fingers in the air—"as well as his money, into it. A corbeille shows what a man is. He must have been collecting it ever since he came to France. I feel proud of him. I want to pat him on his dear old back!"

Not having him there to pat she patted me.

"You are going to be married?"

"Who said I was going to be married?"

"Isn't this your corbeille?"

Annabel lifted herself to my ear.

"It was Madame de Ferrier's!"

"What!"

"I'm sure of it!"

"Who bought it?"

"Count de Chaumont, of course."

"Was Madame de Ferrier going to marry him?"

"Who wouldn't marry a man with such a corbeille?"

"Was she?"

"Don't grind your teeth at your dearest Annabel. She hadn't seen it, but it must have decided her. I am sure he intended to marry Madame de Ferrier, and he does most things he undertakes to do. That inconsiderate wretch of a Marquis de Ferrier—to spoil such a corbeille as this! But Lazarre!" She patted her gloved hands. "Here's the consolation:—my father will be obliged to turn his corbeille into my trousseau when I am married!"

"What's a trousseau?"

"Goood! It's a bride's wardrobe. I knew he had something in this cabinet, but he never left the key in the door until to-day. He was so completely upset when the De Ferriers came into Paris!"

"Are they in Paris?"

"Yes, at their own hotel. The old marquis has posted here to thank the emperor! The emperor is away with the troops, so he is determined at least to thank the empress at the assembly to-night."

"Will Madame de Ferrier go to the Tuileries?"

"Assuredly. Fancy how furious my father must be!"

"May I enter?" said the humblest of voices outside the door.

We heard a shuffling step.

Annabel made a face and clenched her hands. The sprite was so harmless I laughed at her mischief. She brought in Doctor Chantry as she had brought me, to behold the corbeille; covering her father's folly with transparent fabrications, which anybody but the literal Briton must have seen through. He scarcely greeted me at all, folding his hands, pale and crushed, the sharp tip of his nose standing up more than ever like a porcelain candle-extinguisher, while I was anxious to have him aside, to get my money and take my leave.

"See this beautiful corbeille, Doctor Chantry! Doesn't it surprise you Lazarre should have such taste? We are going this morning to the mayor of the arrondissement. Nothing is so easy as civil marriage under the Empire! Of course the religious sacrament in the church of the Capuchins follows, and celebrating that five minutes before midnight, will make all Paris talk! Go with us to the mayor, Doctor Chantry!"

"No," he answered, "no!"

"My father joins us there. We have kept Miss Chantry waiting too long. She will be tired of sitting in the carriage."

Chattering with every breath Annabel entrained us both to the court, my poor master hobbling after her a victim, and staring at me with hatred when I tried to get a word in undertone.

I put Annabel into the coach, and Miss Chantry made frigid room for me.

"Hasten yourself, Lazarre," said Mademoiselle de Chaumont.

I looked back at the poor man who was being played with, and she cried out laughing—

"Did you go to Russia a Parisian to come back a bear?"

I entered her coach, intending to take my leave as soon as I had seen Count de Chaumont. Annabel chattered all the way about civil marriage, and directed Miss Chantry to wait for us while we went in to the mayor. I was perhaps too indifferent to the trick. The usually sharp governess, undecided and piqued, sat still.

The count was not in the mayor's office. A civil marriage was going forward, and a strange bridal party looked at us.

"Now, Lazarre," the strategist confided, "your dearest Annabel is going to cover herself with Parisian disgrace. You don't know how maddening it is to have every step dogged by a woman who never was, never could have been—and manifestly never will be—young! Wasn't that a divine flash about the corbeille and the mayor? Miss Chantry will wait outside half a day. As I said, she will be very tired of sitting in the carriage. This is what you must do; smuggle me out another way; call another carriage, and take me for a drive and wicked dinner. I don't care what the consequences are, if you don't!"

I said I certainly didn't, and that I was ready to throw myself in the Seine if that would amuse her; and she commended my improvement in manners. We had a drive, with a sympathetic coachman; and a wicked dinner in a suburb, which would have been quite harmless on American ground. The child was as full of spirits as she had been the night she mounted the cabin chimney. But I realized that more of my gold pieces were slipping away, and I had not seen Doctor Chantry.

"We were going to the mayor's," she maintained, when reproached. "My father would have joined us if he had been there. He would certainly have joined us if he had seen me alone with you. Nothing is so easy as civil marriage under the Empire. Of course the religious sacrament follows, when people want it, and if it is celebrated in the church of the Capuchins—or any other church—five minutes before midnight, it will make all Paris talk! Every word I said was true!"

"But Doctor Chantry believed something entirely different."

"You can't do anything for the English," said Annabel. "Next week he will say haw-haw."

Doctor Chantry could not be found when we returned to her father's hotel. She gave me her fingers to kiss in good-bye, and told me I was less doleful.

- 171 -

"We thought you were the Marquis du Plessy's son, Lazarre. I always have believed that story the Holland woman told in the cabin, about your rank being superior to mine. Don't be cut up about Madame de Ferrier! You may have to go to Russia again for her, but you'll get her!"

The witch shook the mist of hair at the sides of her pretty aquiline face, blew a kiss at me, and ran up the staircase and out of my life. After waiting long for Doctor Chantry I hurried to Skenedonk and sent him with instructions to find my master and conclude our affair before coming back.

The Indian silently entered the Du Plessy hotel after dusk, crestfallen and suspicious. He brought nothing but a letter, left in Doctor Chantry's room; and no other trace remained of Doctor Chantry.

"What has he done with himself, Skenedonk?" I exclaimed.

The Oneida begged me to read that we might trail him.

It was a long and very tiresome letter written in my master's spider tracks, containing long and tiresome enumerations of his services. He presented a large bill for his guardianship on the voyage and across France. He said I was not only a Rich Man through his Influence, but I had proved myself an ungrateful one, and had robbed him of his only Sentiment after a disappointed Existence. My Impudence was equaled only by my astonishing Success, and he chose not to contemplate me as the Husband of Beauty and Lofty Station, whose Shoes he in his Modesty and Worth, felt unworthy to unlatch. Therefore he withdrew that very day from Paris, and would embrace the Opportunity of going into pensive Retirement and rural Contemplation, in his native Kingdom; where his Sister would join him when she could do so with Dignity and Propriety.

I glanced from line to line smiling, but the postscript brought me to my feet.

"The Deposit which you left with me I shall carry with me, as no more than my Due for lifting low Savagery to high Gentility, and beg to subscribe my Thanks for at least this small Tribute of Gratitude."

"Doctor Chantry is gone with the money!"

Skenedonk bounded up grasping the knife which he always carried in a sheath hanging from his belt.

"Which way did the old woman go?"

"Stop," I said.

The Indian half crouched for counsel.

"I'll be a prince! Let him have it."

"Let him rob you?"

"We're quits, now. I've paid him for the lancet stab I gave him."

"But you haven't a whole bagful of coin left."

"We brought nothing into France, and it seems certain we shall take nothing but experience out of it. And I'm young, Skenedonk. He isn't."

The Oneida grunted. He was angrier than I had ever seen him.

"We ought to have knocked the old woman on the head at Saratoga," he responded.

Annabel's trick had swept away my little fortune. With recklessness which repeated loss engenders I proposed we scatter the remaining coin in the street, but Skenedonk prudently said we would divide and conceal it in our clothes. I gave the kind valet a handful to keep his heart warm; and our anxieties about our valuables were much lightened.

Then we consulted about our imminent start, and I told my servant it would be better to send the post-chaise across the Seine. He agreed with me. And for me to come to it as if by accident the moment we were ready to join each other on the road. He agreed to that. All of our belongings would be put into it by the valet and himself, and when we met we would make a circuit and go by the way of St. Denis.

"We will meet," I told him, "at eleven o'clock in front of the Tuileries."

Skenedonk looked at me without moving a muscle.

"I want to see the palace of the Tuileries before I leave France."

He still gazed at me.

"At any risk, I am going to the Tuileries to-night!"

My Iroquois grunted. A glow spread all over his copper face and head. If I had told him I was going to an enemy's central camp fire to shake a club in the face of the biggest chief, he could not have thought more of my daring or less of my common sense.

"You will never come out."

"If I don't, Skenedonk, go without me."

He passed small heroics unnoticed.

"Why do you do it?"

I couldn't tell him. Neither could I leave Paris without doing it. I assured him many carriages would be there, near the entrance, which was called, I believed, the pavilion of Flora; and by showing boldness we might start from that spot as well as from any other. He abetted the reckless devil in me, and the outcome was that I crossed the Seine bridge by myself about ten o'clock; remembering my escape from Ste. Pélagie; remembering I should never see the gargoyles on Notre Dame any more, or the golden dome of the Invalides, or hear the night hum of Paris, whether I succeeded or not. For if I succeeded I should be away toward the coast by morning; and if I did not succeed, I should be somewhere under arrest.

I can see the boy in white court dress, with no hint of the traveler about him, who stepped jauntily out of a carriage and added himself to groups entering the Tuileries. The white court dress was armor which he put on to serve him in the dangerous attempt to look once more on a woman's face. He mounted with a strut toward the guardians of the imperial court, not knowing how he might be challenged; and fortune was with him.

"Lazarre!" exclaimed Count de Chaumont, hurrying behind to take my elbow. "I want you to help me!"

Remembering with sudden remorse Annabel's escape and our wicked dinner, I halted eager to do him service. He was perhaps used to Annabel's escapes, for a very different annoyance puckered his forehead as he drew me aside within the entrance.

"Have you heard the Marquis de Ferrier is alive?"

I told him I had heard it.

"Damned old fox! He lay in hiding until the estates were recovered. Then out he creeps to enjoy them!"

I pressed the count's hand. We were one in disapproval.

"It's a shame!" said the count.

It was a shame, I said.

"And now he's posted into Paris to make a fool of himself."

"How?"

"Have you seen Madame de Ferrier?"

"No, I have not seen her."

"I believe we are in time to intercept him. You have a clever head, boy. Use it. How shall we get this old fellow out of the Tuileries without letting him speak to the emperor?"

"Easily, I should think, since Napoleon isn't here."

"Yes, he is. He dashed into Paris a little while ago, and may leave to-night. But he is here."

"Why shouldn't the Marquis de Ferrier speak to Napoleon?"

"Because he is going to make an ass of himself before the court, and what's worse, he'll make a laughing-stock of me."

"How can he do that?"

"He is determined to thank the emperor for restoring his estates. He might thank the empress, and she wouldn't know what he was talking about. But the emperor knows everything. I have used all the arguments I dared to use against it, but he is a pig for stubbornness. For my sake, for Madame de Ferrier's sake, Lazarre, help me to get him harmlessly out of the Tuileries, without making a public scandal about the restitution of the land!"

"What scandal can there be, monsieur? And why shouldn't he thank Napoleon for giving him back his estates after the fortunes of revolution and war?"

"Because the emperor didn't do it. I bought them!"

"You!"

"Yes, I bought them. Come to that, they are my property!"

"Madame de Ferrier doesn't know this?"

"Certainly not. I meant to settle them on her. Saints and angels, boy, anybody could see what my intentions were!"

"Then she is as poor as she was in America?"

"Poorer. She has the Marquis de Ferrier!"

We two who loved her, youth and man, rich and powerful, or poor and fugitive, felt the passionate need of protecting her.

"She wouldn't accept them if she knew it."

"Neither would the marquis," said De Chaumont. "The Marquis de Ferrier might live on the estates his lifetime without any interference. But if he will see the emperor, and I can't prevent it any other way, I shall have to tell him!"

"Yes, you will have to tell him!"

I thought of Eagle in the village, and the old woman who blessed her a quarter of an hour, and Paul standing on the seat to be worshiped. How could I go to America and leave her? And what could I do for her when a rich man like De Chaumont was powerless?

"Can't you see Napoleon," I suggested, "and ask him to give the marquis a moment's private audience, and accept his thanks?"

"No!" groaned De Chaumont. "He wouldn't do it. I couldn't put myself in such a position!"

"If Napoleon came in so hurriedly he may not show himself in the state apartments to-night."

"But he is accessible, wherever he is. He doesn't deny himself to the meanest soldier. Why should he refuse to see a noble of the class he is always conciliating when he can?"

"Introduce me to the Marquis de Ferrier," I finally said, "and let me see if I can talk against time while you get your emperor out of his way."

I thought desperately of revealing to the old royalist what I believed myself to be, what Eagle and he believed me to be, and commanding him, as his rightful prince, to content himself with less effusive and less public gratitude to an usurper. He would live in the country, shrinking so naturally from the court that a self-imposed appearance there need never be repeated.

I believe this would have succeeded. A half hour more of time might have saved years of comfort to Eagle—for De Chaumont was generous—and have changed the outcome of my own life. But in scant fifteen minutes our fate was decided.

De Chaumont and I had moved with our heads together, from corridor to antechamber, from antechamber to curtained salon of the lower floor. The private apartments of the Bonaparte family were thrown open, and in the mahogany furnished room, all hung with yellow satin, I noticed a Swiss clock which pointed its minute finger to a quarter before eleven. I made no hurry. My errand was not accomplished. Skenedonk would wait for me, and even dare a search if he became suspicious.

The count, knowing what Madame de Ferrier considered me, perhaps knew my plan. He turned back at once assenting.

The Marquis and Marquise de Ferrier were that instant going up the grand staircase, and would be announced. Eagle turned her face above me, the long line of her throat uplifted, and went courageous and smiling on her way. The marquis had adapted himself to the court requirements of the Empire. Noble gentleman of another period, he stalked a piteous masquerader where he had once been at home.

Count de Chaumont grasped my arm and we hurried up the stairs after them. The end of a great and deep room was visible, and I had a glimpse, between heads and shoulders, of a woman standing in the light of many lusters. She parted her lips to smile, closing them quickly, but having shown little dark teeth. She was of exquisite shape, her face and arms and bosom having a clean fair polish like the delicate whiteness of a magnolia, as I have since seen that flower in bloom. She wore a small diadem in her hair, and her short-waisted robe trailed far back among her ladies. I knew without being told that this was the empress of the French.

De Chaumont's hand was on my arm, but another hand touched my shoulder. I looked behind me. This time it was not an old woman, or a laborer in a blouse, or a soldier; but I knew my pursuer in his white court dress. Officer of the law, writ in the lines of his face, to my eyes appeared all over him.

"Monsieur Veeleeum!"

As soon as he said that I understood it was the refugee from Ste. Pélagie that he wanted.

"Certainly," I answered. "Don't make a disturbance."

"You will take my arm and come with me, Monsieur Veeleeum."

"I will do nothing of the kind until my errand is finished," I answered desperately.

De Chaumont looked sharply at the man, but his own salvation required him to lay hold on the marquis. As he did so, Eagle's face and my face encountered in a panel of mirror, two flashes of pallor; and I took my last look.

"You will come with me now," said the gendarme at my ear.

She saw him, and understood his errand.

There was no chance. De Chaumont wheeled ready to introduce me to the marquis. I was not permitted to speak to him. But Eagle took my right arm and moved down the corridor with me.

Decently and at once the disguised gendarme fell behind where he could watch every muscle without alarming Madame de Ferrier. She appeared not to see him. I have no doubt he praised himself for his delicacy and her unconsciousness of my arrest.

"You must not think you can run away from me," she said.

"I was coming back," I answered, making talk.

My captor's person heaved behind me, signifying that he silently laughed. He kept within touch.

"Do you know the Tuileries well?" inquired Eagle.

"No. I have never been in the palace before."

"Nor I, in the state apartments."

We turned from the corridor into a suite in these upper rooms, the gendarme humoring Madame de Ferrier, and making himself one in the crowd around us. De Chaumont and the Marquis de Ferrier gave chase. I saw them following, as well as they could.

"This used to be the queen's dressing-room," said Eagle. We entered the last one in the suite.

"Are you sure?"

"Quite sure."

"This is the room you told me you would like to examine?"

"The very one. I don't believe the Empire has made any changes in it. These painted figures look just as Sophie described them."

Eagle traced lightly with her finger one of the shepherdesses dancing on the panel; and crossed to the opposite side of the room. People who passed the door found nothing to interest them, and turned away, but the gendarme stayed beside us. Eagle glanced at him as if resenting his intrusion, and asked me to bring her a candle and hold it near a mark on the tracery. The gendarme himself, apologetic but firm, stepped to the sconce and took the candle. I do not know how the thing was done, or why the old spring and long unused hinges did not stick, but his back was toward us—she pushed me against the panel and it let me in.

And I held her and drew her after me, and the thing closed. The wall had swallowed us.

We stood on firm footing as if suspended in eternity. No sound from the swarming palace, not even possible noise made by the gendarme, reached us. It was like being earless, until she spoke in the hollow.

"Here's the door on the staircase, but it will not open!"

I groped over every inch of it with swift haste in the blackness.

"Hurry—hurry!" she breathed. "He may touch the spring himself—it moves instantly!"

"Does this open with a spring, too?"

"I don't know. Sophie didn't know!"

"Are you sure there is any door here?"

"She told me there was."

"This is like a door, but it will not move."

It sprang inward against us, a rush of air and a hollow murmur as of wind along the river, following it.

"Go—be quick!" said Madame de Ferrier.

"But how will you get out?"

"I shall get out when you are gone."

"O, Eagle, forgive me!" (Yet I would have dragged her in with me again!)

"I am in no danger. You are in danger. Goodbye, my liege."

Cautiously she pushed me through the door, begging me to feel for every step. I stood upon the top one, and held to her as I had held to her in passing through the other wall.

I thought of the heavy days before her and the blank before me. I could not let go her wrists. We were fools to waste our youth. I could work for her in America. My vitals were being torn from me. I should go to the devil without her. I don't know what I said. But I knew the brute love which had risen like a lion in me would never conquer the woman who kissed me in the darkness and held me at bay.

"O Louis—O Lazarre! Think of Paul and Cousin Philippe! You shall be your best for your little mother! I will come to you sometime!"

Then she held the door between us, and I went down around and around the spiral of stone.

BOOK III

ARRIVING

I

Even when a year had passed I said of my escape from the Tuileries: "It was a dream. How could it have happened?" For the adventures of my wandering fell from me like a garment, leaving the one changeless passion.

Skenedonk and I met on the ship a New England minister, who looked upon and considered us from day to day. I used to sit in the stern, the miles stretching me as a rack stretches flesh and tendons. The minister regarded me as prostrated by the spider bite of that wicked Paris; out of which he learned I had come, by talking to my Oneida.

The Indian and I were a queer pair that interested him, and when he discovered that I bore the name of Eleazar Williams his friendship was sealed to us. Eunice Williams of Deerfield, the grandmother of Thomas Williams, was a traditional brand never snatched from the burning, in the minister's town of Longmeadow, where nearly every inhabitant was descended from or espoused to a Williams. Though he himself was born Storrs, his wife was born Williams; and I could have lain at his feet and cried, so open was the heart of this good man to a wanderer rebounding from a family that disowned the pretender. He was my welcome back to America. The breath of eastern pines, and the resinous sweetness of western plains I had not yet seen, but which drew me so that I could scarcely wait to land, came to me with that man. Before the voyage ended I had told him my whole history as far as I knew it, except the story of Madame de Ferrier; and the beginning of it was by no means new to him. The New England Williamses kept a prayerful eye on that branch descending through the Iroquois. This transplanted Briton, returning from his one memorable visit to the England of his forefathers, despised my Bourbon claims, and even the French contraction of my name.

"What are you going to do now, Eleazar?" he inquired.

Hugging my old dream to myself, feeling my heart leap toward that western empire which must fascinate a young man as long as there remain any western lands to possess, I told him I intended to educate our Iroquois as soon as I could prepare myself to do it, and settle them where they could grow into a greater nation.

The man of God kindled in the face. He was a dark-eyed, square-browed, serious man, with black hair falling below his white band. His mouth had a sweet benign expression, even when he quizzed me about my dauphinhood. A New England pastor was a flame that burned for the enlightenment of the nations. From that hour it was settled that I should be his pupil, and go with him to Longmeadow to finish my education.

When we landed he helped me to sell my Babylonish clothes, except the white court dress, to which I clung with tenacity displeasing to him, and garb myself in more befitting raiment. By Skenedonk's hand I sent some of the remaining gold coins to my mother Marianne and the chief, when he rejoined the tribe and went to pass the winter at St. Regis. And by no means did I forget to tell him to bring me letters from De Chaumont's manor in the spring, if any arrived there for me.

How near to heaven the New England village seemed, with Mount Tom on the horizon glorious as Mount Zion, the mighty sweep of meadow land, the Connecticut river flowing in great peace, the broad street of elms like some gigantic cathedral nave, and in its very midst a shrine—the meetinghouse, double-decked with fan-topped windows.

Religion and education were the mainsprings of its life. Pastor Storrs worked in his study nearly nine hours a day, and spent the remaining hours in what he called visitation of his flock.

This being lifted out of Paris and plunged into Longmeadow was the pouring of white hot metal into chill moulds. It cast me. With a seething and a roar of loosened forces, the boy passed to the man.

Nearly every night during all those years of changing, for even faithfulness has its tides, I put the snuffbox under my pillow, and Madame de Ferrier's key spoke to my ear. I would say to myself: "The one I love gave me this key. Did I ever sit beside her on a ledge of stone overlooking a sunken garden?—so near that I might have touched her! Does she ever think of the dauphin Louis? Where is she? Does she know that Lazarre has become Eleazar Williams?"

The pastor's house was fronted with huge white fluted pillars of wood, upholding a porch roof which shaded the second floor windows. The doors in that house had a short-waisted effect with little panels above and long panels below. I had a chamber so clean and small that I called it in my mind the Monk's Cell, nearly filled with the high posted bed, the austere table and chairs. The whitewashed walls were bare of pictures, except a painted portrait of Stephen Williams, pastor of Longmeadow from 1718 to 1783. Daily his laughing eyes watched me as if he found my pretensions a great joke. He had a long nose, and a high forehead. His black hair crinkled, and a merry crease drew its half circle from one cheek around under his chin to the other.

Longmeadow did not receive me without much question and debate. There were Williamses in every direction; disguised, perhaps, for that generation, under the names of Cooley, Stebbins, Colter, Ely, Hole, and so on. A stately Sarah Williams, as Mrs. Storrs, sat at the head of the pastor's table. Her disapproval was a force, though it never manifested itself except in withdrawal. If Mrs. Storrs had drawn back from me while I lived under her roof, I should have felt an outcast indeed. The subtle refinement of those Longmeadow women was like the hinted sweetness of arbutus flower. Breeding passed from generation to generation. They had not mixed their blood with the blood of any outsiders; and their forbears were English yeomen.

I threw myself into books as I had done during my first months at De Chaumont's, before I grew to think of Madame de Ferrier. One of those seven years I spent at Dartmouth. But the greater part of my knowledge I owe to Pastor Storrs. Greek and Hebrew he gave me to add to the languages I was beginning to own; and he unlocked all his accumulations of learning. It was a monk's life that I lived; austere and without incident, but bracing as the air of the hills. The whole system was monastic, though abomination alighted on that word in Longmeadow. I took the discipline into my blood. It will go down to those after me.

There a man had to walk with God whether he wanted to or not.

Living was inexpensive, each item being gaged by careful housekeeping. It was a sin to gorge the body, and godly conversation was better than abundance. Yet the pastor's tea-table arises with a halo around it. The rye and Indian bread, the doughnuts fragrant as flowers, the sparing tea, the prim mats which saved the cloth, the wire screen covering sponge cake—how sacred they seem!

The autumn that I came to Longmeadow, Napoleon Bonaparte was beaten on the sea by the English, but won the battle of Austerlitz, defeating the Russian coalition and changing the map of Europe.

I felt sometimes a puppet while this man played his great part. It was no comfort that others of my house were nothing to France. Though I did not see Louis Philippe again, he wandered in America two or three years, and went back to privacy.

During my early noviatiate at Longmeadow, Aaron Burr's conspiracy went to pieces, dragging down with it that pleasant gentleman, Harmon Blennerhassett, startling men like Jackson, who had best befriended him unawares. But this in nowise affected my own plans of empire. The solidarity of a nation of Indians on a remote tract could be no menace to the general government.

Skenedonk came and went, and I made journeys to my people with him. But there was never any letter waiting at De Chaumont's for me. After some years indeed, the count having returned to Castorland, to occupy his new manor at Le Rayville, the mansion I had known was torn down and the stone converted to other uses. Skenedonk brought me word early that Mademoiselle de Chaumont had been married to an officer of the Empire, and would remain in France.

The door between my past and me was sealed. Madame de Ferrier stood on the other side of it, and no news from her penetrated its dense barrier. I tried to write letters to her. But nothing that I could write was fit to send, and I knew not whether she was yet at Mont-Louis. Forever she was holding the door against me.

Skenedonk, coming and going at his caprice, stayed a month in every year at Longmeadow, where the townspeople, having had a surfeit of aboriginal names, called him John. He raised no objection, for that with half a dozen other Christian titles had been bestowed on him in baptism; and he entered the godly list of Williamses as John Williams.

The first summer I spent in Longmeadow there was an eclipse of the sun about the middle of June. I remember lying on open land, my book on its face beside me, and watching it through my eyelashes; until the weird and awful twilight of a blotted sun in mid-heaven sent birds and beasts to shelter as from wrath. When there was but a hairy shining around the orbed blackness, and stars trembled out and trembled back, as if they said: "We are here. The old order will return," and the earth held its breath at threat of eternal darkness, the one I loved seemed to approach in the long shadows. It was a sign that out of the worst comes the best. But it was a terror to the unprepared; and Pastor Storrs preached about it the following Sunday.

The missionary spirit of Longmeadow stirred among the Williamses, and many of them brought what they called their mites to Pastor Storrs for my education. If I were made a king no revenue could be half so sweet as that. The village was richer than many a stonier New England place, but men were struggling then all over the wide states and territories for material existence.

The pension no longer came from Europe. It ceased when I returned from France. Its former payment was considered apocryphal by Longmeadow, whose very maids—too white, with a pink spot in each cheek—smiled with reserved amusement at a student who thought it possible he could ever be a king. I spoke to nobody but Pastor Storrs about my own convictions. But local newspapers, with their omniscient grip on what is in the air, bandied the subject back and forth.

We sometimes walked in the burying ground among dead Williamses, while he argued down my claims, leaving them without a leg to stand on. Reversing the usual ministerial formula, "If what has been said is true, then it follows, first, secondly," and so on, he used to say:

"Eleazar, you were brought up among the Indians, conscious only of bodily existence, and unconscious of your origin; granted. Money was sent—let us say from Europe—for your support; granted. Several persons, among them one who testified strongly against his will, told you that you resembled the Bourbons; granted. You bear on your person marks like those which were inflicted on the unfortunate dauphin of France; granted. You were malignantly pursued while abroad; granted. But what does it all prove? Nothing. It amounts simply to this: you know nothing about your early years; some foreign person—perhaps an English Williams—kindly interested himself in your upbringing; you were probably scalded in the camps; you have some accidental traits of the Bourbons; a man who heard you had a larger pension than the idiot he was tending, disliked you. You can prove nothing more."

I never attempted to prove anything more to Pastor Storrs. It would have been most ungrateful to persuade him I was an alien. At the same time he prophesied his hopes of me, and many a judicious person blamed him for treating me as something out of the ordinary, and cockering up pride.

A blunter Williams used to take me by the button on the street.

"Eleazar Williams," he would say, "do you pretend to be the son of the French king? I tell you what! I will not let the name of Williams be disgraced by any relationship to any French monarch! You must do one of two things: you must either renounce Williamsism or renounce Bourbonism!"

Though there was liberty of conscience to criticise the pastor, he was autocrat of Longmeadow. One who preceded Pastor Storrs had it told about him that two of his deacons wanted him to appoint Ruling Elders. He appointed them; and asked them what they thought the duties were. They said he knew best.

"Well," said the pastor, "one of the Ruling Elders may come to my house before meeting, saddle my horse, and hold the stirrup while I get on. The other may wait at the church door and hold him while I get off, and after meeting bring him to the steps. This is all of my work that I can consent to let Ruling Elders do for me."

The Longmeadow love of disputation was fostered by bouts which Ruling Elders might have made it their business to preserve, if any Ruling Elders were willing to accept their appointment. The pastor once went to the next town to enjoy argument with a scientific doctor. When he mounted his horse to ride home before nightfall the two friends kept up their debate. The doctor stood by the horse, or walked a few steps as the horse moved. Presently both men noticed a fire in the east; and it was sunrise. They had argued all night.

In Longmeadow a man could not help practicing argument. I also practiced oratory. And all the time I practiced the Iroquois tongue as well as English and French, and began the translation of books into the language of the nation I hoped to build. That Indians made unstable material for the white man to handle I would not believe. Skenedonk was not unstable. His faithfulness was a rock.

For some reason, and I think it was the reach of Pastor Storrs, men in other places began to seek me. The vital currents of life indeed sped through us on the Hartford and Springfield stage road. It happened that Skenedonk and I were making my annual journey to St. Regis when the first steamboat accomplished its trip on the Hudson river. About the time that the Wisconsin country was included in Illinois Territory, I decided to write a letter to Madame Tank at Green Bay, and insist on knowing my story as she believed she knew it. Yet I hesitated; and finally did not do it. I found afterwards that there was no post-office at Green Bay. A carrier, sent by the officers of the fort and villagers, brought mail from Chicago. He had two hundred miles of wilderness to traverse, and his blankets and provisions as well as the mail to carry; and he did this at the risk of his life among wild men and beasts.

The form of religion was always a trivial matter to me. I never ceased to love the sacrifice of the mass, which was an abomination and an idolatrous practice to Pastor Storrs. The pageantry of the Roman Church that first mothered and nurtured me touches me to this day. I love the Protestant prayers of the English Church. And I love the stern and knotty argument, the sermon with heads and sequences, of the New England Congregationalist. For this catholicity Catholics have upbraided me, churchmen rebuked me, and dissenters denied that I had any religion at all.

When the Episcopal Bishop of New York showed me kindness, and Pastor Storrs warned me against being proselyted, I could not tell him the charm in the form of worship practiced by the woman I loved. There was not a conscious minute when I forgot her. Yet nobody in Longmeadow knew of her existence. In my most remorseful days, comparing myself with Pastor Storrs, I was never sorry I had clung to her and begged her not to let me go alone. For some of our sins are so honestly the expression of nature that justification breaks through them.

On the western border there was trouble with dissatisfied Indians, and on the sea there was trouble with the British, so that people began to talk of war long before it was declared, and to blame President Madison for his over-caution in affairs. A battle was fought at Tippecanoe in the Indiana Territory, which silenced the Indians for a while. But every one knew that the English stood behind them. Militia was mustered, the army recruited, and embargo laid upon shipping in the ports, and all things were put forward in April of that year, before war was declared in June.

I had influence with our tribes. The Government offered me a well paid commission to act as its secret agent. Pastor Storrs and the Williamses, who had been nurturing a missionary, were smitten with grief to see him rise and leap into camps and fields, eager for the open world, the wilderness smell; the council, where the red man's mind, a trembling balance, could be turned by vivid language; eager, in fact, to live where history was being made.

The pastor had clothed me in his mind with ministerial gown and band, and the martial blood that quickened he counted an Iroquois strain. Yet so inconsistent is human nature, so given to forms which it calls creeds, that when I afterwards put on the surplice and read prayers to my adopted people, he counted it as great a defection as taking to saddle and spur. We cannot leave the expression of our lives to those better qualified than we are, however dear they may be. I had to pack my saddlebags and be gone, loving Longmeadow none the less because I grieved it, knowing that it would not approve of me more if I stayed and failed to do my natural part.

The snuffbox and the missal which had belonged to my family in France I always carried with me. And very little could be transported on the road we took.

John Williams, who came to Longmeadow in deerskins, and paraded his burnished red poll among the hatted Williamses, abetted me in turning from the missionary field to the arena of war, and never left me. It was Skenedonk who served the United States with brawn and endurance, while I put such policy and color into my harangues as I could command. We shared our meals, our camps, our beds of leaves together. The life at Longmeadow had knit me to good use. I could fast or feast, ride or march, take the buckskins, or the soldier's uniform.

Of this service I shall write down only what goes to the making of the story. The Government was pleased to commend it, and it may be found written in other annals than mine.

Great latitude was permitted us in our orders. We spent a year in the north. My skin darkened and toughened under exposure until I said to Skenedonk, "I am turning an Indian;" and he, jealous of my French blood, denied it.

In July we had to thread trails he knew by the lake toward Sandusky. There was no horse path wide enough for us to ride abreast. Brush swished along our legs, and green walls shut our view on each side. The land dipped towards its basin. Buckeye and gigantic chestnut trees, maple and oak, passed us from rank to rank of endless forest. Skenedonk rode ahead, watching for every sign and change, as a pilot now watches the shifting of the current. So we had done all day, and so we were doing when fading light warned us to camp.

A voice literally cried out of the wilderness, startling the horses and ringing among the tree trunks:

"The spirit of the Lord is upon me, and He hath anointed me to blow the trumpet in the wilderness, and sound an alarm in the forest; for behold the tribes of the heathen are round about your doors, and a devouring flame followeth after them!"

II

"That's Johnny Appleseed," said Skenedonk, turning in his saddle.

"What is Johnny Appleseed?"

"He is a man that God has touched," said Skenedonk, using the aboriginal phrase that signified a man clouded in mind.

God had hidden him, too. I could see no one. The voice echo still went off among the trees.

"Where is he?"

"Maybe one side, maybe the other."

"Does he never show himself?"

"Oh, yes," Skenedonk said. "He goes to all the settlements. I have often seen him when I was hunting on these grounds. He came to our camp. He loves to sleep outdoors better than in a cabin."

"Why does he shout at us like a prophet?"

"To warn us that Indians are on the warpath."

"He might have thought we were on the warpath ourselves."

"Johnny Appleseed knows Shawanoes and Tecumseh's men."

The trees, lichened on their north sides, massed rank behind rank without betraying any face in their glooms. The Ohio and Indiana forests had a nameless quality. They might have been called home-forests, such invitations issued from them to man seeking a spot of his own. Nor can I make clear what this invitation was. It produced thoughts different from those that men were conscious of in the rugged northwest.

"I think myself," said Skenedonk, as we moved farther from the invisible voice, "that he is under a vow. But nobody told me that."

"Why do you think so?"

"He plants orchards in every fine open spot; or clears the land for planting where he thinks the soil is right."

"Don't other men plant orchards?"

"No. They have not time, or seed. They plant bread. He does nothing but plant orchards."

"He must have a great many."

"They are not for himself. The apples are for any one who may pass by when they are ripe. He wants to give apples to everybody. Animals often nibble the bark, or break down his young trees. It takes long for them to grow. But he keeps on planting."

"If other men have no seeds to plant, how does he get them?"

"He makes journeys to the old settlements, where many orchards have grown, and brings the seeds from ciderpresses. He carries them from Pennsylvania on his back, in leather bags, a bag for each kind of seed."

"Doesn't he ever sell them?"

"Not often. Johnny Appleseed cares nothing for money. I believe he is under a vow of poverty. No one laughs at him. The tribes on these grounds would not hurt a hair of his head, not only because God has touched him, but because he plants apples. I have eaten his apples myself."

"Johnny Appleseed!" I repeated, and Skenedonk hastened to tell me:

"He has another name, but I forget it. He is called Johnny Appleseed."

The slim and scarcely perceptible tunnel, among trees, piled with fallen logs and newly sprung growths, let us into a wide clearing as suddenly as a stream finds its lake. We could not see even the usual cow tracks. A cabin shedding light from its hearth surprised us in the midst of stumps.

The door stood wide. A woman walked back and forth over a puncheon floor, tending supper. Dogs rushed to meet us, and the playing of children could be heard. A man, gun in hand, stepped to his door, a sentinel. He lowered its muzzle, and made us welcome, and helped us put our horses under shelter with his own.

It was not often we had a woman's handiwork in corn bread and game to feed ourselves upon, or a bed covered with homespun sheets.

I slept as the children slept, until a voice rang in the clearing:

"The spirit of the Lord is upon me, and He hath anointed me to blow the trumpet in the wilderness, and sound an alarm in the forest; for behold the tribes of the heathen are round about your doors, and a devouring flame followeth after them!"

Every sleeper in the cabin sat upright or stirred. We said in whispered chorus:

"Johnny Appleseed!"

A tapping, light and regular, on the window, followed. The man was on the floor in a breath. I heard the mother groping among the children, and whispering:

"Don't wake the baby!"

The fire had died upon the hearth, and they lighted no candle. When Johnny Appleseed gave his warning cry in the clearing, and his cautious tap on the window, and was instantly gone to other clearings and other windows, it meant that the Indians were near.

Skenedonk and I, used to the night alarm and boots and saddle in a hurry, put ourselves in readiness to help the family. I groped for clothing, and shoved small legs and arms into it. The little creatures, obedient and silent, made no whimper at being roused out of dreams, but keenly lent themselves to the march.

We brought the horses, and put the woman and children upon them. The very dogs understood, and slunk around our legs without giving mouth. The cabin door was shut after us without noise, closing in what that family called home; a few pots and pans; patchwork quilts; a spinning-wheel; some benches; perhaps a child's store of acorn cups and broken yellow ware in a log corner. In a few hours it might be smoking a heap of ashes; and the world offered no other place so dear. What we suffer for is enriched by our suffering until it becomes priceless.

So far on the frontier was this cabin that no community block-house stood near enough to give its inmates shelter. They were obliged to go with us to Fort Stephenson.

Skenedonk pioneered the all-night struggle on an obscure trail; and he went astray sometimes, through blackness of woods that roofed out the stars. We floundered in swales sponging full of dead leaves, and drew back, scratching ourselves on low-hung foliage.

By dawn the way became easier and the danger greater. Then we paused and lifted our rifles if a twig broke near by, or a fox barked, or wind rushed among leaves as a patter of moccasins might come. Skenedonk and I, sure of the northern Indians, were making a venture in the west. We knew nothing of Tecumseh's swift red warriors, except that scarcely a year had passed since his allies had tomahawked women and children of the garrison on the sand teach at Chicago.

Without kindling any fire we stopped once that day to eat, and by good luck and following the river, reached that Lower Sandusky which was called Fort Stephenson, about nightfall.

The place was merely a high stockade with blockhouses at the angles, and a gate opening toward the river. Within, besides the garrison of a hundred and sixty men, were various refugees, driven like our family to the fort. And there, coming heartily from the commandant's quarters to receive me, was George Croghan, still a boy in appearance, though intrusted with this dangerous post. His long face had darkened like mine. We looked each other over with the quick and critical scrutiny of men who have not met since boyhood, and laughed as we grasped hands.

"You are as welcome to the inside of this bear-pen," said Major Croghan, "as you made me to the outside of the one in the wilderness."

"I hope you'll not give me such another tramp after shelter for the night as I gave you," I said.

"The best in Fort Stephenson is yours. But your rest depends on the enemy. A runner has just come in from the General warning me Proctor and Tecumseh are turning their attention this way. I'm ordered to evacuate, for the post is considered too weak to hold."

"How soon do you march?"

"I don't march at all. I stay here. I'm going to disobey orders."

"If you're going to disobey orders, you have good reason for doing so."

"I have. It was too late to retreat. I'm going to fight. I hear, Lazarre, you know how to handle Indians in the French way."

"My dear Croghan, you insinuate the American way may be better."

"It is, on the western border. It may not be on the northern."

"Then you would not have advised my attempting the Indians here?"

"I shouldn't have discouraged it. When I got the secret order, I said: 'Bring the French—bring the missionaries—bring anything that will cut the comb of Tecumseh!'"

"The missionaries and the French like being classed with—anything," I said.

"We're Americans here," Croghan laughed. "The dauphin may have to fight in the ditch with the rest of us."

"The dauphin is an American too, and used to scars, as you know. Can you give me any news from Green Bay in the Wisconsin country?"

"I was ordered to Green Bay last year to see if anything could be done with old Fort Edward Augustus."

"Does my Holland court-lady live there?"

"Not now," he answered soberly. "She's dead."

"That's bad," I said, thinking of lost opportunities.

"Is pretty Annabel de Chaumont ever coming back from France?"

"Not now, she's married."

"That's worse," he sighed. "I was very silly about her when I was a boy."

We had our supper in his quarters, and he busied himself until late in the night with preparations for defense. The whole place was full of cheer and plenty of game, and swarmed like a little fair with moving figures. A campfire was built at dark in the center of the parade ground, heaped logs sending their glow as far as the dark pickets. Heads of families drew towards it while the women were putting their children to bed; and soldiers off duty lounged there, the front of the body in light, the back in darkness.

Cool forest night air flowed over the stockade, swaying smoke this way and that. As the fire was stirred, and smoke turned to flame, it showed more and more distinctly what dimness had screened.

A man rose up on the other side of it, clothed in a coffee sack, in which holes were cut for his head and arms. His hat was a tin kettle with the handle sticking out behind like a stiff queue.

Indifferent to his grotesqueness, he took it off and put it on the ground beside him, standing ready to command attention.

He was a small, dark, wiry man, barefooted and barelegged, whose black eyes sparkled, and whose scanty hair and beard hung down over shoulders and breast. Some pokes of leather, much scratched, hung bulging from the rope which girded his coffee sack. From one of these he took a few unbound leaves, the fragment of a book, spread them open, and began to read in a chanting, prophetic key, something about the love of the Lord and the mysteries of angels. His listeners kept their eyes on him, giving an indulgent ear to spiritual messages that made less demand on them than the violent earthly ones to which they were accustomed.

"It's Johnny Appleseed," a man at my side told me, as if the name explained anything he might do.

"It's Johnny Appleseed," a man at my side told me.

When Johnny Appleseed finished reading the leaves he put them back in his bag, and took his kettle to the well for water. He then brought some meal from the cook-house and made mush in his hat.

The others, turning their minds from future mysteries, began to talk about present danger, when he stood up from his labor to inquire:

"Is there plenty in the fort for the children to eat?"

"Plenty, Johnny, plenty," several voices assured him.

"I can go without supper if the children haven't enough."

"Eat your supper, Johnny. Major Croghan will give you more if you want it," said a soldier.

"And we'll give you jerked Britisher, if you'll wait for it," said another.

"Johnny never eats meat," one of the refugees put in. "He thinks it's sinful to kill critters. All the things in the woods likes him. Once he got into a holler log to sleep, and some squirrels warned him to move out, they settled there first; and he done it. I don't allow he'd pick a flea off his own hide for fear he'd break its legs so it couldn't hop around and make a living."

The wilderness prophet sat down quietly to his meal without appearing to notice what was said about him; and when he had eaten, carried his hat into the cook-house, where dogs could not get at his remaining porridge.

"Now he'll save that for his breakfast," remarked another refugee. "There's nothing he hates like waste."

"Talking about squirrels," exclaimed the man at my side, "I believe he has a pasture for old, broke-down horses somewhere east in the hills. All the bates he can find he swaps young trees for, and they go off with him leading them, but he never comes into the settlements on horseback."

"Does he always go barefoot?" I asked.

"Sometimes he makes bark sandals. If you give him a pair of shoes he'll give them away to the first person that can wear them and needs them. Hunters wrap dried leaves around their leggins to keep the rattlesnakes out, but Johnny never protects himself at all."

"No wonder," spoke a soldier. "Any snake'd be discouraged at them shanks. A seven-year rattler'd break his fang on 'em."

Johnny came out of the cook-house with an iron poker, and heated it in the coals. All the men around the fire waited, understanding what he was about to do, but my own breath drew with a hiss through my teeth as he laid the red hot iron first on one long cut and then another in his travel-worn feet. Having cauterized himself effectually, and returned the poker, he took his place in perfect serenity, without any show of pain, prepared to accommodate himself to the company.

Some boys, awake with the bigness of the occasion, sat down near Johnny Appleseed, and gave him their frank attention. Each boy had his hair cut straight around below the ears, where his mother had measured it with an inverted bowl, and freshly trimmed him for life in the fort, and perhaps for the discomfiture of savages, if he came under the scalping knife. Open-mouthed or stern-jawed, according to temperament, the young pioneers listened to stories about Tecumseh, and surmises on the enemy's march, and the likelihood of a night attack.

"Tippecanoe was fought at four o'clock in the morning," said a soldier.

"I was there," spoke out Johnny Appleseed.

No other man could say as much. All looked at him as he stood on his cauterized feet, stretching his arms, lean and sun-cured, upward in the firelight.

"Angels were there. In rain and darkness I heard them speak and say, 'He hath cast the lot for them, and His hand hath divided it unto them by line; they shall possess it forever; from generation to generation shall they dwell therein. The wilderness and the solitary place shall be glad for them, and the desert shall rejoice and blossom as the rose!'"

"Say, Johnny, what does an angel look like?" piped up one of the boys, quite in fellowship.

Johnny Appleseed turned his rapt vision aside and answered:

"'White robes were given unto every one of them.' There had I laid me down in peace to sleep, and the Lord made me to dwell in safety. The camp-fires burned red in the sheltered place, and they who were to possess the land watched by the campfires. I looked down from my high place, from my shelter of leaves and my log that the Lord gave me for a bed, and saw the red camp-fires blink in the darkness.

"Then was I aware that the heathen crept betwixt me and the camp, surrounding it as a cloud that lies upon the ground. The rain fell upon us all, and there was not so much sound as the rustling of grasshoppers in tall grass. I said they will surprise the camp and slay the sleepers, not knowing that they who were to possess the land watched every man with his weapon. But when I would have sounded the trumpet of warning, I heard a rifle shot, and all the Indians rose up screeching and rushed at the red fires.

"Then a sorcerer leaped upon my high place, rattling many deer hoofs, and calling aloud that his brethren might hear his voice. Light he promised them for themselves, and darkness for the camp, and he sang his war song, shouting and rattling the deer hoofs. Also the Indians rattled deer hoofs, and it was like a giant breathing his last, being shot with many musket flashes.

"I saw steam through the darkness, for the fires were drenched and trampled by the men of the camp, and no longer shone as candles so that the Indians might see by them to shoot. The sorcerer danced and shouted, the deer hoofs rattled, and on this side and that men fought knee to knee and breast to breast. I saw through the wet dawn, and they who had crept around the camp as a cloud arose as grasshoppers and fled to the swamp.

"Then did the sorcerer sit upon his heels, and I beheld he had but one eye, and he covered it from the light.

"But the men in the camp shouted with a mighty shouting. And after their shouting I heard again the voices of angels saying: 'He hath cast the lot for them, and His hand hath divided it unto them by line; they shall possess it forever; from generation to generation shall they dwell therein. The wilderness and the solitary place shall be glad for them, and the desert shall rejoice and blossom as the rose!'"

The speaker sat down, and one of the men remarked:

"So that's the way the battle of Tippecanoe looked to Johnny Appleseed."

But the smallest boy thoughtfully inquired:

"Say, Johnny, haven't the Indians any angels?"

"You'll wish they was with the angels if they ever get you by the hair," laughed one of the men.

Soldiers began moving their single cannon, a six-pounder, from one blockhouse to another. All the men jumped up to help, as at the raising of a home, and put themselves in the way so ardently that they had to be ordered back.

When everybody but ourselves had left the starlit open place, Johnny Appleseed lay down and stretched his heels to the blaze. A soldier added another log, and kicked into the flame those fallen away. Though it was the end of July, Lake Erie cooled the inland forests.

Sentinels were posted in the blockhouses. Quiet settled on the camp; and I sat turning many things in my mind besides the impending battle. Napoleon Bonaparte had made a disastrous campaign in Russia. If I were yet in France; if the Marquis du Plessy had lived; if I had not gone to Mittau; if the self I might have been, that always haunts us, stood ready to take advantage of the turn—

Yet the thing which cannot be understood by men reared under old governments had befallen me. I must have drawn the wilderness into my blood. Its possibilities held me. If I had stayed in France at twenty, I should have been a Frenchman. The following years made me an American. The passion that binds you to a land is no more to be explained than the fact that many women are beautiful, while only one is vitally interesting.

The wilderness mystic was sitting up looking at me.

"I see two people in you," he said.

"Only two?"

"Two separate men."

"What are their names?"

"Their names I cannot see."

"Well, suppose we call them Louis and Lazarre."

His eyes sparkled.

"You are a white man," he pronounced. "By that I mean you are not stained with many vile sins."

"I hadn't an equal chance with other men. I lost nine years."

"Mebby," hazarded Johnny Appleseed cautiously, "you are the one appointed to open and read what is sealed."

"If you mean to interpret what you read, I'm afraid I am not the one. Where did you get those leaves?"

"From a book that I divided up to distribute among the people."

"Doesn't that destroy the sense?"

"No. I carry the pages in their order from cabin to cabin."

He came around the fire with the lightness of an Indian, and gave me his own fragment to examine. It proved to be from the writings of one Emanuel Swedenborg.

With a smile which seemed to lessen the size of his face and concentrate its expression to a shining point, Johnny Appleseed slid his leather bags along the rope girdle, and searched them, one after the other. I thought he wanted me to notice his apple seeds, and inquired how many kinds he carried. So he showed them in handfuls, brown and glistening, or gummed with the sweet blood of cider. These produced pippins; these produced russets; these produced luscious harvest apples, that fell in August bursting with juicy ripeness. Then he showed me another bagful which were not apple seeds at all, but neutral colored specks moving with fluid swiftness as he poured them from palm to palm.

"Do you know what this is?"

I told him I didn't.

"It's dogfennel seed."

I laughed, and asked him what kind of apples it bore.

Johnny Appleseed smiled at me again.

"It's a flower. I'm spreading it over the whole of Ohio and Indiana! It'll come up like the stars for abundance, and fill the land with rankness, and fever and ague will flee away!"

"But how about the rankness?"

"Fever and ague will flee away," he repeated, continuing his search through the bags.

He next brought out a parcel, wrapped up carefully in doeskin to protect it from the appleseeds; and turned foolish in the face, as bits of ribbon and calico fell out upon his knees.

"This isn't the one," he said, bundling it up and thrusting it back again. "The little girls, they like to dress their doll-babies, so I carry patches for the little girls. Here's what I was looking for."

It was another doeskin parcel, bound lengthwise and crosswise by thongs. These Johnny Appleseed reverently loosened, bringing forth a small book with wooden covers fastened by a padlock.

III

"Where did you get this?" I heard myself asking, a strange voice sounding far down the throat.

"From an Indian," the mystic told me quietly. "He said it was bad medicine to him. He never had any luck in hunting after it fell to his share, so he was glad to give it to me."

"Where did he get it?"

"His tribe took it from some prisoners they killed."

I was running blindly around in a circle to find relief from the news he dealt me, when the absurdity of such news overtook me. I stood and laughed.

"Who were the prisoners?"

"I don't know," answered Johnny Appleseed.

"How do you know the Indians killed them?"

"The one that gave me this book told me so."

"There are plenty of padlocked books in the world," I said jauntily. "At least there must be more than one. How long ago did it happen?"

"Not very long ago, I think; for the book was clean."

"Give it to me," I said, as if I cursed him.

"It's a sacred book," he answered, hesitating.

"Maybe it's sacred. Let me see."

"There may be holy mysteries in it, to be read only of him who has the key."

"I have a key!"

I took it out of the snuffbox. Johnny Appleseed fixed his rapt eyes on the little object in my fingers.

"Mebby you are the one appointed to open and read what is sealed!"

"No, I'm not! How could my key fit a padlocked book that belonged to prisoners killed by the Indians?"

He held it out to me and I took hold of the padlock. It was a small steel padlock, and the hole looked dangerously the size of my key.

"I can't do it!" I said.

"Let me try," said Johnny Appleseed.

"No! You might break my key in a strange padlock! Hold it still, Johnny. Please don't shake it."

"I'm not shaking it," Johnny Appleseed answered tenderly.

"There's only one way of proving that my key doesn't fit," I said, and thrust it in. The ward turned easily, and the padlock came away in my hand. I dropped it and opened the book. Within the lid a name was written which I had copied a thousand times—"Eagle Madeleine Marie de Ferrier."

Still I did not believe it. Nature protects us in our uttermost losses by a density through which conviction is slow to penetrate. In some mysterious way the padlocked book had fallen into strange hands, and had been carried to America.

"If Eagle were in America, I should know it. For De Chaumont would know it, and Skenedonk would find it out."

I stooped for the padlock, hooked it in place, and locked the book again.

"Is the message to you alone?" inquired Johnny Appleseed.

"Did you ever care for a woman?" I asked him.

Restless misery came into his eyes, and I noticed for the first time that he was not an old man; he could not have been above thirty-five. He made no answer; shifting from one bare foot to the other, his body settling and losing its Indian lightness.

"A woman gave me the key to this book. Her name is written inside the lid. I was to read it if it ever fell into my hands, after a number of years. Somebody has stolen it, and carried it among the Indians. But it's mine. Every shilling in my wallet, the clothes off my back you're welcome to—"

"I don't want your money or your clothes."

"But let me give you something in exchange for it."

"What do I need? I always have as much as I want. This is a serviceable coat, as good as any man need wish for; and the ravens feed me. And if I needed anything, could I take it for carrying a message? I carry good tidings of great joy among the people all the time. This is yours. Put it in your pocket."

I hid the padlocked book in the breast of my coat, and seized his wrist and his hand.

"Be of good courage, white double-man," said Johnny Appleseed. "The Lord lift up the light of His countenance upon you, the Lord make His face to shine upon you and give you peace!"

He returned to his side of the fire and stretched himself under the stars, and I went to Croghan's quarters and lay down with my clothes on in the bunk assigned to me.

The book which I would have rent open at twenty, I now carried unsealed. The suspense of it was so sweet, and drew my thoughts from the other suspense which could not be endured. It was not likely that any person about Mont-Louis had stolen the book, and wandered so far. Small as the volume was, the boards indented my breast and made me increasingly conscious of its presence. I waked in the night and held it.

Next morning Johnny Appleseed was gone from the fort, unafraid of war, bent only on carrying the apple of civilization into the wilderness. Nobody spoke about his absence, for shells began to fall around us. The British and Indians were in sight; and General Proctor sent a flag of truce demanding surrender.

Major Croghan's ensign approached the messenger with a flag in reply.

The women gathered their children as chickens under shelter. All in the fort were cheerful, and the men joked with the gush of humor which danger starts in Americans. I saw then the ready laugh that faced in its season what was called Indian summer, because the Indian took then advantage of the last pleasant weather to make raids. Such pioneers could speak lightly even of powwowing time—the first pleasant February days, when savages held councils before descending on the settlements.

Major Croghan and I watched the parley from one of the blockhouses that bastioned the place. Before it ended a Shawanoe sprang out of a ravine and snatched the ensign's sword. He gave it back reluctantly, and the British flag bearer hurried the American within the gates.

General Proctor regretted that so fine a young man as Major Croghan should fall into the hands of savages, who were not to be restrained.

"When this fort is taken," said Croghan on hearing the message, "there will be nobody left in it to kill."

British gunboats drawn up on the Sandusky river, and a howitzer on the shore, opened fire, and cannonaded all day with the poor execution of long range artillery. The northwestern angle of the fort was their target. Croghan foresaw that the enemy's intention was to make a breach and enter there. When night came again, his one six-pounder was moved with much labor from that angle into the southwest blockhouse, as noiselessly as possible.

He masked the embrasure and had the piece loaded with a double charge of slugs and grape shot and half a charge of powder. Perhaps the British thought him unprovided with any heavy artillery.

They were busy themselves, bringing three of the ineffectual six-pounders and the howitzer, under darkness, within two hundred and fifty yards of the fort; giving a background of woods to their battery. About dawn we saw what they had been doing. They concentrated on the northwest angle; and still Croghan replied only with muskets, waiting for them to storm.

So it went on all day, the gun-proof blockhouse enduring its bombardment, and smoke thickening until it filled the stockade as water fills a well, and settled like fog between us and the enemy. An attack was made on the southern angle where the cannon was masked.

"This is nothing but a feint," Croghan said to the younger officers.

While that corner replied with musketry, he kept a sharp lookout for the safety of the northwest blockhouse.

One soldier was brought down the ladder and carried through the murky pall to the surgeon, who could do nothing for him. Another turned from a loophole with blood upon him, laughing at his mishap. For the grotesqueness and inconvenience of a wound are sometimes more swiftly felt than its pain. He came back presently with his shoulder bandaged and resumed his place at the loophole.

The exhilaration of that powder atmosphere and its heat made soldiers throw off their coats, as if the expanding human body was not to be confined in wrappings.

In such twilight of war the twilight of Nature overtook us. Another feint was made to draw attention from a heavy force of assailants creeping within twenty paces, under cover of smoke, to surprise the northwest blockhouse.

Musketry was directed against them: they hesitated. The commander led a charge, and himself sprang first into the ditch. We saw the fine fellows leaping to carry the blockhouse, every man determined to be first in making a breach. They filled the ditch.

This was the instant for which Croghan had waited. He opened the porthole and unmasked his exactly trained cannon. It enfiladed the assailants, sweeping them at a distance of thirty feet; slugs and grapeshot hissed, spreading fan rays of death! By the flash of the re-loaded six-pounder, we saw the trench filled with dead and wounded.

The besiegers turned.

Croghan's sweating gunners swabbed and loaded and fired, roaring like lions.

The Indians, of whom there were nearly a thousand, were not in the charge, and when retreat began they went in panic. We could hear calls and yells, the clatter of arms, and a thumping of the earth; the strain of men tugging cannon ropes; the swift withdrawal of a routed force.

Two thousand more Indians approaching under Tecumseh, were turned back by refugees.

Croghan remarked, as we listened to the uproar, "Fort Stephenson can hardly be called untenable against heavy artillery."

Then arose cries in the ditch, which penetrated to women's ears. Neither side was able to help the wounded there. But before the rout was complete, Croghan had water let down in buckets to relieve their thirst, and ordered a trench cut under the pickets of the stockade. Through this the poor wretches who were able to crawl came in and surrendered themselves and had their wounds dressed.

By three o'clock in the morning not a British uniform glimmered red through the dawn. The noise of retreat ended. Pistols and muskets strewed the ground. Even a sailboat was abandoned on the river, holding military stores and the clothing of officers.

"They thought General Harrison was coming," laughed Croghan, as he sat down to an early breakfast, having relieved all the living in the trench and detailed men to bury the dead. "We have lost one man, and have another under the surgeon's hands. Now I'm ready to appear before a court-martial for disobeying orders."

"You mean you're ready for your immortal page in history."

"Paragraph," said Croghan; "and the dislike of poor little boys and girls who will stick their fists in their eyes when they have to learn it at school."

Intense manhood ennobled his long, animated face. The President afterwards made him a lieutenant-colonel, and women and his superior officers praised him; but he was never more gallant than when he said:

"My uncle, George Rogers Clark, would have undertaken to hold this fort; and by heavens, we were bound to try it!"

The other young officers sat at mess with him, hilarious over the outcome, picturing General Proctor's state of mind when he learned the age of his conqueror.

None of them cared a rap that Daniel Webster was opposing the war in the House of Representatives at Washington, and declaring that on land it was a failure.

A subaltern came to the mess room door, touching his cap and asking to speak with Major Croghan.

"The men working outside at the trenches saw a boy come up from the ravine, sir, and fall every few steps, so they've brought him in."

"Does he carry a dispatch?"

"No, sir. He isn't more than nine or ten years old. I think he was a prisoner."

"Is he a white boy?"

"Yes, sir, but he's dressed like an Indian."

"I think it unlikely the British would allow the Shawanoes to burden their march with any prisoners."

"Somebody had him, and I'm afraid he's been shot either during the action or in the retreat. He was hid in the ravine."

"Bring him here," said Croghan.

A boy with blue eyes set wide apart, hair clinging brightly and moistly to his pallid forehead, and mouth corners turning up in a courageous smile, entered and stood erect before the officer. He was a well made little fellow. His tiny buckskin hunting shirt was draped with a sash in the Indian fashion, showing the curve of his naked hip. Down this a narrow line of blood was moving. Children of refugees, full of pity, looked through the open door behind him.

"Go to him, Shipp," said Croghan, as the boy staggered. But he waved the ensign back.

"Who are you, my man?" asked the Major.

"I believe," he answered, "I am the Marquis de Ferrier."

IV

He pitched forward, and I was quicker than Ensign Shipp. I set him on my knees, and the surgeon poured a little watered brandy down his throat.

"Paul!" I said to him.

"Stand back," ordered the surgeon, as women followed their children, crowding the room.

"Do you know him, Lazarre?" asked Croghan.

"It's Madame de Ferrier's child."

"Not the baby I used to see at De Chaumont's? What's he doing at Fort Stephenson?"

The women made up my bunk for Paul, and I laid him in it. Each wanted to take him to her care. The surgeon sent them to the cook-house to brew messes for him, and stripped the child, finding a bullet wound in his side. Probing brought nothing out, and I did not ask a single question. The child should live. There could be no thought of anything else. While the surgeon dressed and bandaged that small hole like a sucked-in mouth, I saw the boy sitting on saddle-bags behind me, his arms clipping my waist, while we threaded bowers of horse paths. I had not known how I wanted a boy to sit behind me! No wonder pioneer men were so confident and full of jokes: they had children behind them!

He was burning with fever. His eyes swam in it as he looked at me. He could not eat when food was brought to him, but begged for water, and the surgeon allowed him what the women considered reckless quantities. Over stockades came the August rustle of the forest. Morning bird voices succeeded to the cannon's reverberations.

The surgeon turned everybody out but me, and looked in by times from his hospital of British wounded. I wiped the boy's forehead and gave him his medicine, fanning him all day long. He lay in stupor, and the surgeon said he was going comfortably, and would suffer little. Once in awhile he turned up the corners of his mouth and smiled at me, as if the opiate gave him blessed sensations. I asked the surgeon what I should do in the night if he came out of it and wanted to talk.

"Let him talk," said the doctor briefly.

Unlike the night before, this was a night of silence. Everybody slept, but the sentinels, and the men whose wounds kept them awake; and I was both a sentinel, and a man whose wounds kept him awake.

Paul's little hands were scratched; and there was a stone bruise on the heel he pushed from cover of the blankets. His small body, compact of so much manliness, was fine and sweet. Though he bore no resemblance to his mother, it seemed to me that she lay there for me to tend; and the change was no more an astounding miracle than the change of baby to boy.

I had him all that night for my own, putting every other thought out of mind and absorbing his presence. His forehead and his face lost their burning heat with the coolness of dawn, which blew our shaded candle, flowing from miles of fragrant oaks.

He awoke and looked all around the cabin. I tried to put his opiate into his mouth; but something restrained me. I held his hand to my cheek.

"I like you," he spoke out. "Don't you think my mother is pretty?"

I said I thought his mother was the most beautiful woman in the world. He curled up his mouth corners and gave me a blue-eyed smile.

"My father is not pretty. But he is a gentleman of France."

"Where are they, Paul?"

He turned a look upon me without answering.

"Paul," I said brutally, "tell me where your father and mother are."

He was so far gone that my voice recalled him. He simply knew me as a voice and a presence that he liked.

"With poor old Ernestine," he answered.

"And where is poor old Ernestine?"

He began to shake as if struck with a chill. I drew the blanket closer.

"Paul, you must tell me!"

He shook his head. His mouth worked, and his little breast went into convulsions.

He shrieked and threw himself toward me. "My pretty little mother!"

I held him still in a tight grip. "My darling—don't start your wound!"

I could have beaten myself, but the surgeon afterwards told me the child was dying when he came into the fort. About dawn, when men's lives sink to their lowest ebb with night, his sank away, I smoothed his head and kissed and quieted him. Once he looked into space with blurred eyes, and curled up his mouth corners when I am sure he no longer saw me.

Thus swiftly ended Paul's unaccountable appearance at the fort. It was like the falling of a slain bird out of the sky at my feet. The women were tender with his little body. They cried over him as they washed him for burial. The children went outside the stockade and brought green boughs and August wild flowers, bearing the early autumn colors of gold and scarlet. With these they bedded the child in his plank coffin, unafraid of his waxen sleep.

Before Croghan went to report to his General, he asked me where we should bury the little fellow.

"In the fort, by the southern blockhouse," I answered. "Let Fort Stephenson be his monument. It will stand here forever. The woods around it will be trampled by prowling savages, and later on by prowling white men. Within, nothing will obliterate the place. Give a little fellow a bed here, who died between two countries, and will never be a citizen of either."

"I don't want to make a graveyard of the fort," said Croghan. But he looked at Paul, bent low over him, and allowed him to be buried near the southwest angle.

There the child's bones rest to this day. The town of Fremont in the commonwealth of Ohio has grown up around them. Young children who climb the grassy bastion, may walk above his head, never guessing that a little gentleman of France, who died like a soldier of his wound, lies deeply cradled there.

Before throwing myself down in the dead heaviness which results from continual loss of sleep, I questioned the wounded British soldiers about Paul. None of them had seen him. Straggling bands of Indians continually joined their force. Captives were always a possibility in the savage camp. Paul might have been taken hundreds of miles away.

But I had the padlocked book, which might tell the whole story. With desperate haste that could hardly wait to open the lids, I took it out, wondering at the patience which long self-restraint had bred in me. I was very tired, and stretched my arms across the pillow where Paul's head had lain, to rest one instant. But I must have slept. My hand woke first, and feeling itself empty, grasped at the book. It was gone, and so was the sun.

I got a light and searched, thrusting my arm between the bunk and the log wall. It was not on the floor, or in my breast pocket, or in my saddle-bags.

The robbery was unendurable. And I knew the Indian who had done it. He was the quietest, most stubborn Oneida that ever followed an adopted white man. Why he had taken the book I could not understand. But I was entirely certain that he had taken it out of my hand while I slept. He would not break the padlock and read it, but like a judicious father he would take care of a possibly unwholesome volume himself.

I went out and found the bald-headed and well-beloved wretch. He was sitting with his knees to his chin by the evening log fire.

"Skenedonk," I said, "I want my book."

"Children and books make a woman of you," he responded. "You had enough books at Longmeadow."

"I want it at once," I repeated.

"It's sorcery," he answered.

"It's a letter from Madame de Ferrier, and may tell where she is."

His fawn eyes were startled, but he continued to hug his knees.

"Skenedonk, I can't quarrel with you. You were my friend before I could remember. When you know I am so bound to you, how can you deal me a deadly hurt?"

"White woman sorcery is the worst sorcery. You thought I never saw it. But I did see it. You went after her to Paris. You did not think of being the king. So you had to come back with nothing. That's what woman sorcery does. Now you have power with the tribes. The President sees you are a big man! And she sends a book to you to bewitch you! I knew she sent the book as soon as I saw it."

"Do you think she sent Paul?"

He made no answer.

"Madame de Ferrier does not know I have the book."

"You haven't it," said Skenedonk.

"But you have."

"If she wrote and sent a letter she expected it would be received."

"When I said a letter I meant what is called a journal: the writing down of what happens daily. Johnny Appleseed got the book from an Indian. That is how it was sent to me."

"If you read it you will want to drop everything else and go to find her."

This was the truth, for I was not under military law.

"Where is the book?"

"Down my back," said Skenedonk.

I felt the loose buckskin.

"It isn't there."

"In my front," said Skenedonk.

I ran my hand over his chest, finding nothing but bone and brawn.

"There it is," he said, pointing to a curled wisp of board at the edge of the fire. "I burnt it."

"Then you've finished me."

I turned and left him sitting like an image by the fire.

V

Before I left Fort Stephenson, I wrote a letter to Count de Chaumont, telling him about Paul's death and asking for news of the De Ferriers. The answer I begged him to send to Sandusky, which the British now despaired of taking. But although Skenedonk made a long journey for it twice during the half year, I got no answer.

The dangerous work of the next few months became like a long debauch. Awake, we were dodging betwixt hostile tribes, or dealing with those inclined to peace. Asleep, I was too exhausted to dream. It was a struggle of the white force of civilization with the red sense of justice. I wrestled with Algonquin dialects as I had wrestled with Greek. Ottawas and Chippewas, long friendly to the French, came more readily than other tribes to agreement with Americans.

Wherever I went I pushed the quest that was uppermost in my mind, but without finding any trace of Madame de Ferrier.

From the measure constantly taken betwixt other men of my time and myself, this positive knowledge resulted.

In spite of the fact that many treated me as a prince, I found myself an average man. I had no military genius. In argument, persuasive, graceful—even eloquent—were the adjectives applied to me; not sweeping and powerful. I should have made a jog-trot king, no better than my uncle of Provence; no worse than my uncle of Artois, who would rather saw wood than reign a constitutional monarch, and whom the French people afterward turned out to saw wood. My reign might have been neat; it would never have been gaudily splendid. As an average man, I could well hold my own in the world.

Perry on the lakes, General Jackson in the southwest, Harrison in the west, and Lawrence on the ocean were pushing the war towards its close; though as late as spring the national capital was burned by the British, and a gentleman whom they gaily called "Old Jimmy Madison," temporarily driven out. But the battle on the little river Thames, in October, settled matters in the Northwest.

The next April, after Leipsic, Napoleon Bonaparte was banished to the island of Elba; and Louis XVIII passed from his latest refuge at Hartwell House in England, to London; where the Prince Regent honored him and the whole capital cheered him; and thence to Paris where he was proclaimed king of France. We heard of it in due course, as ships brought news. I was serving with the American forces.

The world is fluid to a boy. He can do and dare anything. But it hardens around a man and becomes a wall through which he must cut. I felt the wall close around me.

In September I was wounded at the battle of Plattsburg on Lake Champlain. Three men, besides the General and the doctor, and my Oneida, showed a differing interest in me, while I lay with a gap under my left arm, in a hospital tent.

First came Count de Chaumont, his face plowed with lines; no longer the trim gentleman, youthfully easy, and in his full maturity, that he had been when I first saw him at close range.

He sat down on a camp seat by my cot, and I asked him before he could speak—

"Where is Madame de Ferrier?"

"She's dead," he answered.

"I don't believe it."

"You're young. I'm going back to France for a while. France will not be what it was under the Empire. I'm tired of most things, however, and my holdings here make me independent of changes there."

"What reason have you to think that she is dead?"

"Do you know the Indiana Territory well?"

"The northern part only."

"It happened in what was called the Pigeon Roost settlement at the fork of the White River. The Kickapoos and Winnebagoes did it. There were about two dozen people in the settlement."

"I asked how you know these things."

"I have some of the best Indian runners that ever trod moccasins, and when I set them to scouting, they generally find what I want;—so I know a great many things."

"But Paul—"

"It's an old custom to adopt children into the tribes. You know your father, Chief Williams, is descended from a white girl who was a prisoner. There were about two dozen people in the settlement, men, women and children.

The majority of the children were dashed against trees. It has been consolation to me to think she did not survive in the hands of savages."

The hidden causes which work out results never worked out a result more improbable. I lay silent, and De Chaumont said,

"Do you remember the night you disappeared from the Tuileries?"

"I remember it."

"You remember we determined not to let the Marquis de Ferrier see Napoleon. When you went down the corridor with Eagle I thought you were luring him. But she told us afterward you were threatened with arrest, and she helped you out of the Tuileries by a private stairway."

"Did it make any stir in the palace?"

"No. I saw one man hurrying past us. But nobody heard of the arrest except Eagle."

"How did she get out?"

"Out of what?"

"The queen's closet."

"She was in the garden. She said she went down the private stairway to avoid the gendarme. She must have done it cleverly, for she came in on the arm of Junot and the matter was not noticed. There stood my emergency facing me again. You had deserted. What made you imagine you were threatened with arrest?"

"Because a gendarme in court dress laid his hand on my shoulder and told me I was to come with him."

"Well, you may have drawn the secret police upon you. You had been cutting a pretty figure. It was probably wise to drop between walls and get out of France. Do you know why you were arrested?"

"I think the groundless charge would have been an attack upon Napoleon."

"You never attacked the emperor!"

"No. But I had every reason to believe such a charge would be sworn against me if I ever came to trial."

"Perhaps that silly dauphin story leaked out in Paris. The emperor does hate a Bourbon. But I thought you had tricked me. And the old marquis never took his eyes off the main issue. He gave Eagle his arm, and was ready to go in and thank the emperor."

"You had to tell him?"

"I had to tell him."

"What did he say?"

"Not a word. All the blood seemed to be drawn out of his veins, and his face fell in. Then it burned red hot, and instead of good friend and benefactor, I saw myself a convict. His big staring blue eyes came out of a film like an owl's, and shot me through. I believe he saw everything I ever did in my life, and my intentions about Eagle most plainly of all. He bowed and wished me good-night, and took her out of the Tuileries."

"But you saw him again?"

"He never let me see him again, or her either. I am certain he forbade her to communicate with us. They did not go back to Mont-Louis. They left their hotel in Paris. I wrote imploring him to hold the estates. My messages were returned. I don't know how he got money enough to emigrate. But emigrate they did; avoiding Castorland, where the Saint-Michels, who brought her up, lived in comfort, and might have comforted her, and where I could have made her life easy. He probably dragged her through depths of poverty, before they joined a company bound for the Indiana Territory, where the Pigeon Roost settlement was planted. I have seen old Saint-Michel work at clearing, and can imagine the Marquis de Ferrier sweating weakly while he chopped trees. It is a satisfaction to know they had Ernestine with them. De Ferrier might have plowed with Eagle," said the count hotly. "He never hesitated to make use of her."

While I had been living a monk's studious, well-provided life, was she toiling in the fields? I groaned aloud.

De Chaumont dropped his head on his breast.

"It hurts me more than I care to let anybody but you know, Lazarre. If I hadn't received that letter I should have avoided you. I wish you had saved Paul. I would adopt him."

"I think not, my dear count."

"Nonsense, boy! I wouldn't let you have him."

"You have a child."

"Her husband has her. But let us not pitch and toss words. No use quarreling over a dead boy. What right have you to Eagle's child?"

"Not your right of faithful useful friendship. Only my own right."

"What's that?"

"Nothing that she ever admitted."

"I was afraid of you," said De Chaumont, "when you flowered out with old Du Plessy, like an heir lost in emigration and found again. You were a startling fellow, dropping on the Faubourg; and anything was possible under the Empire. You know I never believed the dauphin nonsense, but a few who remembered, said you looked like the king. You were the king to her; above mating with the best of the old nobility. She wouldn't have married you."

"Did she ever give you reason to think she would marry you?"

"She never gave me reason to think she would marry anybody. But what's the use of groaning? There's distraction abroad. I took the trails to see you, when I heard you were with the troops on Champlain. I shall be long in France. What can I do for you, my boy?"

"Nothing, count. You have already done much."

"She had a foolish interest in you. The dauphin!—Too good to sit at table with us, you raw savage!—Had to be waited on by old Jean! And she would have had me serve you, myself!"

He laughed, and so did I. We held hands, clinging in fellowship.

"I might not have refused your service; like Marquis de Ferrier."

The count's face darkened.

"I'll not abuse him. He's dead."

"Are you sure he's dead this time, count?"

"A Kickapoo is carrying his scalp. Trust my runners. They have traced him so much for me they know the hair on his stubborn head. I must go where I can have amusement, Lazarre. This country is a young man's country. I'm getting old. Adieu. You're one of the young men."

Some changes of light and darkness passed over me, and the great anguish of my wound increased until there was no rest. However, the next man who visited me stood forth at the side of the stretcher as Bellenger. I thought I dreamed him, being light-headed with fever. He was unaccountably weazened, robbed of juices, and powdering to dust on the surface. His mustache had grown again, and he carried it over his ears in the ridiculous manner affected when I saw him in the fog.

"Where's your potter's wheel?" I inquired.

"In the woods by Lake George, sire."

"Do you still find clay that suits you?"

"Yes, sire."

"Have you made that vase yet?"

"No, sire. I succeed in nothing."

"You succeed in tracking me."

He swam before my eyes, and I pointed to the surgeon's camp-chair.

"Not in your presence, sire."

"Have you lost your real dauphin?" I inquired.

"I have the honor of standing before the real dauphin."

"So you swore at Mittau!"

"I perjured myself."

"Well, what are you doing now?"

"Sire, I am a man in failing health. Before the end I have come to tell you the truth."

"Do you think you can do it?"

"Sire"—said Bellenger.

"Your king is Louis XVIII," I reminded him.

"He is not my king."

"Taken your pension away, has he?"

"I no longer receive anything from that court."

"And your dauphin?"

"He was left in Europe."

"Look here, Bellenger! Why did you treat me so? Dauphin or no dauphin, what harm was I doing you?"

"I thought a strong party was behind you. And I knew there had been double dealing with me. You represented some invisible power tricking me. I was beside myself, and faced it out in Mittau. I have been used shamefully, and thrown aside when I am failing. Hiding out in the hills ruined my health."

"Let us get to facts, if you have facts. Do you know anything about me, Bellenger?"

"Yes, sire."

"Who am I?"

"Louis XVII of France."

"What proof can you give me?"

"First, sire, permit a man who has been made a wretched tool, to implore forgiveness of his rightful sovereign, and a little help to reach a warmer climate before the rigors of a northern winter begin."

"Bellenger, you are entrancing," I said. "Why did I ever take you seriously? Ste. Pélagie was a grim joke, and tipping in the river merely your playfulness. You had better take yourself off now, and keep on walking until you come to a warmer climate."

He wrung his hands with a gesture that touched my natural softness to my enemy.

"Talk, then. Talk, man. What have you to say?"

"This, first, sire. That was a splendid dash you made into France!"

"And what a splendid dash I made out of it again, with a gendarme at my coat tails, and you behind the gendarme!"

"But it was the wrong time. If you were there now;—the French people are so changeable—"

"I shall never be there again. His Majesty the eighteenth Louis is welcome. What the blood stirs in me to know is, have I a right to the throne?"

"Sire, the truth as I know it, I will tell you. You were the boy taken from the Temple prison."

"Who did it?"

"Agents of the royalist party whose names would mean nothing to you if I gave them."

"I was placed in your hands?"

"You were placed in my hands to be taken to America."

"I was with you in London, where two royalists who knew me, recognized me?"

"The two De Ferriers."

"Did a woman named Madame Tank see me?"

Bellenger was startled.

"You were noticed on the ship by a court-lady of Holland; a very clever courtier. I had trouble in evading her. She suspected too much, and asked too many questions; and would have you to play with her baby on the deck, though at that time you noticed nothing."

"But where does the idiot come into my story?"

"Sire, you have been unfortunate, but I have been a victim. When we landed in New York I went directly and made myself known to the man who was to act as purveyor of your majesty's pension. He astonished me by declaring that the dauphin was already there, and had claimed the pension for that year. The country and the language were unknown to me. The agent spoke French, it is true, but we hardly understood each other. I supposed I had nothing to do but present my credentials. Here was another idiot—I crave your majesty's pardon—"

"Quite right—at the time, Bellenger."

—"drawing the annuity intended for the dauphin. I inquired into his rights. The agent showed me papers like my own. I asked who presented them. He knew no more of the man than he did of me. I demanded to face the man. No such person could be found. I demanded to see the idiot. He was shut in a room and fed by a hired keeper. I sat down and thought much. Clearly it was not the agent's affair. He followed instructions. Good! I would follow instructions also. Months would have been required to ask and receive explanations from the court of Monsieur. He had assumed the title of Louis XVIII, for the good of the royalist cause, as if there were no prince. I thought I saw what was expected of me."

"And what did you see, you unspeakable scoundrel?"

"I saw that there was a dauphin too many, hopelessly idiotic. But if he was the one to be guarded, I would guard him."

"Who was that idiot?"

"Some unknown pauper. No doubt of that."

"And what did you do with me?"

"A chief of the Iroquois Indians can tell you that."

"This is a clumsy story, Bellenger. Try again."

"Sire—"

"If you knew so little of the country, how did you find an Iroquois chief?"

"I met him in the woods when he was hunting. I offered to give you to him, pretending you had the annuity from Europe. Sire, I do not know why trickery was practiced on me, or who practiced it: why such pains were taken to mix the clues which led to the dauphin. But afterwards the same agent had orders to give you two-thirds and me only one-third of the yearly sum. I thought the court was in straits;—when both Russia and Spain supported it! I was nothing but a court painter. But when you went to France, I blocked your way with all the ingenuity I could bring."

"I would like to ask you, Bellenger, what a man is called who attempts the life of his king?"

"Sire, the tricks of royalists pitted us against each other."

"That's enough, Bellenger. I don't believe a word you say, excepting that part of your story agreeing with Madame de Ferrier's. Put your hand under my pillow and find my wallet. Now help yourself, and never let me see you again."

He helped himself to everything except a few shillings, weeping because his necessities were so great. But I told him I was used to being robbed, and he had done me all the harm he could; so his turn to pluck me naturally followed.

Then I softened, as I always do towards the claimant of the other part, and added that we were on the same footing; I had been a pensioner myself.

"Sire, I thank you," said Bellenger, having shaken the wallet and poked his fingers into the lining where an unheard-of gold piece could have lodged.

"It tickles my vanity to be called sire."

"You are a true prince," said Bellenger. "My life would be well spent if I could see you restored to your own."

"So I infer, from the valuable days you have spent trying to bring that result about."

"Your majesty is sure of finding support in France."

"The last king liked to tinker with clocks. Perhaps I like to tinker with Indians."

"Sire, it is due to your birth—"

"Never mind my birth," I said. "I'm busy with my life."

He bowed himself out of my presence without turning. This tribute to royalty should have touched me. He took a handsome adieu, and did not afterward seek further reward for his service. I heard in the course of years that he died in New Orleans, confessing much regarding myself to people who cared nothing about it, and thought him crazy. They doubtless had reason, so erratic was the wanderer whom I had first consciously seen through Lake George fog. His behavior was no more incredible than the behavior of other Frenchmen who put a hand to the earlier years of their prince's life.

The third to appear at my tent door was Chief Williams, himself. The surgeon told him outside the tent that it was a dangerous wound. He had little hope for me, and I had indifferent hope myself, lying in torpor and finding it an effort to speak. But after several days of effort I did speak.

The chief sat beside me, concerned and silent.

"Father," I said.

The chief harkened near to my lips.

"Tell me," I begged, after resting, "who brought me to you."

His dark sullen face became tender. "It was a Frenchman," he answered. "I was hunting and met him on the lake with two boys. He offered to give you to me. We had just lost a son."

When I had rested again, I asked:

"Do you know anything else about me?"

"No."

The subject was closed between us. And all subjects were closed betwixt the world and me, for my face turned the other way. The great void of which we know nothing, but which our faith teaches us to bridge, opened for me.

VI

But the chief's and Skenedonk's nursing and Indian remedies brought me face earthward again, reviving the surgeon's hope.

When blood and life mounted, and my torn side sewed up its gap in a healthy scar, adding another to my collection, autumn was upon us. From the hunting lodges on Lake George, and the Williamses of Longmeadow, I went to the scorched capital of Washington. In the end the Government helped me with my Indian plan, though when Skenedonk and I pushed out toward Illinois Territory we had only my pay and a grant of land. Peace was not formally made until December, but the war ended that summer.

Man's success in the world is proportioned to the number of forces he can draw around himself to work with him. I have been able to draw some forces; though in matters where most people protect themselves, I have a quality of asinine patience which the French would not have tolerated.

The Oneidas were ready to follow wherever I led them. And so were many families of the Iroquois federation. But the Mohawk tribe held back. However, I felt confident of material for an Indian state when the foundation should be laid.

We started lightly equipped upon the horse paths. The long journey by water and shore brought us in October to the head of Green Bay. We had seen Lake Michigan, of a light transparent blueness, with fire ripples chasing from the sunset. And we had rested at noon in plum groves on the vast prairies, oases of fertile deserts, where pink and white fruit drops, so ripe that the sun preserves it in its juice. The freshness of the new world continually flowed around us. We shot deer. Wolves sneaked upon our trail. We slept with our heels to the campfire, and our heads on our saddles. Sometimes we built a hunter's shed, open at front and sloping to ground at back. To find out how the wind blew, we stuck a finger in our mouths and held it up. The side which became cold first was the side of the wind.

Physical life riots in the joy of its revival. I was so glad to be alive after touching death that I could think of Madame de Ferrier without pain, and say more confidently—"She is not dead," because resurrection was working in myself.

Green Bay or La Baye, as the fur hunters called it, was a little post almost like a New England village among its elms: one street and a few outlying houses beside the Fox River. The open world had been our tavern; or any sod or log hut cast up like a burrow of human prairie dogs or moles. We did not expect to find a tavern in Green Bay. Yet such a place was pointed out to us near the Fur Company's block warehouse. It had no sign post, and the only visible stable was a pen of logs. Though negro slaves were owned in the Illinois Territory, we saw none when a red-headed man rushed forth shouting:

"Sam, you lazy nigger, come here and take the gentleman's horses! Where is that Sam? Light down, sir, with your Indian, and I will lead your beasts to the hostler myself."

In the same way our host provided a supper and bed with armies of invisible servants. Skenedonk climbed a ladder to the loft with our saddlebags.

"Where is that chambermaid?" cried the tavern keeper.

"Yes, where is she?" said a man who lounged on a bench by the entrance. "I've heard of her so often I would like to see her myself."

The landlord, deaf to raillery, bustled about and spread our table in his public room.

"Corn bread, hominy, side meat, ven'zin," he shouted in the kitchen. "Stir yourself, you black rascal, and dish up the gentleman's supper."

Skenedonk walked boldly to the kitchen door and saw our landlord stewing and broiling, performing the offices of cook as he had performed those of stableman. He kept on scolding and harrying the people who should have been at his command:—"Step around lively, Sam. Tell the gentleman the black bottle is in the fireplace cupboard if he wants to sharpen his appetite. Where is that little nigger that picks up chips? Bring me some more wood from the wood-pile! I'll teach you to go to sleep behind the door!"

Our host served us himself, running with sleeves turned back to admonish an imaginary cook. His tap-room was the fireplace cupboard, and it was visited while we ate our supper, by men in elkskin trousers, and caps and hooded capotes of blue cloth. These Canadians mixed their own drink, and made a cross-mark on the inside of the cupboard door, using a system of bookkeeping evidently agreed upon between themselves and the landlord. He shouted for the lazy barkeeper, who answered nothing out of nothingness.

Nightfall was very clear and fair in this Northwestern territory. A man felt nearer to the sunset. The region took hold upon me: particularly when one who was neither a warehouseman nor a Canadian fur hunter, hurried in and took me by the hand.

"I am Pierre Grignon," he said.

Indeed, if he had held his fiddle, and tuned it upon an arm not quite so stout, I should have known without being told that he was the man who had played in the Saint-Michel cabin while Annabel de Chaumont climbed the chimney.

We sat and talked until the light faded. The landlord brought a candle, and yelled up the loft, where Skenedonk had already stretched himself in his blanket, as he loved to do:

"Chambermaid, light up!"

"You drive your slaves too hard, landlord," said Pierre Grignon.

"You'd think I hadn't any, Mr. Grignon; for they're never in the way when they're wanted."

"One industrious man you certainly have."

"Yes, Sam is a good fellow; but I'll have to go out and wake him up and make him rub the horses down."

"Never mind," said Pierre Grignon. "I'm going to take these travelers home with me."

"Now I know how a tavern ought to be kept," said the landlord. "But what's the use of my keeping one if Pierre Grignon carries off all the guests?"

"He is my old friend," I told the landlord.

"He's old friend to everybody that comes to Green Bay. I'll never get so much as a sign painted to hang in front of the Palace Tavern."

I gave him twice his charges and he said:

"What a loss it was to enterprise in the Bay when Pierre Grignon came here and built for the whole United States!"

The Grignon house, whether built for the whole United States or not, was the largest in Green Bay. Its lawn sloped down to the Fox River. It was a huge square of oak timbers, with a detached kitchen, sheltered by giant elms. To this day it stands defying time with its darkening frame like some massive rock, the fan windows in the gables keeping guard north and south.

A hall divided the house through the center, and here Madame Grignon welcomed me as if I were a long-expected guest, for this was her custom; and as soon as she clearly remembered me, led me into a drawing-room where a stately old lady sat making lace.

This was the grandmother of the house. Such a house would have been incomplete without a grandmother at the hearth.

The furniture of this hall or family room had been brought from Montreal; spindle chairs and a pier table of mahogany; a Turkey carpet, laid smoothly on the polished floor to be spurned aside by young dancers there; some impossible sea pictures, with patron saints in the clouds over mariners; an immense stuffed sofa, with an arm dividing it across the center;—the very place for those head to head conversations with young men which the girls of the house called "twosing." It was, in fact, the favorite "twosing" spot of Green Bay.

Stools there were for children, and armchairs for old people were not lacking. The small yellow spinning wheel of Madame Ursule, as I found afterwards Madame Grignon was commonly called, stood ready to revolve its golden disk wherever she sat.

The servants were Pawnee Indians, moving about their duties almost with stealth.

The little Grignon daughter who had stood lost in wonder at the dancing of Annabel de Chaumont, was now a turner of heads herself, all flaxen white, and contrasting with the darkness of Katarina Tank. Katarina was taken home to the Grignon's after her mother's death. Both girls had been educated in Montreal.

The seigniorial state in which Pierre Grignon lived became at once evident. I found it was the custom during Advent for all the villagers to meet in his house and sing hymns. On Christmas day his tables were loaded for everybody who came. If any one died, he was brought to Pierre Grignon's for prayer, and after his burial, the mourners went back to Pierre Grignon's for supper. Pierre Grignon and his wife were god-father and god-mother to most of the children born at La Baye. If a child was left without father and mother, Pierre Grignon's house became its asylum until a home could be found for it. The few American officers stationed at the old stockade, nearly every evening met the beauties of Green Bay at Pierre Grignon's, and if he did not fiddle for them he led Madame in the dancing. The grandmother herself sometimes took her stick and stepped through a measure to please the young people. Laughter and the joy of life filled the house every waking hour of the twenty-four. Funerals were never horrible there. Instead, they seemed the mystic beginning of better things.

"Poor Madame Tank! She would have been so much more comfortable in her death if she had relieved her mind," Madame Ursule said, the first evening, as we sat in a pause of the dancing. "She used to speak of you often, for seeing you made a great impression upon her, and she never let us forget you. I am sure she knew more about you than she ever told me. 'I have an important disclosure to make,' she says. 'Come around me, I want all of you to hear it!' Then she fell back and died without telling it."

A touch of mystery was not lacking to the house. Several times I saw the tail of a gray gown disappear through an open door. Some woman half entered and drew back.

"It's Madeleine Jordan," an inmate told me each time. "She avoids strangers."

I asked if Madeleine Jordan was a relative.

"Oh, no," Madame Ursule replied; "but the family who brought her here, went back to Canada, and of course they left her with us."

Of course Madeleine Jordan, or anybody else who lacked a roof, would be left with the Grignons; but in that house a hermit seemed out of place, and I said so to Madame Ursule.

"Poor child!" she responded. "I think she likes the bustle and noise. She is not a hermit. What difference can it make to her whether people are around her or not?"

The subject of Madeleine Jordan was no doubt beyond a man's handling. I had other matters to think about, and directly plunged into them. First the Menominees and Winnebagoes must be assembled in council. They held all the desirable land.

"We don't like your Indian scheme in Green Bay," said Pierre Grignon. "But if the tribes here are willing to sell their lands, other settlers can't prevent it."

He went with me to meet the savages on the opposite side of the Fox near the stockade. There the talking and eating lasted two days. At the end of that time I had a footing for our Iroquois in the Wisconsin portion of the Illinois Territory; and the savages who granted it danced a war dance in our honor. Every brave shook over his head the scalps he had taken. I saw one cap of soft long brown hair.

"Eh!" said Pierre Grignon, sitting beside me. "Their dirty trophies make you ghastly! Do your eastern tribes never dance war dances?"

After the land was secured its boundaries had to be set. Then my own grant demanded attention; and last, I was anxious to put my castle on it before snow flew. Many of those late autumn nights Skenedonk and I spent camping. The outdoor life was a joy to me. Our land lay up the Fox River and away from the bay. But more than one stormy evening, when we came back to the bay for supplies, I plunged into the rolling water and swam breasting the waves. It is good to be hardy, and sane, and to take part in the visible world, whether you are great and have your heart's desire or not.

When we had laid the foundation of the Indian settlement, I built my house with the help of skilled men. It was a spacious one of hewn logs, chinked with cat-and-clay plaster, showing its white ribs on the hill above the Fox. In time I meant to cover the ribs with perennial vines. There was a spring near the porches. The woods banked me on the rear, and an elm spread its colossal umbrella over the roof. Fertile fields stretched at my left, and on my right a deep ravine lined with white birches, carried a stream to the Fox.

From my stronghold to the river was a long descent. The broadening and narrowing channel could be seen for miles. A bushy island, beloved of wild ducks, parted the water, lying as Moses hid in osiers, amidst tall growths of wild oats. Lily pads stretched their pavements in the oats. Beyond were rolling banks, and beyond those, wooded hills rising terrace over terrace to the dawn. Many a sunrise was to come to me over those hills. Oaks and pines and sumach gathered to my doorway.

In my mind I saw the garden we afterward created; with many fruit trees, beds, and winding walks, trellised seats, squares of flaming tulips, phlox, hollyhocks, roses. It should reach down into the ravine, where humid ferns and rocks met plants that love darkling ground. Yet it should not be too dark. I would lop boughs rather than have a growing thing spindle as if rooted in Ste. Pélagie!—and no man who loves trees can do that without feeling the knife at his heart. What is long developing is precious like the immortal part of us.

The stoicism that comes of endurance has something of death in it. I prepared a home without thought of putting any wife therein. I had grown used to being alone, with the exception of Skenedonk's taciturn company. The house was for castle and resting place after labor. I took satisfaction in the rude furniture we made for it. In after years it became filled with rich gifts from the other side of the world, and books that have gladdened my heart. Yet in its virginhood, before pain or joy or achievement had entered there, before spade struck the ground which was to send up food, my holding on the earth's surface made me feel prince of a principality.

The men hewed a slab settle, and stationed it before the hearth, a thing of beauty in its rough and lichen-tinted barks, though you may not believe it. My floors I would have smooth and neatly joined, of hard woods which give forth a shining for wear and polish. Stools I had, easily made, and one large round of a tree for my table, like an Eastern tabouret.

Before the river closed and winter shut in, Skenedonk and I went back to Green Bay. I did not know how to form my household, and had it in mind to consult Madame Ursule. Pawnees could be had: and many French landholders in the territory owned black slaves. Pierre Grignon himself kept one little negro like a monkey among the stately Indians.

Dealing with acres, and with people wild as flocks, would have been worth while if nothing had resulted except our welcome back to Pierre Grignon's open house. The grandmother hobbled on her stick across the floor to give me her hand. Madame Ursule reproached me with delaying, and Pierre said it was high time to seek winter quarters. The girls recounted harvest reels and even weddings, with dances following, which I had lost while away from the center of festivity.

The little negro carried my saddlebags to the guest room. Skenedonk was to sleep on the floor. Abundant preparations for the evening meal were going forward in the kitchen. As I mounted the stairway at Madame Ursule's direction, I heard a tinkle of china, her very best, which adorned racks and dressers. It was being set forth on the mahogany board.

The upper floor of Pierre Grignon's house was divided by a hall similar to the one below. I ran upstairs and halted.

Standing with her back to the fading light which came through one fan window at the hall end, was a woman's figure in a gray dress. I gripped the rail.

My first thought was: "How shall I tell her about Paul?" My next was: "What is the matter with her?"

She rippled from head to foot in the shiver of rapture peculiar to her, and stretched her arms to me crying:

"Paul! Paul!"

VII

"Oh, Madame!" I said, bewildered, and sick as from a stab. It was no comfort that the high lady who scarcely allowed me to kiss her hand before we parted, clung around my neck. She trembled against me.

"Have you come back to your mother, Paul?"

"Eagle!" I pleaded. "Don't you know me? You surely know Lazarre!"

She kissed me, pulling my head down in her arms, the velvet mouth like a baby's, and looked straight into my eyes.

"Madame, try to understand! I am Louis! If you forget Lazarre, try to remember Louis!"

She heard with attention, and smiled. The pressure of my arms spoke to her. A man's passion addressed itself to a little child. All other barriers which had stood between us were nothing to this. I held her, and she could never be mine. She was not ill in body; the contours of her upturned face were round and softened with much smiling. But mind-sickness robbed me of her in the moment of finding her.

"She can't be insane!" I said aloud. "Oh, God, anything but that! She was not a woman that could be so wrecked."

Like a fool I questioned, and tried to get some explanation.

Eagle smoothed my arm, nested her hand in my neck.

"My little boy! He has grown to be a man—while his mother has grown down to be a child! Do you know what I am now, Paul?"

I choked a sob in my throat and told her I did not.

"I am your Cloud-Mother. I live in a cloud. Do you love me while I am in the cloud?"

I told her I loved her with all my strength, in the cloud or out of it.

"Will you take care of me as I used to take care of you?"

I swore to the Almighty that she should be my future care.

"I need you so! I have watched for you in the woods and on the water, Paul! You have been long coming back to me."

I heard Madame Ursule mounting the stairs to see if my room was in order.

Who could understand the relation in which Eagle and I now stood, and the claim she made upon me? She clung to my arm when I took it away. I led her by the hand. Even this sight caused Madame Ursule a shock at the head of the stairs.

"M's'r Williams!"

My hostess paused and looked at us.

"Did she come to you of her own accord?"

"Yes, madame."

"I never knew her to notice a stranger before."

"Madame, do you know who this is?"

"Madeleine Jordan."

"It is the Marquise de Ferrier."

"The Marquise de Ferrier?"

"Yes, madame."

"Did you know her?"

"I have known her ever since I can remember."

"The Marquise de Ferrier! But, M's'r Williams, did she know you?"

"She knows me," I asserted. "But not as myself. I am sure she knows me! But she confuses me with the child she lost! I cannot explain to you, madame, how positive I am that she recognizes me; any more than I can explain why she will call me Paul. I think I ought to tell you, so you will see the position in which I am placed, that this lady is the lady I once hoped to marry."

"Saints have pity, M's'r Williams!"

"I want to ask you some questions."

"Bring her down to the fire. Come, dear child," said Madame Ursule, coaxing Eagle. "Nobody is there. The bedrooms can never be so warm as the log fire; and this is a bitter evening."

The family room was unlighted by candles, as often happened. For such an illumination in the chimney must have quenched any paler glare. We had a few moments of brief privacy from the swarming life which constantly passed in and out.

I placed Eagle by the fire and she sat there obediently, while I talked to Madame Ursule apart.

"Was her mind in this state when she came to you?"

"She was even a little wilder than she is now. The girls have been a benefit to her."

"They were not afraid of her?"

"Who could be afraid of the dear child? She is a lady—that's plain. Ah, M's'r Williams, what she must have gone through!"

"Yet see how happy she looks!"

"She always seemed happy enough. She would come to this house. So when the Jordans went to Canada, Pierre and I both said, 'Let her stay.'"

"Who were the Jordans?"

"The only family that escaped with their lives from the massacre when she lost her family. Madame Jordan told me the whole story. They had friends among the Winnebagoes who protected them."

"Did they give her their name?"

"No, the people in La Baye did that. We knew she had another name. But I think it very likely her title was not used in the settlement where they lived. Titles are no help in pioneering."

"Did they call her Madeleine?"

"She calls herself Madeleine."

"How long has she been with your family?"

"Nearly a year."

"Did the Jordans tell you when this change came over her?"

"Yes. It was during the attack when her child was taken from her. She saw other children killed. The Indians were afraid of her. They respect demented people; not a bit of harm was done to her. They let her alone, and the Jordans took care of her."

The daughter and adopted daughter of the house came in with a rush of outdoor air, and seeing Eagle first, ran to kiss her on the cheek one after the other.

"Madeleine has come down!" said Marie.

"I thought we should coax her in here sometime," said Katarina.

Between them, standing slim and tall, their equal in height, she was yet like a little sister. Though their faces were unlined, hers held a divine youth.

To see her stricken with mind-sickness, and the two girls who had done neither good nor evil, existing like plants in sunshine, healthy and sound, seemed an iniquitous contrast.

If ever woman was made for living and dying in one ancestral home, she was that woman. Yet she stood on the border of civilization, without a foothold to call her own. If ever woman was made for one knightly love which would set her in high places, she was that woman. Yet here she stood, her very name lost, no man so humble as to do her reverence.

"Paul has come," Eagle told Katarina and Marie. Holding their hands, she walked between them toward me, and bade them notice my height. "I am his Cloud-Mother," she said. "How droll it is that parents grow down little, while their children grow up big!"

Madame Ursule shook her head pitifully. But the girls really saw the droll side and laughed with my Cloud-Mother.

Separated from me by an impassable barrier, she touched me more deeply than when I sued her most. The undulating ripple which was her peculiar expression of joy was more than I could bear. I left the room and was flinging myself from the house to walk in the chill wind; but she caught me.

"I will be good!" pleaded my Cloud-Mother, her face in my breast.

Her son who had grown up big, while she grew down little, went back to the family room with her.

My Cloud-Mother sat beside me at table, and insisted on cutting up my food for me. While I tried to eat, she asked Marie and Katarina and Pierre Grignon and Madame Ursule to notice how well I behaved. The tender hearted host wiped his eyes.

I understood why she had kept such hold upon me through years of separateness. A nameless personal charm, which must be a gift of the spirit, survived all wreck and change. It drew me, and must draw me forever, whether she knew me again or not. One meets and wakes you to vivid life in an immortal hour. Thousands could not do it through eternity.

The river piled hillocks of water in a strong north wind, and no officer crossed from the stockade. Neither did any neighbor leave his own fire. It seldom happened that the Grignons were left with inmates alone. Eagle sat by me and watched the blaze streaming up the chimney.

If she was not a unit in the family group and had no part there, they were most kind to her.

"Take care!" the grandmother cried with swift forethought when Marie and Katarina marshaled in a hopping object from the kitchen. "It might frighten Madeleine."

Pierre Grignon stopped in the middle of a bear hunt. Eagle was not frightened. She clapped her hands.

"This is a pouched turkey!" Marie announced, leaning against the wall, while Katarina chased the fowl. It was the little negro, his arms and feet thrust into the legs of a pair of Pierre Grignon's trousers, and the capacious open top fastened upon his back. Doubled over, he waddled and hopped as well as he could. A feather duster was stuck in for a tail, and his woolly head gave him the uncanny look of a black harpy. To see him was to shed tears of laughter. The pouched turkey enjoyed being a pouched turkey. He strutted and gobbled, and ran at the girls; tried to pick up corn from the floor with his thick lips, tumbling down and rolling over in the effort; for a pouched turkey has no wings with which to balance himself. So much hilarity in the family room drew the Pawnee servants. I saw their small dark eyes in a mere line of open door, gazing solemnly.

When the turkey was relieved from his pouching and sent to bed, Pierre Grignon took his violin. The girls answered with jigs that ended a reel, when couples left the general figure to jig it off.

When Eagle had watched them awhile she started up, spread her skirts in a sweeping courtesy, and began to dance a gavotte. The fiddler changed his tune, and the girls rested and watched her. Alternately swift and languid, with the changes of the movement, she saluted backward to the floor, or spun on the tips of rapid feet. I had seen her dance many times, but never with such abandon of joy.

Our singular relationship was established in the house, where hospitality made room and apology for all human weakness.

Nobody of that region, except the infirm, stayed indoors to shiver by a fire. Eagle and the girls in their warm capotes breasted with me the coldest winter days. She was as happy as they were; her cheeks tingled as pink as theirs. Sometimes I thought her eyes must answer me with her old self-command; their bright grayness was so natural.

I believed if her delusions were humored, they would unwind from her like the cloud which she felt them to be. The family had long fallen into the habit of treating her as a child, playing some imaginary character. She seemed less demented than walking in a dream, her faculties asleep. It was somnambulism rather than madness. She had not the expression of insane people, the shifty eyes, the cunning and perverseness, the animal and torpid presence.

If I called her Madame de Ferrier instead of my Cloud-Mother, a strained and puzzled look replaced her usual satisfaction. I did not often use the name, nor did I try to make her repeat my own. It was my daily effort to fall in with her happiness, for if she saw any anxiety she was quick to plead:

"Don't you like me any more, Paul? Are you tired of me, because I am a Cloud-Mother?"

"No," I would answer. "Lazarre will never be tired of you."

"Do you think I am growing smaller? Will you love me if I shrink to a baby?"

"I will love you."

"I used to love you when you were so tiny, Paul, before you knew how to love me back. If I forget how"—she clutched the lapels of my coat—"will you leave me then?"

"Eagle, say this: 'Lazarre cannot leave me.'"

"Lazarre cannot leave me."

I heard her repeating this at her sewing. She boasted to Marie Grignon—"Lazarre cannot leave me!—Paul taught me that."

My Cloud-Mother asked me to tell her the stories she used to tell me. She had forgotten them.

"I am the child now," she would say. "Tell me the stories."

I repeated mythical tribe legends, gathered from Skenedonk on our long rides, making them as eloquent as I could. She listened, holding her breath, or sighing with contentment.

If any one in the household smiled when she led me about by the hand, there was a tear behind the smile.

She kept herself in perfection, bestowing unceasing care upon her dress, which was always gray.

"I have to wear gray; I am in a cloud," she had said to the family.

"We have used fine gray stuff brought from Holland, and wools that Mother Ursule got from Montreal," Katarina told me. "The Pawnees dye with vegetable colors. But they cannot make the pale gray she loves."

Eagle watched me with maternal care. If a hair dropped on my collar she brushed it away, and smoothed and settled my cravat. The touch of my Cloud-Mother, familiar and tender, like the touch of a wife, charged through me with torture, because she was herself so unconscious of it.

Before I had been in the house a week she made a little pair of trousers a span long, and gave them to me. Marie and Katarina turned their faces to laugh. My Cloud-Mother held the garment up for their inspection, and was not at all sensitive to the giggles it provoked.

"I made over an old pair of his father's," she said.

The discarded breeches used by the pouched turkey had been devoted to her whim. Every stitch was neatly set. I praised her beautiful needlework, and she said she would make me a coat.

Skenedonk was not often in the house. He took to the winter hunting and snow-shoeing with vigor. Whenever he came indoors I used to see him watching Madame de Ferrier with saturnine wistfulness. She paid no attention to him. He would stand gazing at her while she sewed; being privileged as an educated Indian and my attendant, to enter the family room where the Pawnees came only to serve. They had the ample kitchen and its log fire to themselves. I wondered what was working in Skenedonk's mind, and if he repented calling one so buffeted, a sorceress.

Kindly ridicule excited by the incongruous things she did, passed over without touching her. She was enveloped in a cloud, a thick case guarding overtaxed mind and body, and shutting them in its pellucid chrysalis. The Almighty arms were resting her on a mountain of vision. She had forgot how to weep. She was remembering how to laugh.

The more I thought about it the less endurable it became to have her dependent upon the Grignons. My business affairs with Pierre Grignon made it possible to transfer her obligations to my account. The hospitable man and his wife objected, but when they saw how I took it to heart, gave me my way. I told them I wished her to be regarded as my wife, for I should never have another; and while it might remain impossible for her to marry me, on my part I was bound to her.

"You are young, M's'r Williams," said Madame Ursule. "You have a long life before you. A man wants comfort in his house. And if he makes wealth, he needs a hand that knows how to distribute and how to save. She could never go to your home as she is."

"I know it, madame."

"You will change your mind about a wife."

"Madame, I have not changed my mind since I first wanted her. It is not a mind that changes."

"Well, that's unusual. Young men are often fickle. You never made proposals for her?"

"I did, madame, after her husband died."

"But she was still a wife—the wife of an old man—in the Pigeon Roost settlement."

"Her father married her to a cousin nearly as old as himself, when she was a child. Her husband was reported dead while he was in hiding. She herself thought, and so did her friends, that he was dead."

"I see. Eh! these girls married to old men! Madame Jordan told me Madeleine's husband was very fretful. He kept himself like silk, and scarcely let the wind blow upon him for fear of injuring his health. When other men were out toiling at the clearings, he sat in his house to avoid getting chills and fever in the sun. It was well for her that she had a faithful servant. Madeleine and the servant kept the family with their garden and corn field. They never tasted wild meat unless the other settlers brought them venison. Madame Jordan said they always returned a present of herbs and vegetables from their garden. It grew for them better than any other garden in the settlement. Once the old man did go out with a hunting party, and got lost. The men searched for him three days, and found him curled up in a hollow tree, waiting to be brought in. They carried him home on a litter and he popped his head into the door and said: 'Here I am, child! You can't kill me!'"

"What did Madame de Ferrier say?"

"Nothing. She made a child of him, as if he were her son. He was in his second childhood, no doubt. And Madame Jordan said she appeared to hold herself accountable for the losses and crosses that made him so fretful. The children of the emigration were brought up to hardship, and accepted everything as their elders could not do."

"I thought the Marquis de Ferrier a courteous gentleman."

"Did you ever see him?"

"Twice only."

"He used to tell his wife he intended to live a hundred years. And I suppose he would have done it, if he had not been tomahawked and scalped. 'You'll never get De Chaumont,' he used to say to her. 'I'll see that he never gets you!' I remember the name very well, because it was the name of that pretty creature who danced for us in the cabin on Lake George."

"De Chaumont was her father," I said. "He would have married Madame de Ferrier, and restored her estate, if she had accepted him, and the marquis had not come back."

"Saints have pity!" said Madame Ursule. "And the poor old man must make everybody and himself so uncomfortable!"

"But how could he help living?"

"True enough. God's times are not ours. But see what he has made of her!"

I thought of my Cloud-Mother walking enclosed from the world upon a height of changeless youth. She could not feel another shock. She was past both ambition and poverty. If she had ever felt the sweet anguish of love—Oh! she must have understood when she kissed me and said: "I will come to you sometime!"—the anguish—the hoping, waiting, expecting, receiving nothing, all were gone by. Even mother cares no longer touched her. Paul was grown. She could not be made anything that was base. Unseen forces had worked with her and would work with her still.

"You told me," I said to Madame Ursule, "the Indians were afraid of her when they burned the settlement. Was the change so sudden?"

"Madame Jordan's story was like this: It happened in broad daylight. Two men went into the woods hunting bee trees. The Indians caught and killed them within two miles of the clearing—some of those very Winnebagoes you treated with for your land. It was a sunshiny day in September. You could hear the poultry crowing, and the children playing in the dooryards. Madeleine's little Paul was never far away from her. The Indians rushed in with yells and finished the settlement in a few minutes. Madame Jordan and her family were protected, but she saw children dashed against trees, and her neighbors struck down and scalped before she could plead for them. And little good pleading would have done. An Indian seized Paul. His father and the old servant lay dead across the doorstep. His mother would not let him go. The Indian dragged her on her knees and struck her on the head. Madame Jordan ran out at the risk of being scalped herself, and got the poor girl into her cabin. The Indian came back for Madeleine's scalp. Madeleine did not see him. She never seemed to notice anybody again. She stood up quivering the whole length of her body, and laughed in his face. It was dreadful to hear her above the cries of the children. The Indian went away like a scared hound. And none of the others would touch her."

After I heard this story I was thankful every day that Eagle could not remember; that natural happiness had its way with her elastic body.

Madame Ursule told me the family learned to give her liberty. She rowed alone upon the river, and went where she pleased. The men in La Baye would step aside for her. Strangers disturbed her by bringing the consciousness of something unusual.

Once I surprised Marie and Katarina sitting close to the fire at twilight, talking about lovers. Eagle was near them on a stool.

"That girl," exclaimed Katarina, speaking of the absent with strong disapproval, "is one of the kind that will let another girl take her sweetheart and then sit around and look injured! Now if she could get him from me she might have him! But she'd have to get him first!"

Eagle listened in the attitude of a young sister, giving me to understand by a look that wisdom flowed, and she was learning.

We rose one morning to find the world buried in snow. The river was frozen and its channel padded thick. As for the bay, stretches of snow fields, with dark pools and broken gray ridges met ice at the end of the world.

It was so cold that paper stuck to the fingers like feathers, and the nails tingled with frost. The white earth creaked under foot, and when a sled went by the snow cried out in shrill long resistance, a spirit complaining of being trampled. Explosions came from the river, and elm limbs and timbers of the house startled us. White fur clothed the inner key holes. Tree trunks were black as ink against a background of snow. The oaks alone kept their dried foliage, which rattled like many skeletons, instead of rustling in its faded redness, because there was no life in it.

But the colder it grew the higher Grignon's log fires mounted. And when channels were cut in the snow both along the ridge above Green Bay, and across country in every direction, French trains moved out with jangling bells, and maids and men uttered voice sounds which spread as by miracle on the diffusing air from horizon to horizon. You could hear the officers speaking across the river; and dogs were like to shake the sky down with their barking. Echoes from the smallest noises were born in that magnified, glaring world.

The whole festive winter spun past. Marie and Katarina brought young men to the peaks of hope in the "twosing" seat, and plunged them down to despair, quite in the American fashion. Christmas and New Year's days were great festivals, when the settlement ate and drank at Pierre Grignon's expense, and made him glad as if he fathered the whole post. Madame Grignon spun and looked to the house. And a thousand changes passed over the landscape. But in all that time no one could see any change in my Cloud-Mother. She sewed like a child. She laughed, and danced gavottes. She trod the snow, or muffled in robes, with Madame Ursule and the girls, flew over it in a French train; a sliding box with two or three horses hitched tandem. Every evening I sat by her side at the fire, while she made little coats and trousers for me. But remembrance never came into her eyes. The cloud stood round about her as it did when I first tried to penetrate it.

My own dim days were often in mind. I tried to recall sensations. But I had lived a purely physical life. Her blunders of judgment and delusion of bodily shrinking were no part of my experience. The thinking self in me had been paralyzed. While the thinking self in her was alive, in a cloud. Both of us were memoryless, excepting her recollection of Paul.

After March sent the ice out of river and bay, spring came with a rush as it comes in the north. Perhaps many days it was silently rising from tree roots. In February we used to say:—"This air is like spring." But after such bold speech the arctic region descended upon us again, and we were snowed in to the ears. Yet when the end of March unlocked us, it seemed we must wait for the month of Mary to give us soft air and blue water. Then suddenly it was spring, and every living soul knew it. Life revived with passion. Longings which you had forgotten came and took you by the throat, saying, "You shall no longer be satisfied with negative peace. Rouse, and live!" Then flitting, exquisite, purple flaws struck across milk-opal water in the bay. Fishing boats lifted themselves in mirage, sailing lightly above the water; and islands sat high, with a cushion of air under them.

The girls manifested increasing interest in what they called the Pigeon Roost settlement affair. Madame Ursule had no doubt told them what I said. They pitied my Cloud-Mother and me with the condescending pity of the very young, and unguardedly talked where they could be heard.

"Oh, she'll come to her senses some time, and he'll marry her of course," was the conclusion they invariably reached; for the thing must turn out well to meet their approval. How could they foresee what was to happen to people whose lives held such contrasts?

"Father Pierre says he's nearly twenty-eight; I call him an old bachelor," declared Katarina; "and she was a married woman. They are really very old to be in love."

"You don't know what you'll do when you are old," said Marie.

"Ah, I dread it," groaned Katarina.

"So do I."

"But there is grandmother. She doesn't mind it. And beaux never trouble her now."

"No," sighed the other. "Beaux never trouble her now."

Those spring days I was wild with restlessness. Life revived to dare things. We heard afterwards that about that time the meteor rushed once more across France. Napoleon landed at a Mediterranean port, gathering force as he marched, swept Louis XVIII away like a cobweb in his path, and moved on to Waterloo. The greatest Frenchman that ever lived fell ultimately as low as St. Helena, and the Bourbons sat again upon the throne. But the changes of which I knew nothing affected me in the Illinois Territory.

Sometimes I waked at night and sat up in bed, hot with indignation at the injustice done me, which I could never prove, which I did not care to combat, yet which unreasonably waked the fighting spirit in me. Our natures toss and change, expand or contract, influenced by invisible powers we know not why.

One April night I sat up in the veiled light made by a clouded moon. Rain points multiplied themselves on the window glass; I heard their sting. The impulse to go out and ride the wind, or pick the river up and empty it all at once into the bay, or tear Eagle out of the cloud, or go to France and proclaim myself with myself for follower; and other feats of like nature, being particularly strong in me, I struck the pillow beside me with my fist. Something bounced from it on the floor with a clack like wood. I stretched downward from one of Madame Ursule's thick feather beds, and picked up what brought me to my feet. Without letting go of it I lighted my candle. It was the padlocked book which Skenedonk said he had burned.

And there the scoundrel lay at the other side of the room, wrapped in his blanket from head to foot, mummied by sleep. I wanted to take him by the scalp lock and drag him around on the floor.

He had carried it with him, or secreted it somewhere, month after month. I could imagine how the state of the writer worked on his Indian mind. He repented, and was not able to face me, but felt obliged to restore what he had withheld. So waiting until I slept, he brought forth the padlocked book and laid it on the pillow beside my head; thus beseeching pardon, and intimating that the subject was closed between us.

I got my key, and then a fit of shivering seized me. I put the candle stand beside the pillow and lay wrapped in bedding, clenching the small chilly padlock and sharp-cornered boards. Remembering the change which had come upon the life recorded in it, I hesitated. Remembering how it had eluded me before, I opened it.

The few entries were made without date. The first pages were torn out, crumpled, and smoothed and pasted to place again. Rose petals and violets and some bright poppy leaves, crushed inside its lids, slid down upon the bedcover.

VIII

The padlocked book   In this book I am going to write you, Louis, a letter which will never be delivered; because I shall burn it when it is finished. Yet that will not prevent my tantalizing you about it. To the padlocked book I can say what I want to say. To you I must say what is expedient.

That is a foolish woman who does violence to love by inordinate loving. Yet first I will tell you that I sink to sleep saying, "He loves me!" and rise to the surface saying, "He loves me!" and sink again saying, "He loves me!" all night long.

The days when I see you are real days, finished and perfect, and this is the best of them all. God forever bless in paradise your mother for bearing you. If you never had come to the world I should not have waked to life myself. And why this is I cannot tell. The first time I ever saw your tawny head and tawny eyes, though you did not notice me, I said, "Whether he is the king or not would make no difference." Because I knew you were more than the king to me.

Sire, you told me once you could not understand why people took kindly to you. There is in you a gentle dignity and manhood, most royal. As you come into a room you cast your eyes about unfearing. Your head and shoulders are erect. You are like a lion in suppleness and tawny color, which influences me against my will. You inspire Confidence. Even girls like Annabel, who feel merely at their finger ends, and are as well satisfied with one husband as another, know you to be solid man, not the mere image of a man. Besides these traits there is a power going out from you that takes hold of people invisibly. My father told me there was a man at the court of your father who could put others to sleep by a waving of his hands. I am not comparing you to this charlatan; yet when you touch my hand a strange current runs through me.

When we were in Paris I used to dress myself every morning like a priestess going to serve in a temple. And what was it for? To worship one dear head for half an hour perhaps.

You robbed me of the sight of you for two months.

Sophie Saint-Michel told me to beware of loving a man. To-day he says, "I love you! I need you! I shall go to the devil without you!" To-morrow he turns to his affairs. In six months he says, "I was a fool!" Next year he says, "Who was it that drove me wild for a time last year? What was her name?"

Is love a game where men and women try to outwit each other, and man boasts, "She loves me"—not "I love her"?

You are two persons. Lazarre belongs to me. He follows, he thinks about me. He used to slip past my windows at Lake George, and cast his eyes up at the panes. But Louis is my sovereign. He sees and thinks and acts without me, and his lot is apart from mine.

We are in a ship going to the side of the world where you are. Except that we are going towards you, it is like being pushed off a cliff. All my faith in the appearances of things is at an end. I have been juggled with. I have misjudged.

I could have insisted that we hold Mont-Louis as tenants. The count is our friend. It is not a strong man's fault that a weak man is weak and unfortunate. Yet seeing Cousin Philippe wince, I could not put the daily humiliation upon him. He is like my father come back, broken, helpless. And Paul and I, who are young, must take care of him where he will be least humbled.

I was over-pampered in Mont-Louis and Paris. I like easy living, carriages, long-tailed gowns, jewels, trained servants, music, and spectacles on the stage; a park and wide lands all my own; seclusion from people who do not interest me; idleness in enjoyment.

I am the devil of vanity. Annabel has not half the points I have. When the men are around her I laugh to think I shall be fine and firm as a statue when she is a mass of wrinkles and a wisp of fuzz. When she is a mass of wrinkles and a wisp of fuzz she will be riper and tenderer inside. But will the men see that? No. They will be off after a fresher Annabel. So much for men. On the other hand, I had but a few months of luxury, and may count on the hardness that comes of endurance; for I was an exile from childhood. There is strength in doing the right thing. If there were no God, if Christ had never died on the cross, I should have to do the right thing because it is right.

Why should we lay up grievances against one another? They must disappear, and they only burn our hearts.

Sometimes I put my arms around Ernestine, and rest her old head against me. She revolts. People incline to doubt the superiority of a person who will associate with them. But the closer our poverty rubs us the more Ernestine insists upon class differences.

There should be a colossal mother going about the world to turn men over her lap and give them the slipper. They pine for it.

Am I helping forward the general good, or am I only suffering Nature's punishment?

A woman can fasten the bonds of habit on a man, giving him food from her table, hourly strengthening his care for her. By merely putting herself before him every day she makes him think of her. What chance has an exiled woman against the fearful odds of daily life?

Yet sometimes I think I can wait a thousand years. In sun and snow, in wind and dust, a woman waits. If she stretched her hand and said "Come," who could despise her so much as she would despise herself?

What is so cruel as a man? Hour after hour, day after day, year after year, he presses the iron spike of silence in.

Coward!—to let me suffer such anguish!

Is it because I kissed you? That was the highest act of my life! I groped down the black stairs of the Tuileries blinded by light. Why are the natural things called wrong, and the unnatural ones just?

Is it because I said I would come to you sometime? This is what I meant: that it should give me no jealous pang to think of another woman's head on your breast; that there is a wedlock which appearances cannot touch.

No, I never would—I never would seek you; though sometimes the horror of doing without you turns into reproach. What is he doing? He may need me—and I am letting his life slip away. Am I cheating us both of what could have harmed no one?

It is not that usage is broken off.

Yet if you were to come, I would punish you for coming!

Fine heroic days I tell myself we are marching to meet each other. If the day has been particularly hard, I say, "Perhaps I have carried his load too, and he marches lighter."

You have faults, no doubt, but the only one I could not pardon would be your saying, "I repent!"

The instinct to conceal defeat and pain is so strong in me that I would have my heart cut out rather than own it ached. Yet many women carry all before them by a little judicious whining and rebellion.

I never believe in your unfaith. If you brought a wife and showed her to me I should be sorry for her, and still not believe in your unfaith.

Louis, I have been falling down flat and crawling the ground. Now I am up again. It didn't hurt.

It is the old German fairy story. Every day gold must be spun out of straw. How big the pile of straw looks every morning, and how little the handful of gold every night!

This prairie in the Indiana Territory that I dreaded as a black gulf, is a grassy valley.

I love the garden; and I love to hoe the Indian corn. It springs so clean from the sod, and is a miracle of growth. After the stalks are around my knees, they are soon around my shoulders. The broad leaves have a fragrance, and the silk is sweet as violets.

We wash our clothes in the river. Women who hoe corn, dig in a garden, and wash clothes, earn the wholesome bread of life.

To-day Paul brought the first bluebells of spring, and put them in water for me. They were buds; and when they bloomed out he said, "God has blessed these flowers."

We have to nurse the sick. The goodness of these pioneer women is unfailing. It is like the great and kind friendship of the Du Chaumonts. They help me take care of Cousin Philippe.

Paul meditated to-day, "I don't want to hurt the Father's feelings. I don't want to say He was greedy and made a better place for Himself in heaven than He made for us down here. Is it nicer just because He is there?"

His prayer: "God bless my father and mother and Ernestine. God keep my father and mother and Ernestine. And keep my mother with me day and night, dressed and undressed! God keep together all that love each other."

When he is a man I am going to tell him, and say: "But I have built my house, not wrecked it, I have been yours, not love's."

He tells me such stories as this: "Once upon a time there was such a loving angel came down. And they ran a string through his stomach and hung him on the wall. He never whined a bit."

The people in this country, which is called free, are nearly all bound. Those who lack money as we do cannot go where they please, or live as they would live. Is that freedom?

On a cool autumn night, when the fire crackles, the ten children of the settlement, fighting or agreeing, come running from their houses like hens. We sit on the floor in front of the hearth, and I suffer the often-repeated martyrdom of the "Fire Pig." This tale, invented once as fast as I could talk, I have been doomed to repeat until I dread the shades of evening.

The children bunch their heads together; their lips part, as soon as I begin to say:

Do you see that glowing spot in the heart of the coals? That is the house of the Fire Pig. One day the Fire Pig found he had no more corn, and he was very hungry. So he jumped out of his house and ran down the road till he came to a farmer's field.

"Good morning, Mr. Farmer," said the little pig. "Have you any corn for me to-day?"

"Why, who are you?" said the farmer.

"I'm a little Fire Pig."

"No, I haven't any corn for a Fire Pig."

The pig ran on till he came to another farmer's field.

"Good morning, Mr. Farmer, have you any corn for me to-day?"

"Who are you?" said the farmer.

"Oh, I'm the little Fire Pig."

"I don't know," said the farmer. "I would give you a great bagful if you could kill the snake which comes every night and steals my cattle."

The pig thought, "How can I kill that snake?" but he was so hungry he knew he should starve without corn, so he said he would try. The farmer told him to go down in the field, where the snake came gliding at night with its head reared high in air. The pig went down in the meadow, and the first creature he saw was a sheep.

"Baa!" said the sheep. That was its way of saying "How do you do?" "Who are you?"

"I'm the little Fire Pig."

"What are you doing here?"

"I've come to kill the great snake that eats the farmer's cattle."

"I'm very glad," said the sheep, "for it takes my lambs. How are you going to kill it?"

"I don't know," said the pig; "can't you help me?"

"I'll give you some of my wool."

The pig thanked the sheep, and went a little farther and met a horse. "He-ee-ee!" said the horse. That was his way of saying "How do you do?" "Who are you?"

"I am the little Fire Pig."

"What are you doing here?"

"I've come to kill the great snake that eats the farmer's cattle."

"I'm glad of that," said the horse; "for it steals my colts. How are you going to do it?"

"I don't know," said the pig. "Can't you help me?"

"I'll give you some of the long hairs from my tail," said the horse.

The pig took them and thanked the horse. And when he went a little farther he met a cow.

"Moo!" said the cow. That was her way of saying "How do you do?" "Who are you?"

"I'm the little Fire Pig."

"What are you doing here?"

"I've come to kill the great snake that eats the farmer's cattle."

"I am glad of that, for it steals my calves. How are you going to do it?"

"I don't know. Can't you help me?"

"I'll give you one of my sharp horns," said the cow.

So the pig took it and thanked her. Then he spun and he twisted, and he spun and he twisted, and made a strong woolen cord of the sheep's wool. And he wove and he braided, and he wove and he braided, and made a cunning snare of the horse's tail. And he whetted and sharpened, and he whetted and sharpened, and made a keen dart of the cow's horn.

—Now when the little pig has all his materials ready, and sees the great snake come gliding, gliding—I turn the situation over to the children. What did he do with the rope, the snare and the horn? They work it out each in his own way. There is a mighty wrangling all around the hearth.

One day is never really like another, though it seems so.

Perhaps being used to the sight of the Iroquois at Lake George, makes it impossible for me to imagine what the settlers dread, and that is an attack. We are shut around by forests. In primitive life so much time and strength go to the getting of food that we can think of little else.

It is as bad to slave at work as to slave at pleasure. But God may forgive what people cannot help.

There is a very old woman among the settlers whom they call Granny. We often sit together. She cannot get a gourd edge betwixt her nose and chin when she drinks, and has forgotten she ever had teeth. She does not expect much; but there is one right she contends for, and that is the right of ironing her cap by stretching it over her knee. When I have lived in this settlement long enough, my nose and chin may come together, and I shall forget my teeth. But this much I will exact of fate. My cap shall be ironed. I will not—I will not iron it by stretching it over my knee!

Count du Chaumont would be angry if he saw me learning to weave, for instance. You would not be angry. That makes a difference between you as men which I feel but cannot explain.

We speak English with our neighbors. Paul, who is to be an American, must learn his language well. I have taught him to read and write. I have taught him the history of his family and of his father's country. His head is as high as my breast. When will my head be as high as his breast?

Skenedonk loves you as a young superior brother. I have often wondered what he thought about when he went quietly around at your heels. You told me he had killed and scalped, and in spite of education, was as ready to kill and scalp again as any white man is for war.

I dread him like a toad, and wish him to keep on his side of the walk. He is always with you, and no doubt silently urges, "Come back to the wigwams that nourished you!"

Am I mistaken? Are we moving farther and farther apart instead of approaching each other? Oh, Louis, does this road lead to nothing?

I am glad I gave you that key. It was given thoughtlessly, when I was in a bubble of joy. But if you have kept it, it speaks to you every day.

Sophie Saint-Michel told me man sometimes piles all his tokens in a retrospective heap, and says, "Who the deuce gave me this or that?"

Sophie's father used to be so enraged at his wife and daughter because he could not restore their lost comforts. But this is really a better disposition than a mean subservience to misfortune.

The children love to have me dance gavottes for them. Some of their mothers consider it levity. Still they feel the need of a little levity themselves.

We had a great festival when the wild roses were fully in bloom. The prairie is called a mile square, and wherever a plow has not struck, acres of wild roses grow. They hedge us from the woods like a parapet edging a court. These volunteers are very thorny, bearing tender claws to protect themselves with. But I am nimble with my scissors.

We took the Jordan oxen, a meek pair that have broken sod for the colony, and twined them with garlands of wild roses. Around and around their horns, and around and around their bodies the long ropes were wound, their master standing by with his goad. That we wound also, and covered his hat with roses. The huge oxen swayed aside, looking ashamed of themselves. And when their tails were ornamented with a bunch at the tip, they switched these pathetically. Still even an ox loves festivity, whether he owns to it or not. We made a procession, child behind child, each bearing on his head all the roses he could carry, the two oxen walking tandem, led by their master in front. Everybody came out and laughed. It was a beautiful sight, and cheered us, though we gave it no name except the Procession of Roses.

Often when I open my eyes at dawn I hear music far off that makes my heart swell. It is the waking dream of a king marching with drums and bugles. While I am dressing I hum, "Oh, Richard, O my king!"

Louis! Louis! Louis!

I cannot—I cannot keep it down! How can I hold still that righteousness may be done through me, when I love—love—love—when I clench my fists and walk on my knees—

I am a wicked woman! What is all this sweet pretense of duty! It covers the hypocrite that loves—that starves—that cries, My king!—my king!

Strike me!—drive me within bounds! This long repression—years, years of waiting—for what?—for more waiting!—it is driving me mad!

You have the key.

I have nothing!

IX

My God! What had she seen in me to love? I sat up and held the book against my bosom. Its cry out of her past filled the world from horizon to horizon. The ox that she had wreathed in roses would have heard it through her silence. But the brutal, slow Bourbon had gone his way, turning his stupid head from side to side, leaving her to perish.

Punctuated by years, bursting from eternities of suppression, it brought an accumulated force that swept the soul out of my body.

All that had not been written in the book was as easily read as what was set down. I saw the monotony of her life, and her gilding of its rudeness, the pastimes she thought out for children; I saw her nursing the helplessness which leaned upon her, and turning aside the contempt of pioneer women who passionately admired strong men. I saw her eyes waiting on the distant laggard who stupidly pursued his own affairs until it was too late to protect her. I read the entries over and over. When day broke it seemed to me the morning after my own death, such knowing and experiencing had passed through me. I could not see her again until I had command of myself.

So I dressed and went silently down stairs. The Pawnees were stirring in the kitchen. I got some bread and meat from them, and also some grain for the horse; then mounted and rode to the river.

The ferryman lived near the old stockade. Some time always passed after he saw the signals before the deliberate Frenchman responded. I led my horse upon the unwieldy craft propelled by two huge oars, which the ferryman managed, running from one to another according to the swing of the current. It was broad day when we reached the other shore; one of those days, gray overhead, when moisture breaks upward through the ground, instead of descending. Many light clouds flitted under the grayness. The grass showed with a kind of green blush through its old brown fleece.

I saw the first sailing vessel of spring coming to anchor, from the straits of the great lakes. Once I would have hailed that vessel as possible bearer of news. Now it could bring me nothing of any importance.

The trail along the Fox river led over rolling land, dipping into coves and rising over hills. The Fox, steel blue in the shade, becomes tawny as its namesake when its fur of rough waves is combed to redness in the sunlight. Under grayness, with a soft wind blowing, the Fox showed his blue coat.

The prospect was so large, with a ridge running along in the distance, and open country spreading away on the other side, that I often turned in my saddle and looked back over the half-wooded trail. I thought I saw a figure walking a long way behind me, and being alone, tried to discern what it was. But under that gray sky nothing was sharply defined. I rode on thinking of the book in the breast of my coat.

It was certain I was not to marry. And being without breakfast and unstimulated by the sky, I began to think also what unstable material I had taken in hand when I undertook to work with Indians. Instinctively I knew then what a young southern statesman named Jefferson Davis whom I first met as a commandant of the fort at Green Bay—afterwards told me in Washington: "No commonwealth in a republic will stand with interests apart from the federated whole." White men, who have exclaimed from the beginning against the injustice done the red man, and who keep on pitying and exterminating him, made a federated whole with interests apart from his.

Again when I looked back I saw the figure, but it was afoot, and I soon lost it in a cove.

My house had been left undisturbed by hunters and Indians through the winter. I tied the horse to a gallery post and unfastened the door. A pile of refuse timbers offered wood for a fire, and I carried in several loads of it, and lighted the virgin chimney. Then I brought water from the spring and ate breakfast, sitting before the fire and thinking a little wearily and bitterly of my prospect in life.

Having fed my horse, I covered the fire, leaving a good store of fuel by the hearth, and rode away toward the Menominee and Winnebago lands.

The day was a hard one, and when I came back towards nightfall I was glad to stop with the officers of the stockade and share their mess.

"You looked fagged," said one of them.

"The horse paths are heavy," I answered, "and I have been as far as the Indian lands."

I had been as far as that remote time when Eagle was not a Cloud-Mother. To cross the river and see her smiling in meaningless happiness seemed more than I could do.

Yet she might notice my absence. We had been housed together ever since she had discovered me. Our walks and rides, our fireside talks and evening diversions were never separate. At Pierre Grignon's the family flocked in companies. When the padlocked book sent me out of the house I forgot that she was used to my presence and might be disturbed by an absence no one could explain.

"The first sailing vessel is in from the straits," said the lieutenant.

"Yes, I saw her come to anchor as I rode out this morning."

"She brought a passenger."

"Anybody of importance?"

"At first blush, no. At second blush, yes."

"Why 'no' at first blush?"

"Because he is only a priest."

"Only a priest, haughty officer! Are civilians and churchmen dirt under army feet?"

The lieutenant grinned.

"When you see a missionary priest landing to confess a lot of Canadians, he doesn't seem quite so important, as a prelate from Ghent, for instance."

"Is this passenger a prelate from Ghent?"

"That is where the second blush comes in. He is."

"How do you know?"

"I saw him, and talked with him."

"What is he doing in Green Bay?"

"Looking at the country. He was inquiring for you."

"For me!"

"Yes."

"What could a prelate from Ghent want with me?"

"Says he wants to make inquiries about the native tribes."

"Oh! Did you recommend me as an expert in native tribes?"

"Naturally. But not until he asked if you were here."

"He mentioned my name?"

"Yes. He wanted to see you. You'll not have to step out of your way to gratify him."

"From that I infer there is a new face at Pierre Grignon's."

"Your inference is correct. The Grignons always lodge the priests, and a great man like this one will be certainly quartered with them."

"What is he like?"

"A smooth and easy gentleman."

"In a cassock?"

"Tell a poor post lieutenant what a cassock is."

"The long-skirted black coat reaching to the heels."

"Our missionary priests don't wear it here. He has the bands and broad hat and general appearance of a priest, but his coat isn't very long."

"Then he has laid aside the cassock while traveling through this country."

The prelate from Ghent, no doubt a common priest, that the lieutenant undertook to dignify, slipped directly out of my mind.

Madame Ursule was waiting for me, on the gallery with fluted pillars at the front of the house.

"M's'r Williams, where is Madeleine?"

Her anxiety vibrated through the darkness.

"Isn't she here, madame?"

"She has not been seen to-day."

We stood in silence, then began to speak together.

"But, madame—"

"M's'r Williams—"

"I went away early—"

"When I heard from the Pawnees that you had gone off on horseback so early I thought it possible you might have taken her with you."

"Madame, how could I do that?"

"Of course you wouldn't have done that. But we can't find her. We've inquired all over La Baye. She left the house when no one saw her. She was never out after nightfall before."

"But, madame, she must be here!"

"Oh, m's'r, my hope was that you knew where she is—she has followed you about so! The poor child may be at the bottom of the river!"

"She can't be at the bottom of the river!" I retorted.

The girls ran out. They were dressed for a dance, and drew gauzy scarfs around their anxious faces. The house had been searched from ground to attic more than once. They were sure she must be hiding from them.

I remembered the figure that appeared to me on the trail. My heart stopped. I could not humiliate my Cloud-Mother by placing her before them in the act of tracking me like a dog. I could not tell any one about it, but asked for Skenedonk.

The Indian had been out on the river in a canoe. He came silently, and stood near me. The book was between us. I had it in the breast of my coat, and he had it on his conscience.

"Bring out your horse and get me a fresh one," I said.

"Where shall I find one?"

"Pierre will give you one of ours," said Madame Ursule. "But you must eat."

"I had my supper with the officers of the fort, madame. I would have made a briefer stay if I had known what had happened on this side of the river."

"I forgot to tell you, M's'r Williams, there is an abbé here from Europe. He asked for you."

"I cannot see him to-night."

Skenedonk drew near me to speak, but I was impatient of any delay. We went into the house, and Madame Ursule said she would bring a blanket and some food to strap behind my saddle. The girls helped her. There was a hush through the jolly house. The master bustled out of the family room. I saw behind him, standing as he had stood at Mittau, a priest of fine and sweet presence, waiting for Pierre Grignon to speak the words of introduction.

"It is like seeing France again!" exclaimed the master of the house. "Abbé Edgeworth, this is M's'r Williams."

"Monsieur," said the abbé to me with perfect courtesy, "believe me, I am glad to see you."

"Monsieur," I answered, giving him as brief notice as he had given me in Mittau, yet without rancor;—there was no room in me for that. "You have unerringly found the best house in the Illinois Territory, and I leave you to the enjoyment of it."

"You are leaving the house, monsieur?"

"I find I am obliged to make a short journey."

"I have made a long one, monsieur. It may be best to tell you that I come charged with a message for you."

I thought of Madame d'Angoulême. The sister who had been mine for a few minutes, and from whom this priest had cast me out, declaring that

God had smitten the pretender when my eclipse laid me at his feet—remembered me in her second exile, perhaps believed in me still. Women put wonderful restraints upon themselves.

Abbé Edgeworth and I looked steadily at each other.

"I hope Madame d'Angoulême is well?"

"She is well, and is still the comforter of his Majesty's misfortune."

"Monsieur the Abbé, a message would need to be very urgent to be listened to to-night. I will give you audience in the morning, or when I return."

We both bowed again. I took Pierre Grignon into the hall for counsel.

In the end he rode with me, for we concluded to send Skenedonk with a party along the east shore.

Though searching for the lost is an experience old as the world, its poignancy was new to me. I saw Eagle tangled in the wild oats of the river. I saw her treacherously dealt with by Indians who called themselves at peace. I saw her wandering out and out, mile beyond mile, to undwelt-in places, and the tender mercy of wolves.

We crossed the ferry and took to the trail, Pierre Grignon talking cheerfully.

"Nothing has happened to her, M's'r Williams," he insisted. "No Indian about La Baye would hurt her, and the child is not so crazy as to hurt herself."

It was a starless night, muffled overhead as the day had been, but without rain or mist. He had a lantern hanging at his saddle bow, ready to light. In the open lands we rode side by side, but through growths along the Fox first one and then the other led the way.

We found my door unfastened. I remembered for the first time I had not locked it. Some one had been in the house. A low fire burned in the chimney. We stirred it and lighted the lantern. Footprints not our own had dried white upon the smooth dark floor.

They pointed to the fireplace and out again. They had been made by a woman's feet.

We descended the hill to the river, and tossed our light through every bush, the lantern blinking in the wind. We explored the ravine, the light stealing over white birches that glistened like alabaster. It was no use to call her name. She might be hidden behind a rock laughing at us. We had to surprise her to recover her. Skenedonk would have traced her where we lost the trail.

When we went back to the house, dejected with physical weariness, I unstrapped the blanket and the food which Madame Ursule had sent, and brought them to Pierre Grignon. He threw the blanket on the settee, laid out bread and meat on the table, and ate, both of us blaming ourselves for sending the Indian on the other side of the river.

We traced the hard route which I had followed the day before, and reached Green Bay about dawn. Pierre Grignon went to bed exhausted. I had some breakfast and waited for Skenedonk. He had not returned, but had sent one man back to say there was no clue. The meal was like a passover eaten in haste. I could not wait, but set out again, with a pillion which I had carried uselessly in the night strapped again upon the horse for her seat, in case I found her; and leaving word for the Oneida to follow.

I had forgotten there was such a person as Abbé Edgeworth, when he led a horse upon the ferry boat.

"You ride early as well as late. May I join you?"

"I ride on a search which cannot interest you, monsieur."

"You are mistaken. I understand what has disturbed the house, and I want to ride with you."

"It will be hard for a horseman accustomed to avenues."

"It will suit me perfectly."

It did not suit me at all, but he took my coldness with entire courtesy.

"Have you breakfasted, monsieur?"

"I had my usual slice of bread and cup of water before rising," he answered.

Again I led on the weary trail to my house. Abbé Edgeworth galloped well, keeping beside me where there was room, or riding behind where there was not. The air blew soft, and great shadow clouds ran in an upper current across the deepest blueness I had seen in many a day. The sun showed beyond rows of hills.

I bethought myself to ask the priest if he knew anything about Count de Chaumont. He answered very simply and directly that he did; that I might remember Count de Chaumont was mentioned in Mittau. The count, he said, according to common report, had retired with his daughter and his son-in-law to Blois, where he was vigorously rebuilding his ruined chateau of Chaumont.

If my mind had been upon the priest, I should have wondered what he came for. He did not press his message.

"The court is again in exile?" I said, when we could ride abreast.

"At Ghent."

"Bellenger visited me last September. He was without a dauphin."

"We could supply the deficiency," Abbé Edgeworth pleasantly replied.

"With the boy he left in Europe?"

"Oh, dear no. With royal dukes. You observed his majesty could not pension a helpless idiot without encouraging dauphins. These dauphins are thicker than blackberries. The dauphin myth has become so common that whenever we see a beggar approaching, we say, 'There comes another dauphin.' One of them is a fellow who calls himself the Duke of Richemont. He has followers who believe absolutely in him. Somebody, seeing him asleep, declared it was the face of the dead king!"

I felt stung, remembering the Marquis du Plessy's words.

"Oh, yes, yes," said Abbé Edgeworth. "He has visions too. Half memories, when the face of his mother comes back to him!"

"What about his scars?" I asked hardily.

"Scars! yes, I am told he has the proper stigmata of the dauphin. He was taken out of the Temple prison; a dying boy being substituted for him there. We all know the dauphin's physician died suddenly; some say he was poisoned; and a new physician attended the boy who died in the Temple. Of course the priest who received the child's confession should have known a dauphin when he saw one. But that's neither here nor there. We lived then in surprising times."

"Madame d'Angoulême would recognize him as her brother if she saw him?" I suggested.

"I think she is not so open to tokens as at one time. Women's hearts are tender. The Duchess d'Angoulême could never be convinced that her brother died."

"But others, including her uncle, were convinced?"

"The Duke of Richemont was not. What do you yourself think, Monsieur Williams?"

"I think that the man who is out is an infinite joke. He tickles the whole world. People have a right to laugh at a man who cannot prove he is what he says he is. The difference between a pretender and a usurper is the difference between the top of the hill and the bottom."

The morning sun showed the white mortar ribs of my homestead clean and fair betwixt hewed logs; and brightened the inside of the entrance or hall room. For I saw the door stood open. It had been left unfastened but not ajar. Somebody was in the house.

I told Abbé Edgeworth we would dismount and tie our horses a little distance away. And I asked him to wait outside and let me enter alone.

He obligingly sauntered on the hill overlooking the Fox; I stepped upon the gallery and looked in.

The sweep of a gray dress showed in front of the settle. Eagle was there. I stood still.

She had put on more wood. Fire crackled in the chimney. I saw, and seemed to have known all night, that she had taken pieces of unbroken bread and meat left by Pierre Grignon on my table; that her shoes were cleaned and drying in front of the fire; that she must have carried her dress above contact with the soft ground.

When I asked Abbé Edgeworth not to come in, her dread of strangers influenced me less than a desire to protect her from his eyes, haggard and draggled as she probably was. The instinct which made her keep her body like a temple had not failed under the strong excitement that drove her out. Whether she slept under a bush, or not at all, or took to the house after Pierre Grignon and I left it, she was resting quietly on the settle before the fireplace, without a stain of mud upon her.

I could see nothing but the foot of her dress. Had any change passed over her face? Or had the undisturbed smile of my Cloud-Mother followed me on the road?

Perhaps the cloud had thickened. Perhaps thunders and lightnings moved within it. Sane people sometimes turn wild after being lost, running from their friends, and fighting against being restrained and brought home.

The gray dress in front of my hearth I could not see without a heaving of the breast.

X.

How a man's life is drawn, turned, shaped, by a woman! He may deny it. He may swagger and lie about it. Heredity, ambition, lust, noble aspirations, weak self-indulgence, power, failure, success, have their turns with him. But the woman he desires above all others, whose breast is his true home, makes him, mars him.

Had she cast herself on the settle exhausted and ill after exposure? Should I find her muttering and helpless? Worse than all, had the night made her forget that she was a Cloud-Mother?

I drew my breath with an audible sound in the throat. Her dress stirred. She leaned around the edge of the settle.

Eagle de Ferrier, not my Cloud-Mother, looked at me. Her features were pinched from exposure, but flooded themselves instantly with a blush. She snatched her shoes from the hearth and drew them on.

I was taken with such a trembling that I held to a gallery post.

Suppose this glimpse of herself had been given to me only to be withdrawn! I was afraid to speak, and waited.

She stood up facing me.

"Louis!"

"Madame!"

"What is the matter, sire?"

"Nothing, madame, nothing."

"Where is Paul?"

I did not know what to do, and looked at her completely helpless; for if I told her Paul was dead, she might relapse; and evasions must be temporary.

"The Indian took him," she cried.

"But the Indian didn't kill him, Eagle."

"How do you know?"

"Because Paul came to me."

"He came to you? Where?"

"At Fort Stephenson."

"Where is my child?"

"He is at Fort Stephenson."

"Bring him to me!"

"I can't bring him, Eagle."

"Then let me go to him."

I did not know what to say to her.

"And there were Cousin Philippe and Ernestine lying across the step. I have been thinking all night. Do you understand it?"

"Yes, I understand it, Eagle."

By the time I had come into the house her mind leaped forward in comprehension. The blanket she had held on her shoulders fell around her feet. It was a striped gay Indian blanket.

"You were attacked, and the settlement was burned."

"But whose house is this?"

"This is my house."

"Did you bring me to your house?"

"I wasn't there."

"No, I remember. You were not there. I saw you the last time at the Tuileries."

"When did you come to yourself, madame?"

"I have been sick, haven't I? But I have been sitting by this fire nearly all night, trying to understand. I knew I was alone, because Cousin Philippe and Ernestine—I want Paul!"

I looked at the floor, and must have appeared miserable. She passed her hands back over her forehead many times as if brushing something away. "If he died, tell me."

"I held him, Eagle."

"They didn't kill him?"

"No."

"Or scalp him?"

"The knife never touched him."

"But—"

"It was in battle."

"My child died in battle? How long have I been ill?"

"More than a year, Eagle."

"And he died in battle?"

"He had a wound in his side. He was brought into the fort, and I took care of him."

She burst out weeping, and laughed and wept, the tears running down her face and wetting her bosom.

"My boy! My little son! You held him! He died like a man!"

I put her on the settle, and all the cloud left her in that tempest of rain. Afterwards I wiped her face with my handkerchief and she sat erect and still.

A noise of many birds came from the ravine, and winged bodies darted past the door uttering the cries of spring. Abbé Edgeworth sauntered by and she saw him, and was startled.

"Who is that?"

"A priest."

"When did he come?"

"He rode here with me this morning."

"Louis," she asked, leaning back, "who took care of me?"

"You have been with the Grignons since you came to the Illinois Territory."

"Am I in the Illinois Territory?"

"Yes, I found you with the Grignons."

"They must be kind people!"

"They are; the earth's salt."

"But who brought me to the Illinois Territory?"

"A family named Jordan."

"The Indians didn't kill them?"

"No."

"Why wasn't I killed?"

"The Indians regarded you with superstition."

"What have I said and done?"

"Nothing, madame, that need give you any uneasiness."

"But what did I say?" she insisted.

"You thought you were a Cloud-Mother."

"A Cloud-Mother!" She was astonished and asked, "What is a Cloud-Mother?"

"You thought I was Paul, and you were my Cloud-Mother."

"Did I say such a foolish thing as that?"

"Don't call it foolish, madame."

"I hope you will forget it."

"I don't want to forget it."

"But why are you in Illinois Territory, sire?"

"I came to find land for the Iroquois. I intend to make a state with the tribe."

"But what of France?"

"Oh, France is over supplied with men who want to make a state of her. Louis XVIII has been on the throne eleven months, and was recently chased off by Napoleon.

"Louis XVIII on the throne? Did true loyalists suffer that?"

"Evidently."

"Sire, what became of Napoleon?"

"He was beaten by the allies and sent to Elba. Louis XVIII was brought in with processions. But in about eleven months Napoleon made a dash across France—"

"Tell me slowly. You say I have been ill more than a year. I know nothing of what has happened."

"Napoleon escaped from Elba, made a dash across France, and incidentally swept the Bourbon off the throne. The last news from Europe shows him gathering armies to meet the allies."

"Oh, sire, you should have been there!"

"Abbé Edgeworth suggests that France is well supplied with dauphins also. Turning off dauphins has been a pastime at court."

"Abbé Edgeworth? You do not mean the priest you saw at Mittau?"

"Confessor and almoner to his majesty. The same man."

"Is he here?"

"You saw him pass the door."

"Why has he come to America?"

"I have not inquired."

"Why is he here with you?"

"Because it pleases him, not me."

"He brings you some message?"

"So he says."

"What is it?"

"I have not had time to ask."

She stood up. As she became more herself and the spirit rushed forward in her face, I saw how her beauty had ripened. Hoeing corn and washing in the river does not coarsen well-born women. I knew I should feel the sweetness of her presence stinging through me and following me wherever I went in the world.

"Call the priest in, sire. I am afraid I have hindered the interview."

"I did not meet him with my arms open, madame."

"But you would have heard what he had to say, if I had not been in your house. Why am I in your house?"

"You came here."

"Was I wandering about by myself?"

"Yes, madame."

"I thought I must have been walking. When I came to myself I was so tired, and my shoes were muddy. If you want to see the priest I will go into another room."

"No, I will bring him in and let him give his message in your presence."

When Abbé Edgeworth was presented to her, he slightly raised his eyebrows, but expressed no astonishment at meeting her lucid eyes. Nor did I explain—"God has given her back her senses in a night."

The position in which she found herself was trying. She made him a grave courtesy. My house might have been the chateau in which she was born, so undisturbed was her manner. Her night wandering and mind-sickness were simply put behind us in the past, with her having taken refuge in my house, as matters which need not concern Abbé Edgeworth. He did not concern himself with them, but bent before her as if he had no doubt of her sanity.

I asked her to resume her place on the settle. There was a stool for the abbé and one for myself. We could see the river glinting in its valley, and the windrows of heights beyond it. A wild bee darted into the room, droning, and out again, the sun upon its back.

"Monsieur," I said to Abbé Edgeworth, "I am ready now to hear the message which you mentioned to me last night."

"If madame will pardon me," he answered, "I will ask you to take me where we can confer alone."

"It is not necessary, monsieur. Madame de Ferrier knows my whole story."

But the priest moved his shoulders.

"I followed you in this remote place, monsieur, that we might talk together without interruption, unembarrassed by any witness."

Madame de Ferrier rose. I put her into her seat again with authority.

"It is my wish, madame, to have at least one witness with Abbé Edgeworth and myself."

"I hope," he protested, "that madame will believe there can be no objection to her presence. I am simply following instructions. I was instructed to deliver my message in private."

"Monsieur," Eagle answered, "I would gladly withdraw to another room."

"I forbid it, madame," I said to her.

"Very well," yielded Abbé Edgeworth.

He took a folded paper from his bosom, and spoke to me with startling sharpness.

"You think I should address you as Monseigneur, as the dauphin of France should be addressed?"

"I do not press my rights. If I did, monsieur the abbé, you would not have the right to sit in my presence."

"Suppose we humor your fancy. I will address you as Monseigneur. Let us even go a little farther and assume that you are known to be the dauphin of

France by witnesses who have never lost track of you. In that case, Monseigneur, would you put your name to a paper resigning all claim upon the throne?"

"Is this your message?"

"We have not yet come to the message."

"Let us first come to the dauphin. When dauphins are as plentiful as blackberries in France and the court never sees a beggar appear without exclaiming: 'Here comes another dauphin!'—why, may I ask, is Abbé Edgeworth sent so far to seek one?"

He smiled.

"We are supposing that Monseigneur, in whose presence I have the honor to be, is the true dauphin."

"That being the case, how are we to account for the true dauphin's reception at Mittau?"

"The gross stupidity and many blunders of agents that the court was obliged to employ, need hardly be assumed."

"Poor Bellenger! He has to take abuse from both sides in order that we may be polite to each other."

"As Monseigneur suggests, we will not go into that matter."

Eagle sat as erect as a statue and as white.

I felt an instant's anxiety. Yet she had herself entirely at command.

"We have now arrived at the paper, I trust," said the priest.

"The message?"

"Oh, no. The paper in which you resign all claim to the throne of France, and which may give you the price of a principality in this country."

"I do not sign any such paper."

"Not at all?"

"Not at all."

"You are determined to hold to your rights?"

"I am determined not to part with my rights."

"Inducements large enough might be offered." He paused suggestively.

"The only man in France," I said, "empowered to treat for abdication of the throne at present, is Napoleon Bonaparte. Did you bring a message from him?"

Abbé Edgeworth winced, but laughed.

"Napoleon Bonaparte will not last. All Europe is against him. I see we have arrived at the message."

He rose and handed me the paper he held in his hand. I rose and received it, and read it standing.

It was one brief line:—

"Louis: You are recalled.
Marie-Therese."

The blood must have rushed over my face. I had a submerged feeling, looking out of it at the priest.

"Well, Monseigneur?"

"It is like her heavenly goodness."

"Do you see nothing but her heavenly goodness in it?"

"This is the message?"

"It is a message I crossed the ocean to bring."

"With the consent of her uncle?"

"Madame d'Angoulême never expresses a wish contrary to the wishes of his majesty."

"We are then to suppose that Louis XVIII offers me, through you, monsieur, the opportunity to sign away my rights, and failing that, the opportunity of taking them?"

"Supposing you are Monseigneur the dauphin, we will let our supposition run as far as this."

I saw distinctly the position of Louis XVIII. Marquis du Plessy had told me he was a mass of superstition. No doubt he had behaved, as Bellenger said, for the good of the royalist cause. But the sanction of heaven was not on his behavior. Bonaparte was let loose on him like the dragon from the pit. And Frenchmen, after yawning eleven months or so in the king's august face, threw up their hats for the dragon. In his second exile the inner shadow and the shadow of age combined against him. He had tasted royalty. It was not as good as he had once thought. Beside him always, he saw the face of Marie-Therese. She never forgot the hushed mystery of her brother. Her silence and obedience to the crown, her loyalty to juggling and evasion, were more powerful than resistance.

A young man, brought suddenly before the jaded nation and proclaimed at an opportune moment, might be a successful toy. The sore old king would oil more than the royalist cause, and the blessing of heaven would descend on one who restored the veritable dauphin.

I never have seen the most stupid man doubt his power to ride if somebody hoists him into the saddle.

"Let us go farther with our suppositions," I said. "Suppose I decline?"

I heard Madame de Ferrier gasp.

The priest raised his eyebrows.

"In that case you will be quite willing to give me a signed paper declaring your reasons."

"I sign no paper."

"Let me suggest that Monseigneur is not consistent. He neither resigns his supposed rights nor will he exercise them."

"I will neither resign them nor exercise them."

"This is virtually resigning them."

"The abbé will pardon me for saying it is not. My rights are mine, whether I use them or not."

"Monseigneur understands that opportunity is a visitor that comes but once."

"I understand that the most extraordinary thing has happened to-day that will ever go unrecorded in history. One Bourbon offers to give away a throne he has lost and another Bourbon refuses it."

"You may well say it will go unrecorded in history. Excepting this lady,"—the abbé bowed toward Eagle,—"there is no witness."

"Wise precautions have been taken," I agreed. "This scrap of paper may mean anything or nothing."

"You decline?" he repeated.

"I think France is done with the Bourbons, monsieur the abbé. A fine spectacle they have made of themselves, cooling their heels all over Europe, waiting for Napoleon's shoes! Will I go sneaking and trembling to range myself among impotent kings and wrangle over a country that wants none of us? No, I never will! I see where my father slipped. I see where the eighteenth Louis slipped. I am a man tenacious beyond belief. You cannot loose my grip when I take hold. But I never have taken hold, I never will take hold—of my native country, struggling as she is to throw off hereditary rule!"

"You are an American!" said Abbé Edgeworth contemptuously.

"If France called to me out of need, I would fight for her. A lifetime of peaceful years I would toss away in a minute to die in one achieving battle for her. But she neither calls me nor needs me. A king is not simply an appearance—a continuation of hereditary rights!"

"Your position is incredible," said the priest.

"I do not belittle the prospect you open before me. I see the practical difficulties, but I see well the magnificence beyond them."

"Then why do you hesitate?"

"I don't hesitate. A man is contemptible who stands shivering and longing outside of what he dare not attempt. I would dare if I longed. But I don't long."

"Monseigneur believes there will be complications?"

"I know my own obstinacy. A man who tried to work me with strings behind a throne, would think he was struck by lightning."

"Sire," Madame de Ferrier spoke out, "this is the hour of your life. Take your kingdom."

"I should have to take it, madame, if I got it. My uncle of Provence has nothing to give me. He merely says—'My dear dauphin, if Europe knocks Napoleon down, will you kindly take hold of a crank which is too heavy for me, and turn it for the good of the Bourbons? We may thus keep the royal machine in the family!'"

"You have given no adequate reason for declining this offer," said the priest.

"I will give no reason. I simply decline."

"Is this the explanation that I shall make to Madame d'Angoulême? Think of the tender sister who says—'Louis, you are recalled!'"

"I do think of her. God bless her!"

"Must I tell her that Monseigneur planted his feet like one of these wild cattle, and wheeled, and fled from the contemplation of a throne?"

"You will dress it up in your own felicitous way, monsieur."

"What do you wish me to say?"

"That I decline. I have not pressed the embarrassing question of why I was not recalled long ago. I reserve to myself the privilege of declining without saying why I decline."

"He must be made to change his mind, monsieur!" Madame de Ferrier exclaimed.

"I am not a man that changes his mind every time the clock strikes."

I took the padlocked book out of my breast and laid it upon the table. I looked at the priest, not at her. The padlocked book seemed to have no more to do with the conversation, than a hat or a pair of gloves.

I saw, as one sees from the side of the eye, the scarlet rush of blood and the snow-white rush of pallor which covered her one after the other. The moment was too strenuous. I could not spare her. She had to bear it with me.

She set her clenched hands on her knees.

"Sire!"

I faced her. The coldest look I ever saw in her gray eyes repelled me, as she deliberately said—

"You are not such a fool!"

I stared back as coldly and sternly, and deliberately answered—

"I am—just—such a fool!"

"Consider how any person who might be to blame for your decision, would despise you for it afterwards!"

"A boy in the first flush of his youth," Abbé Edgeworth said, his fine jaws squared with a grin, "might throw away a kingdom for some woman who took his fancy, and whom he could not have perhaps, unless he did throw his kingdom away. And after he had done it he would hate the woman. But a young man in his strength doesn't do such things!"

"A king who hasn't spirit to be a king!" Madame de Ferrier mocked.

I mercilessly faced her down.

"What is there about me? Sum me up. I am robbed on every side by any one who cares to fleece me. Whenever I am about to accomplish anything I fall down as if knocked on the head!"

She rose from her seat.

"You let yourself be robbed because you are princely! You have plainly left behind you every weakness of your childhood. Look at him in his strength, Monsieur Abbé! He has sucked in the vigor of a new country! The failing power of an old line of kings is renewed in him! You could not have nourished such a dauphin for France in your exiled court! Burying in the American soil has developed what you see for yourself—the king!"

"He is a handsome man," Abbé Edgeworth quietly admitted.

"Oh, let his beauty alone! Look at his manhood—his kinghood!"

"Of what use is his kinghood if he will not exercise it?"

"He must!"

She turned upon me fiercely.

"Have you no ambition?"

"Yes, madame. But there are several kinds of ambition, as there are several kinds of success. You have to knock people down with each kind, if you want it acknowledged. As I told you awhile ago, I am tenacious beyond belief, and shall succeed in what I undertake."

"What are you undertaking?"

"I am not undertaking to mount a throne."

"I cannot believe it! Where is there a man who would turn from what is offered you? Consider the life before you in this country. Compare it with the life you are throwing away." She joined her hands. "Sire, the men of my house who fought for the kings of yours, plead through me that you will take your inheritance."

I kept my eyes on Abbé Edgeworth. He considered the padlocked book as an object directly in his line of vision. Its wooden covers and small metal padlock attracted the secondary attention we bestow on trifles when we are at great issues.

I answered her,

"The men of your house—and the women of your house, madame—cannot dictate what kings of my house should do in this day."

"Well as you appear to know him, madame," said Abbé Edgeworth, "and loyally as you urge him, your efforts are wasted."

She next accused me—

"You hesitate on account of the Indians!"

"If there were no Indians in America, I should do just as I am doing."

"All men," the abbé noted, "hold in contempt a man who will not grasp power when he can."

"Why should I grasp power? I have it in myself. I am using it."

"Using it to ruin yourself!" she cried.

"Monseigneur!" The abbé rose. We stood eye to eye. "I was at the side of the king your father upon the scaffold. My hand held to his lips the crucifix of our Lord Jesus Christ. In his death no word of bitterness escaped him. True son of St. Louis, he supremely loved France. Upon you he laid injunction to leave to God alone the punishment of regicides, and to devote your life to the welfare of all Frenchmen. Monseigneur! are you deaf to this call of sacred duty? The voice of your father from the scaffold, in this hour when the fortunes of your house are lowest, bids you take your rightful place and rid your people of the usurper who grinds France and Europe into the blood-stained earth!"

I wheeled and walked across the floor from Abbé Edgeworth, and turned again and faced him.

"Monsieur, you have put a dart through me. If anything in the universe could move me from my position, what you have said would do it. But my father's blood cries through me to-day—'Shall the son of Louis XVI be forced down the unwilling throats of his countrymen by foreign bayonets?—Russians—Germans—English!—Shall the dauphin of France be hoisted to place by the alien?'—My father would forbid it! . . . You appeal to my family love. I bear about with me everywhere the pictured faces of my family. The father whose name you invoke, is always close to my heart. That royal duchess, whom you are privileged to see daily, monsieur, and I—never—is so dear and sacred to me that I think of her with a prayer. . . . But my life is here. . . . Monsieur, in this new world, no man can say to me—'Come,' or 'Go.' I am as free as the Indian. But the pretender to the throne of France, the puppet of Russia, of England, of the enemies of my country,—a slave to policy and intrigue—a chained wanderer about Europe—O my God! to be such a pretender—gasping for air—for light—as I gasped in Ste. Pélagie!—O let me be a free man—a free man!"

The old churchman whispered over and over—

"My royal son!"

My arms dropped relaxed.

There was another reason. I did not give it. I would not give it.

We heard the spring wind following the river channel—and a far faint call that I knew so well—the triangular wild flock in the upper air, flying north.

"Honk! honk!" It was the jubilant cry of freedom!

"Madame," said Abbé Edgeworth, resting his head on his hands, "I have seen many stubborn Bourbons, but he is the most obstinate of them all. We do not make as much impression on him as that little padlocked book."

Her terrified eyes darted at him—and hid their panic.

"Monsieur Abbé," she exclaimed piercingly, "tell him no woman will love him for throwing away a kingdom!"

The priest began once more.

"You will not resign your rights?"

"No."

"You will not exercise them?"

"No."

"If I postpone my departure from to-day until to-morrow, or next week, or next month, is there any possibility of your reconsidering this decision?"

"No."

"Monseigneur, must I leave you with this answer?"

"Your staying cannot alter it, Monsieur Abbé."

"You understand this ends all overtures from France?"

"I understand."

"Is there nothing that you would ask?"

"I would ask Madame d'Angoulême to remember me."

"Louis! You are a king! You are a king!".

He came forward like a courtier, lifted my hand to his lips, and kissed it.

"With your permission, Monseigneur, I will now retire and ride slowly back along the river until you overtake me. I should like to have some time for solitary thought."

"You have my permission, Monsieur Abbé."

He bowed to Madame de Ferrier, and so moving to the door, he bowed again to me, and took his leave.

His horse's impatient start, and his remonstrance as he mounted, came plainly to our ears. The regular beat of hoofs upon the sward followed; then an alternating tap-tap of horse's feet diminished down the trail.

Eagle and I avoided looking at each other.

A bird inquired through the door with inquisitive chirp, and was away.

Volcanoes, and whirlwinds, fire, and all force, held themselves condensed and quiescent in the still room.

I moved first, laying Marie-Therese's message on the padlocked book. Standing with folded arms I faced Eagle, and she as stonily faced me. It was a stare of unspeakable love that counts a thousand years as a day.

She shuddered from head to foot. Thus a soul might ripple in passing from its body.

"I am not worth a kingdom!" her voice wailed through the room.

I opened my arms and took her. Volcanoes and whirlwinds, fire, and all force, were under our feet. We trod them breast to breast.

She held my head between her hands. The tears streamed down her face.

"Louis!—you are a king!—you are a king!"

THE END.